Just Follow the Dream

Susi Farmer

For Heather, Jeanie and Katherine
for just being brilliant.

Chapter One

"Earth to Anna! Earth to Aaaaaannnnnaaaa!" Jenny's amused voice broke thorough Anna's daydream. Anna blinked and looking up found she was sat at her desk and staring at the notice board, detailing the escape route in case of a fire, a reminder to use recycling bins and a poster for last year's Christmas party.

"So where were you this time?" Jenny asked ignoring the phone that had started to ring.

"I was thinking about the best way to tackle the Bedford account," Anna replied innocently a smile playing around her lips.

"And there was me thinking you were daydreaming about OK doing a multi-page spread on your Surrey mansion." Jenny teased reaching for the phone.

"That was yesterday." Anna returned, playing along with the joke. Although scarily Jenny's wild predictions about her daydreams were often far more accurate than Anna let on. But that was the beauty of daydreaming she reminded herself, you could be anyone or anything you wanted to be. You could be adored by the perfect man, have wardrobes full of amazing clothes, your own shoe room, you could cook and bake to perfection, deliver word perfect pitches at work that were a balance of brilliant strategy and subtle wit or decorate your home with infinite style. And when you worked in a beige office talking to obnoxious customers on the phone all day, you needed an escape.

Today's daydream had related to the meeting she had with her boss that afternoon. A man who was memorable for all the wrong reasons, not least the fact that he only ever spoke to her chest and insisted on being called Mr Elvin. Jenny claimed it was because his first name was Horace but Anna had sat through too many of his endless rants about the lack of respect young people had these days to believe her. Realising she was about to drift off into another place Anna pulled her attention back to the present. She looked around the office, in what she hoped was an inconspicuous manner to see if anyone else had noticed she had spent the last however many minutes daydreaming, but luckily no one seemed to have. Jenny was now trying not to sound bored as the customer on the other end of the phone yelled at her for the hundredth time that he needed his delivery that day even though he would not pay for the last one and Tim was smiling to himself, no doubt having found a football web site which had not been fire walled by IT.

Glancing at the clock again she realised there was only half an hour left until her meeting with her boss. On a recent night out for Tim's birthday everyone had been moaning about the fact that the pay rise had been non-existent for the third year running, despite how well the company was doing. Anna had somehow found herself agreeing to be the person to speak to Mr Elvin, for which she blamed the cocktails they had been drinking.

When Jenny had interrupted her, she had been dreaming that the meeting had gone so well she had not only secured large pay rises for the whole team but also gone on to be a renowned negotiator.

However, looking at the blank document on her screen which was meant to list ten reasons why they all deserved a better pay rise, Anna sighed. She could mention the fact they often worked late, although in truth this was normally because she and Jenny had spent slightly too long shopping at lunchtime.

After five more minutes of unproductively staring at the screen Anna enlisted Jenny's help and along with the odd comment from Tim, they managed to cobble together ten fairly good reasons on which to base an argument for a better pay rise.

With five minutes to go, her phone rang, recognising her best friend's number she smiled.

"Good luck," Lucy sang down the phone. "Remember stay calm and try and you'll be fine!"

"Thanks," Anna's nerves were starting to kick in now. She was about to ask Lucy whether she could think of any other reasons for her list but Lucy was already wrapping up the call.

"Sorry I've got to run, I've got a meeting, speak later!"

And with that she was gone.

With five minutes to go, she went into the Ladies to check her appearance.

"Very sexy," Jenny commented walking in, as she tried to secure a long dark strand of hair that had escaped her pony tail and was curling beautifully down the side of her neck.

"Why wouldn't it do this on Friday night?" Anna sighed remembering the battle with the curling iron. "And actually, sexy is the last thing I want if I'm off to see…" She pulled a face making Jenny laugh.

"Talking of which, look at the time!" Jenny held her arm out so Anna could read her watch.

"Great!" Anna hurried out of the toilets, realising she was now late for the meeting. Picking up the list of ten reasons off her desk she scanned through them (she was hoping that being a friendly team would count and that was one of the better ones).

"Give him hell, Love, we're right behind you!" One of the team called.

Glancing back at her work mates, Anna realised they were all smiling at her, all confident she could do this. She wished she felt the same.

Knocking on the door she walked into her boss' office, suddenly feeling very nervous, she swallowed, hoping her voice would sound normal as her throat felt tight.

"Take a seat Anna, I'm sure we can sort out your little problem," Mr Elvin, her boss, murmured smarmily, addressing her chest as usual. Pulled back from her thoughts she sat down and decided not to point out that it was not her problem that was little, but her pay rise. Instead, she took a deep breath hoping to outwit Mr Elvin and secure pay rises for the whole team.

"Mr Elvin," Anna opened the conversation, in what she hoped was a professional manner, "I have worked here for five years now."

Surely it was not that long she thought, but she banished the thought as she needed to concentrate and stay focused.

"And I feel I have greatly contributed to the expansion of the company through my diligence, dedication to detail and hard work." Oh, that sounded good she marvelled, slightly surprised at herself, but she grounded herself again, trying to stay focused so that she did not to ruin it. "And it is not just myself but the whole team that have contributed, and we feel that, in light of the reasons which I will shortly address, our pay rises this year should be reviewed, as we are a great asset to the company." Pleased at how easy this had been so far, Anna moved on "So to run through the reasons............"

"Anna, Anna, Anna." Mr Elvin shook his head sadly and gave her a patronising smile. "Let's not waste our time with your little list. Although well done for trying to show that you think you are valued," he paused, looking at her in pity.

Anna glared back at him, trying desperately to remain calm and professional. He sighed at her response and carried on. "Anna, I know you like to feel you are valued, but really for someone who daydreams all day and spends what little time is left at the computer e mailing her friends I really think that your pay rise was extremely generous."

Don't get angry and stay calm, that was what Lucy had said. Anna took a deep breath, and tried to follow Lucy's advice but it was no good because her voice was naturally rising on its own.

"I don't spend all day daydreaming; I was the best debt collector last month and the MD loved the report I did on how to become a paperless office."

He smiled sadly at her, whilst Anna desperately tried to remember anything else that she had done that had been successful. "Anna that report was over fifteen months ago and the MD just likes pretty girls to brighten up the office. And as for best debt collector, it doesn't say much doing slightly better than that sorry lot out there. Most of them are lucky to even get paid!"

Anna spluttered in outrage, and feeling that for women everywhere she needed to take a stand, she coldly told Mr Elvin if he wanted something to decorate the office then he could, well...... he could buy a plant. It was far from ideal but this was not in the plan. Taking a deep breath, she informed Mr Elvin that her looks should not matter it was her brain that was the important bit, and she wanted him to acknowledge this.

Mr Elvin gave her a withering look in response. Inspiration struck Anna as she decided to threaten to resign. If they all resigned, he would have to take notice. It would be like that film where they all protested for better pay, they might even be on the news. Drawing herself up tall, she pushed her shoulders back, gave Mr Elvin what she believed to be her coolest, haughtiest look and she said in measured tones.

"Well, if you don't feel I am of value to the company, then I will have to tender my resignation, and so will the rest of the team."

Mr Elvin leant back in his chair regarding Anna for a second before he spoke.

"Well Anna I'll be sorry to lose you all but if that is what you feel you must do, then I won't stop any of you," he remarked, thinking that she would be begging for her job back in seconds.

Annoyed and stunned by the turn of events but determined not to back down Anna stood up, and with what little self-control she had left, she informed him they would all finish at the end of the month and if he made any more inappropriate comments then she would report him to HR. She gleaned a certain satisfaction as a look of fear flashed across his face, at the mention of HR, before she marched out of his office.

Once she heard the door click safely behind her, she looked around at all the faces watching her waiting to see if she had been successful.

"He said no," she paused, as a crushed sigh went around the room, "So I told him we would all resign. He'll have to back down he cannot lose a whole team" Anna told them excitedly, but before she could say anymore a horrified sigh went round the room.

"I've got my mortgage to pay!"

"We're expecting a baby!"

"My Jim will go nuts if I walk out on my job!"

"You were supposed to get us more money, not get us all sacked!"

Anna looked at them horrified, "I don't mean actually resign, just threaten to, it'll be like that film. The company will have to back down" She said looking around at them hopefully.

"It's alright for you, single with no mortgage or kids or anyone to think about but some of us have commitments!" One person said angrily.

There was a nod and mutterings from the rest of them as people turned back to their screens.

Looking around Anna spotted Mr Elvin watching through his office window smirking.

Collapsing in her chair she looked sadly at Jenny. "Well, that went well."

"Don't worry he'll have forgotten it all by tomorrow." Jenny told her gently shaking her head.

"I threatened to report him to HR too!" Anna admitted.

"Blimey Anna. I would love to have seen his face." Jenny was now laughing in delight.

However, seeing how woe be-gone Anna looked, Jenny stopped quickly. Feeling slightly guilty for pushing Anna to tackle Mr Elvin about their pay rises, since Anna was the only person Mr Elvin actually seemed to like in the team, she tried again. "Look, I bet you any money you like, tomorrow morning he will call you in to discuss what went wrong and keep you on."

Anna nodded hesitantly wanting to believe what she was being told.

Jenny smiled encouragingly. "Wait till tomorrow and then tell him that your cat died this morning, cry a bit and say it's made you a bit over emotional today."

"Jenny, first I don't have a cat and second that is just plain wrong!" Anna was horrified at the suggestion.

"Mm. You're probably right," Jenny agreed with a shrug, making Anna wonder how many times Jenny had used that excuse before.

"Say you've got the painters in," was Tim's advice. For which, both girls gave him a look of scorn. "Women's problems! You know it's the most believable," he replied looking completely unrepentant.

"Tim, I'll remember this conversation, next time you are drunk and moaning you haven't got a girlfriend," Jenny answered and with that she turned off her computer and suggested they go for a drink to cheer themselves up as it was practically five o'clock and home time.

Looking at the clock Anna could see it was barely past four thirty. She was about to decline, as it was really a bit too early, but Jenny was already running a brush through her sleek blonde bob.

"Hurry up Anna, time to go!"

"Perhaps we should wait until it's nearly five." Anna suggested

"Anna, you have just resigned. What's he going to do? Sack you? Too late for that!"

As she fully comprehended the extent of her actions, Anna struggled to suppress the urge to run into her boss' office and beg for her job back.

Seeing the look of panic on Anna's face, Jenny linked her arm though Anna's and marched her out of the office.

Several drinks later it all seemed fine. Jenny had promised to help her with her CV, and there were always hundreds of finance admin jobs available in London, she was going to be fine, Anna kept telling herself.

Jenny was preparing to fight her way to the bar again when a man approached the table.

"You're early," Jenny accused him. "But now you are here, you can get the drinks in, two gin and tonics for us and whatever you're having."

Anna sat watching, with amusement, as the bloke headed off to the bar without question. She never failed to be amused by the way Jenny always said whatever you're having even though they were the ones paying.

"What happened to Mike?" she asked, aware she was starting to slur, and deciding to make this next drink her last.

"Anna, I'm too young to be tied to one man. I just want to play the field a bit, I'll settle down when I am older."

Jenny was in her early-thirties, like Anna, but unlike Anna, Jenny was confident, assertive, with a great figure, an amazingly dirty laugh and half the men in the county falling at her feet. Years ago, Anna had tried to copy her but now she just sat back and watched in admiration.

She frequently tried to forget the time she had briefly tried to be more like Jenny. Having read a magazine article which told you to stand in front of the mirror every day for five minutes and repeat the mantra "I am a sex goddess", she convinced herself it would work. But when Anna had actually tried it, she had just felt stupid. Although in hindsight, perhaps doing it in tracksuit bottoms, after attempting to jog around the block, was not giving it the best chance of success. Especially, since she had been bright red, sweating and struggling to breathe.

Rob, as the gorgeous drink bearing man turned out to be called, put the drinks down and sat next to Jenny giving Anna the isn't it time you were leaving now smile. Being one of Jenny's friends this was a look Anna could read quite easily, but she quickly went off Rob, since most men usually let you have at least one drink before making you feel like a gooseberry.

Anna stood up to leave, she swayed slightly, definitely time to go, she thought. After saying good bye to Jenny, she turned and smiled at Rob, taking some satisfaction from the fact he would not be around in a week's time.

Outside the pub Anna paused to take a deep breath, unable to face going back to her small bedsit she headed towards her best friend's flat instead.

Lucy answered the door, and seeing Anna she smiled, "So did you turn out to be a brilliant negotiator?" She asked, but her face fell as Anna looked like she was about to burst into tears.

"That bad? I've just opened a bottle of wine. You look like you need a glass."

Accepting the glass Lucy held out she gratefully sank onto the sofa.

"So, what happened?" Lucy asked.

"I lost my job," Anna ruefully admitted.

"They sacked you?" Lucy was surprised.

"No," Anna shook her head and explained the whole story.

After listening to her, Lucy smiled and all she said was, "Good."

"Good, what do you mean? Good? I have no money from the end of the month. How can you say good?" Had Lucy not listened to a word she had just said?

"Anna, let's face it, last week you were moaning that you had had a half hour lecture off the admin lady because you ordered the wrong colour folders for the office. You even asked me where your life had gone so wrong that you were stuck in a job where people worried about things so mundane and tedious."

Before Anna could contradict her Lucy carried on. "You spend your life telling us all, how you would escape the rat race given half a chance. Well, here is your chance."

"But I was making a career out of credit control." Anna protested, scared at the thought of what Lucy had just suggested.

Lucy raised her eyebrows sceptically at Anna. "You hate people shouting at you and threatening you because they don't want to pay their bills. Come on admit it you loathe the job. The only thing you would really miss is going shopping at lunchtime with Jenny."

Anna smiled reluctantly because she knew Lucy was right. And then as she considered what

Lucy was saying, she realised that this could be the golden opportunity she had been waiting for. This was fate. She would now land a top job in the city, have the use of a plush company car, a gorgeous flat, make that penthouse overlooking the Thames, and of course she would meet her dream man. She would just had given a fantastic presentation that had saved the company and made it more profitable than anyone thought possible, whilst looking stunning in a Prada suit, with her perfectly high-lighted hair, or perhaps low lights would look more business-like, and after the MD had given her another huge pay rise, there he would be, her dream man. Of course, after a Hello or OK wedding, they would move to the country from where they could commute to work every day by helicopter or something.

"Anna. One step at a time, find a job you like before you start running the Stock Exchange!" Lucy like Jenny often teased her about daydreaming. However, her smile faded as she noticed the time, "I'm really sorry but I've got to go out shortly. Nick's team all got their bonuses today so we are off to celebrate." Lucy stopped abruptly wishing she had not mentioned her husband's bonus. "Are you going to be ok? Look, I can cancel if you want."

"I'm fine!" She replied with just a little too much exasperation.

"Look I'm only trying to help." Her guilt meant Lucy was getting defensive too.

"Honestly I'll be ok, it's just a job." Anna replied collecting her things together.

"Exactly and this has given you have a real chance to turn your life into what you want it to be now. You always say you want to live in the country but instead you come and live with me in the city. Jenny got you the job so you have never made steps towards the sort of career you would like. You say you want to work outdoors and meet people but you work in an office where you see the same people every day, never need to go anywhere and have no interaction with the public apart from people who won't pay their bills."

"That new salesman at work I told you about was nice, and anyway I am good at maths so finance is the right place for me to work," Anna protested, starting to feel like a failure at Lucy's words.

"But you had nothing in common with the salesman, did you? I was good at French at school but I do not want to live in France," she paused debating whether to continue. "Anna I sometimes worry that you are living my dream, my life and not your own."

Her words were frighteningly accurate. "But I'm happy here," Anna protested again now starting to feel like some sort of hanger on.

"Anna, I know you are and I love having you living so nearby, but now we are starting to grow up a bit, I feel that by asking you to come to London with me I have held you back from making the choices which would lead to where you would be happy." Lucy finally admitted the thoughts she had been harbouring for a while.

"I did come down here of my own free volition. I can make my own decisions." Anna decided arguing was better than facing the truth. When Lucy had invited Anna to live with her, Anna had been living at her parents, drifting along wondering why other people returning from University were all making a success of their lives whilst she had no idea what to do or where to go. Lucy, asking Anna to go and live with her had seemed to be the chance she was waiting for, and it had made the decision for her. She was going to be a career girl. Even when Lucy and Nick had moved in together, she had found herself a little bedsit and convinced herself she was Bridget Jones. The only problem was Mark Darcy was nowhere to be found. Anna now wondered if it had given her the chance to avoid making a decision and decide what direction to take her life in. But the thought of deciding which way to take her life had and still seemed a frightening prospect.

"Look why don't we get a take away and we'll look at your career options," Lucy said, now feeling extremely guilty. But Anna shook her head. The last thing she needed was Lucy sat there all night reminding her life was one big mess and worse still expecting her to do something about it.

As she trudged on to the tube station rather than day dream as normal, she began to get cross.

How dare her boss, treat her like that? Or Lucy, think she had no mind of her own? The more she thought back over what had happened, the angrier she became.

All fired up now and still in her work clothes she braced her shoulders deciding she would show them all. She was going to take action and prove to them all just how successful she could really be.

However, as she looked around, she paused and wondered what to do as all the recruitment agencies were now closed for the day. She was still full of righteous indignation, and she did not want to merely carry on back to her flat. Looking around her she spotted the newsagents, she could at least get the jobs paper she decided, convincing herself it was a start.

Ten minutes later she was back in the flat surrounded by papers, a few magazines, a bottle of cheap wine and a large slab of chocolate, ready to find the life changing job and abandon the rat race.

Two hours later the wine bottle was empty and the chocolate had long gone. The Times did not quite match her job spec or rather and to be more accurate she did not match theirs and the local paper would be great if she wanted part time work for three hours a week.

As she thought about what she wanted to do, it hit her that she did not really want to work in an office anymore. Finally, Anna started to acknowledge that maybe and only maybe Lucy had a point.

She picked up the magazines and idly flicked through Cosmo, quickly by passing ten ways to the greatest orgasm ever, thinking that she'd settle for any old orgasm right now.

Having worked through the jobs in Cosmo, she decided she did not want to become an air hostess, as she was terrified of flying, a clairvoyant, the only time she had dabbled in tarot cards they had predicted a catastrophic event and the next day she had been given the worst haircut ever or a beauty therapist, since she wasn't even that great at painting her own nails. She did want to leave the rat race but it had to be for the right job.

Anna put the magazine down, after quickly reading her stars. However, they were no help. Apparently, she should not rock the boat at work. It was too late for that she thought, annoyed at the astrologer. She really wanted the prediction to say your perfect man would arrive in five days' time and in two weeks' time your perfect job. Was that really too much to ask, she wondered.

She picked up the TV remote and flicked through the channels but there was nothing on. She drummed her fingers then inspiration hit. The internet, how had she not thought of this before?

She worked her way through all the main sites, she read job description after job description and each time convinced herself it was not quite what she wanted. She would send off her CV next week, when she hadn't drunk a bottle of wine and could get Lucy to sense check everything.

Leaning back against the sofa, Lucy's words came back to haunt her. Was this what she really wanted? She had not got excited about anything she had seen. She sat for a moment thinking about what she did want. What was her favourite dream?

Slowly she picked up her iPad again. She opened Google and started to type, 'working with horses.' This time hundreds of jobs and agencies appeared. There were dozens of adverts the wages were fairly poor and they seemed to want anything from a nanny to a home help, rightly believing that horses would lure people in. There were many others though, that genuinely wanted riding instructresses, grooms, stud hands and jockeys. Anna read through the adverts, but many required qualifications which she did not have. And then after half an hour she found it.

The advert was brief but offered what she was looking for. "Yard manager wanted for Riding School in Cotswolds. Must have sound business knowledge and a genuine love of horses."

Anna had loved riding and had spent many happy weekends at the local riding stables during her teenage years. She had even worked there one summer holiday whilst she was at University. The idea was to get a great tan and meet a rich young farmer. Unfortunately, it had rained most of the time and the only farmer she met was a ninety-year-old who turned up on his tractor to deliver hay.

The advert also said there was accommodation supplied as the person would need to live on site, and personality was far more important than qualifications although some experience was necessary.

She read the advert over and over again, a bubble of excitement mounting. But it all seemed too soon, so she left the page open, put the iPad down and wandered into the kitchen in need of distraction. Finding nothing, as the fridge was in its usual state of emptiness, she headed back into the lounge. She flopped down on the sofa still at a loose end and started flicking through the TV channels again but nothing held her attention for long. Her eyes kept straying to the iPad lying innocently on the sofa.

Jumping up she strode across the room and reached for the phone, dialled the number and then hung up as fast as possible, hoping it had not started ringing at the other end.

Anna looked at the phone warily, then at the clock. It was too late she told herself. She sat back down, hesitated, and then decided to do it before she could change her mind. So, she phoned again, with each ring of the phone her heart seemed to beat louder, she desperately wanted to hang up but it felt as if her arm was glued to her ear. The phone had been answered, she panicked. Just say hello, she told herself, but her mouth had gone dry and no sound was coming out. At the other end of the phone line there was a click and then a voice boomed out.

"Obviously I'm not here so leave a message if I need to return your call." The voice was posh and frightening

Lost in thought she realised the phone had beeped and was now recording, she froze, as she had not planned what to say. Instead of hanging up, Anna started gushing "Hi I am phoning about the job, although maybe it has gone." The thought had just hit her, "but hopefully it has not. Anyway, I'm afraid I have no qualifications. Well actually I do have my B test and the ones below it as I was in pony club and I have taught the youngsters at the local riding school." Please shut up she told herself, actually starting to hear what she must sound like as she rambled on without pausing for breath. "But if the job is still available." Please let it still be available, she silently prayed. "My mobile number is…" She started to reel off her number then paused; she had gone completely blank. "Oh no! Sorry it's, it's…." she froze as the numbers which normally tripped off her tongue disappeared completely. She quickly repeated the first few digits and at last remembered it. "It's….." She rattled the numbers off quickly, relief washing over her. "Well, thank you. Bye."

Great, she thought as she hung up and realised how awful her message would sound to the person who had to listen to it. She groaned, dropping her head into her hands. Well at least that was over with, she thought. There was no way they would phone now. At first, she felt relieved, it was a silly idea really. She tried to convince herself that she was a city girl who did not want to work in the country. It could be slave labour; long hours and it would probably rain all the time.

But there was another voice that was getting louder and it told her she did want to do this and now the idea was there she realised she did want to do this very badly indeed.

Chapter Two

Paris stretched out luxuriously, as she heard Daniel turn off the shower. She remained where she was, sprawled across the bed sheets, as he padded in from the bathroom naked. As he turned to pick up a pair of jeans lying on the armchair in the corner of the room, she allowed herself a small self-satisfied smirk. Daniel slid the jeans over his long legs, and she watched as the muscles in his taut back and broad shoulders flexed as he tightened his belt before pulling on a shirt.

Chelsea Pettiford-Reed may have bagged the richest bachelor in the area but she certainly had the best looking one she thought smugly, just one hurdle to go and Chelsea would be well and truly put in her place.

"Well, I can't lie here all day!" Paris announced, although she had still not moved.

"Really?" Daniel turned to her, an amused smile playing on his lips.

"Yes, Mummy is taking me to Brockworth House Spa for the day, she knows how stressed I've been lately." She raised a perfectly manicured hand to her brow to emphasise the point.

"Stressed?" Paris completely missed the warning tone in Daniel's voice as he reached for his watch.

"Daniel, you know I'm desperate for us to move into the Manor." Paris beseeched, from under her eyelashes.

"What and live with my mother?" Daniel asked amused, knowing there was no chance of any of the parties agreeing to that.

"I thought you were going to sort that problem out!" Paris returned trying to hide her annoyance, but seeing the look on Daniel's face she quickly moved on.

"I have so many plans to transform the place." Paris' pouted prettily, knowing Daniel nearly always gave in.

"It doesn't need transforming, its fine the way it is." Daniel gave her a tight smile, hiding his irritation at yet another attack on his childhood home.

Paris suppressed a sigh. "I meant transform it back to its former glory." Cleaning it would be a start she added in her head. She paused, smiling sweetly at him before adding, "And, of course, it would be the perfect place for our engagement party."

"Don't I have to propose first?" Daniel asked, watching the annoyance flash across her face.

"We both know it's what we want." Paris recovered quickly.

Daniel said nothing, merely kissing her briefly and within minutes he was out of the house.

Was it what they both wanted Daniel wondered for the hundredth time, as he started the engine and pulled out of the village, heading for the new site he and Tom were developing into luxury homes? However, he did not dwell on the subject long, but instead he turned his attention to whether the new Cotswold stone would be delivered that day, for once they had brickies on site and no bricks. Daniel had been unwilling to use the first batch of stone that had been delivered as it was too dark a yellow and would look cheap. He and Tom had built up a very successful business building top of the range houses and he wasn't about to compromise now.

As he turned into the development he smiled, still proud that this was what he had achieved, the exclusive estate of eight houses were nearly finished and then they would move onto Broome Hill, their new project, which would really establish them as one of the leading developers in the area. He pulled up alongside Tom's pick-up truck and let George out. He watched as George bounded off, no doubt hoping to find a builder whose breakfast he could finish.

"Late night?" Daniel turned to find Mollie watching him with interest. "You're normally the first one here!"

Daniel smiled. "Maybe!" He replied giving nothing away. "So, to what do we owe the pleasure? Not that it's not lovely to see you!" He quickly amended as Mollie raised her eyebrows.

"My wonderful children! Why is it on a school morning I am forever screaming at them to put shoes on, find socks, and brush their teeth for longer than ten seconds, but today, first day of the school holidays, when I was dreaming of a lie in, the little cherubs woke at six and decided to get dressed!" She half laughed and half groaned at the same time.

"Is that a hint for a coffee?" Daniel asked.

"I thought you'd never offer."

Together they walked over to the office, which Daniel unlocked, as Tom came out of one of the houses.

"The decorators have done a good job," Tom commented catching them up. "You were right to change firms."

While the kettle boiled, Tom and Daniel looked at the plans deciding what needed completing that day.

"I'll make the coffee then, shall I?" Mollie asked no one in particular.

"Thanks," came the joint reply, although they barely looked up.

Spooning instant coffee into the mugs Mollie watched them. They stood together, their stances were the same, the expressions were the same, as was the thick dark blonde hair, although Daniel's was slightly longer, whilst Tom's was fairly short, they both had the same blue eyes, but again Daniel's were more piercing while Tom's were softer. Mollie often joked that Daniel was the air brushed version of Tom, more chiselled, more tanned. Yet, she would not change her husband for the world and much as she loved Daniel as a brother in law, Tom was the one for her.

"Mollie, the love of my life, please, please make me a coffee."

Interrupted from her thoughts Mollie looked up to find Rich the site manager stood in the door, bleary eyed and unshaven. She laughed as he ran a hand through his short dark hair, clearly trying to wake up. "And, which poor woman was it this time?"

"Mollie I'm shocked, I don't know what Tom tells you about me, but you've got it all wrong."

"Course I have." Mollie gently teased him as she handed over the coffee.

"Tom, you are a lucky bloke, if I had a woman like this, I would be happy to settle down."

"Rich I'll have retired before you find a woman who makes you want to settle down!" Tom remarked with heavy irony.

Once Rich had wandered off with his coffee, Mollie turned to Tom and Daniel. "Actually, I'm glad I've got you both together. We need to talk about Rose." Mollie inwardly sighed, as both men looked instantly wary, cross that she was the one that had to deal with this and make them see that they needed to do something, she continued. "I was in the shop yesterday and Lucinda Cottesmore was hinting that there was a problem."

"Tell the nosy cow to poke her nose into someone else's business." Tom replied his normally quiet voice tinged with anger.

"Don't worry I fobbed her off, but things are getting worse. What do you think Daniel?"

Daniel paused and sighed, "I know, even Paris keeps on at me to do something, look Mollie I'm on it, don't worry."

Mollie glanced at him, unable to voice her thoughts but knowing full well that Paris' concern would only be for herself and not Rose. Realising she had made as much progress as was possible that morning she gathered up her bag. "Well, have a good day, I'm off to spend the day at The Fun House, which ironically, for adults, is less fun than the dentist."

Tom laughed, "What drinking coffee, eating cake and gossiping with the other mums?"

Mollie pulled a face at him before rolling her eyes. "Yes, it's great! Spending hours of your life in a room with hundreds of screaming kids and no windows is bliss!" She replied as she headed out of the door.

As Tom and Daniel packed up for the day, Daniel heard his phone bleep and glancing at it he realised there were three missed calls. Waving a hand to Tom he hit the answer phone button.

"Daniel? Are you there? I hate this damn machine." There was a pause and a sigh. "Obviously you are not, well the paperwork has come through to renew my licence and it's ridiculous, how they expect anyone to fill this in is beyond me."

Daniel realised this was his chance to make Rose realise that things needed to change. But he sighed as the enormity of the task hit him.

The phone beeped again and this time the voice was excited and caused Daniel to smile as he recognized it. "Dan, it's Lizzie. I'm going to be back in New York in September. I would love it if you could come out for a visit. At least think about it! Please."

Daniel smiled, thinking it was certainly tempting. He unlocked his truck and watched as

George bounced in, the phone beeped again. "Daniel, honestly this paperwork is beyond belief, you are going to have to help me with it. Phone me when you get this message!"

Climbing into the car Daniel realised he would have to have the talk Mollie had suggested sooner rather than later. It would not be an easy conversation to have with a normal person but his mother was formidable at the best of times, and generally ignored any news or advice she did not want to hear, this was not going to be easy.

"George, we're off for tea and cakes." George, who responded better to the words; tea and cakes, than most dogs do to walkies, sat bolt upright his ears pricked. Daniel wryly smiled, unconvinced whether it was his mother's endless supply of cakes or her Labrador Tilly that held the greater attraction, either way the Great Dane knew tea and cakes meant only one place.

The reason Rose had to renew her licence was because she ran a riding school, although Daniel frequently told her she stood a high chance of being able to register as a charity. Whenever he pointed this out, she would raise an eyebrow and tell him there was more to life than money. Suitably chastised Daniel would give up once more and let her carry on in her own way.

As Daniel drove up the long drive to the house he noticed, not for the first time, that the fence needed repairing in places and that the drive had numerous potholes and it was only a matter of time before someone damaged their car in one. His thoughts briefly returned to the Paris' hints that morning, taking her advice would solve a number of problems. Not wanting to think about it, Daniel turned his attention to the thick hedges brimming with hawthorn flowers, they really needed trimming, he decided. He'd have to send one of their men over to sort it out.

Turning the final bend Daniel could not resist pausing to admire the house, although the windows required painting and the roof repairing, it was still stunning.

The house was balanced with nine sash windows along the first floor and four sash windows either side of the double oak front doors, which were framed by stone pillars. Ivy covered one side of the house, and a climbing rose, with large white blooms, wove around the doors and windows, leaving very little of the Cotswold stone the house was built in showing. If Rose saw a guest arriving, she would fling both doors wide open, otherwise visitors generally made their way round to the kitchen, where after clambering over a pile of wellies and coats in the boot room, they entered a large farmhouse kitchen.

As the doors had not been flung wide open, Daniel made his way round to the kitchen. From the back garden, the stable yard could mostly be seen. Daniel paused to watch as Rose supervised the turning out of the ponies into their various fields. Children led ponies in all directions as his mother tried to ensure no pony ended up in the wrong field.

"Aaron, Pepper cannot go in the same field as Salt."

"This isn't Salt it's Buttons," shouted Aaron as he was towed towards the field by Buttons.

"Oh, jolly good. Well, let him off then." Daniel watched as Pepper and what was hopefully Buttons cantered off down the field together, kicking up their feet in delight at another night's freedom.

Slowly every pony made it to a field, miraculously without a child getting kicked or bitten, which reminded Daniel of the need to check his mother's insurance. Sighing he turned and made his way into the kitchen.

The room was dominated by a vast pine rectangular table around which sat a mixed collection of chairs, each with various coloured and patterned cushions. At one end of the kitchen was a Welsh dresser which displayed a dainty English tea service with blue hand painted flowers. The other end of the room was dominated by a large deep blue Aga which was not only used for cooking but kept the kitchen warm throughout the winter. Two worn old armchairs sat either side of the range, but they were strictly off limits to the humans as they belonged to the dogs who took up residence whenever the Welsh dresser doors were opened, as they generally hid a large selection of shop brought cakes.

The walls were covered in numerous framed photographs and newspaper clippings, alongside some of which were rosettes. All the pictures were old fashioned, and of a colour quality that suggested they had been taken decades ago, a few were even black and white. The pictures were all of horses, usually competing, Rose in her younger days was in many of them, along with Tom and Daniel but in a couple, there was an older man who bore a striking resemblance to Daniel.

Once all the children had been bundled into cars to go home and do the homework, they had neglected that afternoon in favour of the horses Rose made her way into the kitchen, to collect her car keys.

"Daniel! Darling! Why didn't you say you were coming? Now can you stay whilst I drop young Freddie Price home?"

Without waiting for an answer, she had picked up the car keys and was half way through the door, when she called back to him. "Put the kettle on. Is Paris joining us?"

"No," Daniel called to her retreating back. He did not quite catch his mother's reply but it sounded very like the word "Marvellous!"

Sadly, his mother and Paris had never got on. Paris viewed horses as something you grew out of at fourteen when you discovered boys, so she could never grasp what Rose loved about them, and Rose simply did not understand anyone who did not adore horses.

On the few occasions they met socially the conversations had been awkward with neither woman prepared to make any real attempt with the other one. Hearing the old Land rover rattle back into the yard ten minutes later Daniel flipped the electric kettle switch on as Rose burst into the kitchen.

"So, no Paris? Is this a long-term arrangement or is it just tonight that we are to be deprived of her stimulating company?"

"Just tonight, she was busy," Daniel said in a voice that prevented further prying.

"Oh, I am sorry!" Rose replied sounding anything but.

"Now, about renewing your licence." Rose rolled her eyes and looked at her son, as he attempted to change the subject, she had already forgotten about the paperwork and confined it to the kitchen drawer.

She still failed to understand what Daniel saw in Paris. He was good looking, intelligent, had a great sense of humour and of course he rode horses very well, which in Rose's view at least, was a huge bonus.

"The licence?" Daniel raised the point again.

"Yes. Yes. Yes." Rose dismissed the comment with a wave of her hand, keen to change the subject. "I've been thinking that before next winter comes and since Charlie and I are not getting any younger, we are going to need some more help. The local girls who help after school and at the weekend are great, but I think we need a yard manager, they could also sort out the paperwork."

Daniel nearly choked on his coffee. Rose glared at him, daring him to deny it.

"Exactly you and Charlie are getting older and perhaps," Daniel paused refocusing on her earlier comment and knowing what needed to be said but wondering how to get the words out.

"Of course, we are getting older, but you are interrupting me. Now as I was saying a yard manager is just what I need."

"Right," Daniel replied whilst trying to think of a way to talk his mother out of her latest scheme.

"I've already done the advert, so it is too late to change my mind."

Daniel realised he was going to have to try different tactics.

"Are you free on Sunday? I thought you might like to come our see our new development at Broome Hill?"

Rose looked at Daniel, "Well I'm teaching in the morning, but the afternoon would be lovely."

"Great." Daniel replied not quite able to meet his mother's eye. "I'd better be going."

As Rose waved him off, the fears that constantly lurked at the edge of her consciousness came rushing to the fore and whilst she couldn't put her finger on it, for the first time ever Daniel's behaviour had just made her feel very uneasy.

The beautiful sunny day only increased Anna's conviction that the interview she was heading towards was the start of her new life. When the agency had phoned and told her about the job, her excitement had started to grow and now as she drove through the winding county lanes with endless rolling green fields either side, it was reaching new heights. She was already dreaming about how perfect it would be.

She found the place easily. A large slab of sandstone with the name written in copper plate writing adorned the end of a perfect driveway. The long drive went straight up to the yard with smart white post and rail fencing either side. The paddocks either side of the drive were split into neat squares, with two horses allocated to each paddock in rugs which were also spotlessly clean.

The yard was big and impressive and after parking her car in the clearly marked visitor's spaces, Anna was greeted by an old black Labrador, who looked very friendly. Unfortunately, the lady following him did not. She presumed rightly that this must be Pippa, the owner.

As Pippa greeted Anna and confirmed who she was, a look of disappointment came over her face, causing Anna's excitement to dip.

"You are rather thin. Are you sure you will be able to manage hard manual labour every day? You certainly don't look like you are built for it. Well come into the office."

Anna followed her over to a door with frosted glass panels, above it was a sign declaring that this was the office. Anna's heart sank further at the square clinical room, to describe it as sparse would be an understatement. The only item on the walls was a notice board, with a set of laminated typed rules, neatly pinned to it. The desk was clear, apart from a telephone, a large diary and a pen. There was only one hard plastic chair in the room, which did not invite people to relax, although judging by Pippa no one relaxed whilst on her yard anyway. A coffee machine stood in one corner, whilst Pippa made Anna and herself a coffee, Anna read the rule list. Even the paying clients seemed to be expected to comply with Pippa's demands. Having read the rules and thinking how she would do things differently Anna started imagining what the place would be like if she owned it.

Pippa was describing the day which started promptly at seven. Anna smiled pretending that a seven o'clock start was the most normal thing in the world, thinking she did not need to look good for the horses so appearance would not be such an issue.

Almost as if Pippa could read her mind she said, "I expect all my grooms to be tidy and presentable at all times, my clients expect it."

Anna nodded quickly as Pippa continued.

"We pay standard groom fees, not the office wages you are used to at the moment." Pippa glared hard at Anna almost willing her to say no, just so she could berate her for wasting her time.

Anna nodded again before affirming that the pay was fine.

Pippa looked her up and down once more. "You are very thin. How quickly can you muck out a stable?"

Anna managed to conceal an exasperated sigh. Normally she berated the fact, that her thighs and skinny jeans would never be compatible. Yet here it appeared she needed to look like she had been brought up on three solid meals a day. Anna started to wonder if she would ever fit in anywhere.

Bringing herself back to the present Anna quickly guessed at ten minutes per stable, she hadn't mucked out in years and she was sure Pippa knew that.

The interview appeared to be over.

"I will phone you, when I've seen the others," she told Anna as she stood up. Anna had not had a chance to drink her coffee, but one glance at Pippa made her decide to leave it. As Anna said farewell, Pippa gave her an absent wave. Getting into her car Anna acknowledged it was highly unlikely she would hear from this woman again, and her initial excitement completely died.

Driving back home Anna started to wonder at the sense of her idea, and it slowly dawned on her that she had no experience or qualifications so short of becoming a nanny to a horsy family it would not work. She had not even heard anything form the answer phone message she left, not that that was a huge surprise. She had got carried away but it had all been in vain. When she thought about it sensibly the idea was not even viable.

Later that day, she tried to explain this to Jenny and Lucy.

"So basically, Anna after one dud interview with a complete cow, who was probably jealous you were thinner than her, you are telling us you are going to give up and go back to an office job you hate?" Lucy rolled her eyes.

"Don't say it like that," she protested. "Look I've tried and I've looked into it and I've realised that it won't work."

"Anna, you have tried nothing. What's to say you will not end up working on a fantastic yard, meeting a sexy blacksmith and you'll end up living happily ever after?" Jenny winked.

"Well, I'll give it a couple more weeks," Anna conceded her thoughts already on happily ever after.

Chapter Three

The fact Sunday had bloomed into such a lovely warm and sunny day gave Daniel hope that it would not end in disaster. As he drove Rose over to Broome Hill, they talked about their neighbours, both deliberately keeping the conversation light and innocuous.

The new development was beautifully situated on the outskirts of the next village. He and Tom had had to work carefully with the local council and parish council to get the planning, which contained a number of conditions about who could buy the properties.

Pulling onto the site which was only at foundation level, Daniel saw Rose frown. "I know people need houses but it is sacrilege to dig up this gorgeous meadow."

Daniel sighed realising this was going to be the hardest sales pitch of his life.

"Daniel, don't be like that," Rose said misinterpreting his sigh, "I am very proud of you and Tom and what you have achieved. And even I have to admit you do make the developments blend into the villages well but you must see that it is a shame to destroy this."

Wanting to keep her on side Daniel shrugged non-committedly. "Come and have a look. The views are amazing."

Rose got out of the car and followed him, the fear that had engulfed her when Daniel first suggested this trip was still present as they walked around the site, Daniel pointing out its every virtue over and over again. But Rose still could not understand why he had brought her here.

"Well Daniel I'm sure it will do very well. But after all this walking I would love a cup of tea, I take it there is a kettle in the office?"

Daniel nodded deciding he had sowed the seed and hopefully next time he could advance a little further with his plan.

He unlocked the office and held the door open for Rose. The mobile office was covered in plans showing every angle of the development. Along with artists sketches for what the finished development would look like. As Rose looked at the plans Daniel filled the kettle, glad she was taking an interest.

"Daniel." The word was quietly spoken but too late he realised his mistake.

His eyes slowly lifted to see Rose was looking at a picture of the site with two senior residents enjoy a game of golf and underneath were emblazoned the words 'Broome Hill, the Cotswolds Premier Retirement Village.'

Swearing silently to himself, Daniel took a deep breath, "Mum."

"I'd like you to take me home."

"Mum." Daniel tried again.

"Now. Daniel!" The words allowed no discussion.

"Don't you have a key?" Chelsea asked in malicious amusement as she picked her way along the path that led to the back door, in her stiletto heels.

"The front door is stuck and won't open," Paris replied as she pushed at the back door praying Rose had not locked it for once. She smiled back at Chelsea as the door swung open, hiding her relief.

"What an awful kitchen, if you can even call it that!" Chelsea observed to no one in particular as she looked around in disdain. Paris could not help but agree, she never dared sit down in any of the chairs in case they marked her designer clothes.

"Darlings, I can make this soooooo BEE U TI FULL." Fabian, Chelsea's interior designer, sang as he pranced around the kitchen flinging his arms about. "I'm thinking concrete work surfaces, they are just totes amaze."

"I was thinking shabby chic." Paris returned to gain control.

"Shabby chic?" Fabian glanced at Chelsea and they both sniggered. "Darling that's so yesterday."

"Daddy says style never goes out of fashion!" Paris countered back. "And after all he'll be paying for the whole place to be refurbished."

"Can Daniel not afford it?" Chelsea asked innocently.

"Of course, he can," Paris returned, trying to appear nonchalant "Daddy has offered it as one of our wedding presents. After all he wouldn't want me living in this dump." Paris replied looking in disgust at the armchair nearest the Aga which seemed to be covered with an old horse blanket.

Realising just how much commission he might make, Fabian tucked his arm through Paris's, "Now Darling show me everything. This. Will. Be. Amazeballs."

Flashing Chelsea, a smug smile Paris led the way through to the hallway, which was dominated by a huge oak staircase that swept down from vast landings on either side of the hall, before the two staircases met and merged for the final descent. Paris loved it, she had visions of sweeping down the staircase to a sea of admiring guests, all standing in the hall below, once she and Daniel finally moved in. Even Fabian seemed silenced by it for a second, but then he spoke. "Darling I'm thinking steel and glass, this wood has to go!"

Paris was about to disagree knowing Daniel loved the natural oak staircase, but before she could say anything angry voices were heard in the kitchen and the door flew open to reveal Rose.

"What exactly are you doing here, may I ask?" Rose demanded glaring at Paris.

Fabian who seemed oblivious to the icy atmosphere, span round, "Oooh who are you?" he asked regarding Rose's cord trousers, striped shirt and Jodhpur boots with a look of horror. "Interesting outfit Darling, but you haven't quite pulled off the country look. Tweed is in this year."

Rose's initial look of fury, was replaced with one of complete disdain, as she regarded him as though he was something unpleasant on the bottom of her shoe, "And who are you?"

"I'm Fabian and I am here to make this place look spectacular," He sang proudly.

Did he just do Jazz hands? Paris wondered briefly but before she could think any further or more importantly stop him, he waved his arm around the hallway, "For a start all of this needs to go, I don't know who could live in this dump!"

"I would like you to leave my house now!" The words were spoken quietly.

"Excuse me!" Fabian replied, but Chelsea who had watched the proceedings with undisguised glee now stepped forward and linked her arm through Fabian's.

"Darling it's time to go, it would seem Paris has been a little bit naughty and wasn't supposed to be here after all." And flashing Paris a triumphant smile she turned to leave just as Daniel walked into the hall.

"What the.....?" He asked fixing his glare on Paris.

"Hello Tiger!" Fabian was in ecstasy at the appearance of Daniel but seeing the fury on his face, Chelsea quickly pulled Fabian through the front door. As they left Fabian could be heard exclaiming, "How have I never set eyes on that man before?"

And just before the door clicked shut, Chelsea replied, "Well enjoy that glimpse because I doubt, we'll be seeing much of him with Paris after this!"

Back in the hallway Rose turned to face Daniel, "I'm off to feed the horses and I don't want to find either of you here when I get back." And with her head held high she marched from the room.

Daniel turned to Paris, "Just what exactly was that all about?"

"It's called the future Daniel, because believe me I refuse to live in this dump the way it is!" Paris was straight on the attack, her hands on her slim hips, the perfect lips pouting and her green eyes flashing.

"I don't actually remember anyone asking you to live here!" Daniel replied in a low furious tone.

"Well, I'm not living in that tiny cottage." Paris hissed back.

"It would seem we won't be living together then." Daniel stated coldly.

Paris regarded him for a second before stamping her foot in anger, "You may not be able to face what is going on with Rose, but at some point, you'll have to deal with it and then you'll be living here alone! Because this time I won't have you back!" Paris seethed before storming out the front door to her car where she hovered briefly, waiting to see if Daniel would follow her, but when it became obvious, he had no intention of doing that she screamed and wrenched the door open.

Daniel winced as the door to the Porsche slammed hard and the engine revved, though not as loudly as the music that was pouring from the speakers. He watched with relief as the tyres screeched down the drive, the jet-black hair of the driver flying in the breeze before being obscured by the dust the car was churning up.

"Good. Bye. Paris!" he said out loud as he shut the front door behind him, leaving as well,

George, was sat on the passenger seat regarding his master with his head slightly on one side before sighing and slumping down; it was a speech George had heard on numerous occasions in the last ten years.

"You're tired of all the arguments too aren't you mate?" asked Daniel as he rubbed George's head. "I guess she has worn you out as well."

Leaning on the steering wheel Daniel sighed, still unable to believe that Paris had chosen that day of all days to sneak into the house. Although he was aware, he had done the majority of the damage where Rose was concerned, he was still exasperated at the way the day had turned out.

Turning the key in the ignition he pulled away from the house aware that the two women he had upset both needed space to calm down.

But as he thought about it, he released a sigh of relief as he realised there would be no more screaming tantrums about the fact, he could not commit to a marriage proposal. The trouble was Paris had become such high maintenance and lately their whole relationship seemed to revolve around Paris wanting to live in the Manor House.

Yes, it was definitely over this time he reassured himself, he was sure he would not hear from her again.

Lucy and Jenny bounced into Anna's flat, waving bottles of Prosecco and promising her great night to celebrate the fact that her life as a credit controller was now over.

But despite their best efforts the atmosphere was strained. Four weeks after her job search had begun Anna had run out of time and was moving back in with her parents. She had been sure she would find a job, after all she had been to enough interviews. Many of which had been an experience she would rather forget; there had been spoilt children, horrible horses, vicious dogs and one old guy who had mentioned at least three times during the interview that the previous groom never wore a bra, Jenny had jokingly announced she might apply for the job if Anna did not want it.

Lucy poured the drinks and handed them out.

"Right, what shall we drink to?" Jenny asked.

Anna sighed, not missing the look Lucy shot at Jenny.

"Anna it really is not that bad," remarked Lucy trying to lighten the atmosphere.

"Which bit? Moving home to Mum and Dad's, jobless and single to probably end up working back at the pub, I worked at when I was sixteen, or the fact that out of the last six interviews, and I use the term interview loosely not one was in any way legal, ethical or moral?"

Anna was interrupted from saying anymore by her phone ringing. "That'll be my mother asking if I've packed yet!" She said as Lucy rolled her eyes.
She picked up the phone, and it took her a second to realise it was the number from the advert she had left the terrible answer phone message for.

She answered it quickly with a hopeful Hello.

"Hello. You applied for the job at my yard, are you still interested?" The lady was brisk and just as scary as her answer phone message.

"Um, yes, I mean I'm definitely still interested." Anna replied trying to suppress her hope that her miracle had just arrived.

"Right well I suggest you come to the yard on Sunday morning and we can have a proper chat, do you know Upper Sallington?" she asked mentioning a village Anna had never heard of.

"Of course," Anna lied, thinking she would find it on the internet.

"Right, from the centre of the village go past the pub, and after the ford, it is the third drive on the left. If you get lost ask for The Manor and I'll see you at ten."

And with that Anna realised she had hung up.

Lucy and Jenny looked at her expectantly but the phone rang again and Anna groaned as she saw the word Mother flash up. Taking a deep breath, she answered it.

"Darling, seeing as you are coming home your Father and I have decided to come and pick you up on Sunday. We'll be there at half past twelve. Do make sure you are ready not like when we picked you up from university."

"Mum that was different." Anna tried to retake control of the conversation.

"Really? I bet you haven't started packing yet, have you?" She paused and when Anna said nothing, she continued, "Now your Father has spoken to a couple of his golf partners and one of them has offered to help us out by offering you a job as his PA, and Barbara Wyatt's son is back home as well, which will be nice for you."

"Great," Anna replied with a sinking feeling.

"Well honestly darling, you could be a little more grateful you know. After all, you are lucky to have a home to come back to."

"I know. Thank you, Mum. See you Sunday." Anna gave up and unable to converse any further she hung up.

"Well?" asked Jenny.

"I've got an interview with the job I liked on Sunday and my mother phoned to say Adrian Wyatt is back home too." She raised her hands in a sarcastic cheer.

Jenny raised her eyebrows questioningly.

However, Lucy answered with a laugh, "We were at school with Adrian Wyatt. From memory the only thing that turns him on is something containing a megabyte."

"Right," Jenny announced jumping to her feet, "well forget Adrian what's his name we are off to celebrate you getting the interview you wanted."

Anna smiled for the first time that evening and promised herself that no matter how awful this job might be, it was her only chance to escape going back home.

Mollie, Tom and Daniel were all sitting around Rose's kitchen table, the atmosphere appeared relaxed as Daniel had managed to convince Rose he wasn't suggesting she lived at Broome Hill and he had agreed, for now, that help on the yard was the best way forward. No one mentioned the fact that Rose seemed to be running out of candidates for the job.

"How did the interview go today?" Mollie asked tentatively when it was clear Rose was not going to offer up the information willingly.

"She lectured me on health and safety and said the yard would need investment if she was to work here."

"No! Not health and safety." Daniel murmured ironically and wished he had been there to employ her as it would have given him an ally in getting his mother to update her insurance and everything else that needed to be put in place.

"I know what you are thinking Daniel but I don't need some hoighty toighty madam telling me how to run my yard. No one has ever been hurt on this yard, ever." Rose returned with feeling.

From the hallway Billy, Lottie and Josh could be heard giggling and whispering, however Billy was clearly getting frustrated about something, as he rattled a door hard. Standing up Rose went to explain to her grandchildren once again that the study door was locked and she had lost the key. As usual Billy took the news badly and was on the verge of tears when Rose suggested they went in search of cakes. The promise of cake was a more than adequate diversion and all three children came charging back into the kitchen.

"So today was the last interview then?" Daniel asked as casually as he could, as Rose walked back in with Billy and started producing various packets of cakes from the dresser.

Mollie sighed silently, wondering if Billy would go to sleep before midnight with the amount of sugar he had consumed, whilst wishing Rose would just open the study and be done with it. It caused problems every time they came.

Rose paused before answering Daniel's question, to swallow down the fear that the seemingly innocent question had triggered. Despite Daniel's assurances, the trip to Broome Hill had hugely unsettled her. "Actually no, I've another one on Sunday, nice sounding girl, she left an answer phone message a while ago but the old machine must have been playing up as I only picked it up today."

Daniel paused for a second thinking, and then remembered the message. "Not the girl who didn't even know her own phone number. She'd be no use at all." He silently cursed believing he had deleted the message weeks ago.

"Thank you, Daniel, but I am more than capable of knowing who would be good for this yard. And if you are going to listen to my messages, in future please have the decency to pass them on." She fixed him with a glare and was relieved when he looked slightly shame faced, perhaps he had not completely written her off yet.

"Look she might be nice but you need real help. Not someone who couldn't organise a…"

"Honestly Daniel, I'm not about to employ just anyone." Rose said with finality, whilst secretly wishing Daniel had not heard the message. Under normal circumstances she would never have entertained giving the girl an interview, but she had sounded kind and Rose was in need of kindness after recent events.

"Why don't you help interview her?" Tom suggested to Daniel, with a meaningful look.

"Good idea." Daniel replied, thinking a few tough questions would have her running out of the door.

"I can see what you are trying to do," Rose replied.

"Stop being so suspicious, I'm not trying to do anything. I'm just offering to help." Daniel replied innocently.

Rose smiled at her son, she never backed down from a challenge. She was going to offer this girl the job as she desperately needed someone on her side, otherwise she was scared she would lose everything.

Chapter Four

Daniel finished the cup of coffee he had been drinking and picked up his car keys ready to head to the interview that morning. As much as he needed someone to help keep an eye on Rose, after hearing the answer phone message, which the girl they were about to interview had left, he was adamant she was not the person he was looking for.

Deep in thought, he was surprised by a knock at the door. Opening it he was even more surprised to find the woman on his doorstep.

She walked in without an invitation and turned to him, in what he presumed was meant to be a provocative pose.

"Angie, so what can I do for you?" Daniel asked, thinking this was the last thing he needed this morning and wondering how quickly he could get rid of her.

"Don't look so worried Daniel," she smiled batting eyelashes that were clearly false despite the clumps of mascara.

Daniel smiled politely waiting for her to expand upon the reason for her visit.

She smiled in what was meant to be a girlish way, which he simply found annoying. "A cup of coffee would be lovely. Do you have soya milk?" She looked at him expectantly.

"Only full fat dairy I'm afraid." Daniel replied without any hint of remorse, before heading toward the kitchen.

He quickly boiled the kettle and was about to pull two mugs out of the cupboard when he realised, she would no doubt expect fresh coffee. Well, tough, he thought spooning instant into a mug.

"Mugs and instant, how very….." Angie had followed him into the kitchen. "Well, as it's you,

Daniel." She smiled again knowingly as though they were sharing some little secret.

Surely, she wasn't coming onto him, Daniel thought in horror. Not his ex-girlfriend's mother.

"Now I know you and Paris have had a little tiff," she started, somewhat patronizingly. "But I thought I may be able to help."

"Actually, Angie I was just on my way out to a meeting so now really isn't a good time." Daniel handed Angie her drink and leant back against the work surface, not inviting her to sit down.

"I hear young Freddie Prince is having riding lessons at The Manor." Her voice had gone hard now and her eyes glittered maliciously, all pretence of playing nicely had disappeared.

Daniel conceded defeat realising this wasn't just a social visit, and indicated that they sit down, whilst wondering exactly what she was after. Angie had married a man who had turned out to have a penchant for selling second-hand cars, mostly led by his desire to earn as much money as possible. This had taken Angie from a small town no one had ever heard of, to a plush home in the Cotswolds, where she could heavily indulge in her love of fake tan and gold jewellery, especially once the second-hand cars were upgraded to iconic collectibles. Their daughter Paris had been born here and Angie wanted everything for her that life could offer. And there was very little she wouldn't do to make that happen.

Remaining calm, Daniel shrugged, "Don't recognise the name I'm afraid, Mum teaches hundreds of kids." Unfortunately, he was lying and he was pretty sure Angie knew it.

"You know Freddie, proper little troublemaker, he was the one who keyed poor Diana Pennington Smythe's car."

Daniel knew the story, in fact everyone knew the story, Diana had made sure of it.

"Well, it would seem your mother has taken him under her wing and I'd hate to see her get into trouble over it." Angie smiled in what she clearly thought was a caring manner, even though it set Daniel's teeth on edge. "And whilst it's not really my place, I thought, as a friend of the family, you ought to know."

"I'm afraid you've lost me Angie, perhaps you'd better explain." Daniel said hiding his irritation as he realised the interview was due to start.

Anna sat at the crossroads wondering which way to try next, thankful that for once she had left plenty of time. Despite Rose's description on the phone, The Manor was proving extremely hard to find. Having gone up and down what looked like the same lane a dozen times she eventually arrived.

Her heart sank. This was it. As she had driven through the beautiful countryside where the hills gently rose and fell and were interspersed with gorgeous properties all built from Cotswold stone and surrounded by handcrafted stone walls, she had allowed herself to dream about the place she was trying to find, but the sign that let her know she had arrived was a rock covered in moss so the words were barely visible. The driveway ahead of her was supposed to be the pathway to an exciting new life, but not even Anna with her rose-tinted spectacles, could convince herself that this was exactly what she had expected. The driveway looked unkempt with large muddy puddles disguising the potholes, and down each side were overgrown hedges and broken fences, all of which further prevented the entrance living up to the name of the place.

The Manor at Upper Sallington. It had conjured up dreams of a beautiful country house at the end of a perfect gravel drive against a back drop of woodland. In her head she had pictured it swirling in autumn mists making it look even more magical. In a mere twenty-four hours she had built it up to be perfection, as after all, this was the place that was going to change her life.

Well, more accurately, this had to be the place that changed her life as she had run out of options, or rather options that would not want to make her shoot herself.

Anna came back to earth with a bump remembering her mother, she gripped the steering wheel and saying a silent prayer to anyone who may be listening, she put the car into gear and began to navigate her way through the worst of the pot holes.

As she reached the top of the drive, she decided, after her initial disappointment abated, that she liked the feel of the overgrown hedges and the less than perfect drive. They suggested no lined-up wheel barrows and a yard where even the horses were scared to make a mess.

The drive now split in two, to the left was the main house and to the right through an open gate was the riding school, according to a dilapidated old sign. She paused for a second looking at the house in front of her and smiled. The house was breath taking, built in Cotswold stone, with large sash windows along two floors and dormer windows in the loft, and even though it was in need of repair, it still had a charm of its own. Perhaps she had finally fallen on her feet after all.

She drove quickly into the yard and parked. Taking a deep breath Anna realised she had passed the first test and arrived on time, she got out of the car slowly on the look-out for a savage dog ready to maul her, but instead found an old yellow Labrador ambling over to say hello. The wagging tail enabled Anna to release the breath she had not realised she was holding. After being fussed the dog turned around and headed back to where it had come from.

Suddenly a small fat cream pony with its reins swinging loose and its stirrups pulled down and bouncing all over the place, came hurtling around the corner towards her. Following it was a very angry voice yelling for Houdini to be caught.

With a jolt Anna realised the pony was galloping flat out towards the drive, which led to the road. Feeling a bit helpless Anna quickly ran towards the drive. The pony caught sight of Anna and seemed to weigh up his chances before stopping and giving up, to Anna's great relief.

Catching the reins, Anna secured the stirrups and turned to lead the pony back to where it came from only to find a woman watching her.

"Um hi, I'm Anna, I'm here about the job."

Rose looked at her, "Of course you are, I'm Rose, but I'm in the middle of a lesson, we'd better get back before any more of them end up on the floor." She took the reins out of Anna's hands and turned to the pony and in a stern voice said, "Honestly Houdini I thought you could be trusted with Bethany. Fancy bucking her off like that, I am extremely disappointed in you." Houdini merely carried on munching the grass he had just swiped from the verge, completely unbothered by the exchange.

Quickly following Rose, who seemed just as frightening in real life as she did on the phone, Anna passed through an archway and stopped in delight as she entered the stable yard. Built along three sides of a square so all the horses could see one another, the stable block had an old-fashioned air and charm about it. The red bricks had worn away around the edges, the tiled roof dipped at various intervals and the cobbles were uneven. But regardless of these faults, the yard felt loved. Pots of flowers filled the corners with splashes of red, yellow and blue. And the horses looking over their doors all appeared well cared for. Everything seemed quiet and peaceful, and seeing that Houdini had been caught after clattering across the cobbles a few minutes earlier a couple of the ponies sighed and returned to munching their hay.

She hurried on after Rose but in her mind, she was restoring the yard to its former glory. The path now opened out onto fields and an outdoor school where Anna spotted the lesson. A group of children on ponies were standing waiting for Rose to return. Two of the children were having a mock sword fight with their whips, which Rose stopped just in time. In the middle of the school stood a pretty little blonde girl who looked as though she had been crying.

Anna correctly guessed this must be Bethany who had just been bucked off by Houdini and watched as Rose led the pony over to her and crouched down. After Houdini had apologised, during which Anna turned away so she did not laugh, Bethany was put back on board. After she had trotted and cantered a couple of circles each way, she then jumped the jump that had been her undoing only minutes earlier.

"And class Ter rot," immediately all the ponies shuffled forwards at Rose's command. As the lesson continued Anna tried to sum up Rose. She was tall and slim with shoulder length dark grey hair, perfectly set. Not only was her hair perfect but her clothes were also smart. She was dressed in a blue and white striped shirt with the collar turned up, her hair curled neatly over the collar. The shirt was tucked into a pair of slim fitting corduroys and finished with flat leather boots, suitable for wearing in a stable yard. Anna marvelled at her general air of authority and noticed how none of the children kept her waiting as she called them forward to jump the fences.

Finally, the lesson drew to a close and Anna followed them all as they headed back into the yard, leading their ponies.

"Anna, can you help Jemima?" Rose ordered.

"Sure," Anna said a lot more confidently than she felt, especially when she turned to see a young face smiling helplessly at her as a pony dragged her into the stable. Following Jemima into the stable she found her staring at the pony not knowing where to start.

Anna stepped into the stable, and quickly shut the door behind her, not wanting to make a similar mistake to earlier.

Looking at Jemima who still had Pepper's reins in her hand, Anna suggested they take off the saddle. Jemima just looked at her, so Anna started to undo buckles, as she slid the saddle off the girth seemed to catch on something.

"You've not taken the girth out of the martingale," came the accusing little voice on the end of Pepper's reins.

Anna felt all fingers and thumbs, especially after being told off by an eight-year-old, as she removed the girth from the martingale and finished taking the saddle off.

Eventually, she and Jemima emerged from the stable. She followed Jemima into the tack room carrying the saddle and bridle which she had also removed. Pointing her finger Jemima directed her where to put it. Anna glanced at the other children all staggering in carrying their own saddles with the bridles trailing along behind them.

"Don't you want to put this away yourself?" she suggested to Jemima.

"It's not my job" Jemima replied obnoxiously.

Having put the saddle on the rack Anna turned to find an old man in a flat cap, check shirt and corduroy trousers.

"Alright young miss," he greeted Jemima touching his hand to his forehead.

"There you are Charlie, why didn't you help me? She does not know what she is doing." Jemima grandly explained to Charlie, indicating Anna.

Wishing the ground would open up and swallow her, Anna raised her eyes to meet Charlie's kind brown ones. To her surprise she found he winked at her, making Anna feel she had found an ally.

"She looks like she knows what she is doing to me." He spoke with a soft West Country burr; which Anna could not help but like.

"It's so hard to get good staff!" And with that Jemima turned on her heel and walked out of the tack room. As she passed Charlie bowed, which made Anna laugh and they followed her into the yard, where Rose was directing the last of the children to the tack room.

"Can you make sure their parents are there?" she called in Anna and Charlie's direction.

The car park was now full of cars which Anna could see children clambering into, Charlie raised a hand to a couple of cars as they headed off down the driveway.

A brand-new gleaming Range Rover came hurtling up the drive and pulled up taking pride of place in the centre of the drive. A blonde with perfect hair and make-up and in a white outfit was sat in the driver's seat.

"Jemima, darling, come on I have friends coming for lunch," she called as Anna watched Jemima run over to the car. "Thank you, Charlie."

"Anna, I want you to say hello to my mother." Jemima ordered Anna over. Nodding at her to follow him Charlie walked over to the car with her.

"This is Anna. She's come about the job." Charlie introduced Anna even though it was clear Jemima's mother had no interest in her what so ever.

"Well, this place could do with updating. Now come on Jemima."

Anna smiled unsure what to say, feeling slightly awkward at the obvious slur on Charlie and Rose.

"See you next week Mrs Pennington-Smythe" Charlie said with an amused sigh, as the Range Rover roared into life.

As Mrs Pennington-Smythe pulled away she slowed down to acknowledge the driver of the red Maserati just pulling up.

"And here is Bethany's lift," Charlie said sardonically. Anna was wondering what Charlie was trying to imply when Bethany went running past them to where the car had pulled up. Anna had to catch her breath at the man who got out the car.

"Sorry I'm late honey," he said sweeping an ecstatic Bethany up in his arms.

"Sorry Charlie" he called, and then caught sight of Anna, who was trying not to gape. She was not sure whether it was the dark brown eyes and brown hair which gave him a slightly Italian look, or the complete confidence he exuded, but it was not every day she met a man like this.

"Who is this then Bethany?" he asked wondering over to Anna with Bethany still in his arms.

Charlie sighed, flicking his gaze to Anna he made the brief introductions. "Bethany's uncle, Andrew, Anna, she's here about the job."
Anna smiled at the man in front of her.

"Bethany fell off today, you might want to tell her mum to give her a hot bath tonight so she's not stiff tomorrow. See you next week Bethany." And with that he ambled back towards the yard.

Turning to Anna, Andrew smiled admiringly as his eyes slowly ran over her. "It was nice to meet you. I hope I'll be seeing more of you."

And before Anna could form a coherent reply he turned back to the car, where he helped Bethany into the front seat and with another quick smile they were gone.

Realising everyone had left Anna quickly made her way back to the yard, Rose was scary enough without being caught flirting with the customers.

Rose beckoned her over, "I don't know where Daniel is, so we may as well start. Come on."

Anna followed her into the office, which she could not help comparing to the office she had been in for her first interview. The notice board was covered in hastily scribbled notes. Old rosettes covered the walls, apart from the middle of one wall where an old plastic clock had hung, although it looked as though it had not worked for years. A few odd chairs were dotted about the room and the desk was covered with three diaries which were also full of scribbled notes. The rest of the desk contained piles of papers and copies of riding magazines.

Rose examined a couple of mugs and deciding they looked fairly clean, made two cups of strong coffee. She plonked one down in front of Anna and began to drink the other. Seeing Anna glance suspiciously at the mug she laughed. "It's fine, a few germs never hurt anyone. If anything, it will improve your immune system."

Not wanting to appear rude Anna began to drink the coffee, which was so strong she realised she would not be able to sleep for the next week.

"While we are waiting for Daniel, I'll tell you a bit about the job. Charlie and I are not as young as we were, and twenty horses is a lot for us to manage at our age, even with the local teenagers that help out." Anna smiled thinking Rose was the last person she would describe as old but she let her continue. "Also, poor Charlie has hardly had a day off in years and we could do with offering more lessons and bringing the school up to date a bit, there seem to be more and more inspections these days. So really all I need to know is whether you are interested and then you can tell me a bit about yourself."

"The yard is lovely it seems to be just what I am looking for." Anna answered enthusiastically then hesitated wondering where to start. Quickly realising Rose was not the sort of person you could hoodwink by exaggerating her experience, Anna decided to be completely honest. "I currently work in an office, but I want to be outdoors. I want more from life than balancing accounts everyday"

"You work in accounts?"

Anna nodded reluctantly expecting to be told to leave straight away.

Rose however gave a brief smile. "Well although the main job is the horses, it might be useful if you can do accounts. Daniel hates doing them, he always moans at me for losing my receipts.

"Is Daniel your husband?"

"Heavens no! He's my son. My husband is no longer around." Rose replied with the utmost matter of fact tone. "There is accommodation with the job and you are welcome to ride the horses after work, as long as they have not done too much work in lessons. You do ride I take it? It seems an obvious question, but after the last girl I interviewed. Well…" Rose looked at her expectantly.

"Yes, a lot when I was younger but due to being in London, I have not ridden for the last few years so I am probably a bit rusty."

"It's like riding a bike, you never forget. But tell me about when you did ride."

Anna who loved to reminisce about the ponies she had had when she was younger and competing at local shows, happily told story after story.

Rose let her talk until they were interrupted by a knock on the door.

"This must be Daniel, at last!" Rose told Anna, however instead of Daniel, one of the young lads from the stables put his head around the door.

"Sorry Rose, but it's nearly twelve I need to get home." He said in anguish.

"Freddie, I'm sorry I completely forgot. We'd better go now. Anna I'm sorry but I think we covered everything. I'll phone you later."

"Ok. Well thank you for seeing me." Anna replied her face dropping. She had clearly talked too much and would not get the job. Standing up she got ready to leave.

Watching her face fall, Rose felt sorry for her. She fully intended to offer her the job, not only did she like her but she was the first person she had met she thought she could work with. Deciding that if Daniel could not be bothered to turn up, then he did not deserve a say in whom she employed. She turned back to Anna.

"There's no point in dragging this out so Anna I would like to offer you the job. I take it you are interested?"

Anna's face lit up. "That would be great! Do you really mean it? Yes, I would love it."

Feeling slightly embarrassed by Anna's gratitude, Rose moved on. "Right, when do you want to start?"

Anna could not believe her luck; this meant she would not have to go back to her parents. She felt giddy with relief.

"Anna?"

"Sorry, when can I start? Well would today be too soon?"

"Today?" Rose seemed slightly taken aback. "Um... Well, fantastic, I do like someone who gets on with things. But why don't you move in today and we'll start tomorrow?"

"Right. Tomorrow. Great. I will need to go and fetch my things, as I am supposed to be moving out of my flat today."

"Well off you go then. If I am not around when you get back Charlie will show you the flat. See you later."

Chapter Five

Climbing back into her own car, Anna glanced at the clock. It was now ten to twelve, which meant she would be late for her parents. Her joy at the job offer was diminishing fast at the thought of her mother's disapproval and subsequent lecture on her never-ending lateness.

Racing down the lanes, Anna's stress levels escalated as she nearly missed the turning. She turned sharply and due to her speed took the corner too wide. Too late she saw the vehicle coming towards her. It swung out of her way, as she screamed and swerved towards the hedge. She braked hard and looked up to see that her bonnet was just touching the hedge. Luckily it looked as though no damage had been done.

Recovering herself, she took a deep breath and feeling shaken, turned to see what had happened to the other driver. She screamed, as she found a man glowering through the window at her. Smiling a somewhat apologetic smile Anna wound down the window, briefly thinking how good looking he was even though he did look extremely cross. She was about to apologise when he launched into a furious tirade.

"I know what they say about women drivers but you deserve an award for that piece of driving," he fumed at her. "You do know we aren't in France, don't you?"

Anna, who was completely taken aback at the unexpected onslaught, paused for a second and glared at him before replying. "Really? I'd never have guessed." She retorted feeling like a naughty child being told off.

They stared at one another for a few minutes before Anna broke the silence. "Well, is there any damage?"

"Amazingly there isn't, your luck is clearly better than your driving," was the sarcastic reply.

"Well in that case there is nothing more to say is there?" she challenged him.

"No," he replied and swinging on his heel, he turned and stalked back to his car.

Reversing out of the hedge he pulled alongside her and lowered his window. "I'd try driving a little slower in future or maybe get someone else to do it!" And with that he was gone.

Full of indignation Anna reversed out of the hedge and carried on her way, somewhat slower than before and thinking of clever retorts she should have made.

As he neared Rose's, Daniel put Angie to the back of his mind and refocused on the interview he was late for. He hoped his mother had not employed her on the spot, but comforted himself with the fact that no one would be that stupid. She definitely could not employ anyone now he thought, his face turning grim as he went over the conversation he had just had with Angie. He had to do something, there seemed no other option left.

Arriving back at the flat Anna cursed the lack of parking spaces, she never could find one when she was running late. After managing to park two streets away, she ran back to the flat. Bursting into the lounge a few minutes later, red and out of breath, Anna found Lucy serving her parents coffee and biscuits.

Her eyes went straight to her mother. "I'm sorry I'm late."

"That's alright darling Lucy has been wonderful." Anna glanced at Lucy; it was a well-known fact that Anna's mother would love Anna to be more like Lucy. Anna did not hate her mother for this as she often wished she could be more like Lucy too.

"So, darling, why are you late?" As usual Anna recognized the loaded question. Why would she not just say "So, darling, what was more important than being on time for me?"

Taking a deep breath Anna confessed. "I was at a job interview."

"But darling, it's Sunday, who on earth interviews on a Sunday?" Without waiting for an answer or pausing for breath she plundered on, clasping her hand dramatically to her mouth as a thought struck her. "Darling, you are not going to be a barmaid, we did not put you through university for you to be a barmaid."

"Mum what makes you thinks that? And so what, if I am going to be a barmaid?" Anna tried to keep the irritation out of her voice but failed.

"Well public houses are the only places open on Sundays!"

"No, pubs are not the only places open on a Sunday."

Lucy, ever the diplomat, came to the rescue. "So how did the interview go?"

"I got it. They've given me the job. I start tomorrow and I can move in today."

"As what and live where?" Her mother demanded to know.

Anna turned to her, battling with an answer such as a prostitute and a brothel. That would really get her going she thought, but instead she answered honestly.

"Honestly Darling," was all her mother could manage, before giving her father a look prompting him to talk some sense into Anna. But Anna was too quick and started speaking first.

"Dad look, I know you want me to be an accountant, but I hate it and be honest you did too, boring office politics, endless reconciliations of figures. Dad I just want a chance to try something different." Anna glanced up at her dad imploring him to back her up. He smiled and gave in. Anna smiled gratefully back at him as she knew in time, he would talk her mother round.

"Well do you need help moving in?" Her mother now battled to regain control of the situation. "And I don't know how we'll explain to poor Tony either, especially after he was good enough to offer you a job," she sighed theatrically.

"He only said he would see what he could do," Anna's father gently reminded her.

"I'll be fine mum. Why don't you come down in a couple of weeks' time when I have settled in? Here is the address." Anna offered the address knowing it sounded fairly grand and hoping this would be sufficient to pacify her mother for the meantime.

"Well, it will have to do. But one last thing Darling what are they paying you?" Anna went blank at her mother's question wondering whether to admit that she had completely forgotten to ask what the salary was.

And then as though her mother could read her mind, she turned to her father. "She did not ask. I've failed as a mother. Look at how she has turned out!"

Half an hour later and her parents were heading back home without her. Anna sank down on the sofa. "Thanks for coming over and letting them in. I know I need to pack but I want to recover from the interrogation first."

"Look, are you sure this is right?" Lucy asked tentatively.

"You are the one who said I needed to follow my dreams," Anna retorted wondering if anyone would be pleased about her job.

"I know and I don't take that back. But is this job right? I mean don't just jump at it to escape your mother and she only wants the best for you, you know." Lucy lectured her sounding more like an older sister role than a best friend.

"Mmmm," Anna was not convinced. "And yes, the job is perfect. I really like the place and the people seem nice too." Anna did not admit that Rose seemed slightly terrifying, whilst her new work colleagues were an old man and some giggly teenagers or that the customers were obnoxious kids.

Lucy looked sceptical but let it drop, "I just worry about you and I'll be down to visit you know."

"Good because I am going to miss you."

"I'll miss you too." Lucy was quiet for a second. "So, anyone else your own age?"

"Well Rose mentioned her son, but he sounded a bit wet and did not even bother turning up for the interview. I guess I'll meet him later. And there was one nice guy collecting his niece after her lesson."

Lucy raised an eyebrow at Anna's dreamy expression. "Don't make this about a man!" Lucy rolled her eyes in amusement.

"I'm not. Oh, I didn't tell you I nearly crashed on the way home." Anna quickly changed the subject.

"Not again!"

"What do you mean not again? It wasn't completely my fault he was going too fast too! He was really rude and told me I should not be driving."

"Look out for him again in that case. At least he cares about your safety if he thinks you should not drive," Lucy joked. Anna's driving or her lack of attention whilst driving had always been a constant source of amusement amongst her friends.

As the two girls stopped laughing Lucy sighed sadly. "I really will miss you, you know," she said giving Anna a hug.

"Me too," replied Anna and before she started to cry, or worse still lost her nerve, she decided to go. "Well, I'd better pack the car."

Daniel had been dismayed to find Rose had already left the yard by the time he arrived. After a brief chat with Charlie who told him Anna seemed perfect, he groaned. Hoping that Rose had not employed her already, he went in search of her. She was not at Tom's either but finding Tom at home it gave him a chance to talk about the visit he had had that morning.

"It's the way she pretends to be all concerned, that I can't stand." Daniel said trying to keep his annoyance in check. "Apparently it really is time to close the stables and put Mum somewhere more suitable, for her own good of course!"

Tom laughed ironically. "And let me guess, then you and Paris can tie the knot and live unhappily ever after in the Manor house."

Daniel rolled his eyes. "Ange may have hinted at that. Subtly of course," he responded dryly.

"About as subtle as her fake tan, I bet!" Tom chuckled.

"Yep," Daniel sighed. "I have had an awful morning and to cap it all off someone nearly ran me off the road on the way here."

Tom was about to ask for more details when Mollie walked into the kitchen carrying Billy, who immediately wanted to be put down to talk to Daniel.

"Hi Dan, I did not hear you come. Judging by your faces I take it things did not go well?" Mollie asked in concern looking at their serious demeanour, and not commenting on the fact he had put muddy footprints all over her clean floor, which she had spent all morning mopping. She wondered why she bothered.

"No, Angie, Paris' mum dropped in for a little chat so I missed the interview at Mum's and to cap it all off, as I was just telling Tom, on the way back some silly bitch came round the corner on the wrong side of the road and nearly killed both of us."

"Daniel please don't swear in front of Billy, it's bad enough with his older brother constantly doing fart gags" Mollie admonished him. Billy, who had just reached the age where he seemed to repeat everything he shouldn't, started chanting the words silly bitch over and over again to get Daniel's attention.

"Sorry Moll." Daniel replied somewhat guiltily.

"Well seeing as you are still standing, I take it there was no serious damage to the cars."

"Luckily I managed to swerve out of the way and I doubt you'd notice if she damaged her car it was that old."

Any further debate on Daniel's brush with death was prevented by Rose coming through the door.

"Great you can all hear my good news together. I don't know what happened to you Daniel, but Anna is perfect so I have hired her, she is starting tomorrow. I'm hoping you'll take her out and make her feel welcome."

Daniel looked at Tom who shrugged helplessly. Rose was busy making a fuss of Billy but still caught the exchange between her two sons.

"Don't look like that Daniel she is perfect. She was here for nearly two hours. If you did not want me to employ her you should have turned up for the interview. You knew when the interview was. So, where were you?"

"I got delayed." Daniel replied hoping she would not question it.

"Well, you should have phoned then. Right, well, I had better go. Anna is moving in today and has just gone to pick up her things. I'll tell her you'll be in touch Mollie, she's the same age as you, you can show her around." Without waiting for confirmation, she got up and headed towards the hall.

"Is she really moving in today?"

"Yes, Tom, no time like the present, I'll just go and say hello to the children before I go." Rose told them already halfway out of the room.

Watching her disappear up the stairs, Daniel turned to Tom and Mollie. "What are we going to do? This is a disaster waiting to happen."

"If you and Tom had done something when I suggested." Mollie couldn't prevent the exasperation in her voice.

"I know Mollie. You were right, but what do we do now? She can't stay in the house with Mum." Tom said resignedly.

"No, she can't." Daniel agreed, "what with…." He paused not needing to say any more.

"But that only leaves the flat over the stables." Tom said thinking of the damp flat, but as he glanced up and caught the expression on Daniel's face, he shook his head. "Dan that's not fair."

"Look one night in that flat and she'll be gone by eight o'clock tomorrow morning." Daniel said a smile returning to his face.

"I refuse to be a part of this," Mollie replied with meaning before glancing at her husband, "and quite frankly Tom I'm surprised at you!"

"Of course she will have the flat it just needs a good airing!" Rose replied when Daniel suggested it after she had come back from seeing the grandchildren.

Mollie opened her mouth to protest but catching the warning look from Tom she sighed. "What's she like?" Mollie asked instead, glaring at Daniel as Rose gathered up her things.

"Nice girl and with a sensible head on her shoulders." Rose replied, never one to gush.

"So, someone who will do as she's told then," Daniel replied in amusement.

"Honestly Daniel, you make me sound like a dragon, however whilst clearly helpful I would say there is more to her than meets the eye, and she's quite a pretty girl too." She added pointedly looking at Daniel, who deliberately missed her meaning.

"I'll tell her you'll take her out on Friday then." Rose practically commanded. "Let's just hope that she makes it back here," she added to herself as she turned to go.

"Why wouldn't she?" Mollie asked.

Rose glanced up surprised not realising that she had spoken out loud. "Her car is this little old red thing, didn't look like it would make it to the other side of the village let alone to London and back."

"Well not everyone can drive a Land rover Mum." Tom replied with a smile.

"Honestly Thomas!" Rose rolled her eyes. "Well goodbye then." And with that she was gone.

"What's wrong with you Dan?" Tom asked, having seen his brother start at Rose's description of the new girl's car.

"You won't believe this!" Daniel said in horror.

"Believe what?" asked Mollie looking from a horrified Daniel to Tom, who was now nearly crying with laughter having finally made the same link as Daniel

Wiping his eyes and catching his breath Tom explained. "Not only does Daniel not want this girl, I bet she's the one in the old car who just nearly drove him off the road and knowing Daniel, he will have been so sarcastic she will probably never speak to him again. This is going to be fun, whoever said life in the country was boring?"

Chapter Six

Turning up at the stables for the second time that day, Anna realised she had not yet seen the flat she was about to call home. After seeing the main house, she began imagining how quaint her own place would be. Excitedly she knocked on the front door and was somewhat disappointed to find the house empty. There was no one on the yard either but then she spotted a piece of paper pinned to the office door saying the flat was above the tack room, and the keys were on the office desk.

Left to her own devices in the middle of the yard, excitement flooded through her. This was it, the start of her new life. She'd bring the yard back to life, in her head the stables had been painted the yard was bustling with sleek thoroughbreds, after a busy morning, Andrew, who she had met earlier, would drop in for a coffee. She'd look amazing in jodhpurs, her thighs would have shrunk with the exercise, perhaps she could get one of those hats the royals always wore when photographed in the country. Reining in her thoughts, she took a couple of steps backwards, and surveyed the small windows of the flat looking over the yard. It was certainly quaint, although the windows looked like they could do with a clean.

Climbing the brick steps up the outside wall of the tack room which lead to the front door, she took a deep breath and flung the door open, excited to see what was inside. Recoiling instantly, she stepped back, as she was assaulted by an overpowering smell of damp.

Her excitement diminished, she took a deep breath and walked inside. Reminding herself to stay positive she looked around. There was one bedroom with sloping ceilings and dormer windows, the faded flowers on the yellowing wallpaper looked fairly dismal and she ignored the dark stain on the ceiling. The lounge had an old TV and a couple of worn sofas, which had definitely seen better days. Both had different patterns, but with a few throws and cushions it would be fine, Anna reassured herself.

The bathroom was small and fusty but did have a shower she thought thankfully. The only good thing she could say about the seventies style orange bath suite and tiles was that it would wake her up in the mornings. As she walked into the kitchen her heart sank further, the units were old fashioned and well past their prime and the window had mould growing on it but as she looked through it, she smiled as she could see the horses grazing in the fields, it certainly beat the brick wall of the adjoining apartment block which had been her view until today. Feeling slightly more positive she started to unpack the car, having opened all the windows first, and finding the cleaning materials, she started to clean.

Two hours later she was exhausted, but at least she could now face using the bathroom. Deciding a well-earned cup of tea and a biscuit was in order Anna headed towards the kitchen before she remembered, with a sinking heart, that as she was expecting to move home, she had stopped buying food and survived on take aways, and not only had she had no lunch, it was now dinnertime and she was starving. The only thing for it was to go and find a shop.

She headed into the yard but there was still no sign of Rose. Not wanting to bother Rose on her first night or run into the mystery Daniel, Anna decided to take the initiative and go in search of the village shop. After only one wrong turn she came across the village centre.

Spotting the shop, she parked and jumped out pleased with herself that she had not only taken the initiative but also succeeded. She bounced up to the village shop door and pushed, but it resisted. It was then she focused on the sign and the word closed which was staring her straight in the face.

What felt like hours later, after having got lost at least once, she had found an extortionately priced garage, and returned home with some milk, bread, beans and teabags.

Back in the flat she let out a deep sigh as she realised, she had no toaster or microwave to cook with. She was tired and hungry as she had spent half of the day driving, but something inside her ensured the tears which threatened did not fall. After what felt like an eternity Anna managed to get the stove to work, the old dials were broken and the pictures had rubbed away. By holding her hand above each ring, she tried to work out which, if any, was heating up. She cheered as she finally felt some heat coming from the centre of one ring. While the beans cooked, she toasted the bread on the grill, pleased at how resourceful she was.

Well, she thought ruefully looking at her dinner it was hardly the healthy home grown, home cooked food she had dreamt of but then this was only day one. As she settled down to eat, there was a knock at the door. Wondering who it could be Anna gingerly opened the door to find Rose.

"Saw the lights on and thought I'd make sure everything was alright for you?"

"It's great thanks." Anna lied.

"I was going to see if you fancied dinner, but it's probably a bit late now."

"Oh, I've just made something." Anna answered not admitting her food was going cold as they spoke.

"Never mind. Perhaps you could come for a dinner another night. I'm glad you've settled in."

Anna nodded, suppressing thoughts of damp and mould.

"Right, I'll see you in the morning. Eight o'clock sharp."

Back in the kitchen Anna was upset to discover that her meal had now gone cold. Having eaten, she made a cup of tea and decided to watch some TV. Annoyingly, the TV would not tune into anything and she realised she had no Freeview box, still determined to make this work and recapture the feelings of happiness she had experienced earlier she decided she would have a bath and an early night.

Ten minutes later she wanted to cry with frustration as the water ran colder and colder. Giving up again, Anna had a quick wash and got into bed. She was exhausted and considered phoning her friends, but she did not want to admit that she could not cope before she had managed even one day in her dream life.

Instead after flicking through a magazine she had brought with her, she turned out the light, to go to sleep.

Within minutes the light was back on again, as the usual city noises of traffic were replaced by hooting owls followed by eerie silences. She took a deep breath and turned the light off again but due to the lack of street lights, it was pitch black. Turning the light back on Anna finally conceded defeat and the tears started to flow.

Convincing herself that this was a huge mistake and she could go home in the morning, she wondered how to get through the night.

She moved her TV and DVD player into the bedroom and finally fell asleep watching Love Actually.

Too soon the alarm was dragging her from her sleep, opening her eyes Anna was initially confused as to where she was, as Hugh Grant danced across the screen in front of her, the DVD appeared to be on loop. But then she remembered the flat and the new job.

In the light of day Anna decided she could not leave straight away, everyone would say she had not given it a proper chance, instead she would leave it until lunchtime and then tell Rose she did not think it was for her.

Anna spent the morning scrubbing out and filling water buckets, filling and hanging up hay nets and mucking out stables. Mondays as she had discovered was all the horses' day off and the day everything was cleaned thoroughly. By lunch time Anna was shattered, her arms felt like lead from the water buckets, and she felt like each time she made a trip to the muck heap it got further away.

"Right lunchtime," Rose called. Hearing her Anna thankfully put the two buckets down in the stable. As she came out of the stable Charlie waved a hand as he headed off down to the village pub for his lunch.

"Well Charlie will be a while, so I suggest we have a sandwich," Rose said as she turned to Anna. Having had the best bacon sandwich of her life, which Rose credited to the excellent local butcher, Anna felt her dream was getting back on track. Although it had been hard, on reflection, she had enjoyed the morning and Rose and Charlie had been so nice that she decided to leave it a couple more days and see how things went.

"How is the flat?" Rose broke into Anna's reverie.

"The hot water doesn't seem to work." Anna admitted aware she could not survive without hot water to soothe her tired muscles.

"Ah I forgot to say the boiler will need to be turned on, which is easily sorted but surely that cannot be it."

"And the TV does not seem to work," Anna gently added, not wanting to look ungrateful or complaining.

"And…?" Rose asked sensing more.

"Is there a shop nearby?"

"The village shop is good for last minute essentials but there is a supermarket twenty minutes from here, or the farm shop on the east road out of the village. Oh goodness, I bet you have not had time to shop yet. Right let's sort out the water and TV, then you need to go shopping this afternoon, you must eat properly if you are doing manual work all day."

Anna gratefully muttered her thanks.

An hour later with proper instructions she headed off to the supermarket. The water heater was on so she could have a proper hot bath later to soothe her aching muscles, Rose had found a spare Freeview box and had given her the internet password, so she could reconnect with the world.

Feeling happier Anna stocked up on food, as well as throws for the lounge, a microwave and a toaster, plus every cleaning product she could lay her hands on, before returning to the yard. Feeling slightly guilty at having had the first afternoon off, she worked hard for the last hour.

By Friday, she was starting to feel like she knew what she was doing. She had cleaned and cleaned the flat until, whilst not perfect, her heart no longer sank as she walked through the door. There was one stable left to do and Rose had gone back to the house as she had visitors. Noticing that Charlie looked tired, Anna offered to finish off the last horse so he could get off home.

Banging the stable door behind her Anna surveyed the yard, pleased how well the first week had gone. All she had left to do was refresh Pride's water and then sweep up and she could go home to a hot bath, good food and bed.

Picking up the water buckets, she walked around to the water tap, as the water slowly rose, she looked out over the fields and thought how lucky she was. She was so busy dreaming about improving the yard and imagining it as it could be that it was a second before she realised the water was about to overflow. As she lifted the full buckets, a movement caught her eye, Pride was trotting out of the other end of the yard. The door to his stable stood wide open. She watched in horror as he veered off towards the fields, putting the buckets down and grabbing the first head collar that came to hand she ran after him, praying he would not head towards the road.

Luckily on reaching the first paddock he dropped his head and instantly began to graze.

From the kitchen Daniel, Mollie and Tom watched the scene unfold. Only Daniel could not see the funny side of the situation.

"Poor thing," Mollie exclaimed in horror. "We should go and help."

"No," Tom replied. "She is doing fine. Look she's caught him now. Going out there will only embarrass her."

"I don't care if she gets embarrassed. That is an expensive horse and she hasn't got a clue. I thought Mum said she knew what she was doing," Daniel exploded.

"Calm down," Tom replied regarding his brother in surprise. "Blimey Dan, what's got into you?"

Daniel sighed. "Look, I thought she would be gone by now, that flat should have been enough to see anyone off. And the longer she stays the bigger the fall when it goes wrong, and we all know who will be left to pick up the pieces."

Tom was about to reply but stopped as they heard Rose in the hallway.

"Are you all still here? I thought you'd be long gone. Where's Anna?" asked Rose, coming into the kitchen.

"Letting your horses run riot," was Daniel's sarcastic reply.

"Pride got out but she caught him," Tom replied in answer to Rose's puzzled look.

"Honestly Daniel, I do hope you are going to give her a chance," Rose admonished, rolling her eyes.

"I'll go and get her," Mollie said, glad for a chance to escape.

Anna opened the door to her flat and felt relief wash over her. Pride was safely back in his stable, everything else was done and all she had to do was have some dinner and go to bed before getting up again the next day and starting all over again. She started to run the bath, whilst putting a ready-made lasagne in the new microwave. Her dream of casually knocking up beautiful healthy home cooked meals would have to stay that way for now.

Hearing a knock at the door she went to answer it expecting to find Rose. Instead, she found a girl about her own age, on the doorstep.

"Hi! I'm Mollie, Tom's wife?" Anna looked puzzled so Mollie explained further. "He's Rose's son, but you've probably only heard about Daniel!" Mollie rolled her eyes as Anna's expression confirmed the fact.

"Sorry not to give you any warning but we are going to the pub and wondered if you would like to come, meet some of the locals, that sort of thing..."

Mollie looked at her expectantly. Anna thought longingly of her dinner, her bath and her bed but she missed her friends and a night in the pub sounded great.

"I'll need to change though," she ventured. "Do you want to come in?"

Mollie nodded and followed her through to the lounge and looked around in surprise, "Wow! This looks a lot better than the last time I saw it."

"Thanks," Anna said not sure how to reply and not wanting to sound critical of Rose.

"It could still use some decent furniture though. I'll ask Tom if there is any furniture left from the last show house." Mollie said looking at the sagging settee in dismay.

Anna smiled genuinely now, "That would be great. Thank you."

Mollie smiled back, still feeling guilty about the fact Anna was living in the flat, when there were beautiful bedrooms in the main house.

"I'll just get changed." Anna said taking in Mollie's outfit of jeans and a casual jacket. Remembering Mollie had mentioned the local pub, Anna decided to go casual too, and after a quick wash, she put on a plain black top and jeans. After running a brush through her hair and adding a bit of lip gloss, she returned to the lounge, where Mollie was looking at her photos.

"That's not Zanzi Bar is it?" Mollie pointed to a picture.

"Yeah, I love that place." Anna smiled at the group of friends smiling out at her, feeling homesick for a second.

"You know a lot of my friends are back in London." Mollie admitted. "I sometimes wish I was back there, not that I would change Tom and the kids for the world."

As they made their way outside chatting, Anna marvelled at her luck meeting Mollie. Life really seemed to be looking up.

Two men were waiting on the drive for them, she guessed one must be Tom and wondered if she'd finally get to meet Daniel. Horrifyingly as they turned towards her and Mollie, Anna realised her luck had run out.

"Hello again!"

Anna briefly considered pretending not to know him but he clearly knew it was her.

"Hi!" She hoped it sounded more casual than she felt.

"Let's hope you are better with horses than cars!" Daniel's voice was derogatory. "Although based on what just happened with Pride, I'm not so sure."

"Daniel!" Mollie admonished him.

Daniel shrugged, "I'm simply making the point that you can't just read Black Beauty and think you know it all."

Anna's initial mortification about the near crash and the fact he had seen Pride escaping, receded fast as anger started to seep through her at his final insult.

"Pride just got out the stable for a couple of minutes and I certainly did not nearly kill you. If you had been going a bit slower you would not have had to swerve so much," Anna retorted angrily. "And for your information I did not just wake up one morning and decide to work with horses, it's something I have wanted to do for years." Although as Anna said the words, she acknowledged there was some truth in his accusation, not that she would ever tell him that.

Tom laughed at the two of them as they stared angrily at each other both refusing to back down. "Dan she's right you do drive too fast. By the way I'm Tom, and this is Daniel but you can ignore him." Anna gratefully smiled, glad at least he was friendly.

Luckily Mollie started chatting to Anna leaving Daniel to talk to Tom, as they set off for the pub. As the boys walked on ahead of them Mollie dropped her voice. "Don't mind Dan he is normally lovely but has just split up with his nightmare ex. You'll like him when you get to know him. Honestly," Mollie asserted seeing Anna's sceptical face and not giving her a chance to express the fact she was not surprised he was single.

As they neared the pub, Anna's heart sank. People spilled out onto the pavement, Ed Sheeran's latest song poured from the open windows and it felt like they had gate crashed a party.

"Sorry I forgot to mention its Belle Pennington's eighteenth tonight."

Anna's heart sank as they walked through the door to find even more people. The place looked like something out of a magazine shoot. She had never seen so many beautiful people in one space. She glanced around feeling old and frumpy.

"Watch out for the young farmers," Mollie warned her as they made their way to join a table of people Mollie knew.

"Prosecco ok?" Mollie asked signing to Tom at the bar.

Whilst Mollie caught up with her friends, Anna looked around, unable to add anything to the conversation. The pub had a low beamed ceiling and the small areas of the floor that she could see revealed polished oak floorboards. The chunky wooden tables and chairs, and strategically placed large mirrors gave the place a modern twist.

Over at the bar Tom and Daniel were chatting to various people, everyone seemed to know everyone.

"It's usually a bit quieter in here than this. Belle's step-mother is a dreadful snob and is having a marquee put up in their garden and throwing her a ball, but Belle insisted on a pub karaoke night too. I'm sure it was only to annoy her step-mother. Look that's Belle over there."

Mollie pointed at a stunning red head. The short silver dress, she wore, showed off her figure to perfection. Confidence seemed to ooze from her. Anna would have loved even half that confidence now, let alone when she was eighteen.

"Look she's chatting up Daniel. It hasn't taken long for the news he's single to spread. That's one thing you'll have to get used to, everyone knows more about your life than you do." Mollie laughed while rolling her eyes.

The conversation moved on as Tom came over with the drinks. And as she was drawn into the conversations around her, Anna finally started to relax and enjoy herself. The number of empty bottles of Prosecco on the table increased steadily and eventually Anna found herself feeling extremely tired, a bit drunk and very hungry. Making her apologies to Mollie but knowing she would not last another moment she started getting up to leave, until Mollie halted her.

"Hang on, we'll get a lift. We're coming too. Need to get back for the babysitter! Tom find us a lift."

Anna felt relieved, realising she had not thought about how she would get home.

Tom reappeared shortly. "Jim is leaving now and will give anyone a lift who wants one," he declared, as other parents all started jumping up to get back to babysitters and grandparents.

It took a few minutes for Mollie and Tom to say their good byes as they headed through the crowd to the door. As they reached the entrance there was a scream of laughter from the other side of the room as two naked men came running through the bar and disappeared through the door and out into the night.

"Not sure if they are young farmers or the rugby team," Mollie giggled following them out into the car park. "Not a bottom I recognise though."

"I should hope not!" laughed Tom putting an arm around her.

"Wait up," Daniel shouted coming out the door. "I can't believe you nearly left me," he said to Tom as he reached them.

"Thought you were enjoying yourself," Tom replied, a picture of innocence.

Someone caught Anna's arm making her turn. She could not stop the smile as she found herself face to face with Andrew, who she had met at her interview. "Well this is pleasant surprise," he murmured stepping closer to her.

"It is," Anna tried to act surprised, even though she had spotted him across the pub earlier.

"So, you decided to come and work for Rose, very brave." He watched her in amusement making Anna blush.

"Anna we're ready to go." Daniel's voice barked from nearby.

Glancing around, she found Daniel once again glowering at her.

"You could always stay with me; I'll make sure you get home." Andrew said seductively completely ignoring Daniel who was radiating annoyance.

Having dreamed of seeing Andrew all week, but aware of Daniel, Tom and Mollie watching her, Anna reluctantly said her goodbyes to Andrew.

"At least let me have your number," Andrew replied.

She quickly gave Andrew her number, the whole-time aware Daniel's eyes were boring into her back.

Turning to Mollie, she gave her a bright smile and ignoring Daniel she climbed into the mini bus after her.

"Is this safe?" Anna whispered to Mollie, as the bus lurched forwards.

"He's not drunk, he's just a terrible driver and anyway it's not far," Mollie replied with confidence.

As they lurched down the road, two of the occupants started singing. Anna glanced at Mollie and giggled before they both joined in with the song.

"Thanks for a great night" she said with a smile, as they pulled up on the drive.

Trying not to tread on anyone Anna attempted to climb out and was surprised by Daniel jumping out first to help her down.

"Thank you," she said as she made it safely out.

"Well in your state you would have fallen flat on your face," he replied abruptly.

After waving them off, she made her way into the flat. Having navigated the steps, she collapsed on the bed and fell straight to sleep still fully dressed, too tired to think about Andrew's flirting, Daniel's hostility and her fear of country noises.

Chapter Seven

When the alarm sounded the next morning, Anna groaned and bashed the snooze button. As she staggered out onto the yard a short while later Charlie looked her over.

"I take it you were at the knees up last night?" he asked with chuckle.

Anna nodded woefully, her head thumping. "I was but I'm regretting it this morning."

"The fresh air will soon sort you out," Charlie replied. "Right I'm off to bring round some more hay."

The thought of dragging heavy hay nets across the yard when her arms ached as much as her head, caused Anna to sigh. "Could we not put the hay in the other barn? Then we would not have to carry the nets as far?" she asked hopefully.

Charlie thought about it for a moment before nodding. "Makes sense to me." He looked across the yard to where Rose was just appearing. "Anna has suggested we move the hay to the other barn so it's closer. Save us all walking so far."

Rose looked at Anna sharply, making her quake inside. Wishing she had not spoken out as she had probably made Rose think she was lazy, Anna quickly tried to think of a way out of her predicament. "It was only an idea and I'm sure you have a perfectly good reason for having it in the other barn. Sorry," she finished apologetically, wishing she had left well alone.

Rose stared at her for a long moment before turning to Charlie.

"It seems more practical."

Charlie nodded.

"Well done Anna. Any other ideas?" Rose asked. Realising for the first time in her life that she was making a positive contribution Anna felt a huge surge of happiness.

"Well, the tack room could be reorganised so the pony's saddles are near the bottom where the kids can reach them," she tentatively suggested not wanting to mention the whole area needed reorganising.

As though Rose could read her mind she agreed "I have been meaning to do it for ages but just could not face it. It's all yours!"

Anna nodded, hoping that Rose had not taken offence, but she only suggested they went back to work.

The following morning Anna practically bounced onto the yard. "You look better this morning!" Charlie commented laughing.

She smiled in acknowledgement and hoped he didn't notice that she had been up early to make sure she looked her best in case Andrew picked Bethany up again.

As found herself once again helping Jemima to untack her pony, she wondered for the hundredth time if Andrew would turn up.

Coming out of the stable, she heard Rose ask if one of them could ensure all the children were properly collected.

"I'll go," Anna quickly volunteered, trying to ignore Charlie's knowing expression.
Bethany and Jemima were the last two to be collected and Anna chatted to them whilst they waited. Glancing at the drive yet again, she silently groaned as she saw Daniel walking towards them. She could imagine his views on the fact he had caught her standing on the drive talking.

Anna gave him a tight-lipped smile, hoping he would walk straight past her and not make some sarcastic comment. Luckily he nodded briefly to her but made no attempt to stop or say anything. Relief washed over Anna as he walked on. She had not noticed the car pulling up, until the stunning redhead from the party opened the door.

"Daniel, fancy seeing you here?" Belle smoothly folded herself out of her car and casually flicked her long red hair over her shoulder, pushing her designer sunglasses up onto her head, as she called to Daniel.

"Belle, why are you picking me up and not Mummy?" Jemima demanded.

Belle, who up until Jemima spoke, had been smiling at Daniel, flashed a look of annoyance at her.

"Jemima you know I love to see how you are getting on with your riding," she told the sceptical looking eight-year-old, whilst rolling her eyes at Daniel.

"Anna this is my half-sister Arrabella, we have different mummies. My mummy lives with us," Jemima informed Anna.

Belle threw Jemima a look of pure hatred before retaliating. "Well, my mother left because it is so boring round here." Then she paused and looked at Daniel in horror. "You know what I mean."

"Of course," he acknowledged wryly.

"Belle, this is Anna the new groom," Jemima told her, attempting to distract her from Daniel.

Anna smiled at the girl but only got a dismissive hello in return.

"Jemima why don't you go and wait in the car, while I talk to Daniel," Belle said with a wave of dismissal.

Jemima scowled and walked over to the gleaming new Mercedes SLK. As Belle started to explain to Daniel it was her birthday present from her father, Anna moved away and then smiled as Andrew's car drew onto the drive.

Whilst Bethany was openly delighted, Anna tried to be casual about it. "Uncle Andrew, where's mummy?"

"Now there's a welcome," he replied, once again sweeping her up in his arms. "I'm coming for lunch so I told your mum I would collect you."

Hearing Belle shriek with laughter at something Daniel said, Anna and Andrew looked over at them before Andrew turned back to Anna.

"I was hoping to catch you. Are you free on Thursday night?"

"Um yes, definitely," was all Anna could manage as she tried but failed not to look too pleased.

"I'll pick you up at eight." Andrew replied amused, before getting in the car to leave.

As he pulled away Anna turned back to the stables. Belle was laughing at one of Daniel's jokes, but as far as Anna was concerned, she was welcome to him.

By Thursday afternoon Anna was a bundle of nerves, she was full of nervous excitement about her date with Andrew. Unfortunately, it was starting to show as she had put Houdini in the wrong stable and let the water buckets overflow twice.

"Look I don't know what's on your mind but why don't you call it a day, I'll finish off here and you can owe me one." Charlie offered as he looked at the flooded yard.

Feeling bad Anna declined the tempting offer, but Charlie insisted. Five minutes later she was back in the flat, with a bath running.

With five minutes to spare she was ready and started pacing the floor, eight o'clock came and went, as did eight fifteen and eight twenty. Just when she decided he had stood her up there was a knock on the door.

Opening the door Anna found a repentant Andrew stood on the door step. "Anna wow, you look stunning. I'm so sorry that I'm late I was helping Bethany with her homework."

Anna's anger faded, who could be mad at that she thought and smiled, "It's fine, I was only just ready anyway," she lied, although she had the impression Andrew did not believe her. "I'll get my jacket and then shall we go?"

"Sure, I thought I'd drive that way I can get you drunk and have my wicked way with you." Andrew replied with a wink.

Sinking into the cream leather seats of his Maserati, Anna decided she could certainly get used to this lifestyle. She walked into the pub confidently, on one hand she was with Andrew and secondly, she was appropriately dressed this time. She smiled at Andrew as he held the door open for her but her smile faded as she was met by a number of locals casually dressed, she instantly felt self-conscious in her strappy top and too late she remembered she had left her jacket in the car.

Andrew chatted easily to the locals as he ordered their drinks, whilst Anna felt more and more conspicuous. Picking up their glasses Andrew suggested they sit at the table in the corner.

Once out of the public glare of the bar Anna began to relax, Andrew turned out to be a fantastic story teller and had her giggling with his tales of some of village inhabitants. Anna was laughing at a story Andrew had just told her when the last orders bell rang, looking up she realised they were the only people left in the pub.

"Perhaps we had better make a move" she said regretfully.

Andrew nodded. "Sorry Geoff," he called to the landlord standing up and taking their glasses over to the bar. Anna shivered as they walked outside, and Andrew put his coat around her shoulders. Anna wondered if life could get any more perfect.

The car purred to a halt next to her flat and the engine quietly died as Andrew turned to her. Anna started to thank him for a great evening, but Andrew interrupted her.

"Anna……"

"Yes……?" she asked.

Andrew was watching her intently. Anna caught her breath as his eyes darkened and he leant forward to kiss her. The kiss started softly, but quickly deepened and Anna was vaguely aware Andrew's hand which had started on her waist, had moved to her back whilst the other hand ran along her thigh and slowly and tantalisingly up towards her breast. Anna groaned in pleasure as his thumb brushed her nipple, but she was shocked back into the present as Andrew suddenly pulled away.

"What on earth?" he exploded. Turning to see what had diverted his attention, Anna found herself face to face with Rose, who was about to knock on the window.

"Sorry to interrupt you dears but I wondered if Anna could give me a hand. Alfred has colic and we'll need to walk him." Rose shouted through the window, looking distinctly unembarrassed considering the situation.

Looking helplessly at Andrew, Anna apologised to him and opened the door to get out.

"I'll go and make us some coffee while you check the horse," Andrew said also opening his door.

"Oh, I wouldn't bother if I was you. We are likely to be up walking him all night," Rose replied, sounding very perky for someone who was about to lose a night's sleep.

Anna shot Andrew a regretful look and got a tight-lipped smile in reply.

"Sorry but thanks for a great night." She said unsure what to do.

"Anytime," Andrew replied slamming his door, the engine roared into life and she watched disappointed as the tail lights disappeared down the drive.

"Hope I did not ruin your night?" Rose asked looking completely unrepentant.

"He was just leaving anyway," Anna lied. "So how long has Alfred been ill?" She was keen to change the subject now.

"About an hour, I was just off to the phone the vet when I saw the car."

Reaching the stable they looked over the door "Well would you believe it he seems fine now. He was groaning and rolling around like nobody's business ten minutes ago," Rose said cheerfully.

Anna glanced at her suspiciously but all she said was, "Fancy a coffee?" Looking at her face Anna decided she was being unfair as there was no way Rose would deliberately ruin her evening. Nodding her head, she agreed to the coffee and followed Rose into her kitchen.

Within twenty minutes she was yawning. As Anna stood up to leave, she glanced uncertainly through the window. Catching the look of apprehension that crossed her face Rose suggested she took one of the dogs back with her.

"Just don't let her sleep on the bed," she warned Anna, who had decided to take Tilly the younger of Rose's two Labradors back with her.

Turning to Penny the old yellow Labrador, Rose sighed, "Well it looks like it's just you and me tonight. I think we did the right thing though." And with that she turned out the lights and went to bed.

Chapter Eight

Anna woke the next morning, rolled over and nearly screamed as she came face to face with a wet nose and two big brown eyes. "Tilly how did you get in here?" she asked, thinking it was not the pair of brown eyes she had dreamt of waking up next to.

Tilly merely closed her eyes and went back to sleep, making Anna laugh.

The second week went faster than the first, Anna found the water buckets no longer felt as though they were made of lead and she was sure she had got quicker at mucking out the stables. She was also pleased to notice her normally pale complexion was slowly being replaced with a healthy-looking tan and although she was not the type to spend hours in front of the mirror, she had taken a quick five minutes to observe that she was toning up quite nicely.

In fact, there were only two clouds on her otherwise sunny horizon, the first was that she had not yet ridden a horse and the second was that she had heard nothing from Andrew since the disastrous end to their first date.

The first cloud was blown away on Friday when one of the private lessons was cancelled. Anna, who had given up wearing jodhpurs and had taken to wearing jeans, was bringing a couple of horses back into the yard, when Rose called her over.

"Kelly has just called and cancelled her lesson but Murphy is already tacked up, why don't you pop on?"

"Um I haven't got the right clothes on," Anna began.

"Well go and change then."

A few minutes later Anna made her way back onto the yard. There was no sign of Rose or Charlie so she took Murphy out of his stable and made her way over to the mounting block. It had been a few years since she had ridden and although she was desperate to get back in the saddle, she was nervous too and glad she did not have an audience.

Having walked around the edge of the ménage a couple of times she started to feel more confident. After a couple more circuits in walk, she felt even more secure and decided it was time to progress to a trot. She kicked Murphy on and started to trot down the side of the ménage. Twenty minutes later she was enjoying herself so much she decided to have a canter to finish.

As they passed the bottom corner of the school a bird flew up, causing Murphy to run sideways. Anna who had not been expecting this lurched to one side, but as she tried to right herself, the saddle slipped further and further down Murphy's side, until she plopped unceremoniously into the soft sand.

It had all happened so slowly she was completely unhurt, well physically at least, but the embarrassment of what had happened was quickly surfacing. Scrambling out from underneath Murphy on her hands and knees, Anna glanced up to see Charlie watching her shaking his head in amusement. Standing up slowly Anna gave him an embarrassed smile.

"Get back on, you'll be fine," Charlie called and continued on his way to the muck heap.

Anna turned to retrieve Murphy, who was now disappearing in the direction of the yard. As she followed him, fear started to take hold of her. Deciding that the best course of action was to try again tomorrow, Anna felt better. Until she walked around the corner to find Murphy stood in the middle of the yard having been caught by Daniel, who raised an eyebrow when he saw her in her riding clothes, still brushing the sand off her jodphurs.

Daniel said nothing and merely looked at her expectantly, and then at the saddle under Murphy's tummy. Annoyed she had given him another reason to think she was inept, she searched for an explanation. She was about to speak when Charlie ambled over.

"Forgot to say he is a bit spooky in that bottom corner. Leg up?"

Realising that she could not refuse the help to get back on, she agreed. Once back in the saddle, which was now the right way up again, Charlie patted Murphy and leaned forward so Daniel could not hear. "Keep your reins a bit shorter, grip with your lower leg and you will be fine," with that he winked and stood back to let her pass.

She heard Daniel sigh and walk back out of the yard, as she made her way for the second time to the ménage. This time she took Charlie's advice and managed a canter in both directions. Buzzing with what felt like a huge achievement, she rode back into the yard to find Charlie. He walked over to the stable with her while she untacked Murphy.

"Not bad, you're a bit rusty but give it a few weeks and you will be fine," and with that he disappeared.

Smiling at his praise, Anna headed towards the tack room, to put the saddle away. Too late she heard the angry voices as she walked through the door.

"She's just fallen off Murphy, I mean Murphy, who you put all the beginners on, and the saddle was underneath him!" Daniel fumed at Rose. "Look I know you think she has improved things but anyone could have thought to move the hay." He paused, "Mum, admit it you've made a mistake. I'll tell her if you want. She's just a sticking plaster to a problem that is not going to go away."

Anna was shocked, she knew Daniel did not like her but she could not believe he would want to sack her. She turned to go but as she did so Rose caught sight of her.

"Anna I'm sorry you are going to think that Daniel has no manners at all at this rate." She glared at Daniel.

Wishing she had not walked into this argument but realising now she had, she ought to defend Rose's decision for hiring her, Anna spoke up. "You are right Daniel it was terrible to fall off Murphy but I have not ridden for the last few years while I have been living in London. I am a bit rusty, but I'm sure if you give me a chance, I'll prove I can ride."

Daniel who was slightly taken aback by Anna's speech and aware of his mother's glare gave a cynical smile. "We'll see," and with that he left.

"I'm sorry Rose a bird flew up and he shot sideways. I'd forgotten to check the girth; it was my fault."

"Nonsense, like you said you are just rusty. Although I would suggest you try and ride as much as possible. The more you ride the quicker you'll get your seat back."

"That would be great," Anna replied unable to believe her luck at the offer.

Running towards church, for the annual school leavers service, with Billy on her hip, Mollie cursed the fact that she had originally thought she had time to hang out the load of washing that had just finished, she clearly had not, especially as Billy had then needed the loo, lost his socks and various other things that now meant she was going to be stuck at the back.

"Mollie!" The voice calling her made her inwardly groan, but glancing up she forced a smile, as the person ended their phone call.

"Olivia, hi!"

Olivia Walthingstow was the school queen bee; Mollie would quite happily have kept her distance but unfortunately their sons were the best of friends.

"Late again, Mollie?" She asked in feigned surprise, dropping the phone into an enormous designer handbag.

Knowing full well, she would have been the first one there, Mollie smiled, "unfortunately Billy needed the toilet."

"I have taught mine to get that out of the way before breakfast, so much healthier." Olivia smiled a saccharine sweet smile whilst Mollie imagined whacking her around the head with the large handbag.

"I'll bear it in mind." Mollie said through gritted teeth wondering if children could really be taught to poo on demand instead of at a totally inappropriate moment, for example when she was already running late.

"Oh, by the way Josh's reading is really coming on isn't it?"

Ignoring the patronising tone, Mollie agreed, "Yes, he's been trying really hard."

"I could see that when I listened to them read in school, I know I'm a working mum but one does try to do one's bit for the school."

Mollie ignored the dig that as a non-working mum she did not help out and instead merely replied, "How lovely of you."

By now they had entered the church porch, and the church warden started to close the large door behind them.

"Looks like you were the last." Olivia said pointedly. "By the way Mrs May was saying Joshua should move up a reading band soon, which means he'll only be two levels behind Angus." Without waiting for a reply Olivia sashayed up the church to where one of her minions had kept her a seat in pride of place.

"Mollie." Hearing someone hiss her name, Mollie turned and gratefully sank into a seat next to Jane, one of her best friends.

"Wave to Josh and Lottie," She nudged Mollie in the direction of where both her kids were trying to get her attention.

Giving them a wave, she settled down as Lottie and the rest of the reception class stood to sing their song.

Whilst they sang and did the actions, Jane whispered quietly, "So what was your and Olivia's cosy little chat about?"

Glancing at her, Mollie could see she was already laughing, as she felt the same way about Olivia that most parents did.

"The usual, why was I late? Could I not manage my children properly? Isn't Josh reading coming on? But obviously not at the Einstein level of Angus......"

Jane rolled her eyes, "don't worry about it, her nanny does all the childcare and let's face it she pushes poor Angus so hard he'll probably have a nervous breakdown before he's ten."

"I know. Poor Angus! But seriously what is her problem? I'm just trying to raise happy kids that don't turn out to be delinquents. I don't have the energy to compete with all the other parents."

"Do you not want Josh to be the next prime minister?" Jane giggled.

Mollie giggled too, but abruptly stopped when a grandmother turned to glare at her.

"How does she know how Josh is reading anyway?" Jane whispered once the grandmother turned back around.

"She now helps out in school, even though she is a working mother." Mollie whispered back.

"Working mother? She only drops into her husband's work and hangs about to make sure he isn't shagging his secretary, which he probably is." Jane said with irony, and then catching Mollie's eye roll, she added, "Well wouldn't you, if you were married to her?"

"Maybe." Mollie laughed. "I do wonder if I should help in school though?" She added.

"You've got Billy, don't let her guilt you out." Jane raised her eyebrows knowingly, making Mollie smile.

"You're right, I need to stop letting her wind me up." Glancing at Billy she realised he was about to draw in a hymn book with her lipstick. "Billy!" She whispered in horror. Sensing her freeze, Jane quietly took the hymn book and lipstick off Billy and handed him a box of raisins before he realised what had happened and began to cry.

"Thanks." Mollie sighed wondering how a short service could be so stressful.

Josh's class had now stood up and were singing the same song that they had the previous spring. "Shoot me now," muttered Jane. "I hate this song." The grandmother in front, turned and glared at her again.

"No, you don't, you love this as much as I do," Mollie whispered back, smiling and rolling her eyes, knowing that although Jane would never admit it, she never missed a school event.

As they finished and sat down, Olivia rose to do the annual thank you from the parents to the headteacher. Mollie glanced at the head of the PTA whose job it should have been, she sat tight lipped but even she did not cross Olivia. As Olivia droned on talking about how successful the year had been, highlighting her own children's achievements, Mollie noticed other parents start to get restless, especially those trying to keep younger siblings quiet. At last Olivia finished, basking in the returned thank you from the head and the somewhat reluctant applause from the parents.

"Don't tell me you even love that bit! Thank fuck for gin is all I can say." Jane said cheerfully, as the Grandmother in front tutted loudly in their direction.

Sunday morning dawned with bright blue skies and plenty of sunshine. Choosing her outfit carefully, Anna spent a couple of minutes longer doing her hair, hoping that Andrew would pick Bethany up again from her lesson.

Sadly, there was no sign of him.

"Anna, come and meet my mum" Bethany took Anna's hand and led her towards a car, which wasn't Andrew's. Disappointed Anna watched a woman, who looked similar to both Bethany and Andrew, get out of the driver's seat smiling.

"Anna this is my mum."

"Hi!" Anna tried hard to look pleased to meet her.

Bethany's mum smiled kindly. She had the same dark hair and eyes as Andrew. "It's nice to meet you, Bethany's been talking about you non-stop and I did have to wonder why Andrew was so keen to pick her up last week!"

Anna blushed.

"Anyway, we'd better go Bethany, you need to finish your project for school tomorrow."

"Is that the one Andrew was helping her with?" The words came out without Anna meaning them too.

But Bethany's mum laughed as she got into the car. "My younger brother would never do his own homework, so there is no way he would offer to do anyone else's."

As they drove away Anna walked back to the stables confused, she was sure Andrew had been late for her because he was helping Bethany.

"Nice lady," Charlie said falling into step beside Anna, taking in the sad look on her face. Anna just smiled in agreement.

"All done?" Rose asked as they made their way back round to the stables.

"Yes, they've all been picked up. Right, I'm off for my Sunday roast," he replied.

As Charlie ambled off, Rose turned to Anna, "I'm just dropping Freddie back and then I thought we could go for a ride." She said.

"That would be great." Anna replied, thinking it would stop her dwelling on Andrew.

As they trotted down the lane, Anna relaxed as she listened to the bubbling brook that ran alongside them. The trees gently draped their branches over it, adding to the ambience.

She sighed happily. "This is the perfect way to spend a Sunday."

"Definitely." Rose agreed.

They were approaching the outskirts of the village now and Anna was surprised to hear someone call their names. Looking around she saw Mollie waving.

Following Rose's lead Anna turned Murphy round as Mollie beckoned her up the drive, where she was unloading bags and children from the car.

"Look at you two," Mollie said as they got nearer.

Bringing Murphy to a halt Anna grimaced. "Well ,it's only my second go but so far so good."

"Yeah. I heard you had a fall. Are you ok?"

Seeing Anna look slightly taken aback at the news, Mollie apologised. "Sorry Daniel mentioned something. I just wanted to check you weren't hurt."

"Honestly, I will need to have a word with him, gossiping like that." Rose said indignantly.

Glad Rose had defended her, Anna relented. "I think I'm a bit rusty, it's been a while."

"Well, I admire you, I tried riding a few times when Tom and I got together but after one horse took off with me, I realised it just wasn't for me."

"Really?" Anna asked in surprise.

"Yep, I think Rose has just about forgiven me," Mollie replied laughing at Anna's face.

"Well almost! Although, we do need to think about getting Lottie riding soon, unfortunately Josh wasn't keen at all!" Rose replied. "Right, we'd better be off."

As she turned away Mollie rolled her eyes at Anna in amusement. She waved them off, before following the kids into the house, where she found Tom and Daniel in the kitchen.

"Who was that?" Tom asked trying to make out who Mollie had been talking to.

"Rose and Anna." Daniel replied heavily.

"I thought you said she could not ride for toffee Dan?" Tom reminded him.

"I said she fell off. I never said she could not ride. Honestly is there anybody left around here that is not in the Anna fan club?"

"Perhaps you should wonder why you are the only one who does not like her," Mollie replied.

"Well for a start she's very friendly with Andrew."

"Ah that's not good. Does she know about Lizzie?"

"Who knows? But the sooner she goes the better."

Mollie glanced at Daniel's stubborn face.

"Even if she has been seeing Andrew, she is not gossiping about Rose and she could very easily." Mollie pointed out.

Daniel thought about it for a second reluctantly realising Mollie had a point.

Seeing him soften Mollie pushed on. "In the last few weeks there has not been one incident and it doesn't take a rocket scientist to put two and two together here."

"I was sorting it though." Daniel struggled to keep his voice calm.

"No Daniel you weren't and just for once perhaps this was something you could not sort." Mollie sighed, "Look I don't want to fall out with you over this but apart from the obvious, Rose and Charlie are both getting older. Rose won't sell any of the horses so the only option left is for her to get some help. And there will come a point where Charlie needs to cut down or retire full stop!"

Daniel looked about to speak but seemed to admit defeat instead.

Mollie softened her tone, "I don't think you have any other option. Anna is the only person Rose would consider hiring and she interviewed over twenty. There haven't been any problems since she started, some of the mum's have even been praising her on the school run, so whether you like it or not I think Anna's here to stay."

Chapter Nine

As Anna finished tacking up the ponies the following Sunday morning, she decided to run back to her flat for a coat as the black sky threatened rain. As she passed across the front yard, she could see Jemima crying hard.

"Mummy please stay? You always tell daddy you stay but you never do."

"Darling mummy's got things to do, and you are too old to behave like this."

But Jemima cried harder. Sensing Anna and the other parents were watching, Diana Pennington Smythe produced a phone and made a brief phone call.

Turning to Jemima, she smiled tightly. "Of course, I'll stay, now stop crying please."

Jemima was delighted and immediately tugged her mother towards the stables.

Having collected a coat, Anna arrived back to find all the children on their ponies. Rose was supervising girths and stirrups being tightened and altered, but seeing Anna she looked at the black sky.

"Anna can you get some of the ponies in before it rains? It looks like a storm."

Anna watched the lesson head off to the indoor school and picking up a few headcollars went to catch some of the other ponies.

Having put Houdini in his stable, she was taking off his field rug, when someone wolf whistled causing her to jump. She turned around to find Andrew leaning against the stable door.

"Hi I was in the area and thought I'd see if that coffee you still owe me was going free?"

Anna glanced at him, she had not seen him for two weeks, and had heard nothing since the night of Alfred's phantom colic. She really should say no, she thought.

Andrew smiled ruefully, "I know I'm rubbish and I should have phoned." He smiled, the dark brown eyes trying to look repentant and failing.

Anna could not help but laugh. "I can spare five minutes," she tried to sound firm and not look like a complete pushover.

Anna shut the door to Houdini's stable, just as the lesson rolled back into the yard.

"Uncle Andrew, are you picking me up?" asked Bethany dragging Pepper towards them.

"Sorry honey, I'm here to see Anna but I'll pop by later."

"Andrew fancy seeing you here, I did not realise you were into horses." Diana Pennington-Smythe walked over to them.

"I was in the area and unexpectedly free so thought I would pop in for a coffee with Anna."

"How sweet." Diana's voice was acidic. "Come on Jemima, we need to go, give the groom the pony."

Jemima jumped off Spot and handed Anna the reins without a word. She ran after her mother. "Did you see how high I jumped? Do you think I'm good? Can I have my own pony?" She could be heard asking as they disappeared from view.

"Stuck up cow." Andrew muttered. Anna smiled and untacked Spot quickly. As she and Andrew made their way onto the front drive Anna made sure all the children were picked up. As the last parents were preparing to leave, Andrew smiled. "Finally, we can get that coffee."

The shout made everyone freeze. "Someone stop Houdini". Anna felt herself go cold, quickly trying to remember if she had shut the door properly. But luck was not on her side as the fat cream pony came hurtling around the corner. One of the parents had just opened the gate to drive through and seeing his chance Houdini took it. He did not look left or right but galloped flat out towards the gate.

"Stop him." Anna yelled hopelessly at the parent who seemed frozen to the spot. She was running towards the gate but knew she would never make it. She sighed as Houdini disappeared down the driveway.

Rose who had raised the alarm now came running around the corner. Seeing everyone stood staring at an open gateway she took control. "Anna, we need to get that pony quickly. She threw Anna a headcollar and jumped in the Land rover.

"I'll go down the road. Can you head across the fields? That's where he went last time."

The parent by the gate finally started to speak. "I'm sorry I did not know how to stop him. I'm not into horses you see."

Assuring them it was fine, Anna tried as quickly as possible to get them back into the car so she could go and look for Houdini.

Andrew was still on the drive. "I don't suppose you want to help do you?" She asked him hopefully, as the thunder rumbled overhead. Andrew looked at his clean clothes and the imminent rain filled sky.

"Anna I'm sorry but I did say I would pop and see Bethany and anyway I am useless with horses. I would only scare him."

Anna sighed. "I need to go."

Turning on her heel she ran over to the gate and athletically jumped it before running across the field in the direction Rose had told her to go. As she ran which was not easy in riding boots, the rain started to fall. The drops were big and heavy and coming down fast, within minutes she was soaked. She was soon out of breath so she slowed her pace to a jog and finally a walk. The rain showed no signs of relenting and continued to drive down harder than ever. Her hair and her clothes were wet through, but she carried on looking hoping to catch a glimpse of cream through the hedges. After what felt like hours, she realised bringing her phone would have been a good idea as Rose may have found him by now. Seeing a lane behind the far hedge she decided it would be easier to walk around the roads than head back across the fields, as they were so slippery. By now the water was running down the inside of her coat, even her underwear was wet, she thought miserably whilst her feet squelched in her boots.

She climbed the gate into the lane and looked up at the sky, there was still no sign of a let up in the weather. Starting to shiver, she walked briskly along the road, feeling the water ooze between her toes each time she placed a foot to the floor. After walking for a while, she started to worry. The lane was not leading her where she thought it would, acknowledging she may have lost her bearings in the field and come out in a different place she wondered what to do. She was cold and wet and just wanted to go home; Houdini was far from her mind now.

The sky darkened and although the sun was not due to set for hours, the day was getting very dark. The rain was heavier than ever and visibility was decreasing rapidly. Anna began to panic now. She was in the middle of nowhere and not only did she not know where she was but neither did anyone else. Although she did not watch horror films as a rule, Anna had seen a few and her imagination began to run into overdrive. They often started like this a single female on a deserted road in bad weather. Before long someone would drive past and offer her a lift. They would seem kind, harmless and trustworthy, but as soon as she got in the car they would change into a madman and take her to a deserted cabin in a forest and she would never be seen again.

Anna's heart was hammering hard now, she stopped and gave herself a mental shake, scaring herself was the last thing she should be doing.

Her heart lifted as she realised Tom's car was coming towards her. Relief flooded through her as the car slowed and drew up alongside her, but it quickly turned to shock as the window slid down to reveal Daniel.

"Sorry I thought you were Tom."

"No. Look you had better jump in." Daniel said as the water dripped off the end of her nose.

"No, I'm fine." Anna stalked onwards, forgetting that only minutes earlier she had not wanted to be alone lost on a deserted lane, in a thunderstorm.

"Anna, get in the car." Daniel practically ordered.

"I'm fine thanks." Anna replied crossly, not stopping.

The car over took her before stopping in the lane. Daniel jumped out looking set to explode.

"Just get in the car now before we both get soaked." For a second, they stood staring at each other.

Eventually with a shrug Anna got in and sat gingerly on the seat. Daniel got back in as well and let out a long sigh as he lent his head back against the head rest and closed his eyes. Opening his eyes, he turned to her with a baffled look.

Back in the warmth, the dry and the safety of the car, with the rain streaming down the windscreen, Anna realised how silly she had looked refusing the lift. The tense atmosphere, the relief at being safe and the craziness of the whole situation suddenly made Anna want to giggle, which judging by Daniel's face would be the worst thing she could do.

"I'm sorry." Anna just managed to suppress the hysteria, as she realised, he could have driven straight past her, she smiled guiltily up at him through strands of wet hair.

Looking at her, sat huddled in her seat, her big blue eyes staring up at him, Daniel was surprised by a sudden urge to kiss her. Repressing it quickly he glanced at her. "You know you are the most irritating woman I have ever met."

"Well you're….." Anna's tried to think of a suitable come back.

But Daniel held his hands up and smiled, "Look don't you think it's time we called a truce?"

"A truce?"

"Well, we got off to a pretty bad start, maybe not a truce as it's been mostly my fault, but can we try being friends?"

Anna hesitated and then realising he had picked her up, she nodded her agreement slowly.

"What are you doing out in this anyway?"

"Houdini got out. Actually, have you got a phone?"

"Yes, but last time I checked Houdini did not have one." He replied watching her in amusement.

"I meant to phone Rose."

As Daniel went to hand her the phone, he noticed she was starting to shiver. He took off his jacket and gave it to Anna instructing her to put it on and take off her wet coat, while he phoned Rose.

"Mum it's me. I've just picked up a drowned Anna on the side of the road. Have you found Houdini?"

There was a pause.

"Yes."

Another pause.

"Yes." With a sigh.

Pause.

"Good bye."

Anna glanced at him as she struggled into his jacket. Trying to avoid looking at her wet T-shirt, Daniel turned the heating up.

"Mum's found Houdini, came home as soon as it started raining. She said have a hot bath and she'll make you dinner tonight." He declined to add how delighted Rose had been that Daniel had picked

Anna up, after all he would have picked anyone up in this weather, he told himself.

"You know Mum really seems to like you." Daniel commented as the car pulled away.

"I like her too." Anna replied trying not to take offence at Daniel's comment.

"Sorry, what I meant was she thinks most people are idiots." His voice was laced with irony.

Anna laughed, "Maybe…"

"But you're not scared of her." Daniel replied with what seemed like admiration.

"I was to start with but when you get to know her, you can't help but like her." Anna admitted, as Daniel pulled up by her flat.

Daniel paused, staring out the window, as though debating whether to say what was on his mind, Anna was about to speak when he looked up at her.

"It hasn't always been easy for Mum, and some of the village love to gossip about her," for a second his face darkened, "But I appreciate the fact you haven't done that."

Surprised Anna struggled to know what to say, but Daniel seemed to shake his thoughts and smiled, "I'd better let you go and get dry."

Thanking him again Anna slipped out the car, more confused than ever by Daniel.

Having dropped Anna off, Daniel called in at Tom's to drop his car back.

"Keep it till tomorrow," Tom replied, "saves me having to pick you up for work!"

"I'll pick you up, I don't want to be there on my own tomorrow."

Tom looked at his brother in surprise before starting to laugh. "Of course, Eleanor Burrett is coming, isn't she?" He pronounced it phonetically.

"Boreigh." Daniel rolled his eyes making it sound French.

"What's this?" Mollie asked, joining them in the lounge.

"Our nightmare interior designer, she's after Daniel and she's worse than Hyacinth Bouquet." Tom laughed shaking his head

"You're not still putting up with her, are you?" Mollie asked exasperated.

"She's good, even if she is a bit high maintenance." Daniel sighed.

"Make that very high maintenance," Tom added, to which Daniel didn't argue.

"You know," Mollie paused wondering whether to say anything or not. "You know I could do it."

"But Mollie you are busy with the kids and don't need the stress." Tom replied, closing down the suggestion.

Frustrated Mollie nodded, letting it go for now.

"Anyway, its highly entertaining watching Daniel try to avoid her advances."

"Sure." Mollie said with a half-hearted smile, as she got up and left the room.

Daniel waited until they heard her in the kitchen, "She's a good interior designer Tom." He commented defending Mollie. "Better than Eleanor."

"I know, but I don't want her stressed with this," Tom replied pointedly making Daniel realise the subject wasn't up for discussion. "You staying for dinner?"

Daniel nodded and Tom shouted through to the kitchen to let Mollie know.

Mollie stood in the kitchen staring out of the window in frustration, was this all he thought she was good for? "Already done it," she shouted back having anticipated Daniel would stay and made extra.

"Mum I can't find Rapunzel and Josh says he has her and he won't let me have her back." Lottie came charging into the kitchen, crying. "He knows she's my favourite doll ever. I hate having brothers."

"Josh!" Mollie raised her voice so it would carry up the stairs.

"I haven't got it. I don't want her stupid toy!" Josh's voice high and defensive came straight back down the stairs, before she even needed to explain why she was calling him.

"She's not stupid," wailed Lottie.

"Well help her find it!" She yelled back before telling Lottie to go and look for it with Josh, just as Tom wondered into the kitchen.

"Do I have to?" Josh shouted back.

"Tom can you talk to them please?"

"Talk to who?" Tom asked surprised.

"The kids, Josh is winding Lottie up again.

"Josh, stop winding up your sister." Tom shouted up the stairs.

Mollie just sighed.

"Any beers in the fridge, Moll?" He asked opening the door.

"At the bottom." She replied.

"You're the best," he gave her a kiss as he headed back to the lounge with the beers and bottle opener.

Billy wandered in next, "I hungry!"

"Dinner will be ten minutes." She replied, her frustration creeping into her voice. She turned back to the stove as the potatoes started to boil over, having rescued them she turned back to Billy who was sat on the middle of the kitchen table eating an apple.

"Billy!" She said in exasperation, knowing he would no longer want his dinner. Was this all her life had become one long battle of trying to get her husband and kids to eat, sleep and not kill each other. Upstairs she could still hear Josh and Lottie arguing.

"Sorry Mummy, you have some?" He held the apple out to her.

Looking at his big blue eyes and solemn expression, Mollie gave herself a mental shake, she had three gorgeous healthy children, a husband she loved and a beautiful home, perhaps wanting a career too was just selfish.

She picked up Billy and pulled him close, despite the fact he wriggled, planting a kiss on his head she put him in his booster seat and chopped up his apple for him. Turning back to check on dinner she spotted Rapunzel sitting on the kitchen counter. "Lottie Rapunzel is here!" She shouted up the stairs.

"I don't want her anymore," came back the reply, "we're playing Minecraft now."

Rolling her eyes Mollie began to set the table, harmony had been restored for now.

Anna entered the village shop the following day to pick up a few essentials, she did not have long but luckily there was only one other customer in the shop beside herself. Anna had got used to how glamorous some of the locals were, but this girl with her supermodel figure and amazing black hair was in another league.

As Anna quickly threw items into her basket, she could not help but listen to the girl whose voice carried loudly around the shop.

"Mummy has warned him about Freddie Prince but even that has not made any difference. If he'd just stop listening to his wet brother and frumpy sister in law, then this would never have happened."

"Well, I'm not sure that's quite how I'd describe Tom and Mollie," the lady behind the counter replied, casting a nervous glance in Anna's direction.

Anna continued to stare at the products in front of her as though deciding what to get, shocked at hearing Tom and Mollie described that way, whilst silently agreeing with the woman that Mollie was definitely not frumpy and neither would she call Tom wet.

"Come on, she's the classic little housewife. Honestly the other day she was on the school run without a scrap of make-up. You'd never see me let myself go like that." The girl said with contempt.

Anna felt her hackles rise as her dislike for this woman grew. Having got, what she needed she headed towards the till, keen to see who the person was.

The girl turned and Anna was startled by her amazing green eyes, which ran over Anna quickly before deeming her unworthy of any attention. The girl picked up the bottle of champagne she had just brought as though to leave.

"Bye Paris, do wish your dad happy birthday for me." The lady behind the counter said.

Anna started. This was Paris? Surely that could not be who Daniel had been seeing?

Catching her reaction Paris turned to her, the green eyes glittered dangerously.

"I don't think we've met."

"I'm Anna," Anna replied, "I'm working up at the Manor with Rose." She met Paris' gaze defiantly. Paris laughed contemptuously, "Well that shows you how inaccurate village gossip is they said you were attractive!" With a final sneer, she span around and flounced out of the shop.

The lady behind the counter nervously smiled and started to scan through Anna's purchases. "Afternoon Mrs Cottesmore." She looked up and called to the woman entering the shop as the bell over the door rang.

Anna casually glanced up remembering Mollie warning her about the local gossip, she smiled and nodded.

"Twenty-three pounds eighty," the lady said turning back to Anna, as she finished putting her items into bags.

The bell rang again but Anna did not look up this time, she was starting to panic as she rifled through her purse trying to find her bank card. Anna froze, as she finally accepted her bank card was not there, before remembering she had probably left it in her jacket pocket when she had been out the night before.

"Look I'm so sorry, I've forgotten my card. Can I leave this here and I'll pop back later and get it?"

The lady smiled indulgently, "Oh don't worry, I can put in on a tab and then you can pay next time you are in."

"Really?" Anna was surprised as the lady did not know her.

"Well, you're working up at the Manor aren't you so we know where you are?"

"Thank you!" Anna gratefully picked up her bags.

"Everything alright Anna?" Andrew's deep voice was right behind her. "I hope Rose is remembering to pay you," he commented loudly looking concerned.

Aware Lucinda was listening, Anna tried to laugh it off, "Of course she is, I just forgot my bank card."

"As long as you are being treated properly, then that's ok." Andrew returned, as he placed a bottle of wine on the counter. "So, any plans tonight?"

"No, I was just going to have a quiet one," Anna replied without thinking, as he paid.

"Great, then I might just pop round." Andrew said with a wink, and with that he was gone.

Unsure what to say and still very aware of the two ladies watching her, Anna merely smiled and picked up the rest of her shopping, and followed Andrew out of the shop.

Rose replaced the receiver, and wrote the name in the book, the yard was doing well and they were nearly back up to full capacity, if it carried on like this, she would have soon have waiting lists again, like in the good old days.

For a second, she paused, her hands gripping the back of the chair, before she forced herself to relax. It was all going to be alright, all the stress, all the worry, whilst not totally extinguished were far lower than they had been for years. If only she had employed someone like Anna earlier, then things need never have got so bad.

She shook herself, not wanting to dwell on bad memories and instead went in search of Anna to tell her the good news.

Anna had just collected the tack to get the one of the ponies ready for the next lesson, as Rose came over to her. "You must be our lucky charm, because we have four new client bookings for lessons this week."

"That's great," Anna replied though she was not sure it was anything to do with her necessarily, but Rose seemed happy and it was good to feel valued.

"Listen I was thinking if you wanted to do your riding instructress exams then we could definitely fund it through the yard." As ever Rose got slightly embarrassed, when Anna's face lit up. "Well, it makes sense for both of us for you to be properly qualified." She countered thinking it was a small price to pay to keep Anna.

Anna was overwhelmed and was just about to thank her profusely, when Daniel stalked up to them. Anna glanced up to say hi, but the word died on her lips. If she thought she had seen Daniel angry before this was nothing compared to now.

"Can I have a word in private?" he asked Anna, barely acknowledging Rose.

"Honestly Daniel, whatever is the matter?" Rose asked recovering quicker than Anna.

"Mum this is between me and Anna, if you don't mind."

Rose rolled her eyes. "Well don't you dare upset her, I'd be lost without her!" she told him sternly before walking away.

"You couldn't wait, could you?" Daniel rounded on Anna as soon as Rose was out of earshot. "I ask you to keep something quiet and what do you do? Start gossiping as soon as my back is turned. Lucinda Cottesmore has just told me that you were telling everyone in the village shop that Mum is not paying you because, well we all know why!"

"What!" Anna was stunned. "I never said that, Andrew asked if she was paying me…."

"Andrew?" Daniel spat the word in contempt. "I should have known he would be involved."

"Yes, but it wasn't like that…. I don't understand…" Anna tried to find the words to explain that Lucinda had obviously misunderstood.

But Daniel cut her off taking her long pause as a sign of guilt. "Don't bother I've heard enough." And with that he turned and was gone.

Guilt quickly turned to anger at the unfair way she had just been treated. She did not know who she was angrier at, Daniel for not listening or Lucinda Cottesmore for stirring. But her anger deflated as she realised Daniel was never going to accept her being here.

Chapter Ten

As the afternoon progressed Anna decided she needed to talk to Rose and explain before Daniel told her the story. She did not want Rose to think that she had been talking about her behind her back after everything she had done for her. And she still could not work out what Daniel had meant about why Rose was not paying her. She wondered if Rose had money problems. When Rose suggested a coffee at the end of the day, Anna saw her chance.

"Rose, I'm afraid there was a mix up at the shop today with Andrew and then Lucinda Cottesmore said something to Daniel and it seems to have blown out of all proportion."

Rose glanced at her, "Daniel did seem a bit het up and you've been distracted all afternoon, so you had better tell me your side of the story."

Anna quickly explained about forgetting her card, before bumping into Andrew.

"I did say I had just forgotten my card."

"Anna, calm down. I know you are not a gossip and I told Daniel that too. He'll realise that once he's calmed down, he's just hot headed like his father was. And well he has always been a bit over sensitive to village gossip. It was unfortunate it was Andrew though." Rose left the last comment hanging.

"What is the problem there?" Anna asked, relieved that Rose was not mad at her.

Rose sighed. "Andrew and Daniel were best friends for years and then Lizzie came to stay. She and Andrew had a fling which Daniel was furious about and Daniel and Andrew have not spoken since."

"Oh," was all Anna could reply.

Glancing at the clock Rose declared she would need to go and fetch Freddie for the riding lessons that evening.

"How come Freddie's mum never comes to watch?" Anna asked, and for a split second was surprised by a look of unease that flashed across Rose's face.

"Oh she's too busy, his Dad left them, and she works every hour there is providing for him. I just do what I can to help."

Anna could not help feeling yet again that there was more to the story, especially after she had heard Paris mention Freddie too but Rose was halfway out of the door so she let the subject lie.

As Mollie served up the dinner for the kids she silently grimaced at the food. They had asked for fish fingers with chips and baked beans, the whole plate was orange and beige, she really should have done some broccoli, to break up the colour a bit, if nothing else.

Shouting that tea was ready she put the plates on the table. Overhead four sets of feet could be heard stampeding down the stairs, as both Lottie and Josh had a friend over for a play date.

Billy was already in his high chair, as the others ran in.

"Hands!" Mollie called.

"Do we have tooooooooooo!" Josh complained rolling his eyes at Angus his best friend.

"Yes," Mollie said firmly but smiling so Angus would not think she was a horrible parent. "I bet Angus always washes his hands before tea, like we normally do." When I remember she added in her head.

"We never bother," Angus replied happily, "Mum says we should but Laya our new nanny says a bit of dirt never hurt anyone." He sat down and happily picked up his fork, then looked up quickly as a thought struck him. "Just don't tell Mum, or she'll get rid of Laya too."

Knowing that she shouldn't feel quite so pleased that Olivia's house wasn't quite as perfect as she made out, Mollie suppressed a smile and forgetting all about hand washing, she went in search of the tomato ketchup.

"Coooeee." Olivia's head appeared around the door, just as the children were finishing their food. "Oh, this all looks very… um orange… how 70s." She said trying to look wide eyed and innocent but failing to hide her smirk.

Cursing the fact, she had not cooked the broccoli, Mollie pretended she had been indulgent, "Well they fancied it for a treat."

"Treat?" Lottie's voice piped up, "but we had this last night too."

Olivia raised a perfectly shaped eyebrow at Mollie, before the patronising smile came to the fore, "I have a fantastic recipe for homemade baked beans, absolutely no salt or sugar."

"Sounds yucky," Commented Josh, before Mollie could silence him with a glare.

"It is," Admitted Angus sadly.

"Thank you," Mollie managed to force out.

"Sorry to rush off, but it's French class tonight, and they are starting on their verbs. Come along Angus." Olivia became all brisk and business like. "Thank you for having him Mollie, he always enjoys coming here, you are so much more liberal than me!"

Mollie smiled tightly knowing full well by liberal Olivia meant out of control. "Well enjoy French."

They walked to the front door where Angus put his shoes on, as they watched him do it Mollie noticed his hands had pen all over them.

"Oh dear, I see someone forgot to wash their hands before dinner tonight." Olivia commented in a sugary sweet voice. "Never mind!" she wrinkled her nose at Mollie as they left.

Strongly suppressing the urge to scream Mollie walked back into the kitchen and poured herself a large glass of wine.

"Mollie?" A voice shouted from the hallway.

Panicking, Mollie quickly putting the glass of wine in the microwave, before Olivia could see it and add being an alcoholic mother to all her other faults. But as the door opened to reveal Jane rather than the return of Olivia, Mollie let out a sigh of relief.

"Olivia?" Jane asked taking in Mollie's stressed appearance.

"Nightmare," she whispered checking the children were not listening, "she was just commenting on the fact I feed my children orange food."

"Orange food?" Jane asked, walking over to where her son Max sat, she dropped a kiss on his head, even though he batted her away and rolled his eyes at Lottie.

"Chips, fish fingers and beans." Mollie answered.

"It's our favourite, and anyway chips are yellow not orange," said Josh from the table where he was finishing off his dinner, and very clearly listening.

Glancing at the plates of food, Jane laughed, "I call it the Donald dinner, because it's unnaturally orange."

"Donald?" Josh asked in confusion.

"The bright orange man on TV." Max piped up.

"Whose Donald?" asked Lottie.

"Donald Trump, he's the American president and he's always very orange!" Jane explained.

"Donald. Trump?" Lottie and Josh both asked, beginning to snigger.

"Welcome to my world!" Mollie said rolling her eyes and finally relaxing.

Lottie, Max and Josh were now laughing openly. Looking up Josh managed to stop laughing for long enough to explain, "we are definitely going to call this dinner the Donald, as its orange and the beans make you trump," and with that he dissolved into giggles, along with Lottie and Max.

Mollie just shook her head smiling. "Wait till Olivia hears that one!"

"Sorry!" Jane replied looking completely unrepentant.

Mollie finally laughed. "Do you want a drink?" She asked.

Jane grimaced, "I'd love to, but I can't stop, come on Max we need to move."

As Max grumbled that he wanted to stay and play and that Lottie had said they would have banana custard, Jane turned back to Mollie and dropped her voice. "Bit of gossip for you, I popped into the village shop on my way here and apparently Anna, Rose's new helper was in there earlier, anyway she'd forgotten her bank card or something but Andrew was all over it, faking concern that Rose wasn't paying her, before inviting himself round for a drink later. You might want to warn her, he'll eat her for breakfast!

"Come on Max, you don't even like banana custard and you'll see Lottie at school tomorrow."

As Max left with Jane, protesting that banana custard was actually his favourite pudding, Tom and Daniel walked in.

"Hi Love," Tom said giving his wife a hug, before turning to the kids, "has Olivia been winding Mummy up again? I brought Uncle Daniel home just in case to protect me." He did a theatrical scared look around the corner as though Olivia might jump out, making the kids laugh and Mollie roll her eyes at him.

"Yeah, she said we were eating orange dinner, and Mummy got all cross but pretended she wasn't. But it's ok, because Jane said it is called the Donald Trump dinner, because the beans make you fart." Josh started laughing again.

"And because it's orange," added Lottie trying to get in on the action.

Tom laughed too, "Well talking of people getting wound up today, Daniel had another run in with Anna."

"Oh Daniel, I thought you'd admitted you might have been wrong about her." Mollie said in dismay.

Daniel snorted in disgust, wondering how Anna had managed to get her claws into everything in the village. He couldn't go anywhere without people commenting how great it was to see the stables returning to their former glory. He could not understand why no one could see through her, perhaps for a second, he had begun to think differently but then he had realised that he had been right to start with.

"Hold on Jane just said something about a scene in the village shop, is that what this was about?" Mollie asked looking pointedly at Daniel.

Bristling slightly, Daniel bit back, "Well perhaps Anna should stop going around gossiping."

"She didn't, she forgot her card and that was it. It was Andrew who suggested Rose was not paying her before inviting himself over for a drink."

"Really?" Daniel asked. "That wasn't the way Lucinda Cottesmore told the story."

Mollie raised an eyebrow to let him know exactly what she thought of Lucinda. "Well Jane had just come from the shop, and I'd trust her account far more that Lucinda's. To be honest I'm surprised you would even listen to her."

Mollie watched as realisation set in, before continuing. "You know Lucinda is a gossip and Andrew knew full well what had happened he just twisted it, either to wind you up or get Anna into bed. And so far, one of them has definitely worked."

"You mean she…?" Daniel pressed his lips together in an attempt to control his anger. He took a deep breath, aware Mollie was watching him. "Well it's hardly surprising as they seem to be seeing each other," he said with as much nonchalance as he could.

Mollie bit back a smile. "I meant he succeeded in winding you up, but you are certainly playing into his hands right now, if that's what caused the run in Tom was referring to. And actually, I don't think they are seeing each other."

"Beer Dan?" Tom asked opening the fridge. Daniel glanced up. "Um no, actually you know I might just pop over and see Mum."

"Oh okay." Tom seemed surprised by his change of mind.

"By the way, if you were thinking of apologising to Anna while you are there, tonight might not be the best night, Andrew invited himself over." Mollie said as sweetly as she could.

"Right." And with a face like thunder, Daniel was gone.

"Have I just missed something?" asked Tom, as Daniel headed out of the door.

"I'll explain later." Mollie shook her head wondering how Tom could be so unobservant at times. "Right kids, bedtime."

"You forgot pudding! You promised us banana custard." Lottie and Josh said without looking up.

Mollie sighed, not feeling up to an argument. "You can eat it while I bath Billy. Tom can you heat the custard in the microwave?"

As Mollie ran the bath, Tom appeared at the door. "Should I be concerned that there is a glass of wine in the microwave?"

Anna got out of the shower and put her make up on, then after critically assessing her appearance in the mirror, took it off. She did not want to look as though she had made too much effort. Annoyingly, in her haste she rubbed too hard, causing her skin to turn red. Exasperated and getting increasingly nervous she gave up and put it all back on again.

The stupid thing was she did not know if he would actually turn up and if he did what tonight actually was. She also tried to work out what she wanted it to be. By nine o' clock she had just managed to convince herself he would not turn up when there was a knock at the door.

Tilly, who had started barking at the sound, stopped as Anna gave her a stern look and wagged her tail instead.

Opening the door to Andrew, she found him looking repentant and holding up a bottle of wine as a peace offering.

"Anna, I'm so sorry I got caught up with a work thing, I'll totally understand if you'd given up on me." However, despite his contrite appearance, he now smiled lazily his eyes running over her as he walked into the flat.

"Interesting flat!" Andrew commented as she followed him into the kitchen.

"It needs a bit of work," Anna acknowledged.

"A bit!" Andrew mocked. "I hope Rose is treating you properly?"

"Yes its fine," Anna answered quickly not wanting to do anything to wind Daniel up further.

"Good. I'm so glad we decided to do this tonight." Andrew murmured now quickly changing tack.

Had they decided to do this or had Andrew just invited himself over, she wondered, as Andrew stepped closer still and began playing with a lock of her hair. She should probably stop him came a vague thought from somewhere at the back of her mind, but he was so gorgeous and it was so delicious to feel attractive for a change, especially after the way Daniel treated her.

Aware just how close Andrew was now, Anna jumped as something wet nudged her hand. Looking down she saw Tilly sat watching her. Smiling at Andrew she tried to regain control of the situation.

"Would you like a drink?" she said with too much heartiness, she sounded like Mary Poppins she thought in dismay.

If Andrew was bothered by the turn of events, he hid it well. "Of course. I'll open the wine."

As Anna got a couple of glasses out of the cupboard, he located the wine opener and deftly removed the cork.

Andrew handed her a glass, his fingers brushing hers and raised his own in a toast. "To tonight."

Anna smiled nervously, "so shall we go and sit down?"

Andrew caught her arm, "Anna, it's just a drink between friends," he said the words gently but she could not help thinking he was laughing at her.
But as they sat in the lounge chatting, Anna relaxed as Andrew made her laugh with stories about village scandals.

"Seriously, she may act like lady of the manor but Diana is one naughty lady." He said finishing off the story of how Diana had slept with half of the local hunt.

"I don't think I've met her."

"Yes you have, Jemima's mother, Belle's step mother. In fact, they don't get on at all Belle calls her Anna to wind her up."

"Why?" Anna asked trying to see the link.

"She was Anna Smith when she came to the village and was Craig Pennington's PA, same old story! And then they get married and she becomes Diana Pennington Smythe."

"Why Diana?" Anna still struggled.

"She clearly thought it suited her image better and of course Smith became Smythe!"

"But what is wrong with the name Anna?"

"Nothing, it's as perfect as you are." Andrew replied smoothly.

Anna laughed, whilst thinking back to the lady in the Range Rover, immaculate in white.

"But what about her husband, if she is having all these affairs?"

"Always working. Lost his first wife the same way. Although saying that, they both married him for his money. That's women for you."

Spotting her chance Anna asked "What about you? Weren't you married?"

Andrew looked up sharply the smile fading quickly.

"Sorry, forget I said anything," Anna muttered feeling awkward.

"No, it's fine, I'm sure Daniel has painted a very black picture of me."

"No, someone else mentioned it. Daniel and I don't really get on, he doesn't seem to want me here."

"That's because Daniel is an idiot, I however, am very glad you are here," Andrew replied smoothly.

"Rose said you used to be friends." Anna casually mentioned intrigued to know more about what had happened.

Andrew smiled, "let's just say I got fed up with being preached at. But I did not come here to discuss Daniel." He laughed, "Right you need another drink." However, when he picked up the wine bottle Anna realised it was empty. Andrew had been topping up her drink whist they were talking so she must have drunk nearly the whole bottle as he had not drunk that much at all.

"How about a coffee instead?" She offered realising that she needed to sober up a little.

As she made the coffee, she was aware Andrew had followed her into the kitchen. She turned around with a mug in each hand but Andrew took them off her and placed them on the small table next to the door.

"I've really enjoyed this evening." He said softly drawing her closer.

"Me too." Anna agreed, unable to look away from the suggestion in his eyes.

"Good," Andrew murmured, his other hand gently cupping her face and tilting it up for a kiss.

But just as he moved closer, something knocked her off balance.

"Tilly," Anna exclaimed.

"Anna, I think you need to put your dog outside." Andrew said firmly, as a flicker of irritation crossed his face.

Anna called Tilly and shut her in the lounge, she turned back to Andrew.

"Now, where were we?"

The howling started straight away. Andrew sighed.

"Put her outside."

"She'll wake Rose."

"Then take her over there."

"I can't it's late, and anyway I can't just give her back just because…. Well you know."

"You know sounds good to me." Andrew's voice was husky, but as Andrew moved forward, Tilly howled louder.

"Give her something to eat."

Remembering the dog chews in the cupboard, Anna gave one to Tilly, hoping it would keep her quiet for a while.

Returning to Andrew, with Tilly occupied, he slipped an arm around her pulling her in close before tilting her face up to his. His kiss started gently; his fingers gently ran down her throat before continuing lower. The kiss deepened further making Anna moan softly.

Unluckily Tilly chose that moment to come crashing back into the room, knocking the small table and spilling coffee all over them.

Andrew started yelling at Tilly.

"Don't shout at her, it was an accident." Anna snapped in frustration. She paused and regained control of her temper.

"Put her outside." Andrew replied coldly, grabbing a tea towel and unsuccessfully wiping the coffee mark.

"I can't do that." Anna replied imagining Rose's opinion of finding Tilly running around outside barking, especially as it was now raining hard. "Look, are you burnt?" She reached out to help him but Andrew pulled back.

"No. I think I had better go."

Anna just nodded.

Collapsing on the settee after Andrew had left Anna looked at Tilly.

"Oh Tilly."

But Tilly just walked up to her and put her head on her knee and gazed up at her.

"Tilly I am really cross with you," Anna said the conviction in her voice dying as she looked at the pair of big brown eyes, staring lovingly up at her.

Anna sighed, beaten and gave her a fuss, before going to put on her pyjamas and heading into the bathroom for a wash. She was brushing her teeth when Tilly started barking.

"What now?" she asked walking out of the bathroom. Hearing the knock on the door she jumped. Wondering if it was Andrew coming back having calmed down, she opened the door.

"Hi"

"Hi"

Her surprise at finding Daniel on her doorstep, turned to embarrassment as she felt him take in her pyjamas and fluffy slippers in amusement, she hastily tied her dressing gown.

"What are you doing here?"

"Mollie explained about what really happened in the shop and I just thought as I was passing, I'd apologise. I'm sorry I shouldn't have let it wind me up and I certainly should not have taken it out on you."

"Right, thank you." Anna managed to say despite her surprise.

"So, we're ok then?" Daniel asked.

"Yeah," Anna nodded still stunned he had actually come and apologised.

"Great." Daniel responded but did not make any move to leave.

"Do you want a coffee?" Anna found herself asking. She was not tired and after her evening needed some distraction.

"You look like you are off to bed and I've got George with me, so I'll get going."

"George?"

No explanation was needed as the Great Dane bounded into the small kitchen. Tilly who was delighted to see her play mate jumped up too.

"Sit," ordered Daniel and to Anna's amazement they both sat down and stayed put quietly. Anna gave Tilly a hard look, she would behave for Daniel she thought.

"I'm not disturbing anything am I?" Daniel asked. Anna followed his gaze to the empty wine glasses. He'd seen Andrew leave looking annoyed and convinced himself that someone should check Anna was alright.

"No Andrew came round for a drink but he's just gone." She handed Daniel a coffee and headed through to the lounge.

"That's early for Andrew," Daniel commented innocently. He glanced around the lounge, as he sat down. The flat was in a far better state than he had last seen it, but he still felt a spasm of guilt that Anna was living here, hopefully she would never find out it was his idea.

Mistaking Daniel's silence, Anna nodded debating how much to tell him. "Yeah, Tilly jumped on him and spilt his coffee everywhere so he left." She paused but the need to share the horror of the evening was too great. "He was really annoyed." Glancing up she saw Daniel nod and bite his lip.

"It's not funny you know."

"No." Daniel shook his head and tried to keep a straight face. Looking at him Anna felt the laughter well up inside her. It was actually quite funny when you thought about it. Daniel unable to hold it in any longer started laughing and Anna helplessly joined in. The both sat laughing until the tears rolled down their faces.

Finally catching his breath, Daniel shook his head in amusement, "I'm sure that's never happened to him before." And with that he stood up, drained his coffee. "I'd better be going."

Walking with him to the front door, Anna opened it. As he passed her, he paused, looking down at her, his expression softened. "Anna you really are far too nice for Andrew, you know."

But, before Anna could think of a reply he had left, calling George who bounded after him.

Chapter Eleven

The following Monday Anna decided it was time to tackle the tack room, the sun shone brightly, meaning she could completely empty it and rearrange it. For the next hour she steadily cleared out saddles, bridles and various pieces of tack, not to mention the brushes and other random items that were decades old.

"Are you having a yard sale?" Mollie's amused voice came from the doorway.

Glancing up Anna rolled her eyes half smiling, "this has turned out to be a slightly bigger job than I anticipated." She admitted with feeling.

"You can say that again." Mollie commented before dropping her bag and removing her coat.

"What are you doing?" Anna asked in alarm looking at her designer top.

"Giving you a hand, because otherwise you will be here until midnight!"

"Haven't you got Billy?" Anna asked wondering where he was.

Mollie sighed, "He's just started at the local nursery, and to be honest I need something to keep me busy for the next couple of hours, I'm at a bit of a loose end!"

Anna wasn't sure what to say.

"Don't worry, he knows most of the kids as they are siblings of Josh and Lottie's friends and I take him to playgroup there, it's me that's struggling to deal with it. So where do we start."

"Well, it's just this cupboard left to empty."

"What the massive floor to ceiling one that's bursting at the seams?" Mollie asked laughing.

"Yep, just remember you offered." Anna replied with a smile pulling back the doors.

They both groaned quietly as they looked at the jumble of jars and pots, brushes and pads and various tools that caused each shelve to bow in the middle.

"Wow, where do we start?" Anna wondered out loud.

"Anywhere will do," Mollie replied picking up two jars.

They worked side by side for the next half an hour steadily clearing out the cupboard, as they did Anna made Mollie laugh by telling her about the disastrous drink with Andrew.

"So, is that it then between you?" Mollie asked casually.

"To be honest it never got going," Anna paused, "I mean he's gorgeous, but…" she paused.

"But?" Mollie prompted.

"I'm not really sure, it just doesn't feel right." Anna said voicing something she could not quite work out herself.

"Perhaps he's just not right for you. Just because someone is interested in you it doesn't mean you have to feel something back." Mollie replied.

Anna considered her words for a second. "The thing is though I was never convinced he was all that interested. He seemed to blow hot and cold all the time."

Mollie fleetingly rolled her eyes but did not comment.

Anna pulled out a pile of numnahs and to her surprise she found half a bottle of whiskey behind them. "Look at this," she held the bottle up to Mollie. "Whose do you reckon it is?"

Mollie looked at her in consternation, "Anna surely you know."

"Mollie, how lovely to see you." Rose came striding in, she looked at the bottle in Anna's hand. "Well, if you two start drinking that, my tack room will never get sorted out." She said with irony.

"Oh no, it's not mine." Anna was horrified.

Rose just laughed, "it's probably there from last winter, Charlie and I occasionally have a hot toddy to warm up, the wind here can be bitter."

"Oh ok, shall I leave it in the cupboard?" Anna asked.

"May as well." Rose responded, "So any other surprises in here?"

"Just the sheer volume of stuff." Anna responded placing the bottle back on the shelf.

"Oh good," She looked relieved. "I really should sort some of it out." Rose looked at the lines of jars on the floor without much enthusiasm. "But right now, I need to go to the feed merchant, so I'll see you later."

Rose left and Anna pulled the last few items off the shelf. "Right, I'll get some hot water and then we can wipe it down and start putting this place back together."

"Anna….?" Mollie's voice was hesitant.

Anna glanced up surprised. Mollie was biting her bottom lip and looking at her as though weighing something up. She looked like she was about to speak when her phone rang.

Answering it, Mollie had a brief conversation with the person on the end, where both seemed to be reassuring each other that everything was ok and then she hung up. Gathering up her bag and coat she turned to Anna, "Sorry that was the school, Lottie has a stomach ache and they want me to go and get her now. I'm sure it's nothing but I'd better run."

"Absolutely, I hope she's ok." Anna replied, wondering what Mollie had wanted to say.

"She'll be fine." Mollie replied, before glancing at everything, "sorry not to be more any more help."

"Don't worry it was my decision to start it, although I won't be in any hurry to do it again." Anna said with a grimace.

With a sigh she picked up a broom and started sweeping the floor. Once the room was a lot cleaner than it had been before, it was time to put everything back. Using some baling twine, she put up new lines to hang the rugs on, as she hung the last rug, she heard a noise behind her.

"Now this is looking better." Rose walked into the room and looked around, seeming pleased. "What happened to Mollie?"

"She had to go, just after you left, the school phoned to say Lottie had tummy ache."

"Oh no poor Lottie. So, she wasn't here long then?"

Watching her Anna thought she looked a little bit on edge.

"No, not at all." Anna wondered what she was implying.

"Right," Rose smiled at Anna. "You know I was thinking I ought to move that bottle of whiskey, probably not terribly politically correct to have it in the stables, especially with our licence up for renewal."

"Sure," Anna replied laughing, thinking Rose was one of the most un-politically correct people she knew.

"Right, we'd better get those saddles back in." Rose said rolling up her sleeves.

Thump, thump, thump.
Anna woke with a start.
Thump. Thump. Thump.

Someone was hammering on the door of her flat. Throwing back the duvet Anna managed to locate the light as another round of hammering resumed.

"I'm coming," she yelled, thinking that if Houdini had escaped again, she would sell him even if Rose would not. Pulling on her dressing gown, she made her way to the front door. Reaching it, she cautiously called out to see who was there.

"Anna, its Tom. Lottie is ill. You need to help."

Having heard Tom's anguished voice, Anna had started unbolting the door to open it. As they came face to face, she realised the face was more anguished than the voice.

"You need to come now."

"I'll just get dressed." Anna said turning to change, she could hardly go out in the nightdress she was wearing, she thought, cursing the fact she hadn't bothered to do any washing and was only left with a lacy slip from Anne Summers to sleep in. It had been a Secret Santa present at work last Christmas, she was convinced Jenny had got it her.

"No time. We need to go now." His voice was stern as his panic grew.

Looking at his face, Anna realised he wasn't about to compromise, so she quickly kicked on a pair of trainers and followed him to the car, along with Tilly.

As they hurtled back towards Tom and Mollie's house Anna began to panic, wondering what she needed to do to help. Why did men always expect women to know how to deal with these situations she thought, with an angry glance at Tom? Well if she was expected to take charge Tom could help too. She wished Rose was awake she would know what to do.

"How bad is she?" Anna asked.

"She's doubled up in pain," Tom replied, the thought of which caused him to accelerate even more.

Thrown back in her chair, Anna wondered what she could do to help. "Have you got a hot water bottle?" She asked.

Tom gave her a strange look.

"I need to get Mollie and Lottie to hospital and all you think about is your creature comforts. It's not even that cold!" He rolled his eyes. "If I wanted someone high maintenance, I would have phoned Paris up!" he muttered under his breath.

"You're taking Lottie to hospital?"

Tom looked at her like she was mad, then as realisation dawned on him, he sighed. "Sorry Anna, Lottie has suspected appendicitis, the ambulance is on its way and I said I would come and get you."

"Sorry but why have you picked me up?" Anna was still not quite sure what her role was.

"Billy and Josh are asleep, and we don't want to disturb them. Mollie thought you wouldn't mind watching them but I forgot to mention that bit!"

The relief Anna felt was huge, looking after Billy and Josh would be fine. How hard could it be?

"Anna," Anna jumped and turned her attention back to the present. "Thanks for doing this. I've left a message for Daniel to come and rescue you. If he doesn't turn up, just pop Billy in front of Bob the Builder he'll be fine all morning. Don't tell Mollie I said that though, you know what she is like about two hours maximum TV a day."

The ambulance was already at the house. As soon as Mollie saw the car, she raised a hand as the paramedic shut the doors and they were quickly on their way.

Barely giving her and Tilly time to get out, Tom turned on the drive and took off after the ambulance.

As something wet nudged Anna's leg, she glanced down to see Tilly. Standing in the middle of the drive she shivered and hurried into the kitchen. The clock on the wall told her it was three in the morning.

She locked the doors, read Mollie's list, which basically ran through Josh and Billy's breakfast habits and likes and dislikes. And how Anna should help herself to anything and the spare room bed had fresh sheets on it. She finished off saying if the worst came to the worst Anna should stick a film on. Just don't tell Tom, he hates them watching too much TV, she had added. Anna smiled to herself.

Putting the list down she decided to go to bed, as she always felt slightly uneasy in other people's houses when they were not there.

For the second time that night Anna was woken by a thumping sound, except this time it was Billy, banging something against the child gate on his room. Glancing at the bedside clock Anna groaned it was only six. He was annoyingly cheerful and singing away to himself. Anna lay listening for a second wondering if there was ever a time when she had got up that early and been that happy about it. Even with her new job which she loved she still found early mornings hard.

"Mummy..........mummy.........." Billy called out.

Anna got out of the bed, and wrapped a dressing gown around herself that was hanging on the back of the door, once again wishing she was in her usual pyjamas.

She wondered if it was wrong to baby sit in an outfit designed to seduce. Deciding that the best course of action was to get Billy and then find some clothes in Mollie's room, she opened the spare room door.

"Where's Mummy?" Billy asked, not seeming surprised to see her.

"She'll be back soon." Anna opened the gate hoping she could distract him by playing a game.

"Where's mummy?" Billy ran into their bedroom and not finding her Billy began to cry.
Sitting him down on her knee Anna explained that Mummy and Daddy had gone to hospital and would be back soon.

"Is mummy poorly?"

"No, Lottie is."

"Will she die, great granddad went to hospital and he died. He lives in heaven now, with my rabbit."

Remembering the death of the Billy's pet rabbit and how upset he had been Anna quickly changed subject.

"No, they were very old. Lottie will be back before you know it. Now shall we have some breakfast?"

Having managed to negotiate breakfast and having had to eat the porridge too, Anna felt quite proud of herself. Popping Billy in front of the TV she decided to go in search of some clothes. As soon as she left the room though Billy came running after her and started crying.

"Are you going to pital?" Anna trying not to smile at his version of hospital and realised she could not leave him. Taking him with her they went upstairs and into Mollie's room.

Feeling like she was intruding Anna opened the wardrobe, relieved it was Mollie's, she quickly flicked through and pulled out a pair of jeans.

"Mummy's," came an accusatory voice behind her. Billy was looking at her suspiciously, and then started crying again. Picking him up Anna realised that as he would not stay on his own or let her borrow some clothes she would have to stay as she was for now.

In order to distract Billy and not wake up Josh, Anna ran through lists of different things they could do together. All TV was out, Billy's choice, a walk was out, Anna's choice due to lack of clothes and not being able to leave Josh, Lego was out, Billy's choice, and painting was out, Anna's choice after Mollie told her Billy had put painted handprints all over the kitchen wall last time he had painted.

"Cooking?" Anna asked tentatively

"Gingerbread men?" Billy asked, the tears looking like they may abate. Glad she had found something they were both willing to do, Anna readily agreed.

In the kitchen she located Billy's apron and on his insistence one for herself. After managing to find a cook book, scales, ingredients and utensils, they were well away.

Halfway through Josh wondered in, hair tousled and half asleep. Although he appeared fairly nonchalant about Lottie being in hospital, he decided to stay and cook with them, rather than play on his computer.

With the gingerbread made, which took forever as Billy wanted to help do everything, they finally were able to start cutting them out. After more time spent marking on faces and putting on Smartie buttons Anna was feeling quite proud of their achievements. As she put the two trays of gingerbread men in the oven, the phone rang, she answered it to find Tom on the other end.

"Hi, have you survived?"

"Yeah we're fine," Anna answered, her face turning to horror as Billy put his hand in the tin of golden syrup, which she had forgotten to put the lid on, and as he went straight to his mouth with it, golden syrup went everywhere. Anna headed to the sink for a cloth.

"How's Lottie?" she said trying to remain bright and breezy as Billy knocked over the flour. Josh giggled.

"They operated last night, and she's just sleeping now, but thankfully it hadn't burst, so it could have been worse."

"Great!" Anna looked at the devastation in the normally perfect kitchen and wanted to cry.

"Can I say hi to Billy and Josh?"

"Absolutely, they are just here." Anna put Josh on first.

Anna now started to panic. Billy needed a bath as he had golden syrup everywhere and the kitchen was a bombsite. She decided to bath Billy first.

Happier once he had spoken to his dad, Josh decided to go and play Mario Kart. Picking up his glass of milk he turned just as Anna picked up Billy, she felt the glass tip up as they collided.

Her dressing gown was drenched, leaving her no choice but to take it off. Pretending Josh hadn't just gaped in shock at the sight of her in a flimsy nightie whilst he refilled his glass, she took Billy upstairs.

As the bath finished running Anna started to help Billy out of his pyjamas.

"Uncle Daniel," Billy said.

"We'll go and see him later," Anna replied as she wrestled with the pyjama top.

"No need," a much deeper voice than Billy's replied.

Turning to the door Anna found Daniel leaning on the door frame looking highly amused. He had clearly been up all night, he looked crumpled and in need of a shave, but annoyingly he looked more attractive than ever.

"Tom phoned and said you may need a hand but you seem to have it all under control," he said his eyes dancing with amusement. His eyes took in the golden syrup covered Billy and the night dress Anna was in.

"Billy's just having a bath."

"Uncle Daniel stay?" Billy asked hopefully.

"Sure," Daniel sat down on the toilet as Billy told him they had been cooking.

"Oh Shiiiiiiii...ugar." Anna who up until then had been feeling highly self-conscious in the night dress now remembered the gingerbread men.

"Watch Billy I'll be back in sec."

"Anna nearly said a bad word, mummy tells daddy off for that," Billy told Daniel.

Hurtling down the stairs Anna ran to the kitchen and opened the oven door just in time.

"All ok?" asked a voice from behind her. Turning, she found Daniel stood holding Billy who was now wrapped in a towel.

"It's a bit messy," Billy told Daniel. Traitor Anna thought. Taking in the scene of devastation and wisely not commenting Daniel turned to Anna.

"Tom reckoned he'd be about an hour. Do you want to bath Billy or do the kitchen?"

"I'll take the kitchen."

Daniel took Billy up to his bath where she heard endless squeals of laughter. She was just restoring the kitchen to its pre gingerbread men perfection, when Daniel came back in. He watched as she gave the table a last wipe over and wondered if she knew you could see down her dress as she leant over the table. He glanced away before he got caught. Anna started putting away the utensils, feeling like the longer Daniel stood there the smaller her dress felt. Watching her Daniel realised he had never seen her with her hair down or in anything but trousers. As Anna reached up into a cupboard to put a plate away the night dress rose higher.

"Anna." The word came out almost without him realising it.

Something in the tone was different. It sent a shiver of anticipation down Anna's back. Slowly, she turned to face him. Daniel's eyes were fixed on her, her mouth went dry and she wasn't aware of anything else as Daniel moved towards her. His eyes held hers, his expression intense, his intent was obvious as he focused on her mouth, she bit her lip and seeing his reaction, she felt her own breath getting shorter.

He stopped just in front of her. Anna held her breath, his eyes were dark with desire as he bent his head towards her.

"Anna can we have a gingerbread man?" The spell was broken. Josh and Billy stood in the door way.

"Um sure." Anna blushed and moved towards the table where they were cooling.

Daniel turned away frustrated at what he had wanted to happen being stopped and annoyed with himself that he had momentarily completely forgotten Billy and Josh were only in the next room.

He turned to Anna. "I'll sort this, you had better put some clothes on." He winced as it came out far more harshly than he had intended. Anna who had been about to smile, froze. What the hell had she been doing? How could she forget where she was and after Mollie and Tom had trusted her to look after their children?

"I don't have any clothes, as Tom did not give me time to change or grab anything." Anna's voice was strained. Did he think she had tried to seduce him wandering around in the night dress?

"Well borrow something of Mollie's, you can't stay like that." Daniel told her wanting to add it was far too distracting.

"I hadn't planned on it," she retorted.

Watching her angry face Daniel thought she looked sexier than ever.

As she stormed from the room, Anna felt annoyed, with herself. What was she thinking? She was even more annoyed by the realisation of how badly she had wanted something to happen.

Making her way back down the stairs, once she had dressed, she heard Tom's voice, explaining to Billy that Mummy needed to look after Lottie, but that she would be home soon. Glancing up at her, he smiled, "Thanks so much Anna, Mollie is really grateful too. Turns out my useless brother was playing poker all night!" He finished with a jibe at his brother.

"Yeah sorry." Daniel replied his eyes on Anna.

Tom rolled his eyes as he went to answer the knock at the door.

"Anna look…" Daniel stepped towards Anna and started to speak, but Tom was already coming back into the room, followed by Rich. As the phone started to ring, he diverted to the kitchen.

"No rest for the wicked," he could be heard muttering to himself.

"Just came to see if everything was ok as the site is all locked up, and there's a delivery due at nine." Rich explained.

Daniel ran a hand through his hair, "Sorry mate I totally forgot, Lottie got rushed to hospital last night, appendicitis."

"Poor kid, is she ok?" Rich asked, but his eyes were wandering lazily over Anna who he had not yet met. "Looks like my lucky day! We haven't met yet, I'm Rich," he said with a smile.

Despite how corny his opening line was Anna could not help but laugh. "I guessed and Mollie has already warned me about you."

Before she could say anymore Daniel stepped in. "Anna is mum's new yard manager."

"Ahh you're the fit new riding instructress they've all been talking about down the pub. Now I can see why Dan said you were nothing special. He obviously wanted to keep you for himself."

Daniel and Rich were old friends and yet today Rich was trying to work out where Daniel's sense of humour had gone. He put it down to the fact they had been playing poker most of the night.

Hearing the words nothing special, Anna's face fell.

Rich realising his joke had completely backfired decided a quick exit was needed. "Do you want me to go and open up?" he asked.

"That'd be great thanks, and you'd better put the coffee on."

Knowing he had to pass Rose's to get to Broome Hill, Anna saw her chance. "Could you drop me off at Rose's on the way? I should have started work an hour ago," She turned to Tom who had just walked back into the room, "unless you need me to look after the boys?"

"No, I'll grab a shower then we'll all go back to the hospital together. Thanks again Anna."

"Ready then?" Rich asked, thinking his day was looking up after all.

"I was going to drop you back," Daniel interrupted, clearly annoyed.

"Actually Dan, could you watch the kids whilst I grab a shower?" Tom asked coming back into the room.

"Sure." Daniel forced out, as Rich and Anna headed towards the door.

"Oh, just to give you the heads up, Paris was outside your house this morning as I came through the village." Rich said as he opened the door.

As Anna closed it behind her, she heard Tom telling Daniel that Lizzie had phoned the night before looking for him. Clearly, she had just had a lucky escape, he seemed to have half the women in the village falling over themselves.

Chapter Twelve

"You're in a good mood." Charlie commented as he arrived the following morning.

"Sorry was my singing a bit loud?" Anna asked removing her ear buds.

"No, it's nice to have a happy yard."

"So, what do you think?" She waved to the yard she had almost finished weeding.

"Looks better."

"Thanks hopefully it will help with the inspection. I'll just get this last weed out and then we can start getting the ponies in for the first lesson."

"You know my dad used to be head gardener at one of the big houses around here, back in the day. He always said there was no such thing as a weed, they are just plants in the wrong place."

Seeing Anna's sceptical face, he continued. "See this lonely Dandelion here, trying to force its way through a crack in the concrete, it is a sad looking thing, but put it in a meadow with all the other dandelions on a sunny day and their bright yellow faces help create a thing of beauty."

He indicated the meadow opposite, Anna smiled thinking she had never thought about it like that before, but he was right.

"Bit like people really, to thrive and be happy in life you need to be in the right environment, sensible man my Dad." And with that Charlie ambled off to get the head collars.

Anna was sweeping the yard again, when Rose appeared. "She's here!" Rose informed her before turning and heading under the arch to the reception area.

Anna put the broom away and surveyed the yard, it looked good she thought nervously. It still needed work but they had spent the last few weeks preparing for the inspection, doors had been repainted, stables bleached, ponies washed and brushed, saddles cleaned, equipment inspected and that was before the mountain of paperwork they had had to complete.

And now it all came down to this one visit, if they failed to get their licence then the school would have to close. Rose had made half-hearted speeches about how they could become a livery yard, but Anna had seen how worried she was. Not wanting to think about the consequences of not renewing the licence, Anna decided to go and see if she could help Rose.

For the next few hours, they brought ponies out to the school, trotted them up and down the drive, talked through feed plans and training plans, produced records and answered question after question until Anna's head began to thump.

She realised Rose's patience was starting to wear thin and hoped the day could not last much longer, she did not think there was anything else the woman could ask.

"Right, well I think that covers everything." The inspector looked through her notes and nodded to herself, she put down her clipboard and carefully replaced the lid on her pen, before stowing them away in her briefcase.

Anna looked at Rose's clenched fists, and felt her anguish, as the woman carefully zipped up her case.

"Well thank you Rose, it has been a pleasure and I'm pleased to tell you that you have passed."

Anna let out a sigh of relief, glancing at Rose who for a brief second was frozen. "Thank you, that is fantastic news," she said as Rose still seemed incapable of talking. She shook the lady's hand as she collected her bag.

"We'll post out the certificate," she said turning to Rose.

At last the spell was broken and Rose was able to speak.

"Marvellous, well thank you so much and we look forward to seeing in a few years' time." Rose had taken control again and started to walk the inspector back to her car.

Realising that they had done it and that the school was safe, Anna let out a little whoop of joy at the realisation that she still had a job, just as Rose walked back in wreathed in smiles.

She grabbed Anna's hands, "we did it, we really did it!" She seemed almost overwhelmed by the news. Suddenly she caught herself, "Well I was sure we would pass, but it's always a relief to get it over with."

"Absolutely," Anna replied, starting to understand the true depth of Rose's anxiety over the visit.

"Do you know I think we should celebrate tonight?" Rose said thoughtfully. "There is a nice restaurant about twenty minutes from here run by a man whose daughter I taught to ride; I'll see if I can book us a table."

"Sounds good," Anna replied, just as Mollie walked through the door.

"Mollie, how lovely to see you my dear," Rose beamed, "well thanks to Anna here we did it, we have passed the inspection."

"That's fantastic news," Mollie replied genuinely.

"It is, so much so, we are going to go out for a meal tonight, in fact why don't you come with us?" Rose asked.

A host of emotions ran across Mollie's face, before she nodded, "that would be lovely, I've been stuck in the house most of last week with Lottie, but she is a lot better now so why not?"

"You are what?" Tom asked his voice raising.

Glancing to make sure the children were not listening Mollie sighed. "Tom she is delighted they passed and wants to go out for dinner tonight with Anna and they asked me too." Mollie paused. "I couldn't leave Anna to go on her own, just in case… And to be honest I would love a night out."

Tom nodded, "Ok well call me if there are any problems. How are you getting there?"

"Rose mentioned she would drive. You can't take us, because of the kids." She replied but Tom was already on his phone.

"Dan it's me, are you free tonight? Because you need to be!"

As Daniel turned into the restaurant, Anna caught sight of the name on the sign, she glanced over at Mollie who was sat in the back with her. "Is this…?"

"Jean Paul van Houtier's restaurant? Yes, it is."

"Right," Anna replied in surprise, when Rose had mentioned going for dinner, she had expected a village pub not a Michelin star restaurant that half the country wanted to visit. "Isn't there a huge waiting list for this place?" she whispered back whilst Rose and Daniel chatted in the front.

"Apparently not, if you are Rose!" Mollie returned with a shrug and a smile.

Glad she had made the effort and put a dress on, after Rose told her to look smart, she felt a bubble of excitement, she had never eaten in a restaurant like this before.

As the car drew to a stop, they climbed out, Daniel got out too, "I'll come as soon as you need me," he said to Mollie quietly.

"Thank you, Daniel." Rose waved, as she turned to the door which was being held open by a doorman. She glided through it, her wrap trailing in her wake. Anna had never seen her out of riding gear, but was unsurprised how smoothly Rose transitioned and fitted into the world she was now entering.

She turned to briefly thank Daniel for the lift.

He was watching her, his expression unreadable. "I hope you have a good evening; you certainly deserve to. Mum is delighted the licence was renewed so thank you."

"Thanks." She did not know what else to say so turned to follow the others.

"Anna," Daniel's voice stopped her in her tracks and she turned back, "you look stunning by the way."

She was about to respond when Rose called to her to hurry up.

"Did you turn his daughter into an Olympic rider?" Mollie asked, her eyes wide, as they were shown to one of the best tables, where a bottle of champagne was ready and waiting.

"Jean Paul sends his apologies that he cannot be here tonight, but he has requested that you order whatever you would like on the house," The maître de informed them as waiters descended on the table, pulling chairs out for them, placing napkins and filling champagne and water glasses.

"We couldn't possibly…." Rose started.

"Jean Paul insists," was all the maître de said, then with a slight bow he moved away.

"What did you do for his daughter?" Mollie asked intrigued.

"Nothing much, she was having a hard time at school, horses are always so therapeutic." Rose answered vaguely. Realising they were not going to get anything more from her Mollie and Anna grinned at one another as they sipped champagne and perused the menu.

Rose placed her napkin on the table, "Well that meal was certainly far better than what I would have rustled up at home. Excuse me ladies, whilst I powder my nose."

As she walked away Mollie turned to Anna, "Do you know this was exactly what I needed, I feel like I've been trapped in the house forever whilst Lottie recovers." Seeing the surprised look on Anna's face she explained, "Don't get me wrong I want to be the one to look after my children when they are ill, but sometimes I feel as though I have lost me a bit."

Anna smiled not sure what to say, she always thought Mollie had the perfect life. Mollie drew breath as though to say more but a shadow fell across the table.

"Paris." Mollie looked up and greeted her, although her expression was guarded.

"Mollie, what a surprise? I certainly didn't expect to see you tonight." She let the comment linger for a second, "And with Rose too."

"Well we are guests of Jean Paul, Rose taught his daughter to ride." Mollie smiled sweetly, although Anna could feel the dislike emanating from her.

"Well it's very brave of you to bring her out in the evening, I can't imagine Daniel would approve." Her tone didn't attempt to hide the patronising air her words held.

"He dropped us off tonight, so we could all enjoy the fabulous champagne Jean Paul laid on for us." Mollie returned, before deliberately taking a slow sip from her glass.

Paris scowled briefly before her eyes fell on Anna. Then as recognition dawned in her eyes a malicious smile crossed her face. "Of course, you are the new groom, goodness Rose must be desperate for company these days if the only people she can tempt out are a housewife and her own staff. Jean Paul will have to be careful; his reputation will suffer if it gets out that he's letting just anyone in."

"I couldn't agree more Paris, I mean your mother is sat over there and I recently heard she used to clean toilets so she could put you through private school!" Mollie's eyes glittered as she dropped all pretence of playing nicely.

With a tight smile Paris turned and stalked away.

"Bitch." Mollie muttered under her breath taking a large gulp of champagne.

"Don't let her ruin tonight," Anna advised, wondering how Daniel could have ever have been involved with her.

"Sorry, I'm not normally such a cow, but she always was little Miss Perfect when Daniel was around, as soon as he was out of ear shot, she constantly made digs; about me being a down trodden housewife, digs about my size just after Billy was born and even once told me Lottie needed to go on a diet when she was only three. I've waited a long time to put her in her place!"

"But you are Lottie are both so slim." Anna said in shock, before remembering Paris' cruel words in the village shop. Diplomatically she decided not to mention them.

Mollie laughed, "I know but slim isn't size zero! I should not let her get to me but the trouble is there is a small voice in my head that keeps saying I should be doing something more with my life, the problem is I just don't know what. So, when she makes her digs, a tiny part of me is actually agreeing with her."

"But Mollie…"

Mollie laughed, "Don't look so worried I am just feeling a bit sorry for myself that's all. And she's on the war path as Daniel seems to have permanently called time on their relationship, if you could call it that!"

"Really?" Anna asked wondering why the news pleased her so much.

For a second Mollie looked amused as she registered her reaction, "Mmm, I get the impression he's interested in someone else."

"Oh," Was all Anna could say, it was hardly surprising she told herself considering most of the woman in the area looked like super models and were constantly throwing themselves at him.

"Here's Rose. I suggest we have a coffee and call it a night. What do you think?" Mollie interrupted her thoughts.

On Sunday morning, as she tacked up ponies for the lesson, Anna worked through the list of people Daniel could like, but only drew a blank. She thought back to that morning in Mollie's kitchen and went over it again in her mind, had he been interested? Convincing herself she had misread the situation, she tried to focus on the lesson instead.

Anna moved to the next stable to tack up the pony in it. The pony was a Palomino mare, which had only arrived that week and was called Secret. As ponies went, she was very pretty and Anna was sure all the children would go mad over her. Secret had come to the stables after a mother had phoned up Rose asking her to take the pony off their hands. The daughter had lost interest and they did not want to look after it anymore.

As Anna finished tacking up Rose put her head over the door.

"She looks like she might be a bit fresh, so pop Freddie on her until we can get a better idea of what she is like. I had hoped you could sit on her and get her measure but you are far too big."

"Thanks," replied Anna knowing Rose meant no offence with her comments.

As the children started to arrive for their lessons, the new pony caused a stir. Anna was thankful they all acknowledged that Freddie was the best rider, otherwise she would have had a fight on her hands over who got to ride her.

"I like her name. Secret," Bethany said.

"I know a secret," Toby piped up.

"I've got a secret hiding place," Elliot said to better Toby.

Anna smiled at the children's banter around her as she ensured they all got on board the right ponies.

"My sisters got a secret boyfriend," Jemima piped up.

"I bet she hasn't," Elliot said.

"Yes, she has. Belle told me she loves him, but she can't tell because he is older and daddy would be cross."

Anna went cold, Daniel liked someone, and Belle was after Daniel. It all seemed to fit. Anna got through the lesson on autopilot, although she had to concentrate as Secret turned out to be quite a handful even for Freddie.

With the lesson over, they all headed back to the stable yard. As they turned horses out into the field, Anna kept an eye on Secret. She was starting to wonder whether or not the daughter had lost interest or the pony had been too much for them.

As Freddie left to take her to the field, she caught him up. "I'm going to walk with you just in case," she told him.

Although he was not happy with her decision, he said nothing and they walked along in silence. Anna was aware he was not happy at being baby sat but she stayed with him as she could not risk him getting hurt whilst in her care.

The following day began hot and only got hotter. Due to the heat Anna and Rose worked hard to get the work done in the morning as it would be too hot in the afternoon. By half past eleven, everything was finished.

"Right, I am going to take some lunch and drinks up to the field where they are getting the hay in." Rose told her. "Would you mind sweeping the barn?"

Picking up the broom and turning the radio up loud Anna began to sweep. Jenny and Lucy were coming for the weekend and Mollie was having a party for her birthday, it looked like being a great weekend.

Dancing round the barn, using the broom as a microphone she sang along happily. She had turned the music up so loudly that she did not hear anyone approach until a shadow moved across her.

Spinning around, she was horrified to find Daniel watching her in amusement.

"Little Mix, my guilty pleasure!" She admitted reluctantly.

"Mmm I got that impression," he responded dryly, "but don't stop on my account."

"The songs finished." Anna replied, moving to the radio and turning it down.

"Shame!" He replied making her blush. "Actually Anna, I......" Daniel started but they were interrupted by a wolf whistle.

Rich was walking towards them; he lazily took in Anna's shorts and cropped T-shirt. "We thought you'd got lost Dan, but now I see why! What chance do I stand when Dan always gets there first?" He complained, winking at Anna.

"I've heard you don't do too badly," Anna laughed, "Well the barn is ready. Do you need a hand?"

"No, don't worry, the bales are wrapped and you'll get covered in dust." Tom said kindly, who had now joined them as well.

As Tom and Rich made their way back to the tractor, Daniel held back.

"Anna, look...." Daniel started to speak as Anna's phone started to ring.

"I'd better answer that," she told him apologetically having seen Jenny's name flash up.

Pressing answer, she listened as Jenny's excited voice came over the speaker. "We're the next stop! We can't wait to see you."

"Ok, I'm on my way."

Hanging up, she looked at Daniel. "Sorry I have to go and collect my friends."

Daniel sighed.

As they walked back to the yard Anna groaned, looking at the tractor and trailer blocking her car in.

Seeing her face, Daniel handed her his keys, "Take mine." Seeing her hesitation, he raised an eyebrow, "You'll be fine, and then we can talk when you bring the keys back." And with that he went to help the other two.

Pulling into the station Anna could see Lucy and Jenny waiting on the platform. She swung Daniel's truck into a space and jumped out. Waving and shouting she ran over to hug her two friends who were stood in amazement.

"What?" Anna asked wondering if she had hay in her hair.

"Look at you all tanned and toned. You look fabulous babe," Jenny remarked, slightly in awe.

"Come here gorgeous," said Lucy throwing her arms around her.

After the brief reunion, they all piled into the truck and as Anna pulled out of the car park Lucy and Jenny filled her in on a mutual friend's wedding plans and Jenny's latest string of men.

"What happened to Dave he sounded nice when you mentioned him on the phone?"

"Exactly," droned Jenny in a bored voice. "He was lovely marriage material, but that's not what I want." Lucy and Anna exchanged looks they had never believed Jenny wasn't secretly looking for Mr Right as well.

"Anyway, enough about me, what I want to know is where you got a car like this, I didn't think working with horses paid much?" Jenny asked.

"It's Daniel's, I just borrowed it, as mine was blocked in." Anna answered as casually as she could.

"This is the Daniel you hate? The one who you've been moaning about for weeks? Who once told you that you couldn't drive, but has just lent you his car?" Lucy asked innocently. "Is there something we need to know?"

"Sounds like there is," Jenny chimed in, "So is he the man you've been dreaming about all these years, all rippling muscles and even better in bed than Christian Grey," Jenny teased Anna.

"But with a sensitive side." Lucy added pretending to swoon.

Anna suddenly got annoyed with her two friends. "Daniel is just a friend," she snapped.

"Ohhhh dear. I think she's fallen in love," Jenny quipped.

"He's not married?" Lucy asked.

"No, he's not and I'm not in love."

"So, he's a womaniser then?"

"No." Anna paused, thinking of the unanswered questions, Lizzie, Paris and Belle.

"Blimey it does not matter whether you are in the country or the city you still can pick them out at fifty feet," Jenny laughed picking up on Anna's long pause.

"Look you've not met him, we are just friends and he's not interested and neither am I," Anna said still trying to believe she wasn't interested. She wondered again what he wanted to talk about. "Anyway, I do not pick them. If I did pick them, I would be involved with Rich who works for Daniel and who despite being really fit is only committed to staying single!"

"Well, it'll be nice to meet them," said Lucy trying to pacify Anna slightly.

"Really? That's good as there is a barbeque at Tom and Mollie's tonight for Mollie's birthday, which I said we would go to. You can meet everyone then."

"Who'll be there?" Jenny asked.

Smiling at the fact she was always on the lookout for men. Anna replied, "Rose's sons and some friends of theirs, all locals really."

"Oh no will they all be farmers?" Jenny asked giggling, and glancing at Lucy she started doing farmer accents, as they pulled into the yard.

"Just imagine the chat up lines! Hey do you want to see my combine harvester?" Jenny drawled in a West Country brogue.

Drawing to a halt they could see Daniel, Tom and Rich were just finishing unloading the haylage. All three men had stripped down to their jeans and were throwing the heavy bales around as though they were as light as feathers.

"Wow, I see what you mean about the great views around here. It's like a diet coke advert but better." said Jenny leaning forward, her laughter stopping abruptly.

"The taller blonde one is Daniel, the other one is Tom his brother, and the dark haired one is Rich."

"Blimey," was all Lucy could manage.

Seeing the car, Daniel headed over, as the girls got out.

"Thanks for the loan," Anna said as she handed back the keys and made the introductions.

"Anytime, hopefully we'll be seeing you all later at the barbeque?" Daniel said directing the question at Anna.

"Definitely," Jenny replied. "We need to see what it is about this place that Anna loves so much, although it's not hard to guess with what we've seen so far."

Anna glared at Jenny willing her to stop, as a pleased look crossed Daniel's face.

"You'll have to let me know so we can keep her here," he commented not taking his eyes off Anna and making her blush. "I guess now isn't a good time to talk," he said dropping his voice whilst accepting the car keys back from her.

Anna shook her head.

"Ok." He turned to leave.

"Thanks again for lending me the car," Anna shouted after him. He raised a hand to acknowledge her comment but did not turn back.

"So not interested at all then?" Jenny nudged Anna.

Anna had been looking forward to the barbeque for weeks. The weather had been perfect and it had all seemed so enticing. But now stood in front of her wardrobe, which was a better description of the piece of furniture than it was of the jumble of clothes inside, Anna felt complete despair wash over her.

Letting go of the top that she had been holding out from the wardrobe she watched dispiritedly as it swung back into place. She wished she could cancel but having seen Rich nothing would keep Jenny from going.

"Right," Jenny said taking charge of the situation. She looked fantastic in jeans with a shirt tied under her chest showing a flat tanned stomach. Her hair was in two pig tails, which she carried off perfectly, whereas Anna knew she would look stupid if she attempted the same hairstyle.

"What about this red dress with those wedges it'll look amazing."

"It's a bit overdressed."

"You are such a defeatist. Men don't notice overdressed now do you want Daniel or not? Lucy throw me that bag," Jenny produced a number of wondrous products and with Lucy doing her hair by the time they finished even Anna was pleased

"That'll get you Daniel, and if it doesn't, then he must be blind." Lucy said, standing back to admire their work.

The party was in full swing when they arrived and Anna was amazed at what Mollie had achieved. There were fairy lights in all the trees, a professional bar stood at one end of the area, waiters could be seen carrying trays of drinks to happy party goers, nearby professional caterers were manning two large barbeques, next to which a table laden down with salads, rolls and other enticing looking food was being eyed up by a group of young lads. But even more impressive than the party was the amount of people. Anna had thought there were not that many people locally, but there had to be at least two hundred people milling around.

As they made their way through the crowd to find Mollie, Anna said hello to people she knew.

At last Anna glimpsed Mollie behind a group, who had clearly spent the afternoon in the local beer garden and were now trying to play a drinking game that involved a broom and people spinning and staggering off down the orchard, to cheers and whoops from the rest of the crowd.

Skirting the group who erupted with laughter, as someone fell over downing a shot, Anna waved a hand to attract Mollie.

"This is amazing I did not expect anything like this?" she said as she got within shouting distance.

"Thanks," replied Mollie, turning to say hello to Lucy and Jenny.

"I can see why Anna is so happy here? I've never seen so many gorgeous men gathered together." Jenny said her eyes roaming around the orchard.

Mollie laughed. "Yeah, life's not too bad around here, now ladies you definitely look in need of a drink."

"I'll go," Anna offered. She was nervous about seeing Daniel and wanted something to do.

As she wove her way back through the groups of people, Anna was so busy watching that the drinks did not spill, that she nearly walked straight into him. He let out a low whistle.

"You look stunning," he said his eyes sweeping over her. Anna tried not to be too pleased by the fact he had noticed.

"Thanks," she replied nonchalantly, attempting to pass by.

"And you look like you need a hand," he said blocking her path and taking two of the drinks off her. Letting her lead, he followed her back to where her friends stood.

Tom and Rich had now joined them and they all seemed to be getting on well. Handing over the drinks, Daniel took Anna's hand. Turning to Lucy and Jenny he apologised.

"I need to talk to Anna, but I promise I'll bring her back," he told them starting to lead Anna away.

"Be our guest I was beginning to think I'd have to sort you two out," Jenny called after them, to which Anna threw her a look begging her not to say more.

"Sorry to drag you away, but every time I try and talk to you, you seem to find an excuse to run off," Daniel stopped and turned to face her as soon as they were out of earshot.

Anna just smiled not sure what he was about to say, and conscious of the fact Tom, Rich, Mollie, Lucy and Jenny were doing a very bad job of pretending not to watch what was happening.

"You really do look fantastic tonight you know," Daniel told her again moving closer. This time Anna accepted the compliment.

"Daniel, there you are!" Belle declared walking up to them and planting herself firmly between Anna and Daniel. Daniel looked annoyed but turned to say hello.

Feeling like a spare part Anna made her excuses, although Belle barely seemed to notice her leave and returned to the safety of her friends.

As she approached the group, the three girls all looked at her.

"Anna you are hopeless. Now go straight back," Jenny ordered her.

"Look you don't understand he likes her too," she replied wishing Tom, Rich and Mollie were not there to witness her embarrassment.

"No, he doesn't," Mollie replied.

"But you said he was interested in someone," Anna reminded her.

"I meant you, tell her Tom." Tom nodded his head in agreement.

Grabbing a bottle of beer and a glass of wine and putting them in her hands, Lucy gave her a shove in Daniel's direction.

Turning to look at them again, Lucy pointed an arm towards Daniel.

Walking back towards Daniel and Belle, Anna wanted the ground to open up underneath her. This was suicide, she would turn up with the drinks and stand there feeling like a gooseberry. Deciding that if Daniel did not look up, then she would walk straight by and pretend she was looking for someone else.

As she got closer, she got more nervous. Belle was stunning. If she was Daniel, she knew who she would choose.

Putting her head down, she went to walk straight past, when Daniel grabbed her arm.

"Great you've got our drinks! Belle it's great to see you but I need to talk to Anna."

Glancing at Anna, then Daniel in surprise, Belle sniffed then walked away.

"I thought you'd run off again."

"I did. They made me come back."

"Mate, watch out Paris is heading this way," Rich said as he and Jenny walked past them on their way towards the food.

"This is ridiculous. I just want five minutes alone with you. Come on."

Taking her hand again Daniel hurried Anna out of the orchard.

"Damn. She's seen us," he informed Anna and turning the corner of the house, he began running towards the garages. Following along helplessly trying to run in her wedges, Anna started to laugh, as her wine slopped out of her glass.

Opening the side door to the garages and pulling Anna in behind him, Daniel put a finger to her lips. They listened as someone drew closer, and stopped. Anna held her breath but luckily Paris seemed to have given up and was walking away. She looked up at Daniel.

"So, what did you want to talk about?"

Daniel looked down at her his eyes filled with amusement. "Well, I just needed to tell you how sexy you look tonight."

"And you can't do that in public?" She asked smiling.

"Well I could, but I didn't want to stop there." Daniel's voice dropped as he let the meaning of his words sink in.

"Oh!" Anna bit her bottom lip as Daniel's eyes followed her movements, aware they were so close now they were practically touching; Anna dragged her gaze from his mouth back up to meet his eyes. "And what were you planning on doing after?" She asked smiling as his arms slid round her waist drawing her even closer.

Daniel laughed, "Do I really need to explain?" he returned but then the amused look on his face turned serious as his eyes darkened, "How about I show you!"

For a brief second a bubble of elation shot through her as she realised, he was finally about to kiss her. Then his mouth was on hers, softly at first but as she began to kiss him back, his tongue ran slowly along her top lip making her moan with pleasure. In response the kiss deepened as he pulled her even closer making her even more aware than normal of his broad shoulders and defined chest, which tapered to the narrow hips, which were also pressed against hers. She groaned with desire again, realising as he pressed up against her, he was just as turned on as she was.

"You don't know how long I've wanted to do this," Daniel murmured huskily in her ear, his hands were in her hair and his lips moved seductively slowly down her neck. She let her head fall back loving the feel of his lips on her skin.

Anna was so lost in the moment she didn't hear someone knocking persistently on the door.

"Ignore them," Daniel murmured.

But the door opened anyway to reveal Tom. Pulling away Daniel looked over at him. "You are supposed to be on my side."

"Sorry mate, but one of the councillors is here and he wants to talk about a complaint they've had about Broome Hill." Tom gave them both an apologetic look. "We'll be in the kitchen, you look like you need a minute to straighten up," he said with a smirk leaving them in the garage.

Brushing her hair away from her face, Daniel sighed, "I'll be as quick as possible. How long are your friends staying?"

"Until Sunday."

"I guess I will have to wait until Sunday then."

"Until Sunday for what?" Anna teased him now, confident that he really liked her.

"To see you in that sexy nightie again, when Billy is not around," he replied picking up her mood but making Anna blush as they made their way out of the garage.

Finding Lucy and Mollie in the orchard dancing, Anna's smile confirmed that they had all been right about her and Daniel.

"You know for once I think I might approve of your choice in men!" Lucy told her giving her a hug.

"All I can say is, it's about time!" Mollie added. "Although, it's been entertaining to watch you two keep pretending to hate each other."

Anna blushed. "Where's Jenny?" she asked changing the subject.

"We haven't seen her since she and Rich went for food."

"Ahhhhh," Anna and Lucy gave each other knowing looks.

As the night wore on the music got louder and the bar started to run dry. Everywhere people were coupling off, Anna thought she saw Belle with Andrew but could not be sure, but was pleased to realise that whoever Andrew was with she was not bothered.

After Tom and Daniel had re-joined them, they had stayed as a group.

Rich and Jenny reappeared about two in the morning to say goodnight and disappeared again. At which point Tom and Mollie also decided to call it a night.

Daniel offered to walk Lucy and Anna home, and they left the party still in full swing as they walked back up the lane. Daniel took her hand lacing his fingers through hers, his thumb lightly stroked the inside of her wrist as they walked, making it impossible for Anna to concentrate on the conversation. However, at the door Daniel said goodnight and even though Anna invited him in, he declined.

"I'm sure you and Lucy have lots to catch up on, so I'll see you on Sunday." And with another lingering kiss he left.

Going into the flat to find Lucy was making tea, Anna felt that life at that moment was perfect.

"Happy?" Lucy asked laughing.

Anna blushed. "He's great, isn't he?"

"He is, but better than that I've been watching you tonight and you seem different, happier and more confident. Mollie's been singing your praises and you definitely seem to have made a good impression on a lot of people around here. I'm really pleased it has worked out so well for you Anna."

"It's all thanks to you."

"Don't remind me, I still feel bad about that."

"Well you shouldn't because right now I don't think life could get any better."

Chapter Thirteen

As the train pulled into the station Anna hugged Jenny and Lucy, "thank you so much for coming down, it's been fab," she told them as they picked up their bags ready to board.

"Too right it has," Jenny said with a smirk. Rich had spent a lot of the weekend with them and more particularly Jenny, which had given Daniel an excuse to join them too.

Lucy hugged her too, "It has been fantastic, I'm so glad you're so happy."

Anna waved them off before heading back to the car park, Daniel was picking her up in an hour, she thought, nervous excitement spreading through her.

Daniel looked at his watch again in annoyance, the delivery that had been due that afternoon had still not arrived, Tom was with Mollie visiting her parents and he could not get hold of Rich. Reluctantly he pulled out his phone and dialled Anna, "I'm really sorry but I think we are going to have to cancel tonight."

Daniel hung up and switched on the kettle for another coffee, thinking that at least she had not had a hissy fit like Paris would have, but a niggling thought at the back of his mind wondered if she shouldn't have been a bit more bothered.

He stirred the coffee again and sat down to look at the plan for the week as he continued his wait. But the plan quickly lost his attention as his thoughts went back to Anna. Daniel once again felt anger wash over him that the driver was late. Surprised by a knock on the door he realised he had not heard the lorry, he really needed to focus.

"Finally," he muttered getting up to answer the door. However, as he opened the door, he stepped back in surprise to find Anna stood there holding up a bag of Chinese take away.

"Thought you might fancy some food and maybe some company?" She smiled hesitantly, hoping she had done the right thing.

Daniel pulled her towards him smiling too, all his resentment gone, "Definitely," he replied. "I was just thinking about you."

They sat on the floor, chatting as they ate.

At a pause in the conversation, Daniel tucked a piece of her hair behind her ear. "This was certainly not what I had planned tonight, eating a take away on the floor of a porta cabin."

"Really?" Anna asked in amusement.

"Believe me I will make this up to you." Daniel promised, his look making Anna's pulse start to race.

"Well, I can think of a few things that might do it." She replied huskily.

A knock on the door heralded the arrival of the delivery driver. Whilst Daniel supervised the delivery, she cleared away the take away.

Coming back into the office, Daniel glanced around surprised. "Thanks for clearing up, now I feel even worse about how awful tonight has been." He pulled her close to him. "At least let me drive you home as it's getting late."

As they drove back through the village, Anna realised she did not actually know where Daniel lived.

"Do you live in the village?"

"Yes, the one on the end." Daniel indicated the row of cottages on the left. All picture perfect in Cotswold stone.

"It's gorgeous."

"Thank you, I like it, although the tourists staring in during the summer months can be a pain sometimes. As it's still early, I can give you the grand tour, if you are interested?"

Anna paused, the delicious tension that had been simmering just under the surface all night, all weekend and if she was honest for a while flared up between them now.

Daniel smiled, "Don't worry it was just an idea, there's no pressure."

"No, I'd like too." Anna said her voice not quite normal.

Slowing the car, Daniel turned to her, "Are you sure?" His eyes searched hers.

She nodded again her eyes not leaving his, a smile playing around her lips.

"Take a seat in the lounge," Daniel indicated a door, as she heard him in the kitchen. The lounge was cosy with oak beams, two large settees and a wood burner with an oak mantelpiece. A vision of Daniel and her on the rug in front of the fire, flashed though her mind.

"What do you think?" Daniel was stood in the doorway watching her.

"Um…" Anna blushed again hoping he could not read her mind. "The house is beautiful," She managed truthfully as she stood up.

Daniel looked pleased, "Come on I'll show you around while the kettle boils."

As Daniel stood back to show her the kitchen, she noticed the collar of his shirt was slightly up on one side, without thinking she lifted a hand to straighten it. The awareness that had been there all evening magnified even further, instead of removing her hand, she ran her fingers lightly along his jawline and over his lips. They stood staring at each other, their breaths getting shorter, the excitement and longing building. Her fingers dropped now and ran down his face and to his chest. Taking the lead now, Daniel gently kissed his way along her jawline and down her neck. Anna's head dropped back and she moaned as each touch of his lips sent her pulse racing faster. Daniel needed no further encouragement and slipped an arm around her waist, the other plunging into her hair, as his lips came down on hers, Anna gasped again in pleasure.

Wanting to see more of him she started to tug at his shirt, with one swift movement he pulled it over his head, making Anna gasp at the firm body revealed underneath.

"My turn." Daniel's hands now moved to her waist and Anna lifted her arms as he slipped off her top. As it drifted to the floor, he stood staring at her. His eyes were hot and dark with desire. "How about we have that coffee after I show you upstairs?" Daniel asked with cheeky smile.

"That works for me." Anna smiled as she let him lead her upstairs.

A few days later Anna let herself out of Daniel's cottage, smiling to herself as she headed back to the stables. As she shut the door, she became aware of someone staring at her. Turning she found Paris watching her in contempt. "Well, well, well look who it is!"

Anna gave her a tight smile and headed towards her car, but Paris was not letting go.

"Well, well, it would seem it's not only Rose you work for!" Her eyes glittered in contempt and her lip curled in a sneer.

Gasping Anna turned back to her. "What exactly are you suggesting Paris?"

"Nothing!" She affected a look of innocence, "It's just that the whole village is talking about your car being out here every night, but the bit that no one can understand is that Daniel does not seem to want to be seen in public with you!"

Anna's happy mood was evaporating quickly at Paris' onslaught, behind her she heard the door open as Daniel followed her out. She turned back to him, not knowing what to say.

Seeing Anna's face, and then Paris too, he slid an arm around Anna.

"Morning Paris." He said keeping his eyes on Anna and pulling her closer.

"I was just saying to Anna we were all surprised you haven't been out in public together."

Anna felt Daniel still at the implication in Paris' catty remark, but he simply smiled lazily at her, "Well you will on Saturday at the Summer Ball."

Paris practically hissed as she stomped away.

Tipping her face up to his, Daniel searched Anna's eyes, "Sorry are you ok?"

She nodded slowly.

"Would you like to go to the ball on Saturday? I had been meaning to ask but for some reason I struggle to focus around you." He teased.

Anna nodded and smiled, although Paris' words had unsettled her. She wondered if Daniel really did want to be seen out with her and how she would find a dress that was suitable. Getting in her car, she quickly texted Mollie to see if she was free that night.

Answering the door that evening Mollie raised an eyebrow, "Don't I know you?" she joked.

Anna blushed, "Sorry I know I'm an awful friend, I've been meaning to pop around all week but…."

"I heard my brother-in-law had been keeping you busy," Mollie commented innocently.

"Something like that." Anna replied unable to stop the smile that betrayed her.

"Enjoy it, I'm just jealous, I wouldn't change Tom for the world but I love that start of a relationship where you can't stop thinking about them and having sex all the time. Trust me in a few years' time, the fact they never put their boxers in the wash basket will be driving you mad!" She laughed. "Coffee?" Mollie asked taking in Anna's worried look.

"That'd be great!" Anna paused. "Daniel is taking me to this ball on Saturday and I've got nothing to wear and I don't want to let him down, will you come shopping with me? Although I don't know when as it's the day after tomorrow."

"Woah, slow down. Look Daniel won't care if you wear a bin bag from what Tom's said. But as it happens, I have a dress which may well suit you perfectly. Come and try it on."

Sunday's lesson had been moved to Saturday as apparently most parents would not make it out of bed the day after the ball, according to Rose, so Anna decided to take the children around the fields as there were logs to jump, which she thought they would enjoy.

Freddie was still riding Secret who had settled down a lot and was turning into quite a nice pony although Rose would still only let Freddie ride her for the meantime. The others were on various other ponies, which could all be trusted to a certain extent not to run off once they got out in the open fields.

As most of the adults in the village would be going to the ball that evening, they had been happy for the children to stay all morning at the yard, whilst they got their hair done and picked up suits from the dry cleaners.

Anna decided to ride Murphy as she would not be able to keep up with the ponies on foot if they chose to canter off, which she did not quite trust a couple of the children not to do.

Once they had warmed up, Anna let them canter. With Freddie in the lead and her bringing up the rear on Murphy so she could see if anyone fell off, they headed up the first field. She watched as the string of ponies all jumped the first log and then the second. But as they came towards the third jump which had a small ditch in front of it, everything went into slow motion.

Freddie was cantering fast towards the ditch. From where she was Anna could see Secret start to resist. Unable to do anything other than watch, Anna sat staring in horror as Secret started to jump the fence, but on seeing the ditch she swung to the left and dropped her shoulder.

Freddie disappeared down the side of the pony and as it cantered away back towards its stable, Anna could see only his leg as the rest of him was in the ditch.

Immediately the other children started shouting and a couple began to cry. Realising she was on her own Anna tried to take charge.

She rode over to the jump at speed and jumped off to see how badly hurt Freddie was. As she did so she shouted to the other children to all stop their ponies and to stand in a line.

Freddie was conscious, just. But he was very dazed and looking at his leg Anna was sure it was broken. Holding his hand, she told him to lie still and that help was coming.

Turning to the children she debated which one to send for help. Normally her first choice would have been Freddie, she thought ironically.

In the end she settled for Elliot and Jemima. Elliot because he was sensible and a good rider and Jemima because Anna thought she would scream at her if she did not stop telling the others about how her father's friend and broken his leg skiing and had to have it chopped off.

"Elliot, tell whoever you find first whether it is Charlie or Rose, that they need to call an ambulance as Freddie's leg is broken. Now don't canter, just walk back to the yard."

She watched them head off towards the yard, following the path Secret had already taken. Anna turned her attention back to Freddie, who was groaning. She debated whether she should take his hat off, cursing her lack of first aid knowledge.

"Anna, he's not dead, is he?" Bethany asked, unable to see anything other than the leg sticking up out of the ditch. Anna glanced up at her, wondering why children were always obsessed with death.

"No Bethany, he's just hurt his leg," Anna smiled reassuringly at them all.

Looking back down the hill, she could see Rose's old Land rover making its way towards them. As it pulled up Charlie, Rose, Elliot and Jemima all got out.

"Right children," Rose announced. "I want you all to go back to the yard with Charlie and untack your ponies."

The children clearly wanted to stay and watch, but Rose ushered them all off down the hill.

As soon as they were out of earshot, she turned to Anna. "How bad is it?"

"He's conscious but I think he has broken his leg."

Freddie now sat up in the ditch but screamed in pain as he did so, clutching at his leg. Rose was by his side instantly.

"There, there, you'll be fine. Now we need to get you out and take you to hospital."

Freddie nodded and between Rose and Anna they helped him out of the ditch and into the back of the Land rover. Rose carefully drove them back to the yard. But Anna who was sat in the back with Freddie saw him wince in pain at every bump.

Back in the yard the ambulance had arrived and all the children had gathered around. Rose announced she would go to hospital with Freddie.

"I'll phone his mother," Anna offered. At which Rose and Freddie both panicked.

"You'd better leave it to me," Rose answered.

"Don't tell mum, she'll go mad," Freddie pleaded.

"We have too I'm afraid," Rose said sadly.

"I'll say I was playing football." Freddie offered hopefully, whilst gritting his teeth against the pain.

"Freddie you know I can't do that. Don't worry it will be fine." Rose replied trying to look positive.

The paramedics lifted Freddie into the ambulance and Rose got in behind them.

Anna and Charlie got all the ponies untacked and set the children off brushing their ponies until their parents arrived.

"You'd better have some of this, good for shock." Charlie offered Anna the little hipflask that he had pulled out of his pocket.

"Charlie a child in my care has just broken his leg, I can't start drinking whilst looking after the rest of them," Anna retorted.

"Look, first, it's not your fault, if you get involved with horses you can have accidents, it's the same in any sport. And second if you won't have some of this go and get a cup of strong sweet tea. You have had a shock and need to settle your nerves."

Blaming herself heavily Anna did however take Charlie's advice and go and make herself a cup of tea.

Luckily many of the parents were preoccupied with the ball and fairly uninterested in the stories about broken legs that their children were so full of. Charlie quietly dealt with them all telling them it was nothing serious and implying children like to exaggerate.

Wretchedly, the only parent to be late was Jemima's. As Anna waited with her, Jemima asked endless questions as to whether or not Anna thought they would chop Freddie's leg off. Having reassured Jemima that Freddie's leg would not be cut off for what felt like the hundredth time Anna was relieved to see the Range Rover pull into the yard.

But instead of Belle or Jemima's mother, an older man was driving the car.

"Daddy!" Jemima exclaimed in surprise.

As he got out of the car, Jemima asked him if he wanted to see the pony she had ridden and to Anna's surprise he said yes.

As they walked around the yard with Jemima leading the way, Charlie walked over to them.

"Nice to see you Mr Pennington"

"You don't mind do you, Charlie? I just need to be out of the way for a while. The ball is at ours tonight and I've had marquee people, florists, caterers and heaven knows what else traipsing all over the house, there is nowhere left to hide. In addition, Diana and Belle are both running around doing women's things so I thought I'd come and get Jemima for some peace and quiet."

Charlie laughed and offered him a cup of tea. As they sat in the tack room drinking tea and chatting about the village Anna's frayed nerves began to settle.

After an hour Craig Pennington reluctantly declared they should go back home to see if they could help.

After they had gone Anna turned to Charlie, "You know I would never have put him with Jemima's mother."

"Everyone is different, but the trouble is he has always chosen a pretty face over everything. It is a shame because he's a nice man."

Seeing Anna's look of confusion, Charlie expanded his explanation.

"Belle's mother was his first wife, Craig Pennington was good looking and very rich, but not exciting enough, spent all his time working. She took off when Belle was ten. Lives in New York now. He then married his secretary Anna Smith, and along came Jemima."

Anna thought back to Andrew's stories and it all seemed to fit.

As though reading her thoughts, Charlie laughed, "That's new money for you!"

Hearing Rose's Land rover rattle back into the yard they waited anxiously for her to come and tell them the news.

Rose walked around the corner, looking tired and shaken.

"Well, the good news is they don't think the leg is broken just a badly sprained ankle, but they are doing an x ray to make sure. The bad news is his mother has threatened to sue. Though she did take it better than I thought she would."

"She won't sue, once she has had time to calm down a bit." Charlie assured her.

Rose smiled gratefully at him. "I just feel so guilty. I knew she did not want him riding horses after his father ran off, having accrued those huge gambling debts on the races, but he loved it so much it seemed a shame to deny him. And it was keeping him out of trouble."

"Look like I told Anna there is no point in feeling guilty. What's done is done and accidents happen, and what you did, you did with the right intentions."

They finished off the stables early that night, but without their usual banter, as they were all lost in their own thoughts.

As Charlie left for the day, he wished Anna a good time at the ball.

"Of course, the ball I'd forgotten," Rose clapped her hand to her mouth "Anna, have a lovely time. I hear Daniel is taking you?"

Anna nodded glad that Rose was too preoccupied to read anything into it.

Making her way back to the flat Anna sat down and had another cup of tea, it was all she had done all day she thought. Realising she needed to start getting ready, she headed into the bathroom for a shower.

Walking back into her bedroom ten minutes later, she looked at the dress hanging on the back of the door, and then at the matching underwear she had left out ready on the bed. Thinking back to that morning she remembered how excited she had been, laying everything out ready, with high expectation for the evening. Why had she not just taken the children in the ménage as usual, she asked herself for the hundredth time.

Once again, she tried and failed to muster the excitement she had felt earlier. She put the underwear on, did her hair and make-up and pulled the dress over her head, putting her arms through the little spaghetti straps.

She felt the dress catch, the left strap tightened, and then with a pop it flew backwards over her shoulder. Looking in the mirror, she could see the strap hanging limply down the front.

Trying to ignore the thought that bad things happened in threes and she was now on number two, she took the dress off. Searching through her things she found some safety pins. With the strap secure, she carefully put the dress back on and critically surveyed herself in the mirror.

Despite her mood, she was actually quite pleased with her appearance. Giving herself a mental shake, she decided she was going to enjoy the evening, and then tomorrow she would go and speak to Freddie's mum and apologise.

The knock at the door made her jump. Opening it she found Daniel stood on the doorstep in his dinner jacket, he smiled appreciatively. "Wow, you know I vote we miss the ball and just stay here."

Daniel stepped forward to kiss her but wishing he had been there earlier Anna burst into tears.

Looking surprised, Daniel took her in his arms. "Hey, what's wrong? I thought I looked ok in a dinner jacket?"

Anna half smiled before she explained what had happened with Freddie. As she finished telling the story Daniel smoothed away the tears on her cheeks.

"Let's stay here. I'll ring Tom and let him know, but don't worry about Freddie, it will all be fine."

"No, you need to go, you said it helps with opposition to the new site." Anna reluctantly acknowledged. "I'll just go and repair my make up."

"Are you sure? Believe me I am quite happy just to stay in with you." Daniel replied seriously.

Anna nodded and smiled for the first time since the incident. Having patched up her make-up, she was ready to go.

"I said we would drive to Mollie and Tom's and give them a lift then we can walk back to mine later, if that's ok?"

Anna nodded and smiled again. She had been looking forward to this so much; she really wanted to enjoy it.

As Tom and Mollie got in the car, Mollie gave her a hug. "Are you ok? Rose just called, it was broken but it's not serious, he's already back home."

"See," Daniel added.

Anna nodded. They were right. It would all be fine, she tried to convince herself, but underneath the guilt still ate away at her.

Arriving at the ball, Anna gasped, she had been impressed by the barbeque, but this was in another league altogether. No wonder Jemima's father had wanted to escape. The inside of the marquee was nicer than most hotels. Seeing her face Mollie laughed.

"Diana certainly doesn't do things by halves, does she?"

"You can say that again," Anna replied. The marquee did not look like a marquee, there were chandeliers hanging from the ceiling. The floor was covered in what looked like black and white marble tiles. All around the room, between the windows and in the corners were stone pedestals with large flower arrangements pouring out of them. The flower bill alone was probably more than she earned in a month, actually make that a year she thought.

There were three or four rooms with various archways connecting them. But it was the dining hall, as Diana had labelled it, where Anna was completely overawed. The tables were round and covered in crystal cut glass wine glasses, champagne flutes, and water glasses, for each place there appeared to be five different glasses and endless gleaming pieces of cutlery. Now she knew how 'Pretty Woman' had felt, she thought, reminding herself to start at the outside and work inwards. Linen napkins in solid silver rings lay across each place at a perfect forty-five-degree angle. And around each table the chairs were covered in floor length black covers, with large silver bows on the back.

Anna was so overawed by her surroundings it took her a second to realise that someone had wrapped themselves around Daniel. As he gently extracted himself from the arms and legs wrapped around him, Anna's heart plummeted as she realised it was Belle. She was easily the most attractive woman at the party. Her dress was floor length on one side but split up the other side so it fell away showing off her long tanned shapely legs. The top was strapless and the material shimmering gold. With her long red hair falling around her shoulders in ringlets, she looked like a Greek goddess.

As they made their way to the table people stopped to greet Daniel, but he kept hold of Anna's hand, introducing her to everyone. All around them were men in dinner jackets and women in fantastic dresses, some of which would give the Oscars a run for their money.

As they made their way through the throng of people, Anna paused as someone caught her arm. Feeling her stop, Daniel turned in time to see Andrew greet Anna with a kiss. As Anna stepped away, he raised an eyebrow.

"Don't look at me like that, he stopped me." She returned, thinking it was nowhere as near as bad as the greeting he had been given by Belle.

Eventually they arrived at their table. Anna was relieved to find she was sat between Mollie and Daniel and the rest of the table was made up with friends of theirs. The food was gorgeous and the wine waiters kept everyone's glasses full. The banter around the table was light hearted and with Daniel sat next to her, constantly with an arm round her or a hand on her leg, Anna started to relax and enjoy her evening.

After the meal, the dancing began in two of the rooms; a jazz band in one and a disco in the other. Diana had forgotten nothing and catered for everyone's taste, although Anna couldn't even imagine how much it all cost.

Anna and Mollie went off to dance as Daniel and Tom were talking to a couple of locals unhappy about the new development. The disco dance room was fairy-tail like with lights set into the ceiling. As she and Mollie walked in, they saw Belle coming the other way. As she walked past them without acknowledging them, Anna turned to Mollie, "She always makes me feel so frumpy."

"Don't be silly you look gorgeous and Daniel hasn't been able to keep his eyes off you."

Anna smiled her thanks, hoping she was right.

Forgetting about Belle and remembering how much she enjoyed dancing Anna let herself go and she and Mollie had a great time. The dance floor got more crowded and the party revellers more inebriated, Anna kept losing Mollie but as everyone was dancing with everyone, she carried on enjoying herself.

After they had been dancing for a while, Mollie caught her eye, "Come on let's find the boys they can't work all night!"

Making their way back to the tables, they could see Tom who was now chatting to Richard.

As they arrived at the table, Tom looked up. "Didn't Daniel find you?"

Anna shook her head.

"Well he went looking for you a while ago." Saying she would go and find him, Anna turned away from Mollie and Tom.

"Do you want us to help you?" Mollie offered. "I'll be fine he can't have gone far."

Walking from room to room Anna, Anna began to panic; although this was a big place, surely, she should have found him by now.

Heading back into the bar, Anna literally walked into the one person she had not wanted to see.

"Paris."

"Anna."

The two girls eyed each other up. Anna went to walk away but Paris stopped her.

"If you are looking for Daniel, I've just seen him leaving with Belle, he had his arm around her and they were heading for the house."

Anna was stunned, how could he? But then she looked at Paris, smiling at her. She was probably making it up, she tried to convince herself.

Walking on by, she left to carry on looking for him. Seeing Elliot's mother who always seemed very nice, Anna approached her to ask if she had seen Daniel.

Anna saw her face fall and then she shifted uneasily before giving her an over bright smile. "He was with Jemima's sister, but I'm sure he will be back soon," she added kindly. Elliot's father who had not realised that Anna was meant to be with Daniel turned around.

"By the look of those two, we won't see them again tonight," he said with a wink.

Seeing Anna's face drop, Elliot's mother turned and gave him a look.

"Anna…"

"I'm fine, honestly, bye." Anna turned and stumbled away. How could he do this to her? Deep breath, don't jump to conclusions she reminded herself, seeing Lisa who she knew from one of the other yards, she stopped to ask her.

"Sorry mate we just passed him and Belle heading up the house." Lisa's look of pity said it all.

Anna mumbled her thanks and headed towards the exit, she needed to get away from the ball and fast.

Realising someone was walking next to her, she glanced up to see Paris again.

"Look you were right, but if you've come to gloat then please go away."

"Actually, I've come to offer you a lift home, Daniel has done this to me before so I know how it feels."

"Paris, look we both know we are not friends, so please just go away."

"Look I admit when I thought Daniel might be interested in you, I wasn't too happy, but it seems it was Belle he was after, so really we are both in the same boat now."

Anna glanced at her, she was still not sure she trusted her but she was offering a free lift home, and it was a long walk, so Anna nodded her confirmation.

As the two girls made their way out of the exit, Diana came running up to them.

"Have you seen Belle?"

Anna and Paris hesitated looking at one another, before Paris spoke, "She was last seen heading to the house with Daniel."

"Oh," Diana seemed surprised.

Andrew came over. "I can't find her," he told Diana before noticing Anna and Paris.

"Why are you looking for her?" Anna asked.

Diana hesitated, probably to spare her feelings Anna thought, but Andrew spoke up. "She is hopelessly drunk and her father will go mad if he sees her."

Just like her father would go mad if he knew about her secret older man, Anna thought. Perhaps the alcohol had made them less discrete.

"I'm going up to the house to make sure she is ok, apparently Daniel is with her."

"What a surprise." Andrew said contemptuously.

Watching Diana turn and head towards her house, Anna turned to Paris, her was head spinning. "Can we go?"

"Sure, I've told the valet to let the driver know, I'll just say goodbye to Chelsea."

Andrew waited with Anna for Paris to return.

"How was your evening?" Anna asked to trying to be polite and not think about what had happened.

"I've spent the last half hour helping Diana track down her drunken step daughter whilst avoiding her father. I'm now completely sober whilst everyone is getting drunk so time to call it a night." Andrew seemed distracted as well, so Anna did not bother with any more attempts at conversation.

Paris seemed to be taking ages, so Anna announced she was going to start walking home.

"It's on my way so I'll walk with you," Andrew offered.

However, Paris caught up with them on the drive, Andrew smiled, "Night Anna, you look really pretty tonight by the way."

As the large Mercedes glided along the lane, Anna sadly reflected that this was the one way she had not imagined the evening to end. Perhaps if they had stayed at home this would never have happened, but she would have found out about Belle eventually. She would only have been storing up future heartache.

The driver pulled up on the yard.

"Thanks for the lift." Anna climbed out of the car desperate to be on her own.

"Let me see you in," Paris purred, climbing out as well.

Wishing she would go Anna opened the door to the flat, Tilly jumped up to say hello but Paris immediately stepped back. Pausing briefly to fuss her, Anna made her way over to the kettle and flipped the switch.

Realising Paris was not going any time soon, she made two cups of coffee and put them on the table.

"Anna I'm so sorry for you but unfortunately that's what he is like. His father was the same ran off with another woman and caused a huge scandal."

"I never knew." Anna admitted reluctantly.

"He never talked to you about his father then?" Paris asked in fake surprise.

"No." Anna was forced to admit whilst thinking how much Paris seemed to be enjoying herself.

"That's Daniel for you, even I found him secretive, but he is a hard habit to crack, because let's face it there aren't many men like him."

Not knowing how to respond, Anna instead stood up and took a packet of biscuits from the cupboard. Opening them, she offered one to Paris.
Paris looked at the packet in distain. "I don't eat processed sugar."

"I probably shouldn't either, but it's been a bad day." Anna tried to justify wanting the chocolate biscuit.

Paris gave her a patronising smile, but Anna could still not resist the chocolate digestive.

"It's been such a bad day for you, I heard about the Freddie incident. I suppose there is nothing left for you to stay for now?"

"What do you mean?" Anna asked in horror.

"Oh! Rose has not told you?"

"Told me what?" Anna asked, wondering how much worse the day could get. Mollie had said it was all fine, but then she and Rose would say that she thought.

Paris paused, reluctant to say anything, but then began to speak. "Well, you'll find out anyway. Freddie's mum said she would not sue as long as you left. Everyone was talking about it tonight, and a few people were surprised you had even turned up after what had happened to poor Freddie."

Anna was floored, she knew she should not have gone out.

"I'm sorry, I shouldn't have said anything, look it will probably all blow over in a week and it's not like you and Daniel were in a proper relationship, is it? So, there is no need for you to leave." Paris paused, whilst Anna absorbed the impact of what she had suggested.

"Leave?" Anna asked, she had not thought things were that bad.

"No Anna, it's your choice, although if Daniel had made sure I had to live in this grotty flat rather than one of the beautiful bedrooms in the manor, I'd have left a long time ago." Paris left the comment hanging.

"It was Daniel's decision that I had this flat?" Anna asked stunned.

Realising she had hit the bull's-eye, Paris nodded sadly.

"I know he did not want me here at first but…." Anna was starting to feel an even bigger fool as the pieces dropped into place.

"Daniel wants the Manor, it would be worth a fortune, properly done up. He has been trying to put Rose in a retirement home for ages, and let's face it she's a liability." Paris looked at her sadly, before reaching out a hand and placing it on Anna's arm. "Oh dear, you really didn't know, did you?"

Fighting the urge to shake off Paris' hand which felt anything but reassuring, Anna finally spoke, "But why did no one tell me? And surely Daniel would not put her in a home!" Anna could hardly take it in.

"Well, I think when Rose started to like you Daniel realised it would be better to have you on side to help convince her." Paris said sadly. "After all everyone knows Rose listens to you."

Anna hadn't thought she could feel any worse but Paris' final revelation was too much. "So, if I leave, Rose can keep the school?" She looked at Paris who said nothing. "I mean Rose will lose everything if I stay and Freddie's mum sues, and Daniel………." But she could not continue.

"I think you'll be happier in the long run. When do you think you will go?"

"Well I have a month's notice," Anna replied. It seemed like an eternity and she did not know how she would endure seeing Daniel and Belle together.

As though reading her thoughts Paris leant across the table and put a hand on her arm. "Look why don't you go tomorrow; it will save you seeing Daniel and things will die down quicker with the Freddie situation."

Feeling heartbroken at the thought of having to leave but realising it was the right decision Anna nodded.

Paris finished her coffee and assuring Anna she was doing the right thing, she got up to go.

After she had gone Anna made her way back into the lounge and sat down and started to cry, gently at first but then great big sobs. Tilly padded over to her and laid her head on her knee, looking into the big brown eyes staring up sadly at her, Anna managed a weak smile.

"Oh Tilly, I am going to have to leave you too." And putting her arms around Tilly she sank to the floor and cried hard into her coat for a long time.

Chapter Fourteen

Waking up Anna glanced around confused, as she was on the settee in the lounge. Rolling over she looked at the clock, ten o'clock! She needed to be out on the yard. Looking down she saw she was still in her dress and the events of the night before hit her in slow motion. Pulling herself upright she made her way into the bathroom. As she came face to face with the mirror she frowned, her reflection was frightening. Her eyes were swollen with tears and her face was red and blotchy. Having bathed her face in cold water and got dressed, she sat down to write Rose a resignation letter. Explaining about Freddie and saying she was sorry to leave but she thought it was for the best, she finished the letter and put it in an envelope. Looking at it sadly Anna thought back to the week before. She had been so happy; she could not believe it had all changed so fast.

She headed out to the yard, to speak to Rose. She would help get the stables done, and then she could leave. Sensing someone behind her she turned to see Tilly following her, she had stayed with her all morning, if she did not know better, she would think Tilly was looking after her.

Unfortunately, Rose was not around and Charlie was alone. He noticed her face was all swollen, but he decided not to comment. Instead, they worked quietly together bringing in the horses from the fields. It did not take long and they were soon finished.

"So, are you ready to tell me then?" The words came as a surprise to Anna who was miles away.

Glancing at Charlie and nearly but not quite starting to cry again, Anna managed to explain that she was leaving because of what had happened with Freddie.

"Have you spoken to Rose? That does not sound right to me."

"People were talking about it last night, and as long as I leave she won't sue. Look Charlie, I have to go," she added desperately holding back the tears.

"Ok, but can you at least wait to talk to Rose?"

Anna shook her head, "I've written her a letter, which I'll leave in the kitchen."

"Leave the letter with me, seeing as you are in a bit of a rush."

Producing the letter from her pocket she handed it over to Charlie and thanked him.

Smiling in gratitude then almost crying because someone was finally being kind Anna walked back to the flat and quickly threw things into bags. The car was packed in less than half an hour.

With one final look around the flat to make sure she had everything; she pulled the door shut behind her. It banged ominously. She felt as though she was closing the door on everything.

Out on the yard she went and said good bye to all the horses. Charlie watched her walk round. Gossip did not interest him as a rule and generally he preferred horses to people but he still wondered what else had gone wrong. Anna looked incredibly sad and she certainly did not to want to go.

He tried one last time, "Now this is none of my business for sure but you look like you want to stay."

"I do," Anna blurted out the words before she had time to think. "But I have to go. It will be awkward for everyone if I stay."

Charlie raised an eyebrow sceptically.

"You don't understand I have to go."

"Ok, but I think you at least owe Rose an explanation face to face not just a letter."

Anna paused knowing he was right.

"Ok, I've got to drop a dress back to Mollie, then I'll come back and see Rose." Anna replied sadly.

"Stay in touch, things might not be what they seem and you'll always be welcome back. Now don't you go forgetting that?"

Anna nodded.

As she pulled into Mollie and Tom's drive Anna hoped and prayed Tom and especially Daniel would not be around and that she could catch Mollie on her own. Holding the bag with the dress in one hand she knocked on the door.

Opening the door Mollie looked at her slightly shocked, before recovering herself. "Come in, I did not expect to see you today," she was slightly cold and off hand.

Anna followed her through to the kitchen surprised by her demeanour, and wondered if she knew about Daniel and was embarrassed by what had happened.

"So….." Mollie turned to her not knowing what to say.

Hating the strained atmosphere Anna started to pull the dress out of the bag. "Um I am in a bit of a hurry and can't stay. I just came to return this."

"Right, well thanks." As she stepped forward Mollie finally looked at her properly and was shocked. She was not hung over, but she did look terrible.

"Anna what on earth has happened?"

"It's fine, but I'm leaving." She ignored the shock on Mollie's face.

"Leaving as in properly leaving? Look Anna last night was not exactly great but you don't have to leave, I know it will be awkward for a while but………."

Anna was shaking her head. "I can't stay, Rose will explain." She fumbled with the bag, pulling out the dress, "I'm afraid the strap broke."

As the words left her mouth Tom walked in from the lounge. Seeing the broken strap, Tom's face hardened. "Blimey looks like you had a very good night." His words were bitter.

"Hardly," Anna replied fighting to hold back the tears.

"Look Anna we've had some bad news this morning, I'll phone you later." Mollie said gently, her earlier animosity was fading fast.

"Oh, I'm so sorry," Anna turned to leave. "I really didn't mean for any of this to happen. Good bye." She turned and headed towards the front door.

Mollie followed her and was about to say something as she opened the door, but they both paused as Daniel's car pulled onto the drive.

"I'm sorry Mollie I've got to go."

She stepped out of the front door, for a second, she thought Daniel was going to drive off, but then he got out slowly.

He just stared at her, steeling herself Anna stared back and then with a half nod Daniel walked straight past her towards the door.

"Aren't you going to say anything?" Anna asked. The fear at seeing him was now replaced by anger at what he had done and how he was now behaving.

"Like what? What do you expect me to say?" Daniel turned around looking at her in contempt. He was back to behaving the way he had when she first arrived, why had she ever let her guard down?

"Well, you will be glad to know I'm leaving, seeing as you never wanted me here anyway." She said trying to regain some dignity, even if it wasn't much.

Daniel looked briefly shocked, then he shrugged, "well at least something positive has come out of all this. But I've got more important things to worry about this morning." And with that he turned and walked into the house.

Devastated at his behaviour, Anna climbed back in the car. She could not face Rose after this, she thought, but she owed Rose more than just a letter Charlie was right.

Back on the yard, Rose looked up, "Oh there you are! Where on earth have you been?"

Charlie's warning look caused her to stop abruptly. She said nothing but waited for Anna to speak. Finding it even harder to tell Rose than it had been to tell Charlie, Anna suggested they went into the office.

Rose made two cups of coffee, and placed them in front of Anna. Looking at the coffee, Anna thought how ironic it was that her job was ending the same way it had started.

"I can only help if you tell me what the problem is?"

"I need to leave."

If Rose was surprised, she hid it well. "Why?"

"Well Freddie's mum will sue if I don't." Anna said sadly, deliberately omitting the part about Daniel. How did you even begin to tell someone their son wanted to put them in a home?

"Anna, I've told you that what happened to Freddie is not your fault."

"Tom and Daniel are furious about it, apparently everyone was talking about it at the ball."
Rose said nothing but picked up the phone and punched in a number.

"Daniel, it is me, phone me straight away please."

Without hesitating she punched in another number.

"Tom, it's me. Anna says Freddie's mum is threatening to sue? I take it there is no truth in this farce?" Rose's voice was slightly cavalier. However, when there was no reply from Tom, she faltered slightly.

"Tom, I'm relying on you to tell me the truth." The cavalier element to her voice had gone.

Anna did not hear Tom's reply, but judging by Rose's face, she could guess he had confirmed the fact.

"Well then we need to talk to her." Rose was already deciding on the best course of action. "She was angry yesterday but she never mentioned anything about suing anyone."

Tom clearly gave a reply which Rose did not appreciate. "What do you mean, you have other things to sort out this morning?"

Anna watched as the colour suddenly drained out of Rose's face, she said a couple more things about staying in touch and slowly replaced the receiver.

"Jefferson has had a stroke." She seemed shocked to her core.

"Sorry Rose but who is Jefferson?" Anna asked as gently as she could.

"My ex-husband and Daniel and Tom's father."

"Oh I'm sorry." No wonder they had all been so upset this morning, she thought acknowledging she had never heard about Jefferson apart from what Paris had told her. She clearly did not know Daniel at all. She just thought briefly that she had.

Rose remained where she was sat for a long time before looking up slowly at Anna. She looked devastated.

The phone began to ring. Rose looked at it and left it, so Anna picked it up, praying it would not be Daniel.

"Rose?"

"No this is Anna."

"Ah, the so-called instructor! You are just as bad! I'm Freddie's mother. Thanks to you two do-gooders," her voice was loaded with sarcasm, "I have lost my job as I need to look after Freddie, and now cannot afford to pay my bills. In fact, I may lose my home. So, I have spoken to a solicitor and I am going to sue you for negligence." The voice screeched down the phone. "Paris and her mother have been very helpful."

"Look, please don't sue." Anna said desperately, unable to believe Paris was helping her. "I'm leaving, it was my fault. Please don't blame Rose."

"I'm blaming you both." And with that she slammed down the phone.

The phone rang again.

"It's alright I'll talk to her this time." Rose seemed to be regaining some of her spirit.

Luckily Rose had answered as it was Daniel. The conversation was short but the implication was that if Anna left Freddie's mum would not sue. She replaced the receiver. "What a mess!"

"I'm really sorry."

"It's not your fault Anna." Rose had turned in on herself completely. She sighed, "I should never have gone behind Freddie's mum's back like that. It's just that the he loved it so much. He reminds me of Daniel at that age and their situations are so similar." She paused again in sad reflection. Then some of the usual steely resolve reasserted itself. "Now if we just talk to her then I think you will still be able to stay." Anna choked back her tears, and shook her head unable to believe what was happening, but knowing she could not face Daniel.

"Rose we both know that won't work."

Unable to prolong leaving any longer Anna decided it was time to say good bye. As she drove out of the yard, she looked in the rear-view mirror. Her eyes swam with tears and she could only just make out Rose and Charlie stood watching her go. Tilly sat sadly between them.

"I don't know Anna. It does not make any sense, Daniel seemed so genuine."

"Maybe, but remember what Jemima said about Belle's older man, and even Daniel tried to get rid of me at first. I think this is for the best," she concluded.

"What are you going to do now?"

"I don't know yet. I'm on my way to my parents just while I work out what to do." Anna admitted.

"Well don't rush at anything. And think about phoning Rose or Mollie and hearing what they have to say once things have calmed down a bit. Rose may have over reacted." As Anna did not answer, Lucy carried on, "Think about it. Please?"

"Ok." Anna replied, even though she had no intention of doing so.

Ten minutes later the phone rang again. Anna answered it knowing it would be Jenny, bad news always travels fast she thought.

"Ok, what happened?" Jenny asked. Anna recounted the story again, although she was sure Lucy would have told her everything.

"What an absolute…"

"You know me and men," Anna quickly interrupted.

"Look, come and stay with me. I'll get you your old job back, Mr Elvin was sacked, someone finally went to HR about him. The new boss is ok and there are some fantastic new bars opened since you left. It'll be like the old days again"

"Maybe, I'm not sure what I'll do yet." The thought of going back to work, even with a new boss, made Anna depressed. The thought of going back to that office, made her want to cry, and if she did that then she really would have failed completely.

"Well think about it, maybe not the job, but you can come and stay."

After Jenny ended the call, Anna called her parents to tell them she was coming. After being on the phone so long to Lucy and Jenny she was already half way home. As the phone rang out, she prayed her father would answer but it seemed she was not in luck, as her mother's voice gushed down the line.

Anna explained briefly she had left her job and needed to stay for a few days while she planned what to do next, whilst trying not to groan loudly at her mother's delight.

"Thank heavens you've seen sense. You can go back to accountancy now; Mildred's daughter has just qualified as an accountant and she drives one of those BMVs. It's very posh."

"B M W." Her father corrected in the background, with more than a hint of irony.

"No apparently you should pronounce it Bay. Em. Vay." She heard her mother tell her father. "Mildred says that's how they all say it in the City."

"It's called London!" Anna could imagine her Dad rolling his eyes as he walked away.

"Honestly your father is impossible," Anna's mum had reengaged with the phone call, "Since he retired, he is just so out of touch! Luckily Mildred keeps me up to date."

Anna decided not to point out that Mildred's daughter was a pretentious nightmare and not someone to use as a guide on anything, however her mother had moved on to what they would have for dinner that night and now seemed to be wrapping up the phone call.

"Anna I am so glad this silliness is behind you, now you can have a proper career."

Ending the phone call Anna drove on feeling more and more depressed, it was hardly surprising she thought after what had happened with Daniel and having to leave Mollie, Rose, Tilly and all the horses behind but as she drove a realisation hit her that actually she did not want to go back to an office, she did not want to spend eight hours a day staring at walls and computers, occasionally getting a glimpse out of the window knowing she would rather be outdoors than indoors dealing with office politics and endlessly raiding the biscuit tin to try and alleviate the boredom. The problem was what did she do then?

As she parked on her parent's drive, her phone started to ring, she reached for it hoping, well she was not really sure what for but something from Mollie or Rose. Instead, it was a number she did not recognise, she was about to let it ring out when she changed her mind.

"Hello?"

"Is that Anna?" A somewhat resigned woman on the end enquired, Anna barely confirmed it was before she carried on, "you registered with our agency a while ago and I have a fantastic opportunity that has just come up, but they need someone to start straight away." The lady paused almost sensing defeat before Anna could even respond.

Anna stared straight ahead and saw the curtain twitch, suggesting her mother had been looking out for her, and sighed. Jenny's comments about Mr Elvin floated through her mind too, and here she was being offered a way out.

"Look I'm sorry for wasting your time." The lady on the other end seemed about to hang up.

Realising she had not yet spoken, Anna quickly interrupted her, "No I definitely am interested and looking that is."

The woman on the other end perked up, "Really? Look I should warn you the manager can be a bit difficult but it's a lovely yard and comes with your own fantastic flat, and they offer full training."

Relief washed over Anna, as she took down the details.

Mollie made her way slowly down the stairs, the kids were finally asleep and the sun was already setting, only one more week until they were back to school. Suddenly everything felt so depressing, the summer had been fantastic but now Autumn was coming and it seemed so bleak, dark nights, tired kids, a stressed-out husband and Rose, oh goodness Rose she thought, who knew what would happen there. She walked into the kitchen to make a cup of tea, as she flicked on the light, she realised Tom was sat at the kitchen table nursing a beer and staring into space. She had not heard him come home. He blinked at the bright light which suddenly flooded the room, before giving Mollie a sad half smile.

"Did he get off ok?" She asked gently.

Tom nodded slowly.

"Have you told Rich?"

Tom sighed and nodded, before he sat back taking a swig of the beer, realising she did not fancy another cup of tea, Mollie grabbed another beer from the fridge, and sat down opposite him. "Was he surprised?"

Tom shook his head, "No he was in the pub earlier, if it hadn't been for Rich….." He paused, looking at Mollie in sheer bewilderment. "I can't believe that everything was fine yesterday morning and now, well, how did it come to this Mollie?"

She reached across and took his hand, "We'll be fine. And I can always help out with the business with Daniel away."

Tom gave her hand a squeeze, "Thanks Moll but I'm going to be stressed enough, I don't need you stressed too. After all what would I do without you?"

Mollie bit down the frustration, it wasn't worth pushing tonight they would only row, especially after the weekend they had, so she decided to let it go for now.

Daniel stared out of the window as the plane touched down, over the intercom the air hostess welcomed them to New York. Next to him Belle excitedly told him all the things she wanted to do. She had slept for most of the flight. He'd tried to sleep too. But, as he lay there with his eyes closed, his thoughts tortured him, questioning whether he should have left and whether this was the right place to come to.

As they made their way through arrivals, the guilt he felt at leaving Tom and especially Rose threatened to overwhelm him. It had been Lizzie and Tom's idea for him to come and he wanted to be there for Lizzie, but he also knew he needed to escape for a couple of weeks. He flexed his hand, wincing as pain shot through his knuckles. He definitely needed some space. The queue in immigration took forever but he eventually passed through customs and out into the main airport, all thoughts of Tom and Rose were banished though as Lizzie came flying at him and threw her arms around him, "I'm so glad you came. It's been so horrible with Dad."

Daniel gently prised himself out of his half-sister's arms. "Of course, I came. It's good to see you, Lizzie."

Before he could say anymore Belle joined them, having found a porter to help with all her luggage.

"Belle I didn't know you were coming?" Lizzie said throwing Daniel a questioning look.

"Well, when I heard Daniel was flying out, how could I resist?" She smiled at Lizzie, but Lizzie was distracted by something.

"Daniel what have you done to your hand?" She asked, grabbing Daniel's hand and looking at the bruised knuckles, before giving him another questioning look.

"Daniel was defending me." Belle said with a giggle putting her arm through Daniel's.

Chapter Fifteen

Arriving at the new yard, Anna let out a long shaky breath, this was far more like it. Even the sign at the bottom of the drive suggested professionalism, and the lady on the phone had talked about training and qualifications, so perhaps she was finally on the right track, perhaps her adventures in the Cotswolds would be a funny story she would tell people in years to come. Although she was still not ready to laugh about it yet.

Parking in the marked staff spaces on the yard, Anna climbed out of the car to find an effortlessly beautiful blonde lady smiling anxiously. Her long slim legs were encased in spotless cream jodhpurs, and gleaming riding boots. She removed her hands from the fitted quilted navy waistcoat she wore and grabbing onto both Anna's hands shook them vigorously saying how pleased she was to see her.

Delighted by the genuinely warm welcome, Anna unpacked her car with the help of her new boss, Camilla. It was the exact opposite to moving into her previous job and unlike her last flat this was ultra-modern with every comfort imaginable. The bedroom had a King size bed, and an en suite with a huge walk in shower. In the lounge a large sofa sat in front of a flat screen TV under which was every games console and TV box you could ever need. For a second Anna felt a pang for her little flat above the stables, but reminding herself she would be mad to turn this down she smiled and enthused over everything.

"Right, I'll leave you to unpack then and pop back in an hour to show you round and introduce you to all the girls, we are just one big happy family here." Camilla smiled and left the flat closing the door gently behind her.

Although delighted she was so lovely Anna could not help but wonder why she seemed so anxious about Anna being happy. She unpacked quickly realising most of things would not be needed, as Camilla had provided everything.

Sixty minutes later Camilla was once again stood smiling at the front door, before ushering Anna around an immaculate yard.

"We'll get you signed up for your BHS courses shortly, we pay for all staff training as long as they stay for a couple of years after or pay them back." Camilla informed her. "We have a number of staff who have finished training but are still with us." Anna could only nod and smile.

The following morning, she was on the yard at seven thirty sharp. Camilla greeted her warmly, but as a young woman came striding onto the yard, she could feel Camilla's agitation.

"Donna, this is Anna, she is here to replace Jill. Anna, Donna is my yard manager."

Donna was tall and slim, but with a long face and hard small brown eyes. She glanced at Anna dismissively before turning to Camilla.

"We need to discuss where we take Allegro for his next dressage outing."

"Of course," Camilla nodded quickly in agreement, shooting Anna an apologetic smile.

Donna turned to walk away with Camilla trotting after her. Anna's heart sank, she was not going to get on with this girl and suddenly Camilla's over enthusiastic welcome from the day before and the desperation of the agency lady who recruited her, all made sense.

As they were about to walk out of the yard, Anna decided she was not about to be ignored.

"Excuse me, but where would you like me to start?" She called after the two women.

Donna turned and glared at her as though she had just been shouting obscenities at them rather than asking what to do.

"Mandy!" The name was yelled loudly and harshly, but then Anna had a feeling everything she did was loud and harsh or both. Anna was surprised none of the horses reacted to the sudden shouts but reflected they were probably used to it by now.

A head popped out from one of the stables. "Show, thingy here?"

"Anna." Anna said determined not to be belittled

"Show Anna," Donna placed unnecessary emphasis on her name. "What to do, she's new."

The door opened and Mandy appeared. Anna quickly closed her mouth. Mandy had purple hair scrapped into a high pony tail, dirty beige jodhpurs, a hooded top, and was wearing fluorescent pink socks stuffed into heavy duty boots.

She laughed when she saw Anna's face. "I know, Donna is on at me constantly about the way I look, but as I said to her, I work with horses not in some posh bank. Right come on or Miss Whiplash will be back!"

As she and Anna worked their way round the stables, she fell into the routine quickly. Mandy seemed nice enough, although she hardly spoke, but together they worked hard all morning.

Once the stables were finished, they tacked up two horses to hack out.

"So how did Camilla convince you to come to the yard from hell then?" Mandy asked as soon as they turned their horses off the drive and onto the lane and were well out of earshot.

"Well, it seemed a good opportunity." Anna ventured slowly, being careful not to say anything negative. "And they pay for your training."

Mandy looked at her speculatively. "It's been great to have some help today, especially as Helen is on holiday with her bloke and Donna never does any work other than ride the horses. Did they warn you about Donna at the agency?"

"Sort of." Anna conceded. "Although she also talked a lot about the lovely flat and the opportunities. Do you live at the yard?"

"Used to but I'd rather be back at home sharing a room with my sister than knowing Donna could pop up at any moment!" She shuddered.

"Does she have a flat too?" Anna asked.

"No, she lives in the house with Camilla, as she's family." At this Mandy rolled her eyes.

"Oh." Anna's heart sank no wonder she had so much power.

"Oh indeed," replied Mandy as she turned down another lane, making Anna realise she had no idea where they were. "I've worked here for years, long before Donna turned up and it was great, Camilla was always good for a laugh, but then up rocks Miss Whiplash with her Equine degree, undermining Camilla and it all goes pear shaped."

"Why do you call her that? Miss Whiplash I mean?"

"She's knocking off Camilla's husband. Debs once caught them at it, she was just wearing riding boots and holding a riding crop. Dirty Cow!"

"Blimey." Anna responded.

"Yeah, Debs got sacked after that. So, you got a boyfriend?"

"Just split up with someone."

"Oh?"

Anna did not want to go over it again. "Yeah, we realised we weren't right for each other and called it a day."

Mandy looked at her doubtfully. Anna sighed; she was a hopeless liar. "Actually, he cheated. That's why I'm here!"

"They always do. Men are crap, give me horses any day!" And she started to laugh.

The week wore on slowly, Anna learnt if she kept her head down, then generally Donna left her alone. However, that meant not talking to the clients of the liveries, or to Mandy and especially not to Camilla or her husband who occasionally appeared on the yard.

She'd loved being on the yard at Rose's but now she found that the enforced solitude only made her miss Rose, Charlie and the horses more than ever. She finished sweeping the yard realising that there was no going back and picking up the wheelbarrow handles she began to push it towards the muck heap. Anywhere had to be better than this she thought, but aware that walking out on two yards in the space of a week would not be good for her job prospect's she decided to try and make it work for a bit longer.

Lizzie climbed out of the car at the hospital and turned as she waited for Lara to follow her. Instead, Lara turned to Daniel, "So are you going to finally join us today?" She asked pointedly, the one simple question making her thoughts on the matter more than clear.

In a way it was refreshing Daniel thought, Lara was so direct there was never any doubt where you stood.

"Well?" Lara was waiting.

He knew he should but he was still not ready to face the man he had despised for the last twenty-five years. "I need to speak to Tom and then I said to Jake I would come in and meet with the building inspector."

"Ok." Lara conceded, "but we will discuss this later."

Daniel nodded and watched as the mother and daughter headed into the hospital. Turning away from the hospital he headed to his father's office and after a long call to Tom to go over the schedule, he went to meet Jake and the building inspector.

Arriving back at the hospital later to collect Lara and Lizzie, Daniel was surprised to find Lara waiting outside for him already.

"Where's Lizzie?" He asked as he got out and opened the door for her, something he had quickly learnt Lara expected. He watched as the wealthy New York socialite got in. She was so different from Rose, although both were always immaculate, there was a groomed look to Lara that spoke wealth. The hair was perfectly coloured and blow dried and the clothes were elegant and demure but the cut of the garments and the quality of the material left you in no doubt they were designer.

"Elizabeth is not ready yet, but I would like to talk to you alone." Lara met his eye directly indicating that it was not optional. "There is a coffee house around the corner."

"Ok," Daniel nodded and drove, he had expected to hate the woman who had effectively destroyed his parent's marriage, and whom he had never even set eyes on until two weeks ago. However, there was something about her that he actually quite liked, as he drove, he reflected that in some ways Rose and Lara were very similar. Their approach was different but they had the same steel that defied people to argue with them.

Lara watched as the waitress placed the two cups down in front of them, she thanked her and waited for her to leave before she spoke. The coffee house was upmarket and discreet, Lara clearly did not expect to be interrupted.

"Why are you here Daniel, it's clearly not to see your father?"

Daniel was thrown briefly, "Lizzie phoned distraught and Tom and I agreed one of us should come and support her, and as Tom has his family, it was easier for me to come."

Lara nodded, "Ok but Elizabeth seems to be handling it much better now. It was a shock for her but then she is Daddy's little princess!" She gently rolled her eyes, clearly just as indulgent of her daughter as her husband. "We have a driver who can drive us to and from the hospital and Jake can keep the company ticking over for now."

"You mean, it's time for me to go home then?" Daniel replied realising he was no longer needed.

"Oh, you English you are so uptight and defensive." Lara said in despair. "If I wanted you to go home, I'd tell you to go home. I'm American, I don't believe in tiptoeing around the subject."

Daniel smiled acknowledging that was exactly what she would do.

Lara paused, "Daniel your support the last few weeks for both Elizabeth and I is something I will always be grateful for. We would have got through on our own but you make it bearable. And Jefferson and I don't have to worry about the business knowing you are keeping an eye on it, not that Jake is not capable, but we do really appreciate your help. But I only expected you to stay a week and then go, so why are you still here?"

Daniel stared at his coffee for a moment. "I've always felt guilty about what happened with Lizzie and Andrew. This feels like a way to make it up to her."

Lara gave a sad laugh, "Daniel honey, I would gladly string Andrew up in the most painful manner possible after what he did to my daughter, but how is that your fault?"

"Well Lizzie had come to visit us, she was my responsibility and she's my little sister, well half-sister." He amended, he sighed before looking up at Lara.

Lara placed a hand on Daniel's. "Now listen to me, I love Elizabeth but she alone is responsible for her actions, not you or anyone else. If she decided to get involved with this Andrew she would and there would have been nothing you or anyone could have done to stop her."

Daniel shrugged and realising he wasn't convinced Lara continued. "Jefferson has never stopped feeling guilty about leaving you and Tom, so he poured all that guilt into being the best parent he could to Elizabeth, and the result is a fabulous young woman who has grown up knowing she is loved, but, and as a mother this is hard to admit, one who is also head strong and somewhat spoilt. As much as I hate what Andrew did, it taught her humility and made her a better person."

Daniel looked surprised, "I never thought of it like that, I was just so mad at Andrew. He had always been one of my closest friends, we both had our fair share of woman when we were younger." He glanced at Lara who rolled her eyes. "But then he settled down and got married and for a while he was happy, but then his marriage fell apart, he was cheating on her. I warned him not to go near Lizzie but it was hopeless."

"Like I said it's not your fault." Lara paused. "Tom says you and Andrew have not spoken since."

"No," Daniel agreed, and after what Andrew had recently done there was a lot more than just what happened with Lizzie to forgive.

Chapter Sixteen

Anna collected the last feed bucket and bolted the stable door behind her. She felt tired and fed up. Donna had not let up all day with her endless criticism, constant demands and had made Mandy and Anna run themselves ragged. Dreaming of a hot bath and a large glass of wine, Anna nearly walked straight into Donna.

Rather than apologise she merely tutted insinuating it was all Anna's fault.

"Right, I need you to go to this address and collect a saddle." There was no please, no thank you and no acknowledgement of her name.

Anna was about to refuse but realised the address was only fifteen minutes from Rose's yard.

"Well, I have finished for the day." Anna was not about to give in too easily.

"Then you need to go now. You can start an hour later in the morning." Donna grudgingly conceded, knowing full well it would take Anna a few hours to collect the saddle.

Ten minutes later Anna pulled out of the yard and set off to collect the saddle. As she drove along, she argued with herself debating whether or not to call in. She had not spoken to anyone since she had left two months earlier, apart from a couple of text messages with Mollie. She knew Daniel had gone abroad but he could be back by now. She would love to see Mollie, but remembering her last encounter with Tom, she decided against it.

She drove on, the butterflies in her stomach fluttering with increasing intensity as she drew closer to Rose's. The journey alternated between miles which disappeared and miles which lasted forever, as her excitement at seeing Rose dissipated into fear at the welcome she could expect. At last she came to a junction; the destination Donna had intended lay to the right and Rose's yard to the left.

She sat at the junction in indecision, it seemed too good an opportunity to waste, but as memories of her last week at the yard overwhelmed her, she lost heart and turned right to collect the saddle.

Half an hour later with her package safely stored in the boot, she was heading back towards home, if you could call it that. She knew she could not last much longer with Donna's endless demands and cattiness. She had started avoiding calls from her friends and family unable to explain that this job also seemed doomed to failure.

Perhaps her mother was right and she should just accept that her destiny was in an account's office.

Realising she had been on auto pilot for that last fifteen minutes while she mused over the hopelessness of her future, she became aware she was at the bottom of Rose's drive.

The hedges were still overgrown and the entrance was nowhere near as grand as the yard she was currently at but pausing in the lane Anna could not help but feel a pang of homesickness.

Before she had a chance to consider what she was doing she turned the car and headed up the drive. The yard was deserted, for which she was grateful. In the fields she could see the ponies grazing. Houdini in the closest paddock whickered in recognition and ambled over. Having given him a fuss and a treat from her pocket she made her way slowly towards the kitchen door.

Once again trepidation crept through her veins, but unable to stop herself she kept going. She knocked softly at the door but there was no answer. Fear won out and she turned to leave but as she did so she heard a crash from the kitchen and Rose moan.

Forgetting herself, she pushed the door open and ran through the boot room into the large kitchen, to find Rose sprawled on the floor, a saucepan lid nearby was slowly coming to rest having spun across the floor, as it did silence prevailed.

"Rose, are you ok?" Anna moved forwards to help.

"What the hell do you want?" Although the words were harshly said, they were also slurred.

"Rose?" Anna moved more slowly now, as Rose remained slumped on the floor.

"Just bugger off, I don't need some do-gooder telling me how to live my life!" The accusation was hard but aimed at the sky in general.

Anna had the strong feeling that Rose had no idea who she was. With a lot of patience on Anna's part and a large amount of swearing and slurring on Rose's, Anna managed to get her sitting in a chair.

Horrified at Rose's demeanour and clothes, Anna did not know what to say or do. Rose slouched in the chair, clearly unable to sit up straight. Her normally immaculate hair fell about her face, but it was the face itself which disturbed Anna the most. Rose's eyes seemed sunken with heavy black bags below them, her skin looked sallow and patchy and there was a large scratch across one cheek, under which a bruise was fading.

Glancing around the kitchen Anna now became aware of bottles everywhere, gin, whiskey, some empty, some open, all alcoholic. The rest of the kitchen was a mess, the bin was overflowing, dirty plates filled the sink and the floor was covered in mud.

"Oh Rose, what on earth has been going on?" Anna asked in despair.

Rose gave no response but she heard a whimper from behind the door, opening it in bounced Tilly, who was ecstatic to see her. Anna struggled to remain standing as the dog repeatedly launched herself at Anna in her excitement, whilst Penny, Rose's older dog went and sat at Rose's feet and gently nudged her as though to check she was alright.

Fussing Tilly to calm her down, Anna took her eyes off Rose.

"What the hell do you want? Sneaking back in here when you are not welcome." The words were no longer slurred and the venom in them made Anna shiver.

Turning she found Rose glowering furiously at her.

"You are back, are you?" Sarcasm dripped from every word. "Fancy doing some more damage?"

Rose staggered to her feet, and shuffled towards the counter, where she poured a slug of neat gin into a dirty glass. Gulping half of it straight down, she turned back to Anna.

"Sent you, did they? Couldn't be bothered to come themselves, you see." Rose was slurring again.

Feeling completely out of her depth, Anna tried to change the subject, not sure who Rose was actually referring to. "Tilly looks well."

"Well, that's because I look after my animals, not like you young lot, who do not know what responsibility is."

"Shall I make you a coffee?" Anna asked trying to mask the desperation in her voice.

"And that'll make everything alright wont it?" Again, the biting sarcasm.

Anna tried again to steer Rose into a happier place but all she seemed to achieve was to wind her up further.

"Why don't I make us something to eat?"

Rose's glass hit the wall somewhere to the left of her. Tilly slunk away to her basket, her tail between her legs.

"Don't patron, patron, patronise me, my girl." Rose tried to point a finger at her but gave up and slumped back into her chair.

Anna started to clear up the glass, the whole time Rose sat staring at the floor oblivious to everything around her. Anna took the broken glass out to the bin, as she walked back into the kitchen Rose finally looked up and peered at her uncertainly, through her gin induced haze.

"Are you back?" She suddenly barked fixing Anna with a glare, daring her to say no.

"I just popped in to say hello." Anna replied sadly.

"Well, if you are not here to help then bugger off."

Stunned Anna stood helplessly.

"I said, BUGGER OFF." Rose yelled.

Realising there was nothing she could do Anna turned to go, Tilly followed at her heels. Feeling immensely guilty as the two trusting brown eyes pleaded with her to be allowed to come too, Anna gently held Tilly back as she closed the door. Rose remained slouched in the chair muttering to herself.

Anna walked back to the car, she sat in the seat wondering what on earth to do. She could not leave Rose where she was. Peeping through the kitchen window Rose had now fallen asleep in the armchair. Penny and Tilly lay at her feet keeping watch, knowing the storm was over for that night at least.

Relief flooded through Anna as she pulled onto Mollie's drive, Tom's car was nowhere to be seen. For a second, she paused, then she slowly climbed out and knocked quietly on the door.

Mollie opened the door, she looked pale and tired, but surprise flashed briefly across her face as she realised it was Anna. However, after the initial shock she just stared at her, it certainly wasn't welcoming. "This is unexpected," she commented wrapping her oversized cardigan around her and leaning on the door frame.

Stung that she clearly wasn't going to be invited in, Anna began to regret coming. "Um I was in the area and just popped in to see Rose." Anna paused trying to work out what to say but Mollie laughed a humourless laugh.

"Anna, what did you expect?" She asked wearily.

Anna was stunned, before realising that Mollie did not know how bad it was. "Mollie I'm not sure how to tell you this but Rose was in a really bad way. She had clearly been drinking a lot, and not just..." Anna stopped mid-sentence as Mollie just stared incredulously at her. "I'm sorry I just thought you should know."

Mollie shook her head slowly, "Anna, she's an alcoholic, how did you not know? A couple of times you seemed oblivious but then I thought perhaps you were just being kind. Surely you realised when we found the bottle of whiskey in the tack room that day?"

Mollie took in Anna's shocked expression, "You really did not know?" Mollie paused. "I thought that was partly why you left so suddenly."

"No." A strange look crossed Mollie's face not sure what she was thinking Anna returned to the reason for her visit. "Look can't you do something for Rose, she's got a bruise on her face and the kitchen is wrecked, there are bottles and rubbish everywhere, she clearly can't cope."

A bitter smile crossed Mollie's face, "And this is my problem, is it? Good old Mollie will go and sort it out and pick up the pieces yet again. For the last two years I have been on at Tom and Daniel to do something, I've tried to talk to her more times than I can count. And nothing worked but then you turned up and for a while there then things genuinely seemed to be better. Rose did not have any little incidents, no knocks on the door late at night to say she had crashed her Land rover into a hedge or there was the night she decided to ride Alfred through the village at midnight or one of the many other crazy episodes. But then you left, Daniel left, Tom now runs the business on his own, I never see him, everyone gets to live their lives and I'm the one left behind, I'm the one who can sort out drunk Granny and stop it being a problem for everyone else, because why should they have to feel even a brief moment of guilt about what is going on here? And as a housewife I clearly have nothing better to do." Mollie was close to tears as she looked at Anna.

Staring at her Anna realised she was right; she had thought she could just tell Mollie and drive away guilt free. She bit her lip as she cast around for some words not knowing what to say. She was about to speak when her phone rang. She ignored it. "Mollie, look I'm...."

Mollie took a deep shaky breath. "Just go Anna, go and enjoy your life." Seeing Anna about to interrupt she cut her off. "There is nothing anyone can do, she won't admit there is a problem, so go back to your new job and forget us." Mollie said sadly the anger gone.

As Anna climbed back in her car, she wondered if she should go back and check on Rose, but as she did her phone rang again. Answering it she heard Donna's voice hissing down the line asking where she was. Sighing Anna assured her she would not be long and feeling guilty but also somewhat relieved she drove out of the village leaving behind Rose, Tilly and Mollie with all their problems to sort out.

Chapter Seventeen

Daniel looked out over the park, it had been so green when he had first arrived but Autumn had made an impact now and the trees were a sea of reds, oranges and yellows. The leaves were already falling preparing to endure the winter and the snow that Lizzie was so looking forward to. The park had been his haven while he was here, somewhere to breathe away from the craziness of the city, but as winter approached, he was not sure it would offer the same relief.

Behind him Nancy deftly made up the bed that had been delivered that morning, plumping the final pillow she ran a hand over the smooth sheets and turned to Daniel, "Well it's all ready for him now."

Daniel nodded unsure what to say, the old housekeeper had clearly missed Jefferson and nothing seemed too much trouble for his imminent return. Daniel tried to smile, to look more positive than he felt, the trouble was if Jefferson came home there would be no avoiding him. Lara's words though continued to haunt him and he knew it would be rude to go home without seeing him at least once.

His thoughts were interrupted by Lizzie dancing through the door, on seeing the bed she clapped her hands before swinging Nancy around, both of them giggling. Nancy had been her nanny originally and had stayed on with the family as a housekeeper, indulging Lizzie just as much as her parents.

"Daniel I'm so excited Dad can come home tomorrow!"

Daniel tried to look pleased but Lizzie barely noticed as she and Nancy danced around in joy.

The following morning Anna's heart sank as she spotted the magpie sitting outside her flat, she quickly saluted and mumbled the rhyme in her head, praying today would be better than the horrors of the day before. She felt distracted and her mind was very much on Rose and Mollie as she set to work.

"Watch out Miss Whiplash has PMT." Mandy whispered as she passed by carrying the horse's breakfast feeds.

Mandy starting dropping the feed bowls over the stable doors, whilst Anna grabbed the hay nets.

"Have those been properly weighed?" Donna asked derisively striding onto the yard.
She stopped in the centre, hands on hips, looking about her, clearly looking for something to moan about.

"Yes." Anna replied tight lipped.

"Well weigh them again," Donna ordered her, not finding anything else to criticise. She turned to meet Anna's eye, daring her to say anything. "They look too full."

Just about holding her temper, Anna did as she had asked but as the morning wore on Donna's demands got worse. Helen was made to scrub out buckets that were spotless and tack had to be re-cleaned endlessly.

"Mandy, Anna, I want those roses removed. All of them!"

Anna glanced at the plants fading away ready for winter along the side of the barn, however a few rose blooms tried to cheer the place up, so it seemed a shame to cut them.

"But they look pretty."

"They are messy and I want them removed! Having weeds everywhere is not a sign of a professional yard."

"What's got into her?" Anna whispered, as she and Mandy started hacking away the plants.

"Reckon he's," she jerked her head towards the house to indicate Camilla's husband. "Blown her off, make's a change from her blowing him!" Mandy said with a cackle. "He has a guilt trip every so often and tries to end it with her, but it never lasts. I feel sorry for Camilla but at least Miss Whiplash will be bearable again!"

"Shame about the roses though, you know where I used to work there was this old guy who used to say there was no such thing as weeds, they were just plants in the wrong place.

"And they are not the only things in the wrong place around here." Donna snapped from above their heads.

Unable to put up with anymore, Anna stood up. "I suppose by that you mean me?"

Donna stepped back unused to being confronted, but she was still looking for someone to vent her anger at. "Well done you've finally worked it out." She spat.

"Anna," Mandy said gently, trying to help her, but Anna had had enough.

"You are right Donna, I'm never going to be flourish here, with you as the boss."

With a growing sense of conviction, Anna walked over to the house and knocked on the door. Donna was right at her heels.

"Camilla won't believe you; she was saying to me only yesterday, she didn't feel you were pulling your weight."

Anna stared at the door willing it to open, she refused to look at Donna and tried to block out her incessant jibes.

Eventually the door opened and seeing the two girls on her doorstep Camilla's face fell. Anna could not help but think this was a common occurrence.

"Camilla, I'm very sorry but I can't work here, I'm resigning. If it is ok with you, I'll go at the end of the week."

"I want her gone now. She keeps undermining me in front of the others." Donna burst in.

Camilla bit her lip clearly unsure what to do.

"I mean it Camilla." Donna was not letting up.

"Its fine I'll go now." Anna said thinking there was no point in staying. She felt guilty about Mandy and Helen being left with all the work but there seemed little she could do.

A couple of hours later she was packed and driving away from the yard and she knew where she was heading. It was like Charlie had said she needed to be a Dandelion in a meadow and not in concrete.

A feeling of excitement stole through her and she dialled Lucy's number. Lucy answered on the first ring. Excitedly she told Lucy her plan.

"Are you sure?" Lucy asked hesitantly.

Anna was thrown, not anticipating Lucy's reaction, "You think it's a bad idea, don't you?"

Lucy paused as though choosing her words carefully. "I'm just worried you are doing this for the wrong reasons."

"You mean Daniel?" Anna asked.

"Well, yes." Lucy reluctantly admitted.

"Lucy, I know what you think and what it looks like, but Mollie said Daniel left, I don't know where to or for how long and I'll have to deal with that when he returns but the thing is, right now, Rose and Charlie and Tilly and the ponies need me, and what's more I need them." Anna realised the truth in the words as she spoke them. How she would deal with Daniel she did not know, she only hoped it would be a long time before she had to face him.

"You were happy there," Lucy acknowledged.

"I really was," Anna responded, "but this time I feel like I am going in with my eyes wide open, this isn't some crazy dream, I know it's not perfect, but I want to be part of it, actual reality warts and all! I feel like for the first time I know what I want to do and I'm willing to fight for it."

Lucy smiled, "It sounds like you've made your mind up." She paused and then to lighten the mood added, "So I guess in your head by next year you'll have turned Rose's place into one of the leading stables in the country."

Anna laughed, "Well a little dreaming can't hurt!"

"You'll never change, but don't forget I'm always here if you need me."

Anna could not help but feel happy as she turned into Rose's drive, it felt like coming home. She made her way straight around to the yard expecting the lessons to be underway. However, the yard stood dark and silent, but more than that it felt almost desolate, the security light's bulb seemed to have gone and most of the stables were empty although it was mid-November.

She checked on the horses that were in stables, they all had hay and water at least. Taking a deep breath, she headed towards the house. Before she reached the door, there was a crash from the kitchen. Without bothering to knock she ran inside to find Rose slumped against a cupboard, with an upturned glass of gin spreading its way across the floor next to her.

She looked down over Rose. "Rose, Rose, are you ok Rose?"

Rose blearily opened her eyes but was unable to focus properly.

"Back are you? What do you want this time?" She started to try and stand.

Anna stepped forward to help but Rose seemed to have found a previously unknown strength, she rounded on Anna. "Don't you dare touch me. I don't need help from the likes of you."

She stomped away heading towards the open drink's cabinet, there was no attempt to try to hide her habit Anna realised sadly.

The gin glass lay on the floor as Rose pulled out another tumbler and helped herself to the first bottle she could reach.

For a second Anna wondered what to do and then she had a thought, feeling guilty but knowing she was doing it for the right reasons, she pulled out her phone and opened up the camera, setting it to record she held the phone up.

Catching the movement out of the corner of her eye, Rose swung round, the whiskey she had just filled her glass with sloshed out over her hand and wrist. "Now look what you have made me do," She slurred in Anna's direction, before turning back to refill the glass. Once full she shuffled back to the table and slumped into an armchair by the aga.

"You should go, I don't want you here, and you won't stay long, no one ever does." Rose did not quite lift her head enough to make eye contact during the little speech she made but there was no doubting who she was talking to. She raised her hand and flicked it at Anna as though swatting her away.

"Why won't you let me help?" Anna asked desperately, realising she was unable to recognise anything about the woman in front of her.

Anger gripped Rose and she leant forward jabbing her finger at Anna, as she spoke. "Because you don't really want to help, do you? You just don't want to feel guilty."

Rose stared at her hard and then sank back into her chair, the anger gone as quickly as it had come. "Not real help, no one ever does. Do you know what it's like being responsible for all those ponies and knowing no one else cares? Knowing you are getting older and all anyone wants is for you to quietly shuffle off into a nursing home so they can renovate your house, sell the land and pretend you were never there. Can you imagine that? Well, can you?" She glared defiantly at Anna and shook her head. "Of course, you can't, no one can." She muttered in contempt, but as Rose turned away Anna saw a single tear snake down the side of her face.

Anna stood staring, not knowing what to do or say. Eventually she realised the phone was still recording although luckily, she had not noticed she had dropped her arm and the phone was recording the floor. Rose's final humiliation was not on film. Although, even without that, it would be a long time before Anna forgot what she had witnessed tonight.
She jumped as a snore rang out across the kitchen and she realised Rose had fallen asleep. Anna covered her with a blanket and cleaned up the glass and spilt alcohol.

Hearing a whimper, she opened the door to the hall to find Tilly and Penny but this time Tilly did not greet her enthusiastically as she normally would have, she just stared at her as the end of her tail twitched very slightly. Anna gave her some fuss and fed them both, before turning out some lights. Although Tilly had not finished eating and was clearly hungry, she was by Anna's side in seconds. Sighing Anna stopped so she would eat her food, which Tilly did whilst keeping one eye on Anna.

"You poor thing," Anna fussed her a bit more and together they headed out to her car, grabbing her overnight bag, she made her way up the steps to the flat, hoping it wasn't locked.

It was and Anna had no clue where to find the key. There was only one thing for it, Anna turned back to the house. "Come on Tilly," she said needlessly since the dog was almost glued to her side.

Back in the house she made some dinner and then reluctant to poke around Rose's house she cleaned her teeth in the sink and curled up in the armchair opposite Rose, with Tilly lying across her feet. It looked like being a long night.

Tom pulled onto his drive and for a second stared at the house, only the hall light was on suggesting Mollie had gone to bed. Glancing at the clock he sighed, trying to remember the last time he had been home for dinner on time. To start with he had been grateful for the chance to prove he could run the business, but that was over now. It was no fun doing it all on his own, he just hoped Daniel would come back soon. Eleanor Burette, the interior designer, was giving him the run around and if it lasted much longer the show apartment would not be ready on time.

He rubbed a hand across his tired eyes and wearily got out of the car, before heading straight to bed, although he was famished, he couldn't face sitting in the kitchen eating on his own again, even though he knew Mollie would have left him something. He'd make it up to her and the kids once Daniel was back, he promised himself.

Chapter Eighteen

Anna woke to find Rose stood over her. "Anna what on earth are you doing here? It's so lovely to see you!"

"Umm," Anna stirred trying to wake up, conscious that out of the two of them Rose was the one bouncing around the kitchen.

"Honestly, I came down this morning and found you here. I'm afraid I had an early night otherwise I would have been up when you arrived. So, is this a flying visit or can you stay a while?" Rose looked at her expectantly.

Anna was waking up quickly, she shook her head. Had she dreamt last night, she wondered, but she knew she had not. She stared at Rose unable to believe it was the same person as the night before. And then she saw it, a slight flicker across Rose's face and she realised Rose knew and now she could either play along with it or face the problem head on.

"Coffee?" Rose asked turning away from her gaze.

"Thanks." Anna stood up, stretching away the stiffness from a night in a chair. As the kettle boiled Anna asked about the yard, "I was surprised there were no lessons last night, when I arrived."

Rose's hand shook slightly as she spooned coffee into the mugs, Anna wondered if it always had and if she had just never noticed before. "It's been a bit tough since you left, so we've cut back on some lessons."

Anna started to realise that this was far worse than she suspected. "You didn't replace me then?" It had not occurred to her until now that Rose would not have found someone else.

"The girls from the agency were hopeless. The first one kept worrying about breaking a nail, and she wanted to work with horses. Well you can imagine how long she lasted..........."

Anna raised her eyebrows; it seemed the only answer that was needed and she let Rose carry on with her tirade as she sipped her coffee wondering how to steer the conversation where it needed to go.

"The second had an allergy to dust and had to wear a mask. How on earth do you teach children when you sound like Derthman or whatever that science film was about?"

"Darth Vader," Anna supplied

"Yes him, anyway the third.........," and so Rose continued. It was unlike her Anna thought as Rose nervously gabbled on.

Eventually Rose paused. And the silence stretched between them. Be brave Anna told herself. She took a deep breath. "Rose I want to come back." She glanced up seeing relief on Rose's face and forced herself to go on. "But Rose I am worried about the amount you are drinking."

"Honestly Anna not you as well, Daniel was always on at me too!"

Anna was shocked had Daniel tried to stop her? He had said Rose had problems but she had never realised that was what he had meant. Not wanting to think about Daniel she refocused on Rose.

"It's just a generational thing, I occasionally have a Scotch before bed to help me sleep. Honestly it's completely fine."

If Anna had not seen her the night before she would have been convinced by the Oscar winning performance Rose had just put on. But she had seen her the night before she thought pressing onwards.

"Rose it is more than one Scotch though, isn't it?"

Rose pressed her lips together, "Anna, I think it would be best if we changed the subject. Now if you are back, there are horses that need feeding, and Charlie will be on his own out there." The words were stern and brooked no argument.

As Anna followed her out to the yard, she acknowledged this was going to be far harder than she had first thought.

As they rounded the corner, they heard coughing, and found Charlie leaning over a wheelbarrow breathless from the exertion.

"Charlie you really should not be here!" Rose admonished him with exasperation.

Looking up with tears streaming down his face from the coughing, Charlie's face registered surprise as he saw Anna. "Now, you are a sight for sore eyes." He tried to smile but started coughing again.

"Charlie for Heaven's sake sit down and I'll get you some water," Rose ordered.

As Anna helped Charlie to the mounting block to sit down, he turned to her, "Why are you here?"

"I've come back." She told him.

"But there is nothing left to come back to." Charlie said sadly.

"No," Anna shook her head, this was not what she wanted to hear, "Look it's like you said, you need to be where you will thrive in life, you know like the dandelion in the meadow."

Charlie smiled sadly at her, "But Anna the summer is over. Go and find somewhere else to thrive, I doubt anything will grow here now." He looked bleakly around the yard.

Anna stared at him in consternation, if she was honest, she had expected to be greeted with open arms or maybe anger that she had left so quickly but not this defeated attitude. Anna was about to speak again when they heard angry voices. A small determined figure came charging towards them with Rose in pursuit.

"Charles, you promised that you would not come here! And as soon as I leave you alone for five minutes what do you do?" The woman was clearly Charlie's wife and not happy at all.

Rose had caught up by now, and Charlie's wife turned on her. "I'm taking him home now and don't expect to see him again because he has just quit."

Charlie tried to intervene but his wife was not about to let up as she railed on at Rose about how she had taken advantage of Charlie over the years, not that she ever appreciated him.

Charlie started to cough again and she led him away, refusing any assistance from Rose or Anna.

They stood in the now silent yard. Rose looked shaken but as Anna started to speak, she held up a hand, "We still have the stables to do."

Anna looked around her, now she was no longer focused on Charlie and her heart dropped to the floor. In the daylight, she could see the place was a complete mess. Overflowing wheelbarrows sat everywhere and the yard was littered with buckets, hay, straw and mud.

But behind the mess she realised the yard was falling apart, the woodwork was rotting in places, cobbles were missing and the roof looked like it may cave in. How had she never noticed before?

Rose was watching her with a mixture of apprehension and anxiety, Anna took a deep breath, ironically remembering telling Lucy the day before she knew what she was dealing with. She gave Rose what she hoped was a reassuring smile, "I guess we had better get started."

They worked silently all morning. Anna started off by emptying the wheelbarrows and then set about the stables. Charlie and Rose had clearly been overwhelmed as rather than clean out the four horses who were stabled, they had simply been moved on to a clean stable, by lunchtime the right horses were back in the right stables, but only half the stables had been cleared out. Anna offered to sweep up whilst Rose went to make them some lunch. Heading back into the house wondering if perhaps Charlie was right and it was over for the yard Anna felt like crying as she found Rose pouring herself a drink.

Hearing her Rose jumped, a guilty look briefly flashed across her face, but then she smiled and held the bottle up, "Sherry? I always like one before lunch."

How had she never realised she thought once again? She bitterly remembered telling Lucy it was like Christmas everyday with Rose having a sherry before lunch. Anna sighed and braced her shoulders.

"Rose." Anna started but Rose appeared not to have heard.

"Shall we have a sandwich?" Rose interrupted not quite meeting her eye.

"Rose."

"Or we could go to the pub for lunch, my treat."

"Rose, we need to talk." Anna's voice came out far louder than she expected, as frustration and disappointment brimmed over.

Rose looked at her. "It's fine, honestly. I never thought you would stay." Her voice was over bright as she shrugged and knocked back the sherry.

"Rose." Anna struggled to find the words.

"Look this yard is my responsibility, it'll be fine." Rose said stoically.

Anna looked sadly at her trying to work out who Rose was trying to convince.

"Honestly Anna I'll manage I always do."

"But how? You don't even have Charlie now."

"That was a blow I admit, but I managed when my husband left, and when Daniel and Tom left home, and then you and Daniel left, people leave, that's life." Rose tried to brush it off, but Anna saw her hands had started to shake again.

"Rose, you need help."

Rose had started to wring her hands subconsciously, then anger flashed across her face, "Anna look, I know you mean well but it would be better if you left now."

"No, you need help." Anna stood her ground squaring up to Rose. Part of her marvelled at how, she would never have had the nerve to do this a couple of months ago.

Rose stared back for a long moment before sinking into a chair, she dropped her head into her hands, when she eventually looked up, she looked so desolate. "Do you have any idea what is like? All those ponies to look after, not to mention the dogs and there is no one to help share the load, and I'm getting older. Daniel and Tom are not interested in helping out or taking on the stables, they want to close this down and I'm scared, scared of getting too old to fight it, scared of managing this alone, scared of failing the ponies, I'm just so scared." She looked bleakly at Anna for a moment before a glimmer of her old defiance surfaced. "So yes, I do occasionally have a drink, but to be honest I think I deserve it!"

Anna paused, trying to work out what to say, Rose did not want her pity, but the situation could not carry on as it was.

However, seeing the sympathy flash across Anna's face, Rose threw her a look of contempt before continuing, "You have no idea how hard this has been, we managed fine at first when you left, but then the weather got worse and a few of the helpers stopped coming and then of course there was the tack room flood, so I had no option but to close the place down. For the last few weeks, it has just been Charlie and I, so quite frankly I need a little pick me up in the evenings, anyone would."

Aware that she had already opened Pandora's box Anna realised she had to see this through. "Look I should not have left before but the whole Freddie situation and a couple of other things made me run." There was no need to elaborate. "Last time I came here I had my head in the clouds thinking I was walking into this perfect life. This time I know it is far from perfect but I still want to be here, I still want to be part of it, surely that tells you something. We'll sort out the tack room and reopen."

Rose shrugged, "We've lost all the clients."

"Then we'll build the school back up again." Anna tried to remain positive.

"When the boiler in your flat blew up and flooded the tack room, it destroyed most of the saddles." Rose gave a mirthless laugh. "It has been a rough few months."

"Well we will have to see what we can use and then replace the rest as we can afford to."

"Anna I'm not sure we can get the clients back."

Anna paused. "We have to try. After all what's the alternative?"

For a while Rose said nothing, then she looked up, "There isn't one."

Aware Rose was finally talking, Anna pressed on. "Rose if this is going to work, we need to sort out your drinking." As she spoke, she could almost feel Rose's hackles rising.

"Anna you really need to let this go; you make it sound like I have a problem. I do not." Rose said with feeling.

Anna paused, looking at her phone, she knew she had to, but she hated herself. Slowly she picked up the phone and found the video, even then she paused before handing it over.

"Just watch this and then if you still don't think there is a problem, I won't mention it again, I promise."

Rose rolled her eyes, "honestly you young people think your phones can solve everything." She picked up the phone but as her eyes recognised her own face staring back at her she paused and nervously ran her tongue over her top lip.

She pressed play and as Anna heard the recording of her voice from the previous night fill the room, she turned away. She could not watch, but behind her she could feel the effect it was having on Rose.

It had seemed so quick the night before but now the video seemed to stretch on endlessly, and when it finished at last, silence descended over the kitchen. For a while no one spoke, but eventually with her nerves at screaming point Anna turned back to Rose, she bit her lip to stop herself gasping out loud. Rose was staring at the screen and she looked broken, although she had done it for the right reasons Anna could not help but wonder if she had gone too far. Part of her wanted to hug Rose but she looked so brittle Anna stayed where she was.

Eventually Rose let out a long shaky breath and pushed the phone across the table back in Anna's direction, without making eye contact. "I'd," she paused and cleared her throat. "I'd appreciate it, if you did not show that to anyone else." She finally looked up at Anna clearly trying to hold onto the last threads of dignity, that she could muster.

"I'm deleting it now Rose," Anna said glad to get rid of it, "this is between us, I won't be talking to anyone about this."

Rose nodded, "Thank you."

They sat in silence for a while longer, while Anna let the magnitude of what Rose had just witnessed completely sink in.

Eventually Rose spoke, "I guess….. Well perhaps I should cut back a bit."

"Rose." Anna said gently.

"What do you want? If you think I am going to one of those touchy feeling AA meetings with some nosy do gooder then you can think again." The defiance was back but more half-hearted than before.

Anna bit her lip and said nothing.

"I'll talk to my doctor. He's a sensible man." She said at last.

Anna nodded, feeling only relief. She just hoped they could put Rose back together. "I'll phone the doctor."

With the appointment booked, Anna asked Rose if she wanted her to accompany her.

Rose smiled sadly, "You'll have to I'm afraid, Tom confiscated my car keys."

Yet again Anna realised that they were completely at rock bottom. "Things can only get better." She said reassuringly to Rose, whilst praying she was right.

Jefferson leaned on Daniel as he got into the car, Lizzie danced around them, her excitement at Jefferson finally been allowed home made it difficult for her to keep still.

"Thanks son." Jefferson looked at Daniel still unable to believe he was there. Daniel nodded and stepped away allowing Lara room to step forward and fasten his seat belt as his arm was still very weak.

Finally, they were ready and pulled away from the hospital for the short ride back to the apartment. Jefferson watched as his son dealt with the New York rush hour without turning a hair while Lizzie chattered endlessly about the modifications to the apartment that would help him during his rehabilitation.

"Daniel's done an amazing job there is no mess at all, you would not know we'd had builders in at all Dad. Even Mum was pleased."

Lara smiled but let her daughter chatter on, Daniel had done a fantastic job getting their apartment ready, but she was more grateful that he had finally visited Jefferson. She had begun to fear he would go back to England without ever seeing him. Lizzie had let it drop that Daniel was in New York and each day she had seen the hope in Jefferson's eyes that Daniel would be with them, before it died away when he realised Daniel was not there.

Daniel helped him into the apartment and straight to his room, realising like Lara that the journey home and the exertion of leaving hospital had worn him out.

"There we go Jefferson." Daniel helped him onto the bed.

"Thank you, Daniel." The voice was still slightly slurred, but the speech therapist was hopeful it would recover in time. Daniel met his eyes and saw the gratitude and pride in them and nodded slightly embarrassed. He had always thought if he had to come face to face with Jefferson, he would give him a piece of his mind for what he had done to Rose, Tom and himself, but seeing his father weakened by the stroke had made him human again. He was still getting used to the idea of seeing him and repeatedly buried thoughts that he was being disloyal to Rose by even coming out to New York. Tom had maintained a relationship with him from an early age, but then Tom did not remember him leaving. His thoughts returned to Rose, his last phone call to Tom had been worrying, things sounded worse than ever. He would stay another week and then go home he decided.

Chapter Nineteen

Returning from the doctor they sat back down in the kitchen. "So where do we go from here?" Rose asked. She seemed to have given up control to Anna completely.

Noticing how tired she was Anna suggested that she went to lie down, and was surprised when Rose agreed. Whilst she slept Anna cleaned the kitchen from top to bottom, every bottle she uncovered, whether it was from the back of a cupboard, inside a wellie or under a blanket she collected on the kitchen table. By the time Rose returned there were over twenty bottles.

Rose looked at the collection and even she seemed surprised by the number of bottles. "Shall I get rid of them?" Anna asked tentatively.

Rose nodded but turned away as Anna started to pour the contents down the sink.

"At least that'll clear the drains out," Rose said with a small attempt at humour.

By the end of the day Anna felt as exhausted as Rose looked. The doctor had warned her that this would be the case, but she had not appreciated quite how bad it would be. Tomorrow looked like being another momentous day, Anna thought, not only did she have to try and get Rose to her first support meeting, but she also needed to assess just how bad the flooding in her old flat and the tack room was. It had felt too much to face on her first day back.

She was so lost in thought; she had not realised that Rose had stood up and was preparing to go to bed. "Well good night Anna, I'll see you in the morning." Then she paused as she noticed Anna's case by the door. "Anna, where are you going to sleep tonight?"

Anna realised she had not even thought about it. "I'll sleep in here again." Anna said trying to look more positive than she felt.

Rose rolled her eyes, some of her old spirit returning. "I may have become a bit of a liability but I can at least provide you with a proper bed. Come on."

Anna followed her out into the hallway, realising she had never been past the kitchen before. In the hallway was a huge sweeping staircase which split in two before rising up to the second floor. Anna gasped, "Rose this is amazing."

Rose smiled faintly but the pride was unmistakable. "It is rather special, isn't it?" she agreed.

As they ascended the staircase they came onto a long landing with a number of doors. Rose opened the second one, and felt for the light switch and as light flooded the room Anna gasped in delight. The room was large with cream silk wallpaper with tiny violets all over it. At the window were curtains in a deep heavy purple which fell in large swags. The deep cream carpet invited you to walk barefoot, but the centre piece was a large four poster bed.

"Will this do?" Rose asked anxiously. "There is a bathroom through that door, but I'm afraid it is years since it has been decorated. And it could do with a clean," she said, taking in the cobwebs.

"Rose it is gorgeous," Anna said truthfully. Briefly she swallowed the hurt that Daniel had insisted she had the flat rather one of these beautiful rooms.

After Rose had gone, she investigated the bathroom. Although dated, it had clearly been expensively decorated in the past, with a free-standing roll top bath and marble floors. Rose was right it needed cleaning but Anna could not help but smile loving the old-fashioned charm and opulence of the room, perhaps things were not so bad after all.

As Mollie moved around the kitchen that night putting school books back in bags and clearing away the mess of the day, her thoughts kept returning to Anna's surprise visit. She had said Rose was not her problem and she had enough to worry about, but Billy's chicken pox was no longer contagious and he could go back to nursery. She really should go and check on Rose the next day, she could not even phone anymore as the phone seemed to have been cut off. Guilt nagged at her for leaving it as long as she had.

She turned as she heard Tom's key in the door. He came in looking stressed and tired as he now did every night. This was the first time she had seen him this week she realised, as she put his dinner in the microwave to heat it up.

As he sat down at the table, she placed the food in front of him, he smiled gratefully as he picked up the knife and fork. "Thanks Moll."

Making herself a cup of tea she sat down opposite him. "Tom I've been thinking."

He glanced up warily, "What about?"

"I think I should go and check on Rose tomorrow."

Relief flooded across Tom's features, "Thanks that would be great, I just don't have the time at the moment." His eyes dropped quickly from hers. They both knew he could not face dealing with the speed at which his mother had declined.

It was ironic he thought, he had worried about whether he could run the business without Daniel, and whilst he really wanted Daniel to come back, he was pleased to discover he could step out of his brother's shadow. The part about Daniel leaving that really shocked him, was how much and how well Daniel had managed Rose's drinking. He had had no idea just how bad things had become. Confiscating Rose's car keys had been an act of desperation, he simply did not know what else to do.

Chapter Twenty

As Mollie got Billy out of the car and into the pushchair whilst grabbing school bags and lunch boxes, she became aware that other parents were staring. Straightening up she looked across the pub car park where many of the parents parked before completing the short walk to the school. Mothers quickly looked away and hurried past. Rounding the kids up, she followed them out onto the path that led up to the school.

As they walked, she tried to work out what had happened, but as she reached the school playground, Charlie's granddaughter strode angrily towards her. "I hope you are happy, my granddad's in hospital with pneumonia, thanks to your family. He's been doing those horses on his own in the cold, whilst that stuck up cow sits in her big posh house getting pissed. I hate you people, all thinking you are too good for everyone and letting the likes of us work ourselves into an early grave."

Mollie froze in shock, aware Lottie had started to cry, that Josh had gone pale, and even Billy was quiet. Another mother came and put an arm around the now sobbing woman, guiding her gently away, but not before she threw a look of disgust at Mollie.

"Oh goodness Mollie, how shocking!" Olivia's voice was right behind her.

"Bugger off Olivia, no one needs your opinion today." Jane came up beside Mollie as the bell rang. "Right off you go kids, don't worry Lottie and Josh, it'll all be fine." Jane shooed them towards their classes who were now lining up.

Mollie managed a smile and a wave as Lottie glanced worriedly at her before disappearing through the door. Aware she was still the main subject of gossip on the playground that morning she tried to ignore the other mother's as they looked her way, some mildly curious, others more openly judgemental.

"Thanks." She turned to Jane, grateful for her support. "I know things are really bad with Rose but I had not realised it was that bad."

"Apparently Charlie got taken to hospital last night, unfortunately it's all over the village this morning. It was after his wife found him at Rose's yesterday morning, and gave her a piece of her mind."

"Poor Charlie, I'll go round later and see his wife. You know ironically I was going over to check on Rose this morning, I was just waiting for Billy's chicken pox to clear." Mollie told Jane, before pausing. "Well to be honest I've been avoiding it, I just don't know what to do. You know I got mad with Daniel and Tom for not sorting it out, but it turns out I'm no better than they were."

Jane smiled sadly at her. "Come on, let's drop Billy at nursery and rather than go to my spin class, I'll come and check on Rose with you."

"You really don't mind coming?" Mollie asked, wanting to fling her arms around Jane in relief.

"Are you joking, for once I'll know the gossip before Olivia." She laughed, "Now come on before I change my mind."

Anna sat in the car waiting for Rose to come out of her meeting, she really needed to go and buy some food for them, but she did not want to leave in case Rose came out early, having decided that she did not need to be there or that they were all idiots. Anna glanced at her phone and realised that actually the meeting was nearly over which meant Rose had stuck it out. Surprised, she wondered again what the doctor had said to convince Rose to go.

Ten minutes later she watched as people slowly came out of the village hall, Rose had deliberately chosen a meeting, nearly an hour from their village, but Anna could appreciate the need for anonymity. At last Rose came out she looked tired, but she strode across to the car and got in without a word.

Neither spoke as they started to drive back to the village. They stopped and brought food and carried on. Eventually Anna had to ask how it had gone.

Rose paused and considered the question. "Not what I expected, but not quite as bad as I feared. No nosy do-gooders so that was a start!"

Anna nodded. "Will you go again?"

Rose half laughed, "You make it sound like a pottery class, this isn't optional unfortunately, not if I want to beat this and I have to, the ponies need me."

Relieved Anna merely nodded and they drove home in silence, both alone with their thoughts.

Pulling up on the drive Mollie looked at Jane, "You don't have to come in, she can get quite difficult when she's had a few."

Jane just rolled her eyes, "Come on." She said climbing out.

Mollie got out more slowly, fear and dread coursing through her as she headed towards the kitchen door. She paused before she pushed it open, imagining the worst. The door slowly swung open and Mollie forced herself to walk into the kitchen. Tilly greeted her enthusiastically but Mollie hardly noticed her as she looked around in shock. The room was clean and smelt fresh, it was the exact opposite to what it had been just over two weeks earlier when she had last been here.

"I don't understand." She turned to Jane in confusion. "Rose?" She raised her voice, wondering where she was. "Let's try the yard."

The stables were all clean and ready for use and the ponies that were in were all content, and even the yard had been swept and felt more cared for than it had in a while.

"There are five horses and ponies in, and looking at the fields another fifteen, that is a huge amount of work for one person." Jane commented.

Mollie felt guilty, thinking about poor Charlie in hospital, she should have come and helped. Most of the local village kids that liked to help had been stopped by their parents as Rose's drinking had become more noticeable.

"She's not here!" Jane said opening a door. "Oh no."

Coming up behind her Mollie gasped, there was a hole in the ceiling and the water damage was evident everywhere. "It does not look like there is much hope for most of this." Jane commented sadly.

Mollie's heart sank, without saddles and bridles Rose had no riding school left. Fear clutched at her heart. She grabbed Jane's arm, "We have to find her now!"

"Mollie?" Alarm crossed Jane's face at Mollie's sudden anxiety. "Calm down. What's wrong?"

"Think about it, the stables have gone under, she's lost Charlie, the house has been tidied up, what if?" Mollie looked at Jane willing her to understand.

"Sorry! You've lost me."

"Well, you hear about people putting everything straight and then going off and well you know," Mollie watched as comprehension dawned on Jane's face, "Thank heavens we don't have any kids with us."

"Mollie? I didn't know you were coming today." Rose's voice boomed across the yard.

Spinning around Mollie just stared. Rose looked fine and was dressed in clean clothes and had done her hair. She hadn't seen her like that since just after Anna and Daniel left.

"Thank heavens you didn't kill yourself." Mollie exclaimed, before realising what she had said.

"What an odd thing to say Mollie," Rose replied, "as if I'd do something like that, after all who would look after the ponies?"

Beside her Mollie felt Jane suppress a smile.

"Right have you got time for a cup of tea? There are a few things I need to say."

"Sure." Mollie nodded, trying to work out what was going on.

"Come along then, you too Jane, you may as well hear this, then you can put some of the village gossips straight."

They followed Rose back to the house feeling like two naughty school girls. Once in the kitchen, Mollie was surprised to find Anna but before she could say anything Rose took a deep breath. "So, it would seem I'm an alcoholic, well actually a functioning alcoholic, they have to give everything a name these days. I've seen the doctor and Anna is taking me to the meetings, so it's all back under control. Now tell me how are the children? I've missed them so much."

Mollie was jolted by the sudden change of topic, "the children?"

"Josh, Lottie and Billy?" Rose looked at her questioningly.

"Of course, yes, they are fine." Mollie was struggling to keep up, she held a hand up to prevent Rose asking anymore questions. "Rose please, you can't say something like that and move on."

Rose sighed, "What do you want me to say?" She sat down slowly, "I don't know how Tom and Daniel will take hearing that their mother is an alcoholic, not that Daniel cares, seeing as he isn't showing any signs of coming home."

Mollie looked at her in consternation, "Rose they both already know," she said gently.

"I see." Rose nodded stiffly looking as unreachable as ever. "I mean they both said I drank a little too much but we never used that word."

Mollie turned to Jane and Anna, whom she still had not yet spoken to, "Can you give us a minute?"

Outside Jane turned to Anna, "Well I don't know how you did it, but you're a braver woman than me!"

"What do you mean?" Anna asked surprised.

"Mollie has been trying to get Tom and Daniel to do something for the last few years about her drinking. Just before you turned up the last time they were going to try and put her into sheltered accommodation."

Anna looked at her in shock, Paris had been right. "That was the worst thing they could do; it was the fear of losing the ponies and not being able to cope with the yard that was making her drink." The words came out far more harshly than she intended as fury at Daniel consumed her. Anna swallowed, "Sorry, it's just that if that's what they were trying to do, then, they probably made her drinking worse."

Jane looked at her in surprise, "I see what you mean but it was not intentional." For a few minutes they stood quietly, before Jane spoke, "What made you come back?"

Anna half laughed, "A dandelion actually!"

Jane raised an eyebrow. "Please don't tell me you've been drinking too," then she clapped her hand over her mouth, "sorry I shouldn't joke about that considering….."

But to her surprise Anna laughed, "don't worry it's been a tough couple of days, I could do with something to make me smile. And since you are here, do you mind checking out the tack room with me? I want to see how bad it is without Rose; I know she seems strong but I'm not sure how much more she can take at the moment."

Jane gave a tight smile. "We've just been in there, it's not looking good."

"I know, which is why I need to know what I am facing." Anna braced her shoulders as they made their way round to the yard.

Jane looked at her appraisingly. "You know you seem different; you are much more...." She paused searching for the right word.

Anna waited wondering what she would say.

"Don't take this the wrong way but you seem to have grown up." Jane finally said, watching Anna for her response.

Anna smiled sadly. "Last time I was here I was following some crazy dream. This time I know what I'm dealing with. Or some of it." She finished ruefully.

The tack room was still open and Anna groaned as she looked through the door, half the ceiling had caved in and everything was damp and covered in dust and plaster.

"Well, you know what they say, when life serves you lemons..." Jane's voice came from behind her.

"Make lemonade?" Anna finished.

"No make a large gin and tonic!" Jane said with mock indignity. "Oh shit, I've done it again! At this rate I'll be going with Rose to those meetings."

She turned to Anna who had started to giggle. "Can this get any worse do you think?" she laughed sadly.

An hour later Mollie and Jane climbed back in the car to leave. Mollie let out a long shaky breath, "Wow, I wasn't expecting that."

"No, it was certainly better than we hoped." Jane replied.

Mollie started the engine and turned towards the drive, "It was, it is, I don't know how Anna did it, but she's achieved what no one else could. I just hope she doesn't run off again."

"I don't think she will," Jane answered, "she's changed."

Mollie rolled her eyes, "let's hope so." She drove on feeling slightly guilty, last time she had seen Anna she had been really rude and she had not had a chance to talk to her properly with Rose there. She'd have to catch up with her soon, as she had missed having her around, not that she would tell Tom. She bit her lip wondering what Tom would make of what had happened.

"Care to share?" Jane was watching her.

Mollie sighed, "I was just trying to work out what Tom will think about today's events."

"Surely he'll be happy?" Jane looked at her like she was mad.

"He will about Rose, but he still blames Anna for Daniel going."

"Ah I'd forgotten about that!" Jane replied. "It's funny she just doesn't seem the type to do what she did."

"I know," Mollie replied, "to be honest I still wonder if there is more to this story than there seems."

Jefferson leaned on Daniel as they came through for lunch. Daniel helped him into his chair before sitting down as well.

The meals had changed since Jefferson returned home, they were all easy to eat and required nothing more than a spoon for Jefferson. Once again Daniel had to acknowledge just how much Lara cared for Jefferson, outwardly life appeared normal and he was made to feel head of the house, despite the fact he was still recovering. Daniel silently recognised his mother would never have had that patience and forethought unless it was for an animal. Perhaps Jefferson had been right to go, selfish but right, Daniel amended in his head. It had come as a surprise but he realised he actually quite liked his father which was something he had not expected.

But his thoughts were returning increasingly to home now, he wondered how to break the news to the people sat around the table. However, he was spared by his phone ringing, and excusing himself he took Tom's call.

After a brief conversation he hung up and stared out of the window for a long time. Tom had been at a loss to explain why Anna had returned. Only that her return meant that Rose had finally admitted she had a problem. He knew he should be pleased but why did it have to be her? How could he go home now? And how could he face her and thank her for doing what he couldn't. The anger that he thought he had conquered surged through him. He paced the room for a while, until he got his temper back under control.

Realising that the others must be wondering where he had got to, he walked back through to the sitting room where Nancy had just served coffee.

"Guess what Daniel? It's meant to snow next week, and the ice rink opens soon in Central Park, we have to go ice skating." Lizzie beamed up at him. "And we have just been talking and we'd love you to stay for Christmas, oh please say yes Daniel, it'll be so much fun."

He felt a brief pang for Christmas back home but forced himself to smile.

"Then count me in." He replied as Lizzie launched herself across the room at him screaming excitedly.

Chapter Twenty-One

It took Anna two weeks to pluck up the courage to go and visit Mollie, partly because she did not want to leave Rose but also because she was worried about the reception she would get after their doorstep row. Tom had visited Rose, but Mollie and the kids had still not been near the house.

Getting out of her car, Anna walked over and knocked on the front door. She sadly thought that she used to happily go round to the kitchen but that seemed intrusive today. Tom opened the door and looked at her.

"Hi Tom, how are you?" She asked, surprised by his hostility. He had been off with her when he came to the house but she had put that down to his being worried about Rose, now she was not so sure. "Is Mollie in?" She faltered slightly beginning to wonder whether she should have come.

"Sure, come in," he turned and she followed him through to the lounge.

"Visitor for you. I'll take George for a walk," and with that he walked out the room.

Anna watched as Mollie's face dropped as Tom walked away.

"Sorry I'll go, it's obviously not a good time." Anna said starting to turn.

"Please stay, things have been difficult with Rose, well before you came back. And he's really busy with Daniel still in New York."

"New York?" Anna asked not realising Daniel was abroad.

"He's been out there since Jefferson's stroke. Lara and Lizzie would never have coped without him, we were hoping he would come back now Jefferson's out of hospital but he's decided to stay out there for

243

the time being. Apparently, Jefferson is still quite weak after the stroke."

Anna nodded, remembering Lizzie was always leaving messages for him, before briefly wondering who Lara was but now was not the time to ask. Instead, she changed the subject knowing talking about Daniel would do her no good.

"Look I owe you an apology, when I turned up the other day telling you to sort out Rose................." She paused. "It was wrong of me, I'm sorry."

"I'm sorry too, I never realised you did not know about the drinking." Mollie left the comment hanging in the air.

"I think there were a lot of things that were not as they seemed." Anna replied. "But it is good to be back."

"Well, I'm glad you are back, but how on earth did you get Rose to face facts?"

"Do you mind if I don't say, I promised her I wouldn't." Anna did not want to talk about the video ever again.

"Sure." Mollie replied, torn between asking more questions and respecting Anna's request. Acknowledging that the important part was that Rose was addressing her problem, not why she was addressing it, she smiled and moved the conversation on. "How about a cup of tea and you can fill me in on what you have been up to while you have been away."

Finally, on safe ground both of them relaxed and the conversation began to flow as Anna made Mollie laugh with stories about Donna and the yard she had been working at.

"I thought I might bring the kids over after school tomorrow." Mollie said looking at Anna to see what she thought. "We weren't sure to start with, but Tom's spoken to her every day and each time he's seen her she's been sober."

Anna looked at Mollie's unhappy face thinking how much this affected them all. "Rose would love to see them, for all she says its fine, I think she has missed them and we've had a tough couple of weeks. The tack room was a mess and because it was left for a few weeks, things that could have been saved have been ruined too. I'm not sure how we'll replace it all and the thought of reopening at the moment seems a little too ambitious. And before we can, the ponies need tidying up, poor Houdini has got mud fever. We've got a long way to go yet." Anna tried not to think about everything that needed doing or it would overwhelm her.

Mollie sighed, "We knew it was bad but not quite how bad."

"I still don't understand why they closed though." Anna said, hoping Mollie would answer the question Rose had evaded. "Was it because of what happened to Freddie? Was it my fault?"

"Freddie?" Mollie looked confused for a second, "Oh no, don't be silly, Daniel sorted all that out with Sarah before he left. Angie and Paris were behind it. Paris had plans for her and Daniel to live in the Manor."

Anna sighed sadly; she had thought she was helping Rose by leaving but instead she had made things worse for her. Mollie was watching her curiously, so Anna returned to the subject of why Rose had closed the school.

Mollie sighed, "I don't think Rose meant to but the night the tack room flooded she got really drunk and drove down to the village and announced it in the pub. Apparently she was ranting it was all over and that the whole place would close. Thankfully Craig Pennington was there and he took her home. He then brought the car keys round to Tom." Mollie let out a shaky breath. "It's a miracle she didn't hurt herself or someone else. Anyway, Tom was so mad he went round and told her off and said he was keeping the keys. Rose refused to admit she was drunk so had to stand by her decision to close. After that, even the few kids that were still helping out were stopped by concerned parents. Everyone abandoned her but Charlie."

The two of them fell silent, thinking of the price Charlie had paid for his loyalty. Mollie paused before carrying on. "I have been to visit him. It turns out it wasn't pneumonia just a nasty chest infection, although it sounds as though it was still pretty serious."

"Yeah, he told me the same. I went to visit too, I snuck in on Sunday morning when his wife was at church." She added with a guilty smile.

Mollie laughed ruefully, "I wish I'd thought of that, I got the full force of her views on what happened." Although, she had not been as angry as her granddaughter, Mollie acknowledged. "So how is Rose doing?" She asked suddenly looking serious, "I mean really."

"She's finding it tough, but she's determined to beat it and the groups seem to be helping not that she ever discusses what goes on in them, but the fact she has not written them all off as a bunch of idiots gives me hope."

"Perhaps she really does mean it." Mollie mused.

"I do find this weather depressing," Rose commented looking out at the overcast afternoon sky. It was only mid-afternoon, but it was almost dark.

Anna flicked on the kettle for a cup of tea before they started the evening feeds, all the horses were stabled again, but twenty horses for two people was proving hard work and it was only the start of the winter.

Hearing a noise, she glanced out of the window to see Josh, Lottie and Billy running along the path to the back door. With a crash it flew open to reveal three happy faces.

Rose jumped up delighted, embracing all three children at once, as Mollie followed them in carrying coats and a scarf which had clearly been dropped on the wet path.

"We missed you." Lottie said, "Daddy said you were poorly, but you've been poorly for a long time."

"Well, it is a long-term illness," Rose replied.

"Dad told Mum you were an alcoholic, when they thought I was asleep!" Josh added before smiling, "but that's ok because Dillon's Dad says his Mum is an alcoholic and is always pissed on Friday nights. What does pissed mean?"

"It would seem I'm in good company then." She commented, secretly relieved how unfazed the children were.

"Ummm," Mollie started to interrupt but Josh seemed to have forgotten his question as he began to tell Rose about what they had been doing.

Leaving Rose to enjoy seeing her grandchildren Anna headed out to the yard, with Tilly at her heels. It was nearly dark and had started to rain. Anna switched on her head torch as the flood in the tack room had blown all the electrics on the yard. Anna mixed feeds and gave them out to the horses eagerly waiting at their doors for them. She topped up water buckets and replaced hay nets and skipped off the stables. For some reason tonight it seemed to be taking ages. Tired she picked up a large pot of cream and went to apply it to Houdini's legs. They were covered in lesions from the mud fever, he felt so sorry for himself and was so glad to be in a warm dry stable he had made no attempt to escape in over a week.

As Anna sat in the dark stable, tiredness washed over her whilst she applied the cream with only the light from her head torch as a guide, she wondered how they were ever going to get the stables back up and running. She suddenly felt trapped, she had promised everyone she would see this through, but she had no idea how to make this work. Aware her phone was ringing, she was surprised to see Mandy's number, wiping the excess cream on her coat she answered the call.

"You are not going to believe this," Mandy launched straight into conversation without even a hello, "Camilla caught Miss Whiplash and Dick going at it, and she kicked them both out."

"Poor Camilla," Anna thought, having some idea how she must have felt.

"Nah, she's happier than she has been in months, I think she is secretly relieved. Anyway, she wants to get the yard back to normal, back to the good old days. I've already moved back in and she asked me to see if you fancied coming back?"

Anna paused; this was the last thing she had expected.

"Come on, we'll have such a laugh, you know you want to." Mandy coaxed.

Did she want to though? Anna was flummoxed, here she was sat in the dark lonely yard, which may never get back on its feet, being offered a chance to go back to a pristine yard, with fantastic facilities, where she would be surrounded by girls her own age, she could have a laugh with. She thought of the wash down stable complete with a shower and bet Camilla's horses never got mud fever. But as she looked at Houdini gently sniffing at the cream on his leg, and thought of Rose back in the kitchen, she realised she did not want to go anywhere, even if it did mean spending the winter rolling around an old mansion with a recovering alcoholic.

"I'm sorry Mandy it would have been great but I belong here."

"It must be some yard!" Mandy commented.

"Not really, but hopefully it will be one day."

They chatted for a couple more minutes and then Anna hung up, gathering up the cream and brushes she started as she heard a noise. Tilly was somewhere in the yard so it could not be a stranger Anna thought, as Mollie's head appeared over the door.

Mollie held her hands up as the torchlight blinded her. "Just thought I'd see if you needed any help? Why aren't the lights on?" She said looking at the cream smeared all over Houdini's legs.

"The electrics went with the tack room roof. Rose has had no electricity out here since the flood."

"Oh." Mollie looked horrified.

"It's not that bad, it's light in the morning." Anna commented giving Houdini a pat. "Rose wasn't ready to have the place crawling with workman, so I haven't pushed her."

Mollie shook her head sadly. "Oh Anna, I'm surprised you've stuck it, most people wouldn't have."

Anna paused feeling guilty. "I've just been offered my old job back actually."

Mollie looked uncomfortable, "I know, I heard you on the phone. Sorry I didn't mean to eavesdrop."

"Don't worry, it's tempting but I'm not going anywhere, however I do need to think of a way we can start to get this place back on its feet." She commented as they made their way back to the house.

"Leave it with me." Mollie said. Regardless of what Tom thought about Anna, she needed some help.

The following morning Anna was out in the rain again, having just fed the horses. Rose hadn't been up when she came out so she had made a start on her own. They had warned her she would sleep a lot when she first stopped drinking but Anna had completely under estimated just how much she rest she would need.

Sighing she picked up the wheelbarrow to start the first stable, briefly her mind cast itself back to the call from Mandy, perhaps she was crazy not to take the job.

"Morning!" The voice came from behind her making her jump.

Spinning around Anna found herself face to face with Rich. "Hi, what can I do for you?" She asked wondering why he was there.

Rich merely smiled and winked, making Anna roll her eyes, although she did smile, "That's better, actually Tom has sent me here to see what needs to be done."

"What do you mean?" Anna asked in surprise, as two more men appeared carrying what looked like tool boxes.

"I heard that the tack room flooded and you've lost the electrics."

Anna just looked at him and wanted to cry.

"Come on Anna, it's usually when I say I'm leaving that woman cry not when I arrive, I'm actually here to help." Rich said amused.

Anna pulled herself together. "Right well let's start with the tack room."

"Blimey," was all Rich said as he took in the caved in ceiling and water damage. If he was fazed by it, he hid it well. "Leave it with me."

Unable to believe her luck Anna started the stables feeling happier than she had since her return. She worked steadily all morning, as she turned the ponies out into the paddocks away from the hammering and sawing. As she finished off Alfred's stable, there was a flicker, a flash and the yard lit up.

"What on earth is going on?" Rose's voice boomed across the yard. "Oh, Richard I should have known you would be involved."

Anna started to come out of the stables to explain but Rich beat her to it.

"Tom sent us. Apparently, you have been looking after the horses in the dark!"

"Well yes the boiler blew up and flooded the tack room, it has been somewhat inconvenient."

Rich laughed, "You know Rose, most people would not put up with that and would have called an electrician straight away."

To Anna's surprise Rose chuckled, "Yes Richard but I am not most people. Your generation might not be able to cope without all the mod cons but I've spent many winters snowed in up here with no electricity. Charlie used to say it only took a sparrow to fart near an electricity pylon and the whole village would black out."

Rich laughed out loud, so leaving them to it Anna moved on to the next stable. She had just finished when Rose called her over to see what had been done. Looking into the tack room, Anna could see the old ceiling had been completely removed. Heaters had been set up to dry everything out, making Anna wonder why she had not thought of it.

"We need to leave it a couple of days to dry out but then we'll put a new ceiling in, plaster and paint it and you'll be back in business. What's the other side of this wall?"

Rose opened the door to the office, whilst not as bad, the office also had water damage too. Rich looked at the space, "you know you could use a proper counter in here, we'll knock you one up while we are sorting this out. We'll see you tomorrow ladies, we should be done in a week."

Anna and Rose just looked at each other in delight after the men had left, "You know, I had begun to think it was hopeless Anna, but perhaps we can save this place after all."

After the initial excitement of the new tack room and office, the winter dragged on, the bitter wind blew across the yard each day, chilling Anna to the bone. The ponies looked better, and they had started to get the yard repaired, doors were replaced, walls repainted and even the roof retiled. Christmas was just over a week away when Mollie appeared at the yard one morning.

"Is Rose here?" she asked looking around. "Wow this looks better every time I come."

Anna smiled pleased before answering. "No, she's gone to pick up the feed. Do you fancy a coffee? I could do with a break!"

As they walked into the office Anna talked about the need to get some more help in, but when she realised Mollie was not listening, she paused.

"Sorry Anna I was miles away, look, the thing is…." Mollie bit her lip, annoyed at Tom and Daniel for leaving this to her to sort out yet again. "Um, what are your plans for Christmas?"

"I'm staying here. I can't leave Rose all this to do on her own." She replied not adding that it saved her having to be lectured by her mother all Christmas about her career choice.

"Well the thing is, Jefferson has asked us to go out to New York for Christmas with the kids, he's never met them and we've never met Lara."

"Lara?" Anna couldn't help herself.

"Jefferson's wife, Tom's step mother." She paused as though considering whether to say more. "That's who Jefferson went off with when he left Rose."

"Oh, I never knew." Was all Anna could say, she had always wondered what had happened but it was not the sort of conversation you could have with Rose.

"I thought Daniel might have told you about it." Mollie suggested leaving the comment hanging.

Anna laughed a short bitter laugh. "No."

Feeling more than ever that perhaps there was more to the night of the ball than anyone had realised she pressed on. "I'm surprised he didn't."

Anna's face fell, but instead she shrugged "Well it's not like it was anything serious, we didn't talk that much." Or rather Anna had but Daniel had not shared anything.

"That wasn't the impression I got." Mollie could not help but try.

Feeling herself close to tears Anna changed the subject. "New York for Christmas, sounds lovely." She tried to smile, they could all be one big happy family with Daniel and Lizzie at the centre of everything.

Images of Daniel and Lizzie danced around in her head, the pair of them ice skating in Central Park, Daniel with his arms around her as they watched them light the huge Christmas tree that was in all the films, she shook her head to try and get rid of the thoughts.

Mollie watched her, thinking she looked hurt more than guilty, but she clearly didn't want to discuss it today. "How do you think Rose will take it?" She asked instead.

Lara put down the phone and smiled at Jefferson who was dozing in a chair. She decided not to wake him to tell him the news knowing how much he needed his rest. She just hoped having the whole family for Christmas would not tire him out too much. Instead, she set about working out where everyone could sleep, Daniel had the annex but perhaps if took one of the spare rooms then Tom, Mollie and the kids could have the annex.

Looking up she realised that Jefferson was awake, he smiled at her. "Are they coming? I thought I heard you on the phone?"

"Yes, they are." Lara moved over to sit on the arm of his chair, he placed a hand on her thigh and patted it gently.

"Thank you for doing this."

"I'm looking forward to it and I know how much it means to you to finally have Christmas with your family."

Jefferson nodded, "I just wonder how Rose will take it." He said with a sigh.

"You are what!" Tom almost cowered at Rose's reaction. Mollie had refused to tell her, which he knew was fair but didn't stop him from wishing she had done. Mollie would have been fair better at this than him.

"So, first Daniel and now you!" Rose was clearly not happy. "And will you stay out there permanently too?" She demanded.

"No of course we won't." Tom said in a tone that made clear he thought the idea ridiculous. Then realising that he was being unfair he softened his tone. "Mum I know it's not good timing for you, but Jefferson had a stroke and…."

Rose looked at her son and hmphed, "Well he is your father, I suppose and you've never spent Christmas with him, well not since he left."

"Thank you." Tom replied meaning it. He paused for a second.

"Well spit it out Tom." Rose said irritably.

"Well, this won't, I mean you won't, it's just that you have been doing so well." He finally spluttered."

Rose glared at him; she had guessed this was what he wanted to say but had hoped he had more faith in her. "You mean will I start drinking again because my sons have abandoned me at Christmas?"

"Mum…" Tom pleaded.

"Don't worry I'll be fine and anyway I have Anna here; she is staying for Christmas."

Tom bit his tongue and decided not to point out that if Anna had stayed away then Daniel would probably be home by now.

"I don't want to go to school tomorrow." Lottie said quietly.

Mollie was half paying attention as she navigated through the heavy Christmas traffic, wondering why the whole world had all decided on a dark foggy afternoon to go shopping. The glare of the lights in the murky twilight hurt her eyes as she quickly went over the present list in her head. Having been ready for a Christmas at home she was now panic buying presents that would fit in suitcases. She had gone to collect a toy she had reserved earlier, but after struggling to park, they arrived at the shop ten minutes before it was due to close, only to be told they were too late, she had begged, pleaded and demanded to see the manager, only to discover the ten year old spotty boy she was talking to was the manager.

"Mum I just said I don't want to go to school tomorrow." Lottie sounded indignant.

"But it's the last day of term, it'll be fun." Mollie said wishing she had just paid to have the toy delivered.

In the back-seat Billy and Josh were fighting over a Spiderman figure.

"Mum Billy's stolen my Spiderman!" Josh declared.

"I just looking!" Billy shouted crossly whilst refusing to release his grip on it.

"Lacey said I am stupid." Lottie shouted. "I am never going to school again."

"Josh let him have a look at it." Mollie answered distractedly watching the traffic, in the hope someone would let her out of the junction. She turned to Lottie and softened her voice, "Lottie, love, you know you are not stupid and I know you are not stupid, so does it matter what Lacey says?"

"I knew you wouldn't understand," Lottie pouted folding her arms.

In the back Josh was trying to grab the figure off Billy, Mollie was about to say something when the car behind her beeped its horn, realising someone had flashed her out, she slammed the car into gear and shunted forwards, then she nearly screamed as Josh's foot slammed into the back of her chair, as he struggled to get Spiderman back.

"Boys sit still." Mollie said through clenched teeth. Trying to ignore the boys she resumed the conversation with Lottie, "Everyone gets called stupid sometimes!"

"You don't, Daddy doesn't, Josh and Billy don't." Lottie yelled before bursting into tears.

Mollie sighed, every end of term was the same, it was like Groundhog Day. They all got over tired and argued with their friends, it would all be forgotten by the next term. Mollie turned on the radio, hoping she could distract the kids with some Christmas songs.

"Simply having a wonderful Christmas time!" The radio belted out the happy tune.

The argument over Spiderman was escalating on the backseat, as Spiderman's web shot through the seats. It hit Lottie on the side of the face, shrieking she turned round, "Billy you are such a stupid boy." And she burst into tears.

"Lottie, don't talk to Billy like that." Mollie admonished gently, rolling her eyes at the irony of Lottie calling her brother stupid having just complained about being called stupid herself.

"I not stupid!" came back the tearful reply from Billy, in the mirror Mollie could see his lip beginning to quiver.

"Don't be a cry baby Lottie!" Josh added making Billy laugh instead.

"Simply having a wonderful Christmas time." Sang out the radio joyfully, making Mollie want to punch Paul McCartney. As she finally turned onto the main road that led away from the town, she accelerated hard desperate to get home.

"Lottie's a cry baby." The boys sang, as Billy now joined in, copying his brother.

"Simply having a wonderful Christmas time," the radio proclaimed even more joyfully.

"I wish I didn't have stupid brothers," Lottie screamed at them making the boys laugh and sing louder.

"Boys be quiet." Mollie shouted feeling she was losing her grip.

"Simply having…" the radio seemed louder and more joyful than ever.

"I hate boys…" Lottie was screaming at her brothers.

"Waa Waa…" The boys were now doing impressions of her crying which got louder as they delighted in winding up their sister.

"Wonderful Christmas time…." The radio mocked again.

At break point and without thinking Mollie pulled over to the side of the road slamming on her brakes hard. She turned off the radio unable to take any more, "That is it! Christmas is cancelled! There will be no presents, no Santa, no nothing." She glared at all three children.

"No Thomas train?" asked Billy starting to cry.

"It's not is it Mummy?" Josh asked in trepidation.

"We are sorry Mummy." Lottie offered.

Mollie looked at all three faces, their lips were trembling and the tears were ready to fall. Guilt hit her hard, "Christmas is not cancelled." She tried to smile reassuringly. What was wrong with her? With a sigh she went to pull away but realised a car had pulled up in front of her and the driver was getting out.

Praying it was not an angry driver and she was about to be embroiled in a road rage incident, Mollie wondered if her day could get any worse, but as the driver turned to her car, she recognised Rich.

"Are you ok?" He asked drawing level with the window.

"Fine, just a small fight over a toy Spiderman!" Mollie replied over brightly.

"Mummy's just cancelled Christmas." Lottie informed him sadly.

Rich bit back a smile.

"The kids were just arguing and I've had a bit of a nightmare day!" Mollie attempted to explain to someone with no kids how she could just have threatened to cancel Christmas.

Rich looked at her for a second. "Look there is a kids soft play and pub just round the corner, who fancies dinner out?"

The kids shouted their agreement, and before Mollie could refuse, Rich smiled, "my treat, you look like you need a break!"

As Rich placed a glass of wine in front of her, Mollie looked at him in trepidation. "You must think I'm an awful mother."

"Absolutely, I watch you ferrying the kids from parties to clubs, see the cakes Tom brings in that you have made with them and I think those poor poor kids what a terrible life!" Rich replied with irony.

"But then I threaten to cancel Christmas!" Mollie sighed, looking dejected.

"Yeah, wait till your dad gets home might have been a better option," Rich agreed. "It certainly worked for my mum."

"It's just that sometimes it feels endless; the bickering, the moaning, the ingratitude. And then other times, they are just amazing; funny, loving, sweet and I feel guilty for getting cross with them."

Rich looked down at his beer for a second, before meeting her eye, "Mollie, do you know what I think you need?"

Mollie laughed and rolled her eyes, "Let me guess? A bloody good shag?"

Holding up his hands Rich laughed, "You have no faith in me, and I think too much of Tom, although…." He raised an eyebrow at her.

Mollie mock glared at him.

"Only joking, but seriously I think you need something for you. Whenever I talk to you, it's always about the kids or Tom or the dog or the house, but never about you."

"Oh," Mollie was flummoxed. "Are you trying to say I've got boring?" She asked in consternation.

"No, you'll never be boring but I think you need to do something for yourself."

"But what? I'm not really a gym person, they hate it when you ask for cake instead of a smoothie after a work out!" She giggled. "And I tried working but it was a nightmare with childcare." She looked at Rich sadly. "It's a bit hopeless, but thanks for trying to help I do appreciate it."

"Sorry but you don't get off that easily. Did you ever meet Eleanor Burrett?"

Mollie thought for a second, "Oh you mean the nightmare interior designer that was after Daniel?"

"Yep, poor Dan!" Rich chuckled before looking serious. "Now Daniel is out of the picture, she is really messing Tom around with the designs for the new show flat and entrance hall. He needs some help. And let's face it, the last show house was not great either, as you well know."

Mollie smiled glad she wasn't the only one who thought the last show house had been a bit over the top and not the understated elegant look Tom and Daniel usually produced.

"I've seen your work in the past, and your house is amazing, we both know you would do a far better job."

Mollie's face fell, Rich was saying everything she wanted to hear, but it would not work. "Rich I've tried, Daniel was willing to give me a chance but Tom said no, he does not want me involved in the business."

"Since when is that going to stop you and if this was something you really wanted Tom wouldn't stand in your way, you know that!" Rich responded firmly before softening his tone. "Look come over tomorrow to the site, Tom won't be there and I'll show you the plans for the flat and then do a design thing…."

"Mood board," Mollie put in.

"Yeah, that's it and then if you don't fancy it no one need ever know."

Mollie thought about it, she couldn't deny that the thought of being involved was exciting, and something she had dreamed about for months, but it had been so long, it was one thing to decorate your own home, but this was Tom's business, could she really still do this?

"You know, you can do this Mollie." Rich said firmly reading her thoughts.

Chapter Twenty-Two

Rose stood next to Anna straight and tall as the choir made their way back down the aisle after the vicar, who was smiling at the parishioners and wishing them a Merry Christmas. Rose must be aware of the interest her presence at Midnight Mass was causing Anna thought as she calmly met the eye of another person openly staring. She smiled pointedly and the lady dropped her gaze first.

With the service over they turned to leave. Whilst not obviously hurrying they were the first out of the pew, heading towards the back of church where Rose would no doubt thank the vicar and then out of the door and home. Anna longed to be back in the safety of the kitchen, she had tried to persuade Rose not to come but she had been adamant it was time to face the village.

However as much as the locals liked to gossip about Rose, Anna had forgotten how terrified of her they all were and therefore no one made a comment. Craig Pennington caught up with them before they reached the vicar, who was nervously regarding Rose.

"Rose, how delightful to see you out and about." Craig smiled shaking Rose's hand and looking as though he meant every word he said.

"Thank you, Craig, well one cannot miss Midnight Mass." Rose nodded. "Have a lovely Christmas."

As she spoke the church warden's wife, bustled up with a tray full of mulled wine and mince pies. "Mr Pennington Smythe, you'll join us in a Christmas drink, I'm sure." She offered the tray towards him.

Craig hesitated, "Ladies first, Rose?"

Anna watched in desperation, as Craig ever the gentleman deferred to Rose, the church warden's wife went pale and then started to talk as though she would never stop, but Rose merely smiled graciously.

"Thank you this looks delightful, but we must be going. However please don't let me stop you Craig. Merry Christmas everyone."

She swept away and Anna hurried after her, smiling at the on lookers, muttering something about a lovely service to the vicar, before heading out the door after Rose. However, before she was completely out of the door, she felt a hand on her arm.

"Anna that is no greeting for an old friend."

She turned to find Andrew, who immediately leant forward and kissed her on the cheek. "You look fabulous, I'm so glad you are back."

Anna could only nod, desperate to catch up with Rose and as people built up in the porch behind Andrew, she realised yet again far too much attention was on her.

Smiling and wishing Andrew a Happy Christmas, she turned and ran to catch up with Rose, who was already in the Land rover, she had not even closed the door before it rattled into life.

"Well, that will give them something to talk about over Christmas lunch tomorrow," Rose muttered grimly as they headed home.

The children jumped excitedly around the room, as Mollie tried to put on hats, gloves and scarves. "Tom, please can you help?" She said with exasperation as Josh pulled off his hat and rugby tackled Daniel back onto a chair.

"Right, enough." Lara stood in the middle of the room and clapped her hands. Mollie watched in shock as all three kids stopped immediately. She didn't want to know what the glamorous New York socialite thought of her parenting skills, Lara must be wishing they had never come.

However, Lara turned to Daniel, "You need to sort Josh out, Lizzie," she turned to Lizzie who had just come bouncing through all wrapped up ready to go ice skating, "you've got Lottie," at this Lottie beamed as she adored her young aunt, "And Tom you have Billy. Right, I am taking Mollie out shopping and then for lunch we will meet you all back here later."

"Oh but…" Mollie interrupted she was so tempted but the thought of the children ice skating without her, Billy would probably get cold and what if Lottie or Josh fell and broke something.

"They will be fine Mollie. You need some time out."

"Go on Moll, you deserve a break, with the hours I've been working." Tom said.

"But just remember Billy is only little he'll get cold quickly."

"We'll be fine." Daniel replied, once more picking up that things might not be going quite as well at home as Tom was claiming.

As they left the apartment and Jefferson resting, Mollie paused.

"Mollie the kids will be fine." Lara rolled her eyes.

"Actually, I was going to say would you mind if we went to the Guggenheim, they have an exhibition of the Thannhauser collection. It has some of Degas and Picasso and Gaugin." Mollie paused, and laughed self depreciatingly, "sorry I just didn't think I would get a chance to go and…"

"Of course, we can," Lara smiled. "But on one condition, I am on the board of trustees so you need to give me some fantastically clever insights I can make at the meeting next week. Genevieve Borghese, who as you may have guessed comes from an Italian family influential in the art world, even if it was on her husband's side, always treats us all like philistines and I would love, just once, to put her in her place."

Mollie chuckled, "it's a deal."

As they made their way up the spiral walkway Mollie felt a bubble of excitement rise, she'd forgotten how much she loved art museums and being inspired. Maybe Rich was right, maybe she did need to find a way to indulge her passion for being creative from time to time. She still hadn't taken him up on the offer of doing some designs. She'd told herself there was not time before they had left for Christmas, but she knew she was scared. But at the back of her mind the idea of designing the flat simmered gently, ideas were starting to form and as much as she told herself she shouldn't, the desire to see if she could do it was getting stronger.

"Here we are." Lara commented, pausing as they reached the correct floor before following the signs.

"Is Jefferson into art?" Mollie asked.

Lara laughed kindly, "Goodness no, he likes a nice home but I could just as easily have a twenty-dollar picture from The Ranch on the wall as a masterpiece for all he'd care." She glanced at Mollie shrewdly. "I'm guessing it's not Tom's scene either then?"

"No, not really." Mollie admitted.

"And I'm also guessing that Tom has kept up with his hobbies throughout your marriage."

Mollie paused not wanting to be disloyal. "He still plays a bit of Rugby but work and kids get in the way." She did not mention Tom had signed up to coach Josh's team next season.

"I see." Lara commented, but rather than say anymore she turned to a painting by Picasso. "Explain to me what is so special about Picasso."

Glad of the change of subject Mollie paused wondering where to start. "That depends on your point of view, some, in fact many people think he is a genius, but others don't like his work at all."

"And you?" Lara asked.

"He's not one of my favourites but his work is clever, you see in this picture he uses a style known as cubism, which means he paints the same scene from different angles and then puts it all together in one picture. Look, here, the lady's nose is painted from the front and here from the side."

Lara nodded slowly, staring intently at the picture and a smile slowly spread across her face. "It's kind of like an early panoramic picture."
Mollie paused, "I've never thought about it like that before but yes I guess it is."

"You know until now I never got Picasso at all. And whilst I'm still not sure it's my sort of thing at least his pictures make sense now." She smiled at Mollie pleased.

They slowly made their way around the whole exhibition with Mollie becoming more animated as she talked and explained the different styles and the different artists. She was so busy answering Lara's questions that Lara was sure she had not realised a small group of people were somewhat indiscreetly listening in.

"Oh, that's it." Mollie seemed almost disappointed to reach the end.

"We've been here two and half hours." Lara pointed out, before laying a hand on Mollie's arm at her shocked face, "I have loved every minute of it as have the other people who have been listening in."

Mollie looked around confused, but the listeners had quickly dispersed apart from an elderly couple who thanked her.

Lara smiled as if to say I told you so.

"Lara I'm sorry, I hope I haven't bored you to death. I get a bit carried away sometimes. And I haven't even checked my phone." She fished in her bag and retrieved her phone to find a text from Tom and a picture of three happy kids with rosy red cheeks drinking hot chocolate.

"I take it they are fine?" Lara asked amused. When Mollie nodded looking relieved and slightly embarrassed that she had made a fuss earlier, Lara continued, "So as it seems that they can manage without you, perhaps you can escape a little more from time to time." At Mollie's look of horror, she raised a hand, "I don't mean abandon your kids but you need some time for you every once in a while, all mothers do." She paused. "Mollie I've loved this morning, listening to you, you clearly love your subject, you aren't pretentious or obnoxious and I get the impression you would like to have something for yourself. At least think about it."

Mollie bit her lip considering her words before she replied, but before she could her phone beeped. Tom was asking if they wanted to join them and the kids for burgers. She relayed the message to Lara.

"You know I hate burgers and I think Tom can manage for a little longer on his own. It'll be good practice for him when you are back in England!" She said with a wink. "Now there is a very nice Italian on the corner of the park where we could have lunch, my treat."

"That sounds lovely, but I'll get this." Mollie replied, thinking Italian sounded far better than a burger.

"After everything you have taught me this morning, I owe you big time. I cannot wait for next week's meeting."

The restaurant had tall ceilings from which beautiful glass chandeliers quietly shimmered. The rest was tastefully decorated in black and white and felt like a peaceful haven from the bustling streets outside.

After the waiter had brought their drinks, Mollie glanced around discreetly trying to work out what the lady on the table across from them was eating as it looked amazing.

"Tell me about Anna?" Lara said putting her menu down having chosen what she wanted.

"Anna?" Mollie asked surprised, bringing her attention back to Lara. "Well, she works for Rose, she's the one who got Rose…"

Lara rolled her eyes in slight irritation, "I know who she is, but what is she to Daniel?" She asked fixing Mollie with a stare that indicated she would not be fobbed off.

"Why, what has he said?" Mollie was intrigued.

"Nothing, he clams up and gets all moody and intense whenever any of you mention her and let's face it, as much as I adore him, and I really do, I know it's not us keeping him out here."

Mollie smiled and shook her head. "I honestly don't know what is going on with either of them. Tom has taken Daniel's side but I think there is more to it."

"Really? Tell me everything." Lara replied, so Mollie did.

The story lasted throughout lunch and during coffee.

Lara blew out a long breath, "Wow. I agree with you. But knowing how proud Daniel can be, he is unlikely to make the first move and nothing will get solved whilst he stays in New York. We need to get him back home."

Chapter Twenty-Three

Anna had ridden out that afternoon to distract herself from the fact that it was New Year's Eve. She deliberately quashed the self-pity that was whispering negative thoughts about her lack of social life at the moment. She had had invites to a couple of parties but knew someone needed to stay with Rose, even though an exasperated Jenny had told her she may as well just become a nun and have done with it.

She also quashed the thoughts about whether Daniel would come back with Tom and Mollie and if he did how she would feel.

Instead, she refocused her thoughts onto the fact tomorrow was a new year and she needed to start planning how to reopen the riding school, replacing all the lost equipment seemed to be the first task, but that required money.

Back at the yard, she was surprised to find Vicky, she worked at one of the other yards but Anna only knew her to say hello to.

As she put Alfred, the horse she had been riding back in his stable, Vicky chattered about local gossip. Anna could not help but notice that she seemed slightly on edge.

"Is everything ok?" Anna eventually asked when she paused for breath.

Vicky looked at her in consternation, "I need a massive favour."

"Ok." Anna replied, as various possibilities ran through her mind.

"I've got my cousins coming tonight for the New Year's Eve party at Callaghns. It's always amazing. I had booked a B&B but they cancelled this morning. Problem with the boiler. Personally, I reckon she got a better offer. The old bag." Vicky muttered angrily. "And the thing is I've already leant my room to someone else, and there is no way Louisa will sleep in a car or the horsebox for that matter, soooooooooooo" Anna's heart dropped as she realised what was coming. "Look is there any chance we could borrow your flat just for tonight, I'd owe you forever, pleeeeaaase Anna." By now she had hold of Anna's hand and was staring at her beseechingly.

"Vicky I'm really sorry but it got flooded, it's totally uninhabitable, I'm staying in the manor now." Anna said sadly.

"Oh," Vicky looked beaten, but then she perked up. "There must be spare rooms in the manor. That would be amazing!"

"I don't know." Anna couldn't begin to imagine what Rose would say.

"It's just one night and we'll pay you what we would have paid the other place." She mentioned a figure which Anna realised would be a start to replace some of the equipment they had lost.

Sensing she was tempted Vicky flung her arms around Anna, "Oh Anna you are the best we'll see you at four. And don't worry about breakfast, we won't need it."

Breakfast was the least of her worries Anna thought, watching Vicky bounce happily back to her car. She wondered how on earth Rose would take the news.

"You've done what?" Rose looked outraged.

"Look they will be here in a couple of hours and they can have my room and we need another two rooms as well. They are willing to pay and the money will help replace some of what we have lost." Anna was regretting her decision already, and for the hundredth time she wondered what had possessed her say yes.

"Well as long as it is only for one night." Rose sighed, still far from impressed. "We'd better see what we can do." She strode out of the room. "Well come along there are other rooms. You've got the best one, but a couple of the others may be suitable, without you needing to sleep on the settee!"

Anna ran after her. Reaching the landing Rose paused and glanced at Anna before opening the bedroom door. Anna gasped as she walked into the room. It was just as beautiful as her room. The walls were papered with a subtle pink flowered pattern, the curtains were made from a heavy cream brocade and matched the bed spread. All the bedroom furniture was in matching dark wood, and sat on the deep rose-coloured carpet.

Rose was watching Anna's face in amusement, as Anna slowly walked around the room, running her hand over the dressing table. "Rose it's just beautiful, who decorated the house?"

Rose's voice was full of pride. "I told you they would be suitable! My mother loved decorating, she always believed in timeless pieces as they do not date. The furniture is all French antiques and the wall paper is silk."

Anna was impressed by the room, but also delighted that apart from cleaning, the room was ready to be used. The next three rooms were equally fantastic, and all had their own colour themes, pale blue, lemon and burgundy. "Rose this house really is gorgeous."

For the next two hours Anna polished furniture, changed bed sheets and cleaned. It was not perfect but the rooms looked presentable.

"You'd better put these out," Rose walked in with a couple of toiletry gift sets. "You'd be amazed how many of these I get for Christmas," she said before Anna could thank her.

The doorbell rang and Rose turned to her, "I'll leave you to handle this I'm off to do the horses."

Vicky and her cousins were enchanted with their rooms. "You should turn this place into a bed and breakfast." Vicky said, to which Anna could only smile, thinking it would be over Rose's dead body.

"Why don't you come tonight, you'll have a great time?" Vicky asked as they headed back down the staircase, leaving the others to get ready. Anna needed to help with the stables and Vicky had left her straighteners in the car.

"Yes, why don't you?" Rose was stood at the bottom of the staircase.

"Um, I'll let you know." Anna told Vicky as she headed off to her car.

"You should go out. It can't be much fun babysitting me every night." Rose told her as they headed back into the kitchen.

"Honestly I'm not bothered." Anna said slipping her foot into a wellie, ready to go and do the stables.

"Anna, look you cannot watch me twenty-four hours a day, otherwise we will both end up alcoholics! And to be honest sitting here feeling guilty that I am ruining your life is not doing me any favours so please go out."

Daniel picked up the beers from the bar and returned to the table where Tom and Jefferson sat. Placing them down he looked for the right words to start the conversation he needed to have with Tom. However, he decided to keep it light to start with. "So how is mum?"

Tom paused for a second and then continued. "She genuinely seems better. She is going to meetings regularly and she has been sober for eight weeks now."

"How did she do it?" Daniel deliberately avoided mentioning Anna's name so Tom did not either.

"I don't know, she told Mollie she had promised Rose she would not say."

"I guess we should be pleased."

Tom merely rolled his eyes and sipped his beer.

"So how is Broome Hill coming on?"

"Good." Tom nodded. "Yes, all good. We're on target."

"Rich ok?"

"Yep, same as ever."

Daniel was getting frustrated, comments that had been made by all of them, but especially the kids, about Tom never being at home worried him. But Tom clearly was not going to tell him what was really happening. He glanced at Jefferson but he merely raised his eyebrows.

"I'm thinking about coming home." Daniel said instead. Was that relief on Tom's face or was he just being hopeful?

"We'll all be pleased to have you back, especially Mum."

"I hope so." Daniel replied wondering if everyone would be pleased to see him.

"I that deserves another drink." Tom said rising to go to the bar.

They watched him walk away before Jefferson turned to him. "You are right he is struggling."

"Which is why I need to go back," Daniel replied.

Jefferson hesitated.

When he did not speak Daniel prompted him, "You don't think I should?"

Jefferson seemed to consider his words very carefully. "Over the years whenever I have spoken to Tom, I have noticed that if he had a problem you solve it."

"So, you are saying I was wrong to look out for him," Daniel responded in annoyance.

"No Daniel, Tom has been very lucky to have you, especially as I wasn't there. But I think just sometimes it would help him to stand on his own two feet and make his own decisions. You are so capable it is easy for him to leave it to you."

"He does make his own decisions; he is very clear that Mollie should not be involved in the business. I think she should but I've let him take the lead on that one."

Jefferson nodded in defeat. "It was just an observation."

They fell into silence as Tom returned from the bar but Daniel could not help but wonder if there was any truth in what Jefferson had just said.

Anna walked into the party feeling excited. It was just so good to be out again. She could see why Vicky had been so panicked about not having a room. Her cousins were definitely were not the type to slum it for a night. But they were fun and generous and at least they did not keep asking about Rose like a lot of other people around the room. Having just extracted herself from another conversation, with a local whose thirst for gossip was not quite masked by the concern they pretended to have, Anna bumped into Andrew.

"Anna, you look stunning," he exclaimed leaning forward and kissing her on the cheek. "Vicky mentioned she was trying to get you to come tonight, I'm glad she convinced you."

For a second, she found herself smiling into Andrew's eyes, but a flash of light to her left made her turn. She could not see anything that would make a flash but as she turned back to Andrew, she caught Jane's eye, who winked at her.

"Well, well, well this all looks very cosy," Anna turned to find Paris watching her. "What a surprise to see you back Anna!"

"Is it, Paris?" Anna struggled to hold her temper, "It turns out Rose needs help reopening the school. Apparently, Sarah decided not to sue." Anna glared at Paris.

Paris glared back before a cruel smile played around her lips, "Apparently not, Daniel managed to sweet talk her before he and Belle headed off to New York together." And with that she turned and walked away.

"Come on you look like you need a drink," Andrew commented bringing her back to the present.

By two in the morning, despite having had a brilliant night, Anna was exhausted and was relieved when the others decided to call it a night. They headed home and sat in the kitchen eating toast and laughing about the evening. Anna had smiled all evening but now she just wanted to go to bed. The news about Daniel being in New York with Belle had hurt more than she wanted to admit. She groaned as she looked at the clock, it was now three o'clock, and she needed to be up in a few hours to help Rose with the stables. A while later still unable to sleep, she heard Vicky and her cousins, crashing and giggling up the stairs. Her heart sank even further Rose was going to be furious.

It felt like only seconds before the alarm was blaring, struggling out of bed, with her head screaming in protest, Anna threw on some old clothes and headed down to the kitchen.

A coffee sat waiting on the side for her, which she gratefully drank, guessing Rose was already on the yard she slid on her wellies and a warm coat and scarf and armed with her coffee, she hurried outside.

Rose was briskly mucking out, having already done the breakfast feeds when Anna put her head over the door.

"Thanks for the coffee," she said gratefully. Rose merely nodded not breaking her stride. Feeling somewhat chastised Anna collected a wheelbarrow and began to muck out as well. By mid-morning the yard was finished but Anna felt awful. As she had worked, she acknowledged how insensitive she had been filling the house with people drinking when Rose could not, combined with the lack of sleep and the inevitable hangover, she longed to crawl back to bed.

As she swept the yard, Vicky appeared. "We're off now but thank you for saving me last night."

"It was nothing," Anna replied, hanging the broom back in its normal place. "And I had fun, it was good to get out."

"Good." Vicki glanced around the yard, "Wow, this place is looking better. Do you plan to reopen soon?"

"Hopefully!" Anna sighed, although that would depend on whether she had just set Rose back. She walked back to the house with Vicki and waved to her cousins as they headed off somewhere for breakfast. Bracing herself she walked back into the kitchen.

"Rose, I'm so sorry," she started.

Rose turned. "Whatever for?"

"Well last night, the noise, having a load of people drinking in the house. I didn't think."

Rose smiled sadly. "Oh Anna, don't be ridiculous. I'm a recovering alcoholic not a nun. And I do vaguely remember what it is like to be young" She said with a heavy dose of irony. "Vicky's cousin just said this would make a fantastic B&B and I've been thinking we need some income to get the place back up and running, so perhaps we should open as a B&B for a while," she added watching Anna carefully for her reaction.

"Really, I'm not sure, well it would be a lot of stress and…" Anna tried to buy herself some time.

"It's not like you to admit defeat," Rose observed wryly.

"I know Rose but…." Anna wondered how to tell Rose she should not take on anything new whilst she recovered.

"I know what you are thinking, but you see, while I was lay in bed last night, listening to you all come staggering up to bed I finally understood what has been bothering me. This house is meant to be filled with laughter and happiness. After Tom and Daniel left it became a mausoleum, and as the house shut down so did I. I'd forgotten what a beautiful house it is, well was. It needs to be enjoyed. It needs to be brought back to life, a bit like me! So, what do you say?"

Anna looked at Rose who met her gaze unflinchingly, "Ok let's do it."

Having slept in late, Mollie was enjoying a coffee with Lara, glad they had let the kids stay up for Midnight. They were sleepily watching a film and she did not need to go anywhere. The phone next to her buzzed and Daniel asked her to pass it over to him. She could not help glance at the screen as she picked it up.

Her heart sank as a picture of Anna smiling up at Andrew was staring back at her, under which Paris had written, 'Happy New Year'.

As Daniel looked at the phone, she saw his face harden as he took in the picture.

Mollie sighed, wondering what to say to Daniel.

"She's obviously keeping a close eye on Mum." He muttered.

"That's not fair Daniel and you know it."

Daniel looked like he was about to say more but instead he flew across the room, catching Jefferson who had tripped on one of kid's toys and was about to hit the ground.

Lara was right behind him, helping Daniel get Jefferson back on his feet and into a chair. Realising it was Billy's toy that had done the damage, Molly began to apologise profusely, but Lara simply shook her head.

"It was an accident, Mollie. Tom, can you get some water. Lizzie," she called.

As Lizzie came into the room, the colour drained out of her face as she took in the scene, Jefferson's breathing was shallow and his head was bent over.

"Lizzie," Lara's voice was firm, "He's alright but can you phone the doctor so we can get him checked over?"

Lizzie nodded and rushed out of the room as Tom returned with the water.

Jefferson raised his head, attempting to smile. "I'm fine, please stop worrying."

Mollie heard Lottie give a muffled sob and turned to find all three kids looking white faced and frightened. "Come on let's go and play in the other room." She held out a hand to Billy who ran over and clung onto her leg.

"Kids, come here." Jefferson called them over. "Look I'm fine but like you three, late nights don't agree with me, and you know what the adults are like for worrying!" He rolled his eyes theatrically making Josh and Lottie laugh, although somewhat nervously.

"Right so what film are we watching?" he asked. "I'm probably going to be told off by the doctor and Lara won't let me leave this chair for a while, so you three are in charge of entertainment."

As the children excitedly chose a movie, the adults started to sit back down but the relaxed atmosphere had dissolved.

Later as Jefferson rested, the doctor having given him the all clear, and the kids started another film, Daniel turned to Tom, "I think I should stay out here a bit longer. Jefferson needs more help."

The look of shock on Tom's face was temporary. "Of course, you should, we'll be fine."

Mollie's heart sank as her eyes met Lara's. Lara raised her eyebrows in acknowledgement, it looked like Daniel would not be coming home for a while yet.

Chapter Twenty-Four

Anna wrote the latest reservation in the diary. She still could not believe that in the few weeks since they had opened, they were now fully booked. The demand and the speed at which it had happened had taken her by surprise, and she knew Mollie's help had been invaluable.

Mollie had returned from New York and embraced the idea, finding a website designer, making a couple of tweaks to the rooms, helping Anna turn the dining room into a breakfast room for the guests. She initially felt guilty at the amount of time Mollie had given them but Mollie assured her she had loved every minute.

"Another booking?" Rose asked coming through the door back from another meeting.

Anna nodded, "Yes we are fully booked now for the next few weeks."

"I'll call the saddler this afternoon, there is no reason now not to replace all the saddle's and bridles and get this place properly back on its feet. Also, I called into Hodgett's on the way home and he is going to come and sort out the hedges on the drive, and I've asked Tom to send someone round to discuss sorting out those potholes."

"Sounds good," Anna agreed, as more than one guest had moaned about the drive.

"You know I'm enjoying being back in control and it so lovely seeing the place come back to life." Rose admitted. "Daniel and Tom were always offering to sort things out but then they would forget and I suppose it started to make me feel helpless.

Anna looked at her in surprise, Rose was the last person she would ever describe as helpless. But on reflection, Rose had a point, although she had regained the authority that had terrified Anna to start with, she was softer and lesser abrupt. Anna had to wonder if some of the abruptness had stemmed from anxiety.

While she was in such a good mood, Anna broached something that had been on her mind, the hall was beautiful but they needed a more official welcome area. "Rose I was thinking we could really do with a reception area or an office for the B&B."

Rose glanced at the locked door off the hall. "Perhaps it is time." The words were so soft Anna was not sure she had heard correctly, but Rose had already turned away.

Anna raced up the driveway glad the potholes had finally been filled. Along with the perfect hedges the place was barely recognisable, but she did not notice that as she pulled onto the drive, before groaning that Mollie was already there. It was hardly surprising since she was late. Anna had been frustrated by Rose demanding she went out to pick up more horse feed first thing that morning. But more than that she was worried, Rose had been behaving very strangely.

Mollie smiled as she got out of her car. "We did say ten, didn't we?" Mollie asked taking in Anna's flustered appearance.

"Yes, we did. Sorry Rose was being all weird, and insisted I went out for feed." Anna told her.

Mollie's smile vanished. "Oh."

Anna sighed, "I know, I had the same thought."

Together they walked into the kitchen, but a noise from the hallway made Anna's heart sink.

"There should not be any guests until later," Anna said as calmly as she could to Mollie, as they headed straight towards the hallway. Rose, who was just closing the front door, turned guiltily to them.

"Rose, what's going on?" Anna asked, trying to remain calm.

But before she could answer there was a knock on the door. Rose reluctantly opened it.

"Sorry love, almost left my keys." The man picked up the keys, smiled at Anna and Mollie and disappeared back through the front door Rose was holding open.

Turning to Rose, they waited for response. Rose huffed, "Oh stop being so dramatic you two! Look there is nothing to see, I just lost the key for the study and so I got a locksmith to come and sort it out."

Turning they realised the door now stood open. Inside they could see the place was covered in dust. Rose looked embarrassed. "Right, I had better get on, it needs a clean."

"But no one has been in here for years," Mollie said walking into the room. "Why now Rose? You'd never let Billy in here and yet you never normally say no to him?"

Rose sighed and clasped her hands together and stared at them, before speaking quickly and dismissively. "It's all a bit embarrassing. Jefferson had some trophy in here that he loved, and I was a bit cross when he left so I...., well I....," she paused and looked up. "I threw the key on the muck heap. And then when I calmed down it was too late to retrieve it."

Relief washed through Anna but she did not dare look at Mollie as she tried to suppress the giggles that rose up inside her.

"So why did you not just say that?" Mollie asked, also trying to remain serious.

"It was such an undignified thing to do and then Daniel and Tom got it into their heads it was out of respect or grief for their father so I could not say anything. And we were talking about forgiveness yesterday at my meeting made me realise it's time to get that trophy back to Jefferson."

Mollie looked at Rose standing proudly trying to mask her embarrassment and smiled fondly. "I do love you Rose," she remarked.

Unable to hold it back any longer, Anna giggled, Rose rolled her eyes at her. "Well, I am glad I have amused you two. Now, we had better get this place cleaned up," she added firmly, although a smile hovered around her lips.

Jefferson looked at the parcel in surprise, he recognised the handwriting but could not think why Rose would be sending him anything. They had not spoken in years. "Would you mind?" he asked Daniel. The package was too well wrapped for him to open, as his hand was not yet back to full strength.

Nodding Daniel made short work of the tape to reveal a box. He removed the lid and took out a trophy. Hearing Jefferson gasp he looked up. "My dad's trophy!" Jefferson said struggling to control his emotion, "you know I never thought I would see this again."

Daniel handed it over along with the folded piece of paper. The note was simple, wishing him a quick recovery and acknowledging the trophy should have been returned years earlier.

Jefferson turned the trophy over fondly in his hands. "I wonder why she has finally returned it now?" He asked out loud half to Daniel, and half to himself.

"Tom called me yesterday, it appears that she threw the key onto the muck heap when you said you were leaving and then Mum being Mum, she was too proud to admit it." Daniel told him.

He was still struggling to understand it himself. This meant that Rose was no longer some heartbroken woman left fending for herself and her kids, whilst keeping her ex-husband's office as a shrine to him, but someone who had moved on and forgiven Jefferson. It also meant her drinking had not been Jefferson's fault, in which case whose fault was it Daniel wondered, not wanting to consider the answer to closely.

"It's good to have it back." Jefferson replied trying to gauge Daniel's mood. It was just the two of them in the apartment as Lara and Lizzie were both out. "My Dad won it out in America horse racing, and then he came over to Britain to become a trainer and met my mother and stayed."

Daniel smiled sadly he remembered the story although he hadn't heard or thought about it for years.

"You know leaving your mother was one of the hardest things I ever did." Jefferson said tentatively, until now they had never discussed the past.

Daniel stared hard at his father, not sure he wanted to have this conversation. His mother could be difficult to help, he knew that more than most, but it still did not excuse his behaviour.

"Well, it seemed to work out for you." Daniel was shocked at how bitter he sounded.

Jefferson looked down at his hands for a long time, before looking up at Daniel squarely. "Yes, it did. I struggled being married to Rose. It will sound pathetic but she was so capable I felt surplus to requirements. She ran the yard, looked after you two and I was just hovering around in the background, unnoticed.

When Daniel said nothing, Jefferson carried on. "I'm not proud of what I did but when Lara turned up, suddenly someone saw me again. I was no longer someone who got under Rose's feet, or who got an eye roll, because I had done something wrong with a child or a horse, and for once I was someone who somebody actually wanted to be with. Not just the person they fell asleep on at the end of the day, after everyone else had had their time, love and energy."

"You know she cried for weeks after you had gone." Daniel finally spoke.

"Really?" Jefferson was visibly shocked. "I never knew."

They were quiet for a while, before Jefferson spoke again. "I do regret not making more effort though to see both you and Tom."

"Mum can be quite determined when she wants to be." Daniel admitted knowing Rose would never have allowed it. She allowed a phone call once a week, but any mention of a visit was firmly shut down, especially as Jefferson was half way round the world.

"I still should have tried harder, I still remember you standing next to her as I left, telling me that I would never be your father again. For a five-year-old you were quite determined." He said sadly. "You are very like her, strong, dependable and capable. When you said you did not need me, I quite believed you."

Daniel remembered that too, and that feeling had stayed with him for the next thirty years. Luckily, they were interrupted by Lara's return, as Daniel did not know what to say to his father's last admission, he had been convinced that Jefferson would have forgotten his angry outburst or if he had remembered then he would not have cared.

Mollie sighed as she heard the front door. She glanced at the clock; it was gone ten.

Tom walked in and slumped down in the chair and let out a long sigh. "I've had a rubbish day," he said, leaning back and closing and his eyes.

Mollie looked at him in frustration, she already knew, Rich had let her know Eleanor Burrett had insisted he drove down to her office in London.

"How awful for you!" The sarcasm in her voice was unmistakable.

Tom opened his eyes and stared at her in surprise. "Oh, I'm sorry! I thought my own wife might care!" His sarcasm matched hers, tiredness making his patience disappear.

Months of anger and frustration were rising now, and as hard as she tried, Mollie could not suppress them. "Don't act the victim. Not when you won't let me help with the business. Not when you would rather run all over the country chasing that stupid woman, than let your own wife help."

"Oh, not this again." Tom's dismissive words fuelled her anger further.

"Yes Tom, it is this again, except this time we are going to properly discuss it." Mollie had not planned to do this tonight but it was too late to pull back now.

"It's a no Mollie. It's bad enough that I'm tired out with all this. It would be no good for the kids if you were in the same state too. And anyway, we agreed, my childhood was terrible, Daniel was the parent, Dad was not around and Mum was always with the horses. My children are not being raised the same way."

"We agreed?" Mollie choked over the words. "We agreed I would not work when the kids were small but you seem to have taken the decision on yourself about what happens now."

Tom stood up wearily, "Mollie today's been hell and tomorrow looks worse. I need to go to bed, we'll discuss this at the weekend."

"Yet another decision you are making then." Mollie muttered to herself as Tom left the room.

She sat rigid with anger as she heard him clean his teeth, and then ten minutes later as the gentle rumble of his snoring drifted down the stairs, she got angrier still. She was not sure what she was going to do yet, but she was fed up with Tom taking her for granted.

Chapter Twenty-Five

Anna ended the call and looked at the list in front of her. So far, she had phoned over thirty customers to say the riding school was reopening and lessons were going to resume the following week. The response had been mixed but so far no one had actually booked a lesson.

She debated whether to give up for now and try the others later. And whilst she had not anticipated this being easy, she had hoped that there would have been a couple of people wanting to come back. Surely the success of the bed and breakfast had proved to people they were back on their feet.

"Any joy?" Rose asked, hope etched across her face.

Anna paused, not wanting to tell her that it did not look good. "People seem pleased we are able to offer lessons again, they are just checking diaries before they confirm."

"Right jolly good." Rose smiled, trying to sound hearty and confident, but not quite managing it.

As Rose disappeared again, Anna picked the phone back up. She would not stop until she either had a firm booking or had phoned every last client.

The next person on the list was Jemima Pennington Smythe. Anna groaned, she would be the last to return, if at all. She was tempted not to bother for a moment, but with a sigh she dialled the number. The phone rang out for a while, Anna was about to give up when Craig Pennington abruptly answered. Anna's heart sank further.

"Hello," she gabbled, "It is Anna from Rose's, I was just wondering if Mrs Pennington Smythe was there. We are reopening the riding school and are phoning all our old clients to see if they would like to start lessons again."

When the line remained quiet, Anna spoke again. "Look I'm sorry for bothering you, if you could just let your wife know, I'd be very grateful."

Craig cleared his throat. "There is no need to speak to my wife, Jemima keeps saying she is missing her riding, so yes she would love to come back."

Anna took a second to recover herself, "We are starting next Sunday, it will still be at eleven if that suits you?"

Craig confirmed it did and Anna ended the call. She did not have much luck with the rest of list but they had one and that was a start.

Diana Pennington Smythe walked into her house in a happy mood, having spent most of the day at her private spa. Remembering she still had not phoned the agency to replace the housekeeper she decided they would eat out that night.

As she dropped her handbag on the hall table, Craig came out of his study.

"Good day Darling?" she asked heading into the lounge for a drink.

"Not really, I've spent most of the day taking calls for you."

"Anything interesting?" She ignored the irritation in his voice.

"Only one interesting one, the nice girl from Rose's called so say they are reopening the stables." Craig said watching his wife.

She laughed a harsh unkind laugh, making Craig grit his teeth. "I hope you wished them luck, as no one in their right mind will go back after what happened."

"On the contrary, I booked Jemima back in for next Sunday."

"You did what?" Diana's good mood was rapidly evaporating, as she turned to her husband.

"You heard me." Craig replied.

"Well then you will have to phone back and say you made a mistake." She said in icy tones.

"No, this is non-negotiable."

Diana was shocked, Craig never said no to her.

She forced a smile, "Come on Darling, Jemima is far too precious to be left in the care of a drunk." She affected a concerned look.

Craig watched her, questioning why he had not seen through her games years ago. His face hardened, as he spoke, "It never bothered you before, I know you never stayed to watch Jemima ride." He watched his wife's face harden. "Now Rose and Anna are trying exceptionally hard to start the stables up again. And you do not need me to remind you the part we played in its downfall. We owe them our support."

"I hardly think we had anything to do with that." Diana replied in contempt.

"Belle told me everything, but even before that Jemima had let a few things slip too and of course you were always repeating his Lady Godiva joke." Craig told her in disgust.

Diana pouted, not the pretty pout that had originally won Craig over, but a spoilt annoyed one.

"Diana I am warning you, if I hear so much as a whisper that you have not gone out and told all your little cronies to sign their children back up, then I will be talking to my lawyer." The tone of Craig's voice left a shocked Diana in no doubt that this was not an idle threat.

The New York skyline looked ominously dark as they stepped out of the apartment block, Daniel debated whether it was sensible to continue with the short walk he and Jefferson were about to take. The wind felt icy, even though it was March and although

Jefferson was properly wrapped up, he still felt that it was not wise to stay out too long.

They walked slowly across the road into the Strawberry Fields tribute to John Lennon, on the edge of the park. It was slowly coming back to life as small buds appeared on the bare branches of the trees and shoots tentatively started to appear in the empty flower beds.

Tourists milled around, some absorbing the atmosphere, whilst others took photos. "I often used to come here first thing, if I needed to think things through." Jefferson said as they walked.

Daniel could understand why, the place had a tranquillity that enabled you to relax and work through your problems.

"They often have these cards and plaques for sale with John Lennon's famous quote, something about him telling a teacher he wanted to be happy when he grew up."

Daniel smiled but said nothing.

"It sounds so easy doesn't it?" Jefferson continued. "And yet for a long time those words mocked me."

"You weren't happy?" Daniel asked looking at Jefferson.

He shook his head, "That was the problem, I was happy, very happy, but I did not feel I deserved to be, after walking out on you all. I still wished and wanted to play a much bigger role in both yours and Tom's lives."

Daniel nodded slowly not sure what Jefferson was trying to tell him.

"I'm not telling you this to try and make you feel sorry for me. I'm telling you because I don't think you are happy and for some reason, you seem reluctant to reach out for it. Instead, you constantly look out for everyone else. I just wish there was someone special looking out for you."

"There is no one at the moment and looking out for your family is what you do." Daniel was slightly defensive, so Jefferson said no more as they walked slowly on. "Not everyone can have what Tom and Mollie have."

Jefferson said nothing.

"And you are hardly in a position to lecture me about relationships."

Jefferson paused, "No you are right I am not. I took the easy decision and left my wife."

"Exactly!" Daniel returned. The old anger resurfacing quickly.

Jefferson paused and sat down on a bench and started to speak quietly. "It wasn't easy at all actually, the guilt at leaving you and Tom constantly made me question what I was doing. I knew I loved Lara, but after one failed marriage I was not sure I could make it work. I was a divorcee, following a young woman nearly ten years my junior back to New York. You can imagine what her parents thought. They had pinned all their hopes on her marrying a Harvard graduate, and I certainly did not fit that bill."

Daniel sat down too. "So how did you win them over?"

"I didn't for a long time, in fact they cut her off for a while, it was not until Lizzie came along that they reconciled. As a parent now, I completely understand why they tried to stop her seeing me. You see I was living in Brooklyn, which was very different in those days and trying to start up my business developing houses. One night I was camped out at the house I was renovating, to make sure the tools and materials were not stolen and there was a knock at the door. Lara was stood there with an overnight bag and two hotdogs, that was the moment that I realised this was it, she was the one."

An image of Anna stood at the office door with a Chinese flashed through Daniel's mind, but he quickly quashed it, Lara had given up her parents for

Jefferson, it was hardly the same as getting a takeaway. Anyway, Anna had proved she was not the one, despite what he may have thought.

"Come on, we had better head back, before Lara sends out a search party." Jefferson said jovially, but as they headed back Daniel noticed his pace had slowed even more and his breathing was laboured. He would be out here for a while longer, he decided.

The following morning the phone kept ringing, as Rose booked another child back in, she looked up at Anna. "Good old Craig, I should have known he would have helped us," she said happily.

Anna nodded pleased, he obviously must think a lot of Rose she told herself, they now had a third of their clients booked back in. It was a much better start than she had hoped for, she thought going to clean the bedrooms ready for the guests that night.

She had just finished when Mollie called in with the children. Leaving them all having tea with Rose, Anna frequently came and went as she checked people in, before getting ready to do the evening stables.

"I hope you don't mind me saying but you both look exhausted," Mollie said as she packed up the kids and prepared to leave.

"Cleaning the bedrooms takes more work than we anticipated, especially when there is such a quick turnaround. And with horses and customers to feed…"

"Then get a cleaner in, you can certainly afford it and you'll need some help now the lessons are restarting."

"It makes sense." Rose relied looking at Anna.

"By the way I'm not going to be around this weekend." Mollie said as she zipped up Billy's coat.

Anna looked at her in surprise.

"Just going down to see my parents." Mollie replied vaguely, although Anna was not entirely sure she believed her.

"I think she's right." Rose said after they had left. "About getting some help?" Rose prompted when Anna did not respond.

"Yes." Anna replied, putting the uneasy feelings she had about Mollie to one side. "Me too, but where are we going to find a cleaner?"

"How about an advert in the local shop?"

Agreeing that was the easiest course of action, Anna wrote out the advert. The shop did not shut for another half an hour, so she took it straight there.

As she entered the bell tinkled, but the two women at the counter did not look up.

"I'm sorry Sarah, but I cannot put this on credit again. Look if you can pay for these items you can have them and settle the bill later."

She watched as Sarah counted out the change in her purse. "Thanks for this. As soon as I get another job, I'll settle the account."

"I know you will," the assistant said kindly. "Any luck with finding anything?"

"No, and I'm willing to do anything. I still cannot believe I got fired for taking a few days off when Freddie was injured."

"I know it's disgusting. I don't know how that Mr Allan has the nerve to show his face in this village."

Anna, who up until this point had not paid much attention, looked up sharply at the mention of Freddie's name. Sarah must be his mother, and looking at her Anna could see the family resemblance, they had the same eyes.

Sarah had now said good bye to the lady behind the counter and was walking towards Anna. Noticing how tired she looked Anna felt guilty at her part in it.

Without thinking it through she stopped her. "Sarah, umm I'm Anna I work with Rose. I'm afraid it was me who was taking the lesson when Freddie fell off. I'm so sorry about what happened."

The woman looked at her, the weariness was replaced with anger as her words sunk in. "Not as sorry as I am, believe me!"

Taken aback but not surprised Anna followed her as she stormed out of the shop. "Look perhaps I can help. I was just about to put up a job advert in the shop but if you'd like first refusal, then the job is yours."

Sarah paused and glared at her. "I don't do horses and I certainly don't want to work with them. So, take your little charity case job somewhere else!" She snapped turning to go.

Anna was getting annoyed it was impossible to help some people.

"It isn't working with horses. We've set up a bed and breakfast and need someone to manage the bookings, clean the rooms and do the laundry. You need a job and we need some help, but as you are not interested then I'll stop bothering you."

Sarah paused, "Wait." She looked at Anna uncertainly. "Can you give me some time to think about it?"

Anna nodded hoping she would not need too much time.

"Thanks, I've heard about B&B, everyone's saying how well it's doing" Sarah admitted, although she did not add that it had generated a huge amount of gossip in the village, and even more so when people realised Anna and Rose were actually making a success of it. "If I do take it though, I can only work during school hours, I don't want Freddie around the stables."

"But he is such a good rider. It was a freak accident. I can't say he will never get hurt again, but

294

it seems a shame to stop him when he loves it so much."

"You don't understand do you, he lied. Just like his father always did about money. I can't let him turn out like his father." Sarah's anger had returned in full force, the job seemed out of the question as she turned to go.

"Sarah," Anna called, she stopped but did not turn around. "At least think about the job."

Anna thought she said something but did not catch it. The advert was still in her hand, she put it back in her pocket deciding to give Sarah a couple of days.

Heading back to her car, she heard her own name called. Turning she saw Andrew walking over to her.

"I see you have finally escaped. I was beginning to think I was going to have to come and rescue you."

"You make it sound like I was being held against my will." Anna replied with a roll of her eyes.

"Well Rose is a bit of an old dragon." Andrew said with a wink.

Anna gave him a pointed look.

"How about dinner on Friday night?" Seeing Anna hesitate he carried on. "Just friends, I'll be on my best behaviour."

"Thanks, but we're really busy at the moment, with the B&B."

"Come on its Friday?" Andrew cajoled.

Anna hesitated.

Andrew raised his eyebrows.

"Ok, why not?" Anna replied thinking she had not been out for weeks.

Tom arrived home much earlier than usual from work. The guilt he had been carrying around since he and Mollie had argued was eating away at him, and he wanted to apologise. He was stressed out with the designs for the flat and knew he needed to do something; he just did not know what. He was so tempted to phone Daniel but he could not bring himself to admit he had failed. But first before any of that, he needed to apologise to Mollie.

Glancing at the house in confusion, he realised there were not any lights on. Surely, they were not out at this time of night. Billy should be in bed by now he thought, opening the front door.

Inside the house it was silent. The warm welcoming kitchen where dinner would normally be waiting was cold and dark. Tom walked from room to room, trying to work out where they were. Starting to get annoyed he dialled Mollie's mobile, but it just rang out. Panic started to set in, as the fear that they had been in an accident crossed his mind.

Finally reaching his bedroom, he walked in and noticed an envelope on the pillow. He tore it open and as he digested the contents he sank down heavily on the bed. He phoned Mollie again, but again it rang out. He sent three texts and waited but there was no response.

He sat where he was for a long time, before realising Mollie was not going to respond. Although no longer hungry, he made his way down to the kitchen for something to do. There was no meal ready or beer in the fridge. His appetite had completely disappeared but the thought of sitting alone in the house seemed just too depressing so he picked up his car keys.

Arriving at the local pub he hoped to find Rich propping up the bar, before remembering Rich had been whistling all day as he had a big weekend planned, for a second a horrible thought seized him but he dismissed it quickly.

He paused in the doorway wondering if this was actually a good idea, when a movement caught his eye. It was Craig Pennington offering to buy him a drink. Grateful for some company he nodded.

"What'll you have?" Craig asked as he reached the bar.

"Pint of the usual, thanks." He said to the barman.

"I don't often see you in here on a Friday night." Craig commented as they moved over to a table.

"Mollie is not around this weekend." Tom commented.

"So, you have been left to fend for yourself too?" Craig replied. "Diana is out with friends and Jemima is at a sleepover and as we've just lost another housekeeper, I figured this was my best chance of a decent meal."

Tom smiled sadly. "My thoughts as well."

They talked about inconsequential things as they ate, and Tom was glad he did not have to explain himself. As the waitress was clearing away their table, Craig saw Tom's face fall. Turning he saw Anna had just entered the pub with Andrew.

"Not just me that can't stand the sight of him then?" Craig said with a poor attempt at humour.

But to his surprise, Tom did not smile. "Oh, we all know what Andrew is like, it is Anna I've got to thank for my wife's disappearing act."

"Anna? But I thought she had helped Rose get back on her feet."

Tom laughed bitterly, "Oh she has. The only problem is it cost us Daniel."

"Ahhh that." Craig looked at him. "I really am so sorry."

"Don't worry it's hardly your fault." Tom said.

"What has she done to Mollie?" Craig asked moving the subject swiftly on.

"It's a long story." Tom said shaking his head.

"I have nothing else planned tonight. If I can help I will." Craig answered.

Tom looked at him, fed up of carrying the burden of the business alone, he began to talk. "So, you see, we have to start decorating soon, but there are no designs, if Daniel was here, it would have been sorted out by now and Mollie and I would not have argued." He concluded despondently.

To his surprise Craig laughed. "Blimey Tom that's a first."

Irritated that Craig found it funny, Tom sighed and picked up his car keys, "Thanks for dinner," he said starting to rise from his chair.

Craig held up a hand, "Sorry I did not mean to laugh but do you not realise how lucky you are?"

Tom sat back down looking at Craig incredulously, wondering how much he had drunk. Craig paused, "Tom I mix with men every day, whose wives only care about their work in as much as it provides them with the lifestyle they enjoy. You have a wife who not only loves you but also wants to help you with your business."

Tom sighed, "Yes but last time she worked it was a nightmare with the kids. She was burning out running up and down to London, and trying to be a full-time mum."

Craig paused, "Mollie is not Rose you know. I remember Daniel practically raising you, but Mollie is not as single minded as Rose. She's a good mum. She's not talking about working full time, just helping you out."

Tom looked at him for a long time. "I know," he said with a sigh. "I just wanted to prove I could do something on my own, getting my wife to bail me out feels like failing."

"Asking for help is not a sign of failure, it's a sign of strength. Battling endlessly to make something work that doesn't and never will, now that is failure."

For a while Tom said nothing as he finished his drink, eventually he looked up, "So what shall I do about Eleanor?"

Craig chuckled, "Send her contract over, my lawyer will have a field day with it!"

As they left the pub together, Tom paused, "Thank you."

Craig gave him a brief smile of acknowledgement which faded as he caught Anna laughing at something Andrew was saying out of the corner of his eye. If only he could take his own advice he thought.

Chapter Twenty-Six

The next morning Anna was up before five to feed the horses before coming back in to help Rose with the breakfasts. They would then need to muck out before returning to change bed sheets, it felt endless. And what was worse she had to keep changing and showering as you couldn't prepare a room for a guest straight after mucking out. It was always stressful, but for some reason, the morning was proceeding in an even more chaotic way than normal.

The lessons restarted in a few days and she was starting to worry about how they would cope. Anna looked down at the plate she was carrying, she knew they would never win awards for their breakfasts but they were certainly edible. Today though, the toast had burnt twice and one customer had just sent back his scrambled eggs.

As she pushed open the door to the kitchen, carrying a pile of empty plates, she stopped in shock. Rose was stood clutching the table, a bottle of gin in front of her. Not knowing what to say Anna just stared in horror, unsure if Rose was even aware she was there.

"Don't worry." Rose said without looking at her but seeming to snap out of her trance. Without a seconds thought she marched over to the sink and quickly unscrewed the cap and poured the entire contents of the bottle down the sink. The smell of gin pervaded the kitchen, masking the aroma of cooked breakfasts.

Staring at the drain it had disappeared down, Rose sighed, then speaking so quietly that Anna had to move closer she apologised. "Sorry what with Daniel last night and then this morning being so hectic…. I was looking for a saucepan to redo the eggs…… and there it was at the back of the cupboard…………. I'd forgotten it was there…… but for a second I was so tempted."

Anna wondered how many more bottles were hidden in the house.

"There aren't anymore." Rose said with a sad smile, reading her thoughts and making her blush in embarrassment.

Anna tried to be positive instead. "Would going to a meeting help?"

"Yes, but we just don't have time today." Rose replied resignedly. "Don't worry I'll go as soon as I can."

They both looked at each other knowing how close she had come to opening the bottle and how important the meeting was. A knock at the door made them both jump, before it swung open slowly to reveal Sarah Prince.

She stood in the doorway; nervous, slightly embarrassed and looking like she would rather be anywhere else. "Ummm…"

"Sarah, it's good to see you," Anna said ushering her into the room.

Sarah still had not spoken and looking at her face Anna realised it had taken a lot to come to see them.

"Have you thought about what I said?" Anna asked tentatively.

"That's why I am here."

"You are going to let Freddie start riding again?" Rose asked in confusion.

"Heavens no!" Sarah looked shocked. "He will be having nothing to do with horses. Sorry no offence."

"None taken!" Rose replied tightly.

Anna watched the exchange thinking it had been a really bad idea to offer Sarah the job.

"I'm here about the housekeeping job for the B&B." Sarah said looking at Anna for conformation.

"That would be marvellous," Rose said, the relief immense as she realised, she could go back to her ponies. "When can you start?"

"As soon as possible, my electric has just been cut off." She tried to make a joke of it but it clearly wasn't funny.

"Now?" Rose said half joking.

"Now suits me." Sarah said rolling up her sleeves.

"Really?" Rose asked brightening. "Can you cook eggs by any chance?"

"I'm a trained chef." Sarah replied moving towards the Aga.

Rose and Anna looked at each other in astonishment, before Anna finally found her voice, "Well we need some more scrambled eggs on toast."

Two hours later breakfast had finished, Sarah had quickly taken over the running of the kitchen freeing up Anna and Rose to sort out the stables. Rose was heading off to her meeting, leaving Anna to show Sarah where they everything was.

"Sarah, I hope you don't mind me asking but how are you going to manage this with Freddie?"

"It'll be fine." Sarah said slightly defensively and then gasped as Anna opened the first bedroom door.

"I know its stunning, isn't it?" Anna replied, deciding not to push the issue with Freddie.

"I had no idea; no wonder Paris was so keen to get her hands on the place." Sarah stopped suddenly, "Sorry I didn't mean…" She stopped midsentence.

"But Paris said Daniel wanted to develop this place to sell." Anna said confused.

Sarah laughed, "No way! Daniel loves this house. It was Paris who wanted to be Lady of the

Manor. I take it you haven't heard about the time she snuck in with an interior designer and got caught by Rose."

Anna sighed as much as she wanted to hate Daniel, Sarah's version of events made sense than Paris's.

Sarah looked like she wanted to say something but the silence was broken by her phone ringing. As she turned away to answer it, Anna stepped back to give her some privacy. Initially she paid no attention to the call, but as Sarah's voice started to get more agitated, she could not help but overhear what she was saying.

"Please just give me one week and then I can start paying back what I owe, I have got a new job now," her voice was pleading and desperate. She stood tensely listening to the person on the other end of the call.

"No, I know you have been patient and I do really appreciate it but I just need one more week."

Again, the other person was responding to her pleas.

"But you can't my contract says a month." Sarah was close to tears. "Hello? Hello?"

The person on the other end had clearly hung up on her. Sarah put her head in her hands as though she was about to cry, but then she seemed to remember where she was and turned to Anna.

"I've got to go, sorry but I can't take the job." She started to hurry down the stairs with Anna in pursuit.

"Sarah stop, look perhaps I can help?" Anna struggled to keep up with her.

In the kitchen Sarah paused to collect her bag and jacket. Anna tried one more time, "Please don't go, we are desperate. We need help, the riding school reopens next week, half the village are expecting us to fail, and I can't let that happen. Rose has tried too hard; it would kill her."

Sarah stopped and sighed, "I've got to move out of my house by Sunday, I missed a few weeks rent payments which I've been trying to pay back. After living there five years the landlord knows I'm reliable, it's just been a hard few months. But now he has found someone who will pay, so I'm out. I have two days to find somewhere for Freddie and me and I've lost the deposit as I owed rent."

"Oh," Anna did not know what to say, Sarah's problems were definitely worse than hers.

"Don't worry, the council will have to give us something. It just won't be in this village and I have no car, so you see I can't take the job."

Anna watched Sarah leave wondering how she was going to break the news to Rose, when a thought hit her. Without giving herself time to think about it, she started after Sarah. Realising she must have walked from the village, Anna jumped in the car and caught up with her at the end of the lane.

"Wow you walk fast," Anna called pulling the car alongside her. Sarah turned to look at her, tears were streaming down her face. Stopping the car, Anna pulled over so Sarah could get in.

"Anna, please leave me alone." Sarah stopped but made no move to get in the car.

"Please just listen and if you don't like my idea then I promise I will not hassle you anymore."

Jefferson replaced the receiver gently, and stared out of the window. It was funny he thought, before his stroke they would never had dared to approach him and yet now they were sure he would cave in. Part of him knew he would be sensible to consider the offer but after all those years, to sell the business that he had worked so hard to build to his biggest competitor felt like a failure.

And then there was Daniel, he was still here and although he knew it was futile to hope, Jefferson had begun to dream that they could go into partnership together. He could keep his business and pass it on to his son. It was a dream that until recently he had never even entertained.

"How did it go?" Lara asked coming into the room.

"It's a good offer," Jefferson told her honestly.

"Well, that's more positive than I thought it would be!" Lara said amused.

Jefferson laughed, "Oh believe me, a part of me was still tempted to tell him where to go."

"So how did you leave it?" Lara sat down, her eyes fixed on him, her earlier banter quickly forgotten.

"I said I would think about it." Jefferson did not quite meet her eye.

Lara sighed, "He won't stay Jefferson, at some point he will deal with those demons that are haunting him and he'll go back. And I want a husband left when he does. Look I know you are not happy about selling the business, but don't focus on what you are losing concentrate on what you are gaining. We could travel to England and visit Tom and Daniel, take vacations and just enjoy life. You deserve this, we deserve this."

Jefferson regarded her seriously, he knew she was right.

"Just give me a little more time, please?" He asked.

Lara merely nodded, hoping that he would reach the right decision quickly.

Rose arrived back from her meeting, once again acknowledging not only how much she needed the sessions, but aware she could no longer avoid speaking to Daniel. It had seemed so easy when they had discussed it in the group, but now she was back home the reality was very different. She walked into the kitchen to find Anna and Sarah sat at the table waiting for her.

"Is everything ok?" Rose asked looking from one to the other.

"Sarah is having trouble with her landlord so I suggested she move in here too, it would make it easier to do the job, and as Freddie will be here too, she can help with breakfasts."

"That works for me" said Rose distractedly.

Sarah stood up, "Before we talk about this anymore there is something I need to say." She paused, taking a deep breath, her hands were knotted tightly in front of her. She bit her lip, as though debating where to begin.

When she still did not speak, Rose stepped in. "Look I realise I overstepped the mark; I should have told you about the lessons," Rose said earnestly. "I'm sorry I decided I knew what was best for Freddie, it was wrong of me." Rose sat down, realising the call to Daniel would have to wait.

But rather than looked relieved Sarah burst into tears. "I knew about the lessons and you were right it was best for him. He calmed down a lot once he started riding." She paused before continuing, "I did not know at first, but then Paris made some remark about why you and Daniel were always so keen to help Freddie and me, and that was when Daniel let slip about the lessons."

"But if you knew…" Anna could not help but burst out.

Sarah hung her head. "This is why I wanted you to know…Look its better if I go. I really am sorry."

"Hold on," Rose's voice made her stop in her tracks. "Why did you not just admit that you knew?"

Sarah went red. "Because I could not afford to pay for lessons."

"But you made me leave." Anna seemed to be finding this harder to accept than Rose. "You said you would not sue if I left."

Sarah looked shamefaced. "I was angry at first at I admit, Freddie was hurt and I did not know how I would balance work and looking after him. Then Paris and her mother turned up telling me I should sue and talking about the kind of money that would give me more security than I had ever had."

"So why didn't you do it then?" Anna asked unable to keep the anger out of her voice.

"Daniel and I talked, he explained it was an accident and Freddie kept saying the same. Daniel said you had told him you were leaving anyway, so I could save face."

Anna thought back to that morning. He was right she had said that to him, but she had been trying to jolt some response out of him.

"I didn't realise you knew Daniel so well." Rose said.

Anna's head snapped up now, as she realised what was going on. Sarah was certainly attractive, even without much make up and her hair scrapped up into a haphazard ponytail.

"Daniel often used to give me a lift, if I was at the bus stop."

"Oh. Were you?" Rose floundered unsure how to phrase the question.

Sarah laughed and to Anna's relief shook her head. "Heavens no, although Paris implied it, especially as both you and Daniel were helping us out. No, it started when I was walking home from work one day in the rain, he offered me a lift and then after that he would give me a lift if we were going the same way." Sarah glanced up at the two women looking sceptically at her.

Anna thought back to Paris comment about Daniel always disappearing off, was Sarah just a good actress?

Sarah started to speak again quietly, and Anna quickly tried to refocus. "I think the thing was that Daniel worried about you a lot and the fact you were..." she paused and bit her lip.

"You mean the fact I'm an alcoholic, or rather a recovering one?" Rose asked intently focused on Sarah.

Sarah nodded, "Before Joe left, he was struggling with his gambling addiction but he also started drinking. Well Daniel and I used to talk about how..." she paused again.

"Go on..." Rose insisted.

"Well how difficult it is to help people you love and not knowing what to do. I think Daniel just needed someone to talk to. And Paris was... well...." She paused.

"Daniel did care." Rose said quietly to herself.

Sarah looked at her incredulously, "Rose he used to drive over most nights to make sure you were safely in for the night. Paris used to go nuts at him about it. He just did not know what to do to stop you. He blamed himself. I think this was probably the first time in his life he could not fix something. Taking you to Broome Hill was an act of desperation, he just did not know how else to help you."

"I see," Rose replied quietly lost in thought. "Thank you for being so honest, you don't know how much that has helped me." She got up, "I need to make a phone call."

Just as she was about to leave the room, she turned, "You are staying, aren't you?" she asked Sarah.

Sarah nodded warily, "You still want me to after that?"

"Absolutely, I think we can all help each other." With that Rose quickly left the room.

Anna and Sarah turned hesitatingly to each other.

"I really never said you needed to leave, I'm so sorry." Sarah said sincerely.

"Its fine, I did tell Daniel I was going," Anna told her trying to smile.

"If it's any consolation, he seemed really upset you were leaving." Sarah said.

Anna looked at her, whilst Sarah's words may have helped Rose, Anna knew better.

Daniel looked at the caller ID on his phone in surprise. Rose had not once called him since he had come to New York, he phoned her once a week, but their conversations were brief and often awkward.

"Mum, is everything ok?" He asked, briefly hoping she had not relapsed.

"Yes, fine thank you." Her tone suggested it could not be otherwise.

"Good." Daniel replied wondering why she had called. "I hear the stables are reopening next week."

"Yes, yes they are but that's not why I called." Rose sounded agitated now. "I have been going to these sessions and as part of my recovery I am supposed to talk to various people."

"Right," Daniel was amazed Rose had not written the idea off as ridiculous, but as she seemed to be taking it seriously then he did too.

"Am I one of those people?"

Rose paused. "Yes. Sarah Prince has just told me that you used to come and check on me, quite a lot by the sounds of it."

"Sarah Prince?" Daniel asked shocked, wondering how the two of them had even ended up in the same room, let alone speaking to one another.

"Yes, she is coming to live with us, but that's not the point."

Realising that he would have to catch up with Tom later to find out how that had happened, Daniel paused, "I used to call in when I was around to check everything was ok."

"I don't remember." Rose admitted sadly.

"I know. I tried to tell you there was a problem, but every time I mentioned your drinking you laughed it off." Daniel answered honestly. "I did not know what to do. I spoke to therapists, doctors, discreetly of course," he quickly added knowing Rose would not thank him for going behind her back.

"Thank you, I never realised, well how much you cared." Rose said simply.

"What!" The word shot out of his mouth before he could stop it.

"You always seemed cross with me and I felt like such a liability."

Daniel put his head in his hands.

"Daniel?" The voice was uncertain.

"I'm still here Mum." He replied.

"Oh good," her voice was shaky. "I'm not very good at these talks.

Daniel laughed quietly "I don't think either of us are. I wasn't cross with you; I was cross with me. I did not know how to fix things. The stables seemed too much for you, but I just did not know how to make things better."

"Is that why you left?" Rose asked.

"No, you had seemed better when I left, Tom could manage the business. Lizzie needed help and I just wanted to escape for a while."

"Why?" Rose sounded perplexed.

"Sometimes village life gets a bit much, I've enjoyed the anonymity of New York. I can walk through the park and no one has a clue who I am. No one is offering me advice on what I should do about anything."

"You mean no one is making jokes about your alcoholic mother?" Rose said it in a very matter of fact way, Daniel could not respond.

"I'm not here forever I just needed some time out."

"Really? You are starting to sound American with that time out nonsense!"

Daniel chuckled. "Mum, do you mind me spending time with Jefferson?" He asked, glad to have a chance to finally clear the air.

Rose paused. "No Daniel, it's long overdue. I never thought it was healthy that you never wanted to have a relationship with him."

"But after what he did to you?"

"I was very upset when he left, but after a while, I realised I preferred it. The stables is, and will always be my first love. Not having a husband making me choose between the two suited me."

"Oh." Daniel seemed shocked. "So that's why you never remarried?"

"Well maybe if the right person had come along, but they never did. And over the years, even I acknowledged that I had to accept some of the blame for my marriage failing. I never put him first, never discussed anything with him, never considered what he wanted." Rose paused. "Well, what's done is done."

When Daniel said nothing Rose continued, "So what are your plans now?"

"I'm not sure." Daniel admitted.

"Daniel, I would love you to come home, but I want you to be happy. You've always looked after everyone else. Perhaps it's time to decide what you want."

"Jefferson said the same thing too."

"Oh!" Rose seemed surprised initially then she sighed. "Well, he does talk sense sometimes and he obviously isn't all bad otherwise I would not have married him in the first place.

Daniel ended the call smiling; she had not changed and more importantly he realised that perhaps he had not failed her after all.

Chapter Twenty-Seven

Mollie arrived home on the Sunday afternoon to find Tom's car on the drive. Not sure whether she was pleased about that or not, she helped Billy out of the car, and opened the front door. Lottie and Josh kicked off their trainers and ran to find Tom, whilst she helped Billy with his shoes before he too ran after his brother and sister.

Hearing them tell Tom about their weekend, she slowly took off her coat and hung it up, before returning to the car for their bags. Eventually with no other excuses to delay her, she finally made her way into the kitchen.

Tom looked up immediately, "Hi," he said apprehensively.

"Hi," she replied, her tone cool.

"Cup of tea?" Tom asked.

Mollie nodded and started to move to the kettle.

"Sit down, I'll do it." Tom stopped her and whilst chatting to the children he made tea. As he did, she realised that the table was set and that she could smell a roast cooking in the oven. On the hob sat saucepans of vegetables simmering gently.

Catching her looking Tom spoke up, "Your mum said you left an hour ago, dinner will be ready in about thirty minutes."

Mollie nodded but said nothing. The children talked on about their weekend, delighted to see Tom for a change. She and Tom would need to talk once the children were in bed she realised, but for now she let their children provide a distraction.

With Billy asleep and Lottie and Josh, reading in their beds, Mollie knew it was time to face Tom.

Dinner had been surprisingly good, Mollie grudgingly acknowledged although it would take her forever to clear up as he had used every pan in the place.

But when she reached the kitchen, Tom had already tidied up, the dishwasher was running and everything had been put away. He hovered uncertainly watching her.

"Tom, we need to talk." Mollie said slowly.

"I know, can I go first?" He asked.

Mollie nodded, hopefully if his spiel on how she should be a stay at home mother was anything like last time, then it would make what she had to say much easier.

They sat down opposite one another, and she waited for Tom to begin.

"I've been a complete jerk." Tom came straight out with it, looking at her directly.

"Yes, you have." Mollie acknowledged, surprised but not letting on.

"What I said the other night about you needing to stay at home, I'm sorry I never should have said that. I'd forgotten about what was important and what really mattered."

"And what is that Tom?" Mollie asked tentatively.

"You, the kids and us." He ran a hand through his hair. "I've done a lot of thinking this weekend and I realised how selfish I've been. I've chased my career whilst forgetting you might want one too. I've spoken to some agencies and we can get a cleaner and a nanny. Then you are free to focus on what you want to do. I'd like to say I'll be a full-time dad so you can pick up your career, but I know that I couldn't do that, my work is part of who I am, but I had forgotten that yours is part of who you are too. But I will make more effort to help with the kids and be around more."

Mollie nodded, she had been so sure that their marriage was over and now there seemed like a glimmer of light at the end of the tunnel, but would Tom have forgotten all this in a couple of weeks?

"Talk to me Mollie, please?" Tom practically begged.

She looked at him, his whole body was tense. "It's not that I don't want to be a mum," she started slowly. "It's just that I'm fed up of being taken for granted. It's not all the time, but sometimes I feel invisible. Sometimes I feel like all anyone cares about is my ability to get the right child to right place in the right outfit at the right time. Or to make sure there are always clean clothes available and there is always food to eat. But there is never any thanks, just criticism if it isn't exactly as everyone expects it to be. I just wish occasionally you would say 'What would you like to do this weekend?' I just want to be seen as a person again Tom, not a housekeeper." Mollie finished sadly.

Tom reached out for her hand across the table but her arms remained folded. "Mollie you must know I think you are amazing; I know I don't say it enough, nearly enough obviously. I know how lucky I am to have you and what a great mum you are, and I know I've neglected you and the kids whilst trying to prove that I can be as good as Daniel." Mollie's head jerked up at this. "That doesn't matter anymore, what matters is that you are happy and the kids are happy."

"But why don't think you are as good as Daniel?" Mollie asked in confusion.

"I said it wrongly. I just meant that all my life Daniel has bailed me out and looked after me. When he went away, I thought I could finally prove I could do it on my own, but it turns out I can't."

"But the development is nearly finished and you've kept the village protestors happy."

"Only just! I've spent far too much time talking to Janice Endsworthy about the fact that she won't be able to see the development from her house and that it is unlikely a retirement village will have loud music late at night."

Mollie laughed sadly.

"Yes, but that time I should have spent with you and the kids and I still have no show flat, so while I can build houses, I can't sell any."

"Well, I still don't know why you are chasing Eleanor Burrett all over the country." Mollie said getting cross, perhaps they could not rescue their marriage after all.

"I'm not anymore actually," Tom said with a smile. "Craig Pennington's lawyer sent her a letter on Saturday informing her she has breached the terms of her contract so we are terminating it."

"Really?" Mollie asked, this time unable to hide her surprise.

Tom nodded looking relieved, "Yes I won't have to waste any more time on that woman."

"Daniel must be relieved too." Mollie replied thinking it would have been his idea.

"I haven't told him yet." Tom admitted.

"You decided to do this on your own?" Mollie asked incredulously.

Tom nodded not sure whether to be amused or offended, "Yes I realised I'm never going to step into Daniel's shoes because I'm not Daniel, I'm me, so as Daniel is not here, I need to run it my way and a way that allows me to be able to focus on my family."

"So, who is going to do the designs now?" Mollie asked tentatively, desperately trying not to hope, but aware how much was riding on his answer.

Tom took a deep breath, "This will probably sound like a cheek after all I have said and if you've gone off the idea then I understand but I wondered if, and only if you still want to, but I'd really like you to do them."

Mollie could not speak for a second.

"Mollie?" Tom prompted.

Mollie paused, "I suppose if I am being completely honest part of me got scared, and it was easier to blame you rather than risk trying to get back into designing."

"Ok." Tom said tentatively. "But you know you'll be brilliant, you always are," he met her eyes, the sincerity of his eyes stopped the words being a throw away cliché. "I guess we both let our insecurities defeat us for a while there."

"I guess we did." Mollie acknowledged

"And we'll get a cleaner and a nanny if you want one."

"I would love a cleaner, but I still want to be a mum I don't want someone else bringing up my children. I just wanted to be more than a taxi service."

"I know and I'll help too, I'll be home early and help with dinner. You know I'd forgotten how much I like cooking, if I hadn't been so scared, I was going to lose you I would really have enjoyed making dinner today." Tom added his smile reminiscent.

Mollie smiled too remembering how he'd often cooked when they first got together, but like a lot of things that had petered out over the years.

They sat silently for a second lost in thoughts and memories. "I still can't believe you've sacked Eleanor," she finally said, shaking her head trying to make sense of it.

"I told you Mollie, you are what matters."

"Well in that case you've got yourself a new designer. I'm going to do it. If you can stand up to Eleanor, I can do this." Leaving her seat Mollie walked round to where he sat.

He looked up at her. "That's great but do I also still have a wife?"

Mollie nodded and finally smiled, before she held out her hand, taking it Tom rose from his seat and happily followed his wife upstairs to bed.

Chapter Twenty-Eight

Anna sipped her tea and gave a contented sigh, relaxing back into the thick cream cushions of the sun lounger. The sun had turned into a deep red ball as it slowly sunk and dipped behind the far hills. The small terrace leading off their private lounge was now one of her favourite places. Sarah had worked her magic on it and brought it back from being a tangle of weeds to secluded haven, somewhere they could relax away from the guests who were staying.

The evening air was calm and still. The birds chattered gently to one another as they wound down for the day. Anna closed her eyes, simply enjoying the moment.

"Care for some company? I brought drinks!" Sarah was stood there with a large jug of Pimms and two glasses. "It was on offer in the village shop so I couldn't resist. It's so nice to finally have some extra money for the odd treat."

"If you're bringing drinks, then you are always welcome." Anna laughed.

"This. Is. Bliss." Sarah sipped from her glass slowly, savouring the drink. "You know if you had told me a few months ago we would be sat here drinking Pimms together, I'd have told you, well something not very polite." She laughed and Anna joined in.

"Yeah, I wouldn't have had you down as my ideal drinking partner," Anna smiled ruefully leaning across from her sun lounger and clinking her glass against Sarah's, in a toast to their current happiness with life, the gorgeous spring evening and friendship.

"It's funny how things turn out, there's certainly been a lot of changes in the last year."

"Mmmmm." Sarah agreed thoughtfully. "There certainly has, Freddie is happier than he has been in ages. Apart from the fact I won't let him ride yet."

"Yet?" Anna asked hopefully.

"I'm thinking about it," she admitted, but before Anna could say anything she changed the subject. "So how was last night?

Anna paused, thinking back to the previous evening when Andrew had taken her out. He had become a regular visitor, dropping by for coffee or asking her out for dinner. "Great thanks."

"So, are you two an item then?" Sarah probed gently.

Anna paused and shook her head. "No, we're just friends."

"You know sometimes you can spend so long wanting something, that you fail to see that there is something better waiting to be noticed."

"Maybe." Anna conceded. She knew there was no future with Daniel, maybe it was time to move on now.

Sarah smiled now. "Sorry I didn't mean to upset you. You've just helped me so much, I wanted to try and help you."

"You do, and I'm just as happy single as you are." Anna replied.

"Who said I was happy being single? I'm just waiting for Craig Pennington to realise what a complete nightmare his wife really is." Sarah giggled and winked.

Anna started to giggle too, glad the subject seemed closed.

On Sunday Anna was preparing for the lesson, when she saw Sarah and Freddie come onto the yard. Noticing Freddie was in riding clothes she looked at Sarah questioningly.

Sarah nodded. "Yes, I've finally given in."

Freddie, who was beaming from ear to ear, asked if he could ride Secret.

Anna hesitated before suggesting as it was his first-time riding for a while, he would be better off on a quieter pony. Freddie reluctantly agreed before going to get the saddle and bridle for the pony he was riding.

"Are you going to stay and watch?" she asked Sarah, as Freddie ran off to the tack room.

"If you don't mind?"

"You should, I think you'll be pleasantly surprised by how good he is."

Anna realised she had an audience as Diana Penington Smythe had also decided to stay and watch that day. Luckily the lesson went well and all the children were pleased to see Freddie back, but nowhere near as happy as Freddie was to be back riding.

Afterwards she made her way to the car park to check the children were all being collected. Anna was so happy that Sarah had just acknowledged how good Freddie was, it took her a second to realise there was a small commotion. She looked up to see what the children were making noise about, only to find Andrew stood by his car, with a bouquet of roses.

"Ok you lot, see you next week," Anna called dispersing the children to waiting parents. Aware of the interest Andrew was generating from the parents as well, she walked over to his car with Bethany.

"It's an early birthday present." Andrew handed her one of the largest bouquets of flowers she had ever seen.

"Thank you," was all Anna could manage.

"Actually, they are also a bribe. I want to take you out for your birthday, somewhere special. You deserve it."

Anna looked at the red roses, "I thought this was friends only."

Andrew smiled, "Anna, I think we both know it can be more than that."

Anna hesitated, aware of Andrew's fingers caressing her arm. Most women would think she was mad, to take more than a second to consider this. She thought back to her conversation with Sarah, was that what she had meant, was Andrew waiting to be noticed.

"Well?" Andrew's voice was low and seductive.

Anna smiled. "Yes."

Andrew was about to say something, when a voice next to her drawled, "Flowers, how romantic!"

Diana Penington Smythe was looking at the flowers in contempt, making Anna feel like a silly school girl with a crush. But as she attempted to think of a suitable reply, Diana turned and fixed Andrew with a cool look before turning away and calling Jemima.

"Pay no attention to her," Andrew replied watching her leave. He turned back to Anna and dropped his voice. "I'll pick you up at eight on Saturday. I've got something special planned."

Anna now checked all the children had been collected and did not see Rose approaching. "Where on earth did those come from?"

"Andrew." Anna admitted.

Rose pursed her lips.

Thankfully they were distracted by Freddie running around the corner, followed more slowly by Sarah. "Guess what Rose? Mum let me ride today."

Rose turned to Sarah "Good girl." Then giving her full attention back to Freddie she smiled in delight. "Right, you can come and help me tack up for the next lesson and tell me how you got on."

Sarah rolled her eyes at Anna, "I do love Rose but sometimes she makes me feel like a four-year-old."

Anna laughed, "Oh, she does that to me too. Actually, I don't suppose you know where any vases are do you?"

Sarah nodded and together they walked back to the house, as they entered the kitchen, she was surprised to find Mollie there.

"Ooh, nice flowers." Mollie walked over to look more closely at the bouquet. "So, who is the secret admirer?" she teased.

"Umm," for some reason Anna didn't want to answer.

"Andrew." Sarah supplied, but her happy tone seemed forced.

"Oh," Mollie said in surprise.

Anna gave her a quick smile. "I had better get on."

As she disappeared out the door, with her vase of flowers, Sarah groaned. "Sorry, that may be my fault I said to her last night that she might miss something good whilst she waited for someone who might never come through. I think she misunderstood who I meant."

Mollie shook her head. "It's not your fault. She's always had a soft spot for him," she said sadly wondering if Daniel had been right after all.

Chapter Twenty-Nine

Daniel watched as Jefferson poured the wine, placing a hand lightly on Lara's shoulder as he refilled her glass. His father seemed happy tonight, and his health was improving more quickly now, especially as the spring weather enabled Jefferson to leave the apartment more regularly. Jefferson was finally in a position where Daniel felt happy to leave. The question was where to and for what.

"Guess who I saw today?" Lizzie said.

"Who?" Lara asked.

"Belle, apparently her Mum has just moved into the next block, so we're now neighbours."

Daniel wondered briefly if he would ever be free of that night, then realised Jefferson had said something and was waiting for an answer.

"Sorry." Daniel shook his head.

Jefferson cleared his throat. "Actually, Daniel I have a proposal for you...."

Frustratingly he did not manage to finish his sentence as the doorbell rang.

Lizzie jumped up out of her seat, stopping Daniel from prompting their father to continue.

"Nancy will get it." Lara cut across her. "Your father was talking." She gave Lizzie a pointed look and she sank down in her chair.

Jefferson was about to speak again, when Belle and another girl came in giggling.

"Sorry to interrupt."

She looked anything but sorry, Lara thought in annoyance, knowing how much tonight meant to Jefferson

Belle continued. "After we saw Lizzie today, we had to call over and I just had to introduce

Melanie to Daniel." She smiled at Melanie, who was staring at Daniel.

"Melanie this is Daniel who saved me from my wicked step mother and then punched Andrew for cheating on me with her."

Melanie was giggling and saying something to Daniel, which was both complimentary and flirtatious but Jefferson and Lara watched as the look on his face changed from mild amusement to horror.

Ignoring Melanie, who was starting to look a bit affronted, as she was clearly not used to men not giving her their full attention, Daniel stood up and turned to Belle.

"You said Andrew was with Anna."

"Yes, he was." Belle replied wondering why Daniel was being so weird.

"But you just said your stepmother." Daniel's intensity heightened. "Which was it?"

Belle rolled her eyes, "What do you mean which was it? I told you he was with Anna. My stepmother!" She looked at him as though he was mad.

"But her name is Diana." Daniel seemed to be struggling to hold his temper in check.

"Her birth certificate says Anna. I like to remind her she's a fake." Belle pouted.

"So, it wasn't my Anna then?" Daniel interrupted abruptly needing to be sure.

Belle looked confused for a second, then her confusion cleared. "The groom?" She gave a contemptuous snort. "Andrew wouldn't be with her, he said she was frigid." She laughed, a short derisive nasty laugh, but Daniel didn't care.

Belle was bored now with the whole situation; she'd expected to show Daniel off but he had been acting really strangely. "Come on Melanie shall we go? Lizzie, we're off to the Ice Bar if you want to join us?"

Daniel barely noticed Lizzie leave. He sat in shock wondering how he could have got it so wrong.

Returning from showing them out, Nancy asked if she should bring the champagne in. She glanced at Daniel who was sat staring at the table and then at Jefferson who sadly shook his head. "Just coffee thanks Nancy."

Daniel looked up and seemed to be struggling for words.

"I take it you will be heading back to England." Jefferson said sadly.

Daniel nodded, "If it's not too late."

"You know it might help to talk about it." Lara suggested handing him a coffee.

Daniel started talking and did not stop until he had told the whole story. "You know she even turned up with a take away after I cancelled our first date because a delivery was late." He said finally.

Jefferson chuckled, "I told you it was a sign," he smiled taking Lara's hand.

"I'd forgotten about that," Lara replied softly.

"I never did." Jefferson returned.

Feeling like he was now intruding, and keen to get home, he excused himself to go and look at flights.

As he left the room, Lara turned to Jefferson, "I'm so sorry."

"It was always a long shot asking him to stay and be my partner." Jefferson replied, but he suddenly looked tired and weary.

Anna stared at her reflection in the mirror, tomorrow was her birthday, another year older she thought, critically eyeing the fine lines that were starting to appear around her eyes. However, as she thought back to her last birthday, she could not help but feel happier. At least she would not be running to the corner shop on the way to work to pick up the obligatory birthday cakes only for Mr Elvins to make some sarcastic comment.

Life was good she thought as she looked around her little flat. In the end the attic conversion had been too much, and as Sarah said it would be easier to have Freddie in the house they had taken over Tom's room as well. Rose had had her flat repaired and redecorated, the flowery wallpaper was a distant memory and she even had new furniture.

Yawning she went to lock up, gave Tilly a treat and got into bed. Briefly she wondered what Andrew had planned for Saturday night, but she was distracted by her phone beeping, picking it up she read the text.

"Happy Birthday for tomorrow, hope it brings everything you want!!!! ;-) Xxx"

Daniel. The thought came from nowhere, and Anna quickly quashed it. She sent Lucy a smiley faced emoji and climbed into bed. Sleep however evaded her.

She lay staring at the ceiling and sighed loudly. This was all Sarah's fault she had been perfectly happy, until she had started her probing the other day. She really was happy she told herself as she drifted into an uneasy sleep.

Jefferson walked with Daniel into the airport, and waited while he checked in. He watched the girl on the desk try to flirt with him as she checked his bags, but Daniel hardly seemed to notice. Jefferson hoped he would get to meet Anna soon, before acknowledging that six months ago it would just have been a futile hope.

Daniel was walking back over to him now, tucking his passport and boarding card into his jacket.

"I'm sorry to see you go son," Jefferson said. "I hope you can come back out and visit or perhaps Lara and I could come to England. It would be nice to see the village again."

Daniel nodded. "I'd like that."

The two men stood staring at each other, silently realising just how far they had come.

"Thank you for everything. You'll never know just how grateful I am, and Lara too."

"I've enjoyed being here. Real estate in New York has taught me a lot." Daniel replied, wanting to say more but not sure how.

"Well, you had better get that plane," Jefferson said with a sad smile after a long pause.

"Yeah," Daniel was about to turn away when he stopped.

"Thanks Dad, I'm glad…." The words seemed stuck.

Jefferson just nodded, unable to speak either and Daniel knew no more needed to be said.

As he got back in the car, Lara glanced at him in concern. "Hunny?" She questioned, taking in the tears in his eyes.

For a second Jefferson could not say anything.

"I'm so sorry," Lara murmured, "I know how badly you wanted him to take over the business."

Jefferson just shook his head and smiled, "Oh that was just a pipe dream. I think I always knew his heart was in England. You are right it is time to sell up and enjoy our retirement. We have earned it. How would you feel about a trip to England once it is all sorted?"

"What and miss all those museum meetings," she laughed ironically. "I'd love too," she added sincerely linking her arm through his as the driver pulled away from the curb.

"I am lucky to have you," Jefferson said placing his hand over hers.

She smiled back, "I'll get on to the travel agent tomorrow," she said, still concerned by how emotional he looked.

But he smiled, "I am fine Lara, honestly." He paused. "He called me Dad. Lara I never thought I would hear him say that ever again. He called me Dad." And he gripped her hand a little tighter.

Anna lay staring at the ceiling as the early morning light began to seep around the edge of the curtains. Sleep had completely evaded her, so she climbed out of bed and headed to the yard with a cup of coffee. It was a beautiful morning. The sky was a pale golden yellow on the horizon where the sun had begun to rise, and a couple of pink wispy clouds still lingered.

Grabbing a headcollar she went and caught Alfred and was soon heading down the drive. She rode for over two hours, meandering along the lanes, before turning off onto a bridleway through open fields that offered her the chance to go for a long gallop. As she pulled up at the top of a hill, she finally felt better. Sarah was wrong she did not need a man, this was perfect.

Feeling relaxed at last and aware that Alfred was tiring she decided to cut back through the neighbouring farm. The only problem was, it meant going past the empty cottage that had been for sale for years. Giving herself a mental shake, she turned up the track to the cottage, trying not to think about the rumours that it would not sell because it was haunted.

The sky had now turned bright blue. Anna smiled thinking it was going to be a scorching hot day and the best thing was she could spend it out of doors. She definitely had everything she wanted she told herself, but maybe Sarah was right it would not hurt to give Andrew another chance.

As she approached the cottage, she heard a strange noise. Ignoring it, she kicked Alfred forwards but stopped as she heard another moaning sound. Briefly she considered turning back, but Alfred seemed unfazed and animals usually had a sixth sense. Knowing she should get back she pressed on towards the cottage.

An even louder moan broke the silence. Anna decided she had had enough and started to turn Alfred around, they would have to go the long way home, but the moaning had stopped now and instead someone was shouting the words, "Harder. Yes. Andrew. Yes."

Her fear receded fast and more than slightly intrigued Anna pushed on towards the cottage.

As she rounded the corner, she was surprised to see both Andrew's and Diana Pennington Smyth's cars parked outside. From the upstairs window Diana's voice could be heard screaming 'Yes' repeatedly.

Nudging Alfred on, she quickly passed by the cottage, but as she did so a bird flew out of the hedge squawking causing Alfred to jump and his hooves to clatter on the cobblestones, glancing up she saw Andrew's shocked face appear at the window. She definitely would not be going out with him now she thought to herself shaking her head in bemusement.

Chapter Thirty

Back at the yard, Sarah had set out a fantastic breakfast for them all. "Poor Freddie was gutted you weren't back before he left for school."

"Sorry he missed it, but I just fancied getting out on my own this morning!"

"Are you ok? You look a bit…" Sarah looked at her in concern.

"I'm fine." Anna reassured her as the door flew open.

"Happy birthday!" Mollie sang, crossing the room and giving her a hug.

Anna opened her presents whilst Sarah dished up the pancakes. They were about to eat when once more the door flew open, however the person in the doorway had certainly not come bringing presents.

"I need to speak to you now." She announced glaring at Anna.

"Don't come all high and mighty with us Diana!" Rose spoke as though she was telling off one of her pupils. "It's Anna's birthday, so you will have to come back another time."

"This is urgent." Diana completely ignored Rose.

Sighing Anna got to her feet at the same time as Rose. "It's ok Rose. We'll go to the office."

As the office door clicked shut, Diana rounded on her, "Right you listen to me. No one will ever believe you if you say anything, so don't even attempt to cause trouble! Because if you do, then I'll ruin you and this whole little set up." She waved her arm grandly to indicate the house.

Anna stared at her in shock, she had expected Diana to plead with her, get embarrassed or turn on the tears, but not to be quite so vicious.

"You know it really is pathetic following Andrew around and snooping on him. By the time I have finished with you the whole village will think you are some mad jealous stalker."

Shock was quickly being replaced by anger, "Is that so? Even when everyone knows what Andrew is like, and everyone saw him give me flowers last week, including you." Anna was enjoying the fact Diana had no come back.

Diana opened her mouth to speak but Anna beat her to it.

"Look I have no desire to get involved in your smutty little affair, but unless you leave immediately and stay well away from me, then I may be tempted to mention it."

Diana watched her unsure what to do, she opened her mouth to speak again but Anna pointedly opened the door.

"You'd better keep quiet if you know what's good for you." Diana spat as she swept out of the door.

"Always a pleasure Anna!" She pointedly called after her.

Back in the kitchen three expectant faces turned to her.

"What on earth was that about?" Rose demanded. "I'm tempted to go and see Craig and tell him to get his wife under control!"

"There's no need." Anna assured her.

"I think there is some very juicy gossip to be had here!" Mollie said speculatively watching Anna.

"Honestly Mollie, I thought you were above all that nonsense," Rose admonished her.

Anna shook her head. "Nothing exciting at all." She picked up the maple syrup and drizzled it over her pancakes.

"Well, you are no fun!" Mollie chided her, popping a piece of strawberry in Billy's mouth before helping herself to another pancake.

"It's very honourable of you not to gossip, Anna." Rose told her as she stood up. "I'm off to get the ponies in. Now Anna, I have everything covered today. All you need to do is relax and enjoy your day!" And with that, she sailed out of the door.

As soon as the coast was clear, Mollie smiled at her, "Who did you catch her with?"

"Mollie!" Anna half complained.

Sarah laughed pouring them all another cup of coffee. "My guess would be Andrew in the haunted cottage!"

"Well judging by your face Anna, Sarah is spot on!"

"I never said a word," Anna held up her hands in mock protest.

"Come on then Sarah dish the goss," Mollie laughed pulling her chair closer to the table.

"Why do you think I got fired from my last job?" Sarah asked.

"No, what a cow!" Both Mollie and Anna were stunned.

"Yep, she is a nasty piece of work," Sarah replied. "Don't cross her Anna."

"Hold on but you didn't work for her!" Mollie was confused.

"Yes, but I caught her and Andrew once. So, she decided to discredit me. She is very good at putting a word in the right ear, all very quiet and civil. And then there was the whole incident with Freddie allegedly keying her car. The only thing was the night it happened he was at home with me, but who do you think everyone believed. To be honest it wouldn't surprise me if she did it herself!"

"I can't believe she did that to you." Anna said in shock.

"I could be wrong about that, but it's the only thing that makes sense. Craig let slip, when I went to plead Freddie's case, that her new car was already on order so she knew it wouldn't be a problem for her!"

"What a…." Mollie exclaimed, just stopping herself saying too much in front of Billy.

"Well, it all worked out for the best. But you've also got to feel sorry for John Dennis, he's been unable to sell that cottage because everyone thinks it is haunted thanks to that rumour which was started by her and Andrew to keep people away."

"Someone should tell him," Anna said sadly.

"He knows, but he likes Craig Pennington, everyone does. That's the real reason she gets away with it." Sarah said.

"I still can't believe it," Anna replied.

"Surely you've heard people say that the only person she won't take her knickers off for is her husband!"

Mollie laughed, "Even I have heard that one."

They sat chatting for a while before Sarah announced she had rooms to prepare for guests due later. Anna was surprised she had been sure that there weren't any bookings for that night.

"Right, I'll just Billy at nursery and then I'll pick you up for our spa day." Mollie told her starting to retrieve Billy's things from around the room. "By the way," Mollie asked picking up Billy's Paw Patrol rucksack. "Why did you call her Anna when she left?"

"Oh, it's a silly thing Andrew told me that Belle used to do, something to do with her real name, but apparently it really winds her up."

"So, Belle called Diana, Anna?"

"Yeah."

"And this thing with Andrew has been going on a long time?" Mollie confirmed with Sarah.

"Years." Sarah confirmed.

"I've got to go." And with that Molly collected up Billy and swept out the room.

Chapter Thirty-One

"I don't want to talk to you."

"Anna, don't be like this. I just wanted to see how you are?"

"Fine, why wouldn't I be?" Anna replied, determined not to make it easy for him.

"It's just after you saw Mrs Pennington Smythe and I at the cottage earlier I was worried you may have got the wrong idea." Andrew's natural charm was slightly strained.

"And what wrong idea would that be?" Anna asked innocently.

"Diana asked me to go with her to the cottage as she is thinking of buying it to help poor John Dennis out. For some reason he just can't sell it." Andrew shook his head sadly at John Dennis's bad luck.

"Because people are spreading rumours that it's haunted?" Anna asked and then tried not to laugh as Andrew missed her dig completely.

"Exactly, apparently some local youths had been using it to smoke pot, and had spread the story about it being haunted to keep people away."

"How awful!" Anna commented lightly.

"Well, you know what teenage lads are like." Andrew laughed indulgently, sounding far more confident.

"So, the noises that people heard, that they thought were ghosts, were just kids messing around?" Anna asked.

"Absolutely," Andrew laughed, "can't blame them for trying though!"

"It's so odd though, because you went there thinking that people were faking ghost noises and yet the only thing I could hear being faked when I rode past, was an orgasm!" Anna replied sweetly.

Andrew forced a laugh.

"And I am pretty sure it was you who told me about the cottage being haunted." She added smiling even more sweetly.

Andrew paused, "Look Anna after my divorce I was a mess, people make mistakes."

"That is your excuse for everything isn't it? Your divorce!" She rolled her eyes.

"Diana has been very supportive." Andrew said crossly, his normal charm failing him.

"This has been going on a while, hasn't it?" Andrew looked slightly guilty now.

"She's a married woman! When did you meet?" Anna paused for breath, but the pieces of the puzzle were quickly slotting into place. "You met her while Jemima was having lessons, didn't you? That's what she was up to when she was meant to be watching her daughter learn to ride, isn't it? No wonder it was always you two who were always late. I can't believe you would meet her then come and ask me out!"

Anna thought she would explode with anger, as images of Diana and Andrew turning up late after lessons ran through her mind.

"Look I made a mistake. I know I need to change. Let's go out for dinner tomorrow and we can talk." Andrew reverted to his normal charming self.

Anna looked at him like he was mad.

"Diana and I are over." Andrew seemed to really believe it.

"It sounded that way this morning." Anna's voice shook with anger.

Andrew had the grace to look slightly shame faced. "She got jealous, when I gave you the flowers the other day."

Anna let out a bitter laugh, wondering how much worse this could get. "Andrew just go."

"Ok, I'm going." Andrew replied. "I am sorry you know," he added as he left.

Anna shut the door on him and walked back into the kitchen. Frustration and annoyance ran through her and her happy mood was ruined. He had not even remembered it was her birthday she thought angrily.

Hearing the door open, anger surged through her. Spinning around fast, she took a deep breath ready to give Andrew another piece of her mind but it was not Andrew stood there.

Daniel was stood there instead. Everything she had tried to convince herself over the past few months was forgotten, as she stared into the blue eyes.
She knew she should tell him to leave but her voice would not work. No one had warned her he was coming so she had had no chance to prepare.

"Can I come in?" He asked, his smile was warm, despite the fact he looked slightly apprehensive.

Say no her head screamed but she found herself opening the door instead.

"I didn't know you were back." She faltered.

"I just flew in." He replied.

Looking at him she could see dark smudges under his eyes.

"What do you want?" Anna asked, trying not to hope too much.

Daniel raked his hand through his hair, he had not planned on getting straight to the point but now there seemed no other option. "Anna, I owe you an apology. The night of the ball, I made a mistake, I was looking for you and I bumped into Belle and she."

"I know." Anna snapped, not wanting to hear anymore. He had been with Belle she realised. There was no other explanation. Hurt exploded and she sat down, using all her willpower not to cry.

Daniel wanted to reach out to her but it was clear it would not be welcome. He tried again to explain. "Anna I'm so sorry, I can't believe I was so stupid. It was totally my fault, but is there any way we can try again? I haven't stopped thinking about you the whole time I have been away." He watched her but her expression remained frozen.

Anna was in shock. Had he seriously, just turned up and asked for a second chance? She had dreamed of him coming back and saying there had been a mistake and he had not been with Belle, but not to admit he had and then pretend it did not matter.

She wished it wasn't so tempting, despite everything to give him another chance. She wished there was another explanation but the fact that he had dismissed what happened as just a mistake made her realise for him it was not a big deal. And if he could do it once he would do it again. The risk was not worth it. She had worked hard to get the riding school and the B&B up and running and it was a success. She was happy, life was good. She could not risk that all, not even for Daniel.

She shook her head slowly. "I'm sorry Daniel, but I can't."

His eyes met hers and Anna had to look away. "That's a definite no then?"

"It wasn't just one mistake, was it? You took her to New York."

"Only as a favour to Craig, he was worried about her and she was going to visit her mother so we flew out together."

"Right." Anna's voice was full of contempt, it all seemed too convenient.

Daniel was about to say Belle had not deliberately misled him and Belle was a victim in all this too, but judging by Anna's face that would not help.

"And of course, then there was Lizzie, when you were supposedly thinking about me." Anna spat, wondering why she was even giving him the time of day and wishing seeing him did not hurt so much.

"Lizzie?" Daniel shook his head, was Anna suggesting what he thought she was. "Anna, Lizzie is my half-sister."

"Oh right." Anna replied feeling wrong footed before sadly acknowledging that it did not change anything.

"I've missed you." Daniel said.

Anna bit her lip, willing herself not to speak. He seemed so genuine, but she could not let her guard down now. She could not let him hurt her again.

"Look I know I let you down, but...." Daniel tailed off.

"Let me down? Do you have any idea how much what you did hurt me?" Anna retorted as anger started to replace the feeling of sadness. "You never wanted me here, and you put me in the flat in an attempt to get rid of me, or do you deny that?"

Guilt flashed across Daniel's face. "No but I did not know you then. Anna, please believe me, I never wanted to hurt you. You have no idea how much I wish I could change what happened."

Anna's anger evaporated as fast as it had come on. "But you can't," she told him hoping she would not cry.

"No, I can't."

"Look you need to go." Anna told him starting to turn away.

Finally seeming to realise that she really meant it Daniel nodded.

He watched walk to the front door, but when she paused at the door, he could not help himself. "By the way, I'm really grateful for what you did for Mum. You were the only one who could fix her."

Anna shook her head, "I didn't. I just found her when she was ready to fix herself."

Daniel looked sceptical, and remembering Sarah's words about him blaming himself, she carried on. "Only Rose could fix herself, she just wasn't ready to before."

Daniel stayed where he was, unable to believe how badly the conversation had gone. He had just blurted out what he wanted to say without thinking. Except he had been thinking about it the whole flight home, but giving Anna a chance to take in the fact he was back would have been sensible. Hearing a noise behind him, he turned to find Sarah Prince coming through the door.

"Now, you're a sight for sore eyes." She said giving him a hug, "Rose will be over the moon you are back and there's another person who will be very pleased to see you!"

"How is Freddie?" Daniel asked.

Sarah laughed, "Freddie is fine, actually he is more than fine, he spends half his life out on the yard so things could not be more perfect for him right now. But it wasn't Freddie I was referring to." At Daniel's look of surprise, she continued, "I take it you have come to see Anna?"

"I did." Daniel sat down heavily, his shoulders slumped. "But I don't think she was pleased to see me."

Sarah was about to say more, when Rose's voice rang out across the kitchen. "Daniel how marvellous to see you, I did not know you were coming back!"

As Rose took him around the house and the stables, he could not fail to acknowledge what a difference there was. The whole place had been revived.

"Well Anna has worked a miracle, hasn't she?" Rose finally said as they walked back to the house.

"She certainly has," Daniel replied, whilst wondering if he could feel any worse.

Chapter Thirty-Two

Mollie walked into the nursery and watched as Billy happily ran off to play with one of his friends. She waited for the nursery nurse to finish talking to another parent, so she could let her know Tom would be collecting Billy.

When Tom had first apologised, she had wondered how long it would last. However, he had involved her more in the business since then and had kept his word about helping with the children and getting home earlier. It was not every night but it was a definite improvement.

"Is there anything I can help with?" Mollie had been so deep in thought she had not noticed the other nursery nurse come up to her.

Turning she realised it was Charlie's granddaughter, she must be new as she had never seen her there before. Briefly she wondered if it was safe to leave Billy with a woman who hated their family so much.

She looked as shocked as Mollie. "Sorry I didn't realise it was you. Has Rose told you my eldest has started riding? A natural she is too according to Rose."

Rose hadn't mentioned it but Mollie nodded as though she knew all about it. She certainly did not want to upset her again if she was leaving Billy with her.

"Granddad took her, he even said he might go back and do the odd day here and there. Nan's hoping he will, he keeps getting under her feet since he's been home." She nattered on as though they were old friends, although Mollie could not help but notice she kept tucking her hair behind her ear in a nervous gesture.

"Well, I know Rose has missed him," said Mollie truthfully whilst reeling at her change in attitude. The pair of them had managed to avoid each other on the school run quite successfully for the last few months.

"Look about Grandad," she said tucking her hair behind her ear again. "Well…." She looked up at Mollie anxiously.

"We're just all glad he is better now." Mollie replied, knowing it had been fear and worry that had caused her to yell at her in the school playground, and also knowing they should not have left it all to Charlie.

She smiled gratefully and Mollie relaxed, they were going to be fine.

Daniel knew he should go home to bed as he left Rose's. He had not slept for over twenty-four hours now, but he felt restless so instead he turned towards Broome Hill, where he knew Tom would be.

"I didn't expect to see you again today!" Tom remarked, as George bounded over to Daniel. "Things not go well with Anna?"

"No." Daniel did not want to talk about it, instead he focused on giving George a fuss, at least he was pleased to see him.

Tom felt uneasy he knew he would need to apologise to Anna too. Mollie had said as much when she had phoned earlier and confirmed what Daniel had told him about Diana.

"So, let's see what you have been up to then." Daniel straightened up now.

Together they walked round the development. It was nearly finished now and all the units had sold. It was not hard to see why, the location was fantastic and the show flat Mollie had designed was perfect.

"Mollie really has done a great job," Daniel commented glancing over to Tom to see his reaction.

He suppressed an amused smile as Tom swelled with pride.

"I know, I should have stopped being a jerk a long time ago." For a second Tom went white. He would never forget that conversation with his mother in law the morning Mollie had returned with the kids. She had made it exceptionally clear that if he did not get his act together then he would lose Mollie, no matter how much she loved him.

"Everything ok?" Daniel asked in concern, watching Tom's face. He had known something wasn't right at the time, but over the phone Tom would never talk about it.

Tom nodded, "It is now, but if it hadn't been for Craig Pennington, making me see sense, and then a warning from my mother in law, then I would probably have lost Mollie."

Daniel started to protest, but Tom looked at him. "Things were pretty bad. She was honestly thinking about leaving me."

"Why didn't you say anything?" Daniel asked, trying not to think about the fact Tom always came to him for help.

"You had enough on with Dad, and I wanted to sort this out on my own." Tom said looking both defiant and guilty at the same time.

Daniel laughed, "Am I that bad?"

Tom paused before he started to speak. "Don't take this the wrong way, but I think your leaving was a good thing we had all become too dependent on you. I guess we all needed to stand on our feet again."

Daniel nodded, wondering where he would fit in now, he was back.

As if reading his mind, Tom smiled, "That doesn't mean I'm not really glad you're home." He glanced at his watch. "How about lunch at the pub?"

Daniel chuckled, "So basically you just missed having a drinking partner!"

"Yeah, what else was there to miss?" Tom replied, glad things were back to normal.

Walking into the pub Daniel nearly walked straight into Paris' parents, he nodded briefly but kept talking to Tom as other locals came over to welcome him back.

They had just ordered food when the door burst open, to reveal Paris standing dramatically in the entrance. Tom raised an eyebrow at Daniel but he merely carried on their conversation. He was aware of a hush over the pub and he could hear Paris' stiletto heels hitting the floor as she walked over to them.

It was her angry walk, Daniel thought, whilst wishing she had not decided to do this in public. Her mother must have phoned her straight away.

"Well look whose back!" She practically spat.

Daniel turned slowly. Paris was glaring at him, in her typical pose, one hand on her hip, the large handbag over the other arm, and he felt nothing.

"Hello Paris, nice to see you too." He turned back to Tom to continue the conversation, ignoring her sharp intake of breath.

"Aren't you going to ask me how I've been?" She asked her voice dangerously quiet.

Daniel was too tired to care, but he'd also prefer not to have a scene, so with a deep breath he turned back to her. "How have you been Paris?"

She thrust a hand in front of him. Daniel stared at it trying to work out what he was meant to do.

"Congratulations Paris, I heard about the engagement." Tom spoke up to help him out.

At once Paris changed, she giggled and glanced at Tom, "I know I am just so happy." She gave Daniel a triumphant look.

"Congratulations," he said, "Being engaged clearly suits you."

"Of course, it does, Alistair dotes on me, nothing is too much trouble."

Daniel nearly choked on his drink. "Alistair Arrol-Forsythe?" He asked.

Paris looked like the cat that got the cream, "Who else?"

Daniel looked at her in disbelief, she had taken her best friend's (if you could call Chelsea that) fiancé.

"You won't be able to talk me out of it, no matter how hard you try." Paris murmured silkily, leaning right into Daniel, having misread his shock.

Daniel leant away from her and laughed, "Believe me I have no intention of it. Why would I want to be with a woman who tried to destroy my mother's business, I know all about you trying to get Sarah to sue."

"I was doing you a favour." Paris spat. "We all know..."

"Know what?" Daniel had stood up fast.

Paris took a step back, realising she had gone too far. Recovering quickly, she gave him a smug grin, "Well I hope you haven't come back for Anna, from what I hear she and Andrew are very cosy these days." And with that she spun on her heel and flounced out the pub.

"She's not." Tom said quickly.

Daniel merely nodded suddenly feeling very tired. "I'm going to head back to mine."

"Sure, I need to get going too. I've got to pick up the kids."

Chapter Thirty-Three

Mollie arrived home and quickly grabbed her bags, looking forward to the spa. She was about to leave when the doorbell rang. Opening it she found Jane on the doorstep.

"Sorry I know you are off on your spa day but you have got to hear this. Craig Pennington has just kicked out Diana."

"Noooo." Mollie said in shock, briefly wondering if it had anything to do with Anna catching them that morning.

"Yes, apparently Lucinda Cottesmoore saw them both leaving the haunted cottage in a rather a hurry. She was busy telling everyone in the village shop when Craig walked in. Lucinda was so full of her story that she did not see him until it was far too late. Well Craig just wished everyone good morning and left."

"Poor   Craig."   Mollie   muttered sympathetically.

"I know but then an hour later Diana turns up at Andrew's with a suitcase. Andrew is having kittens as you can bet. He certainly does not want to have someone keeping tabs on him."

"What a mess!" Mollie shook her head feeling sorry for Craig.

The phone started to ring and Mollie glanced at the clock, she was supposed to pick Anna up in thirty minutes.

She quickly answered it, in case it was the school.

"Darling, at last I have found you!"

Mollie recognised the voice immediately.

"Genevieve, how are you?"

"Marvellous, but I'll come straight to the point. I've heard you are back."

Mollie hesitated. "Only a show flat for Tom."

"I've just been to see it and its perfect. I've also just signed the contract for a complete refurb for Attingham Park Hotel."

"Wow." Mollie wasn't surprised, Genevieve was brilliant. But even so Attingham was the one of the best known hotels in the country.

"Attingham needs an amazing entrance. I'm thinking chic, elegant, modern but with a classic twist." As she spoke Mollie knew she would be striding around, her arms gesticulating wildly as saw the new design in her mind. "We need a nod to country life in a way that is palatable to the London market they are trying to attract. Mollie this has your name written all over it. I'll pay you whatever you want, just come and consult on it. I have enough minions to track down samples and anything else you need. What do you think?"

"I don't know," Mollie replied overwhelmed.

"Mollie I never beg, you know that."

Mollie smiled in acknowledgement.

"But please consider this?"

"I will, but I need to talk it through with Tom." Mollie answered.

"Well Darling, this has been lovely, but I must go. I expect to hear from you within a week. Remember any hours you want." And with that Genevieve had hung up.

Mollie put the phone down thoughtfully, catching Jane's questioning look.

"My old boss wants me to consult on a job she's doing, I said I'd think about it."

"What job?" Jane asked shrewdly having heard the conversation and realising this was pretty special.

"Attingham Park Hotel."

Jane's eyes lit up in delight, "Of coursed Hamish Knights is where you used to work. Oh, this is brilliant."

When Mollie looked at her in surprise Jane continued, "Olivia was boasting at school this morning that she is having them in to do her house as they are going to be remodelling Attingham. She was saying how exclusive they were and how they never normally take commissions outside of London. I knew the name was familiar."

"I only said I would think about it." Mollie said, although she already knew she wanted to do it.

Jane just gave her a look. "It's such a shame you won't be on the school run though, Olivia will have a fit when she hears that Hamish Knights has a new designer," she replied in gleeful amusement as they walked to the front door.

"Jane…" Mollie warned.

"Don't worry, I won't go too far." Jane promised with a grin as she left which did nothing to dispel Mollie's anxiety.

She quickly texted Anna to say she was running late, and was relieved when Anna texted back to say she would come to her instead.

Glad to escape the house and avoid bumping into Daniel again, Anna got in her car to drive to Mollie's. As she drove along the lane, Anna passed Rich going the other way. She lifted a hand to wave to him, and was sure she saw someone in the passenger seat duck out of sight. What was wrong with the men in this village? She snorted in disgust, as she wondered whose wife he was with. She had definitely done the right thing telling Daniel to go. Between Daniel, Andrew and Rich she decided she was sworn off men. She was glad Jenny had not wanted anything serious from Rich and for the first time ever she began to think Jenny was right in her approach to men.

Daniel let George into the house and followed him inside. He needed to go to the shop as the cupboards were bare, but he could not be bothered. Instead, he headed straight for the lounge collapsing on the settee and staring up at the ceiling.

Once again, he cursed the fact that he had not questioned Belle properly that night. He sighed wearily going over the situation endlessly would solve nothing.

A knock on the door jarred him from his depressing reflections. Answering the door, he was surprised to find Craig Pennington.

"I heard you were back and I wondered if you had five minutes?" Craig seemed rather tense as Daniel opened the door wider to let him in.

They walked through to the kitchen, "Sorry I only got back this morning. I think there may be some coffee here, but there is no milk." Daniel said looking in the cupboard.

"I'm fine thank you." Craig replied somewhat stiffly.

"What can I do for you?" Daniel asked looking at Craig, Daniel knew he was not at his best after being on a plane and having no sleep, but Craig looked a lot worse on closer inspection.

"I owe you an apology." Craig came straight to the point. "When I asked you to escort Belle to New York I was fairly sure that Andrew had been with my wife, well soon to be ex-wife."

Daniel looked at him in surprise, but Craig carried on. "Instead, I allowed you to believe that it was your Anna instead."

"Right." A wave of anger washed over him at what had happened.

"I'm sorry Daniel it was wrong of me, I let my pride stop me from seeing what was right in front of me."

Daniel took a deep breath and looked at Craig, but he was a victim in all this too. The families had been friends for years and it must have been hard for him to admit the truth. "It was not your fault, I would have gone anyway and it gave me a chance to get to know my father."

"That's good, I'm glad something positive came out of this."

"It did." Daniel replied acknowledging it for the first time.

"Well, I had better go, I need to pick Jemima up. Perhaps now my wife has gone we might be able to hold on to a nanny or a housekeeper for longer than five minutes!" He tried to make a joke of it. "It'll save me being eaten alive by the mothers on the playground." He finished with a grimace.

"Tom is picking up the kids today, so you'll have one ally." Daniel watched relief flood Craig's face. "I am sorry about Diana."

Craig gave a self-depreciating smile. "You can lie to yourself but when you discover it's Lucinda Cottesmoore's favourite topic of conversation, you have to face facts."

"You shouldn't pay any attention to her you know." Daniel replied forcefully, anger flashing across his features.

"Sorry I forgot you've had to put up with her gossiping too. I don't really care what she says. I've known for a long time, Jemima used to let slip that her mother never watched her lessons. And then of course there was the Lady Godiva joke...." Craig stopped abruptly realising what he had said.

"Don't worry." Daniel said realising it no longer mattered.

Chapter Thirty-Four

Anna sank into the Jacuzzi and let out a contented sigh. Next to her Mollie smiled, they had had massages and pedicures and Anna had loved every minute of it.

"I know this is your birthday treat, but I'm really enjoying it." Mollie said happily. "Although I half expected you to cancel on me, after Daniel's visit," she gently probed.

Anna did not say anything for a moment. "No."

"He's really sorry you know, about what happened."

Anna just nodded.

"So do you think.."

"No." Anna cut her off. "I can't let him do that to me again."

"I honestly don't think he ever would," Mollie began, but seeing the look on Anna's face she quickly changed the subject.

"So, thanks to Lucinda Cottesmoore Andrew has a new flatmate." Mollie laughed finishing the story.

"At least Diana can't blame me then!" Anna replied with a slight feeling of relief.

"I think Lucinda was annoyed as she has always had a soft spot for Andrew, not that anything would ever happen. She was always repeating his jokes about Rose, especially the Lady Godiva one."

Anna looked at her confused.

"Surely you have heard it?" When Anna shook her head, Mollie continued. "Before you came Rose rode through the village one night at midnight. Andrew told everyone in the pub that night they should all be glad she had not channelled her inner Lady Godiva."

"I can't believe that." Anna said thinking she had just had a lucky escape.

"You can imagine Daniel's thoughts on that one."

For a second Anna felt a pang of pity for him, before pushing it to one side.

"Right, we need to get out and get ready for tonight!" Mollie said her eyes sparkling. "You did bring something special to wear, didn't you?"

Anna slipped on the little black dress and appraised herself in the mirror. Even she had to acknowledge the dress really suited her. Running the yard and being outdoors so much kept her in much better shape than when she had worked in an office.

For a moment she felt her spirits flag, half wishing she had given Daniel a second chance, half wishing he was picking her up tonight and taking her out, but then she reminded herself she would just be waiting and wondering if he would cheat again. And if he did, would she want to stay?

She thought of Rose and Charlie, of Sarah and Freddie, of the horses whickering greetings on frosty mornings when she came onto the yard, of riding out in the Autumn as the mist swirled across the fields, of summer evenings watching the ponies laze in the fields and nights spent in the local pub beer garden. It really was not worth gambling it all.

Rousing herself she applied a second coat of lip gloss and filled her clutch bag. As she finished doing the buckle on the tiny strap of her shoes, whilst admiring her perfectly painted toes, Mollie walked back into the room.

"You look gorgeous, are you ready?" Mollie asked with a mysterious smile.

Anna nodded and grabbing her clutch.

"Are we eating in the restaurant here?" Anna asked curious now.

"No, I booked the room so we could get ready properly. I just need to check us out then we are off," she replied mysteriously.

They got in the car and Mollie looked at her in consternation, "I'm meant to put a blindfold on you but that will ruin your make up. Just don't pay too much attention to where we are going."

As they drove, Anna considered different possibilities but was surprised when they eventually pulled up at Rose's, where the driveway was full of cars

Anna looked at her confused.

"Come on," Mollie linked her arm through Anna's and steered her across the yard, before opening the door of the barn with a flourish.

"Surprise." About a hundred people shouted. Anna recognised friend's faces, as she struggled to take in the fairy lights strung from the beams, the bar at one end and the music that had now started pouring out of two large speakers.

Jenny came running through the crowd and threw her arms around her, "Happy birthday gorgeous, this has been such a hard secret to keep! And then I thought you had seen me when we passed you in the lane earlier!" She laughed as she pulled a horrified face.

Anna stared at her, "Hold on, was that you ducking out of sight?" She asked slowly.

"Who did you think it was?" Jenny asked raising an eyebrow.

"Hold on that's who you have been seeing? You said there was someone but it was not serious." She replied in her defence.

"It's not! Rich just knows he's not allowed to mess around!" She smiled at him and to Anna's surprise Rich just pulled Jenny in close and kissed her.

Slightly bemused and almost jealous of what she had just witnessed, she turned to Lucy to distract herself from wishing she and Daniel had made it to that stage.

"Happy birthday!" Lucy flung her arms around her whilst rolling her eyes at Rich and Jenny, making Anna smile. "Good surprise?"

Anna nodded, thinking today had been one surprise after another, but tonight was a good surprise and she was going to enjoy it.

Mollie reappeared with a glass of Prosecco, but before she could say anything, Rose's voice boomed over the microphone.

Turning she saw Rose standing next to the DJ on the make shift stage, she was even wearing a skirt, touched at the all the effort she had made Anna smiled to herself.

"Good evening everyone. Now I am not one to make speeches but I just wanted to thank you all for coming tonight for Anna's birthday surprise. As you know Anna joined us nearly a year ago after deciding to follow her dreams, but not only has she changed her life, hopefully for the better," she paused and Anna readily nodded, "but she has also changed quite a few of ours too. And I will always be grateful that she chose to come here." Again, she paused and looked over at Anna who swallowed hard to try and get rid of the lump that had formed in her throat, as people started to clap Rose broke eye contact and then looking almost embarrassed, she lifted her glass. "So, I'd like you all to raise your glasses and wish Anna a very happy birthday."

Around the room a chorus of Happy Birthday rang out, the DJ played the first few bars of the song and everyone started to sing as Rose beckoned Anna over to the stage, where Sarah was wheeling out a large cake covered in candles.

Anna leaned forward and blew out the candles as everyone gave her three cheers.

Someone shouted 'speech' from the back of the room, as she straightened up. Looking around she saw the faces of Lucy and Jenny her oldest friends, but also Rose, Mollie and Sarah her new friends and then there were acquaintances and parents of the children she taught to ride and people from the village. Even her parents were there, her Mother smiled proudly at her.

"Wow, I don't really know what to say, except thank you all so much, this is fantastic." She smiled at everyone as she glanced around the room. And there at the back of the room smiling wistfully at her was Daniel, for a second their eyes locked before she forced herself to look away, aware everyone was watching her. She heard her voice speaking on autopilot as she thanked Rose and Sarah and Mollie for the surprise.

Leaving the stage, she made her way back to her friends deliberately avoiding Daniel, on the way people stopped her to wish her happy birthday, but all she was aware of was the feeling of Daniel's eyes on her. She smiled and danced and chatted, determined to enjoy the party, after all there was nothing more to be said to Daniel.

Craig looked around the room and reflected on the reception he had received that evening. When Jemima had come out of school that afternoon full of the party and the fact her other friends were going, he had baulked at the idea. After the debacle in the shop earlier that day, the thought of attending the party had filled him with dread. His plan had been to lock himself away for the evening and hide from the world.

However, he was glad he had come. Everyone knew of course, but rather than be treated as an object of pity, people had been warm and friendly, as the evening wore on and the free bar loosened the adult's tongues, he realised just how unpopular his wife was and how pleased people were to see her get her comeuppance. And rather than pity him for a second failed marriage they seemed to admire him for finally standing up to her. There had naturally been one or two snide comments but he decided he could live with those.

"Jemima seems to be having a great time," Sarah Prince's voice shook Craig from his thoughts.

He looked over at his daughter raiding the pick and mix with her friends, a bottle of some fruity drink in her hand, that he was sure was pure sugar. "She is, although I think she'll be awake until the early hours with the amount of sugar she has consumed." He rolled his eyes theatrically to show he didn't really mind. "Tonight has been good for her, it was a shock for her to find out that Diana and I were splitting up."

"It is tough," Sarah admitted. "How are you?"

"This will sound odd, but now it's over I feel...." He cast around for the right word.

"Relieved?" Sarah supplied.

"Yes, that's it." Craig glanced at her in surprise.

"When my marriage ended, it had been so bad for so long that there wasn't any grieving left to do." Sarah said sadly.

Craig was about to say something when Jemima walked over, "Daddy I feel sick!"

He smiled wryly at Sarah, "Come on then let's get you home. It's getting pretty late."

They said their goodbyes and as he pulled his car out of the drive, Jemima turned to him, "Daddy am I going to get a new mummy like Belle?" Her normal confidence had deserted her.

Stopping the car, he turned to her, "Jemima right now I have absolutely no plans to remarry ever again."

She nodded relieved and settled back against the car seat, starting to nod off in the darkness. "I'll look after you Daddy," she murmured as sleep claimed her.

Rose checked the horses on the yard, and made her way back towards the house. The party was still in full swing, she thought, pleased with how well it had gone. As she headed back towards the house and a cup of tea in the tranquillity of the kitchen, she could hear a few people leaving, although she could not make out the whole conversation snippets floated across to her.

"Surprised to see Daniel back...."

Knowing it never paid to eavesdrop Rose put her hand on the kitchen door ready to push it open.

"Let's hope he doesn't mess Anna around again, I'm telling you that's what made her leave last time,"

"I think you are right, that whole Freddie thing seemed a bit far-fetched, if you ask me."

The voices drifted away down the drive so that Rose could no longer make out the conversation, but it did not matter, she did not need to hear anymore. She stood frozen with her hand on the door. She had been so pleased to have Daniel back, but was he the reason Anna had left? She thought of the times in the past when she had smiled as she watched girls and women throw themselves at him. If she was truly honest, she had taken a sort of pride in having a son who was so clearly such a good catch but now the knowledge that that could be the very thing that could jeopardise her future made her feel silly for ever valuing such a trait.

She had always insisted that her sons treat women with respect but had she tried hard enough? She had seen girls who chased him, made excuses to talk to him, and even took up riding to get near him, as silly and weak. After all who would chase a man who was clearly not interested? But the thought that Anna may have joined that club made her feel terrible.

She stumbled into the kitchen, and sat at the kitchen table her head in her hands. She would have to talk to Daniel, make him realise that anything he had learnt from her, even subconsciously was wrong, and that he should have pity on women who fell for him. But as she sat there, the realisation that Anna would not thank her for telling him to take pity on her or even intervening, became apparent.

There was nothing she could do, except hope that Anna was no longer interested. As she sat there, the cup of tea long forgotten, the old feelings of helplessness and fear began to gather and swirl around her. The thoughts grew stronger, what if Anna left again? Surely Anna wouldn't leave again, but then she had done it before and Rose had not even seen it coming. She had been so pleased that Daniel was back but what if it was actually the last thing Anna wanted?

The panic in her chest rose, threatening to engulf her. She sat gripping the table whilst her panic kept increasing, and then she noticed it. Someone had left half a bottle of gin on the side, the girls had been laughing and joking as they got ready earlier that night. She tried to ignore it and thought about the steps, but at the back of her mind the underlying panic grew and festered, until one thought overrode all others, she could have a drink, just one drink. It would help her sleep and then tomorrow she could try and make sense of this mess.

Standing up, she opened the dresser and took out a glass. The steps, everything she had learnt in class receded into the background and she was aware of the feeling that she had lost control. She shrugged off the knowledge. It would just be a little one, she thought, picking up the bottle. She unscrewed the lid and the familiar smell invaded her senses, she breathed in the fumes deeply, already starting to feel calmer. The bottle hovered over the glass, just a small one, just to help her sleep, that was all it was.

Still the bottle hovered, her hand started to shake, and Rose was aware of tears forming in her eyes. Before she could think it through, she quickly crossed the kitchen to the sink and poured the gin away.

Grasping the edge of the Belfast sink with both hands, she held on tightly to stop her hands shaking, as she took deep breaths, trying to stop the panic and regain some control.

"Are you ok?"

The voice made her jump, but Rose didn't turn.

"Fine, fine, just…" Had she seen what happened, Rose wondered.

"You did the right thing…." Sarah said softly appearing beside her.

Rose dropped her head, "You know I always used to think I was a strong person, but I've realised that I'm not. I'm really quite ashamed of myself."

Sarah laughed but kindly, "Rose, believe me, raising two boys on your own, whilst running a stables and keeping half the village in a state of awe and fear is only undertaken by a strong person. What you've discovered lately isn't that you are weak, it's simply that you are human. Welcome to the club." She finished with a rueful smile.

After a moment Rose smiled back and finally managed to let go of the sink. "Bit of a bugger though, isn't it? Being human I mean!" She replied, some of her spirit returning, as her demons started to retreat into the shadows.

Suppressing a wry smile Sarah nodded. "It is, but as I found out, if you let people help you, then it's easier to stay strong and it turns out being human is not so bad after all."

Rose nodded deep in thought, as Sarah flicked on the kettle. "Cuppa?"

Placing the drinks down on the table and taking a seat opposite her, Sarah asked the question, "So what triggered this?"

Rose looked slightly taken aback at her forthrightness.

Sarah was not prepared to back down though. "This is the most stable home I've had in years, and I don't want that to change, so therefore you need to talk to me so I can help you."

Rose nodded, finally acknowledging that if she slipped up with her drinking, it wasn't just her future she was risking. "I eavesdropped on a conversation and didn't like what I heard."

Sarah looked at her, unable to guess at what she had heard.

Rose sighed, "Apparently Anna is a bit taken with Daniel and that's what made her leave last time."

"She's not a bit taken she's in love with him."

"You knew?" Rose asked, slightly irritated that she had missed what was going on.

"You're his Mother, she wasn't going to discuss it with you." Sarah responded gently.

"True," Rose replied with a shrug. "Do you think she will go again?"

Sarah thought for a second, giving Rose false hope would benefit no one in the long run. "I don't know, even Anna cannot answer that, but what I do know is this, Daniel asked Anna to give him another chance and she said no, because of all this and you." She waved her arm to indicate the house and yard

"I see." Rose looked taken aback. "Well, I guess we will just have to leave them to it." She said as much to herself as Sarah.

"We will," Sarah said with a smile, thinking Rose would struggle not to say something to one or both of them. "But don't forget, whilst we would struggle without Anna, you have a lot of people around you wanting to help, not least Freddie and me."

Rose reflected on her words; she was right. The stables, the house, Rose's future was no longer completely dependent on Anna. She looked up at Sarah, "You are right, I have so much here, I'd be stupid to risk losing it again. To be honest I thought this was just my battle but it affects us all, doesn't it?"

Sarah nodded, "I'm afraid so."

"We're going to be ok though, aren't we?" She said thoughtfully.

Sarah nodded, not that Rose seemed to need a response.

Rose was silent for a second longer then stood up, looking more like her normal self, but then she paused and cleared her throat. "I'm still struggling with this whole touchy feely, talking about everything nonsense. But thank you for tonight Sarah, I really am grateful. I think we've all been lucky to find each other." And looking slightly embarrassed, she nodded and left the room.

Sarah put the cups in the sink and headed up to bed as well, smiling to herself, none of them were perfect she thought, but at least they were muddling through together. She put her head around Freddie's door to find he was fast asleep. She placed a kiss lightly on his forehead so she didn't wake him and then pulled his door closed with a contented sigh.

Chapter Thirty Five

Aware that Anna was definitely ignoring him, he wasn't particularly welcome amongst her friends and with exhaustion washing over him, Daniel decided to call it a night. He would just slip away quietly he thought, saying a quick goodbye to Tom and Mollie and then Rich, he stood to leave. Anna was across the room chatting happily to her parents.

It would be best to leave her to it, that way she could enjoy her party, he thought heading towards the door. But when she glanced up and saw him, he changed direction towards her.

"You look like you are having a good time." He said smiling as she moved towards him, swaying slightly after one too many drinks. He just managed to stop himself putting out a hand to steady her.

She giggled and moved closer still, but taking in his jacket, she stopped. "You're not leaving, are you?" Her eyes fixed questioningly on his.

Did she want him to stay Daniel wondered, before reminding himself she had only turned him down a few hours earlier. "Jetlag." He said by way of explanation.

She nodded slowly. "Well thanks for coming."

For a moment they stood staring at each other, before Daniel gave a half smile. "Enjoy the rest of your party. And sorry I did not say it earlier but Happy Birthday."

Anna nodded and watched him walk away. Disappointment washed over her, but acknowledging that keeping Daniel at arm's length was the best thing to do she forced herself to turn away.

Deciding she needed another drink, Anna headed to the bar for a refill. With her mind still on Daniel as she waited for her drink, she did not notice Tom had come over to her.

"Anna, have you got a minute?" He looked uncomfortable and almost embarrassed.

Unsure what he was about to say, but seeing as this was the most, he had spoken to her in months, she nodded hesitantly.

"I owe you an apology." He glanced up to see confusion settle across her features. "The thing is when Daniel said you were messing around with Andrew, I believed him. Mollie said I should have questioned it but Daniel seemed so sure and well Belle was so upset...." He paused again knowing he was making a mess of things.

But Anna was shaking her head, "Sorry Tom what do you mean, I wasn't messing around with Andrew and why was Belle upset?"

Tom began to wish he'd never started the conversation. He knew he'd been rude to Anna but maybe he should have waited until they were both sober. And now she was looking at him expectantly so he tried to explain again.

"At the ball when Daniel was looking for you but then he found Belle in tears saying she had caught Andrew with Anna, and he put two and two together and made five as it turns out. I took his side. Well, I'd just seen you leave with Andrew and he is my brother!" Tom's voice was slightly defensive on the last statement, before he paused. "I'm sorry. I should have given you the benefit of the doubt."

Anna stared at him trying to make sense of what she was being told, as the truths she had believed for the last six months became jumbled and settled into a different pattern.

"Belle was upset about Andrew?" Anna asked trying to make sense of everything.

Tom looked around for Mollie, he'd wanted to apologise but he hadn't expected this. Unfortunately, Mollie was over the far side of the room, Jane still seemed to be telling her about Olivia's reaction to finding out Mollie was being head hunted by her old firm. Deciding that he needed to wrap up the conversation he quickly told her what he knew. "Apparently Belle had been seeing Andrew." Anna was starting to look upset. "Look you are better off asking Mollie about this." Tom replied uneasily.

"But I thought Daniel was with Belle. Elliot's mum and dad said they saw Daniel and Belle together and that he had his arm around her and they were laughing, as they headed into the house."

"Look I wasn't there but I saw Daniel just after that and as he put it, he was covered in tears and snot."

"Oh…." Anna wanted to believe Tom so much but it seemed too much to hope for.

"Are we ok?" Tom asked now desperate to end the conversation, as the whole situation was far messier than he had realised.

Anna glanced at him distractedly, "Yeah, course."

Tom decided it was time to escape, but Anna caught his arm.

"When Daniel apologised about the Belle thing was that because he thought that I was with Andrew?"

Tom shuffled uneasily. "Yes, but look he'll only be at the end of the drive by now, why don't you have this conversation with him?"

Anna looked horrified, "I can't…. I mean…." She paused and looked at him, "Can I?"

"Yes, you can, and actually it's him you need to talk to not Mollie."

"Ok I'm off." She said without moving, but instead glanced towards her friends.

"You'll be fine and I'll let everyone know where you've gone." Tom said kindly.

Anna headed out of the marquee hesitantly, and paused for a second looking down the long drive. It was really dark and what if Tom had got it wrong? Just then a wet nose touched her hand. Glancing down she realised Tilly had sidled up to her. "Ok let's do this."

Halfway down the drive she became aware that her heels were far from ideal, but knowing that if she went back to change them her courage would fail. Luckily there was a full moon, and away from the lights of the party it was not as dark as she first thought. In fact, the night was clear and mild and the stars were dotted across the sky, it certainly felt romantic she thought, realising she had drunk too much, as she was getting overly sentimental. Her feet were starting to hurt though and she realised she would need to pick up her pace if she was going to catch up with Daniel.

Daniel walked back towards his house feeling shattered, the jetlag had kicked in, but what really bothered him was Anna's friends, they had been so hostile, he was sure he was missing something. Lost in thought he slowly became aware George had stopped and was staring intently at the road behind them. Probably a fox he thought, calling him.

He turned to go but turned back swiftly as he heard something approach fast, in the moonlight he could just make out an ecstatic Tilly hurl herself at George. Great he thought, now he'd have to take her back.

"Come on you two," he called them both ready to retrace his steps when he looked up to find Anna stood a few feet away, staring at him.

She was out of breath, and her hair fell about her face, his hand twitched with the urge to tuck it behind her ear. Daniel had wanted to talk to her all night and now here she was alone with him on a quiet lane, standing in the moonlight, but reminding himself it was not him she was here for, he sighed.

"I'm guessing Tilly was missing her playmate, come on I'll walk you back." He deliberately kept a slight distance from Anna as they turned to go back the way they had come. Anna still had not said anything, perhaps she didn't want to be alone with him on a deserted lane, but then he wasn't going to leave her to walk back on her own he thought.

"Look I'll see you back safely and then I'll go." He said despondently, she merely nodded.

Anna fell into step beside him. Perhaps Tom had got it wrong, he hardly seemed pleased to see her and seemed to be determined to keep as far away as possible. They walked along in silence. Daniel did not seem to want to talk, her brief attempts at conversation were met with one syllable answers. Anna bit her lip wondering how to start the conversation she had wanted to have. But luck it seemed was not on her side as they had already reached the bottom of the drive.

"I'll be fine from here." Why had she said that? She turned to face Daniel. "You must be tired."

"Yeah, I've not slept since Thursday." His eyes searched hers, making her catch her breath, but then he sighed, "Well, see you around."

Frustration ran through her. "See you around?" The words came out before she could stop them, they sounded angry and indignant.

Daniel had started to turn away but now he turned back in surprise, "Look Anna I've apologised and if I could change what happened that night believe me I would, more than anything, but I can't." He ran his hand through his hair but still she could not get any words out. "I don't know what to do to make this right."

Was Daniel suggesting she was punishing him? She tried to make sense of what he had just said.

"Goodnight Anna." His words sounded final and defeated, as he started to walk away, Anna realised she had still not spoken.

"It wasn't Tilly who came after you it was me." Anna called after him, causing him to turn back around but he kept his distance a few feet away.

"It's just that I had misunderstood something about that night and the thing is…." She was staring down at her hands, not daring to look at him. "The thing is…." She wrung her hands wondering where to start.

"The thing is...?" Daniel had somehow moved so he was right in front of her, he gently took her hands in his linking their fingers, dropping them to his side so they were facing each other.

Her heart hammered in her chest and as she looked up at him, she lost her train of thought.

"The thing is...?" he prompted again his voice barely a whisper. His eyes locked on hers for a second before dropping to her mouth. The message was clear.

She let go of his hands and pulled back slightly, it would be so easy to forget what she needed to say but she needed to be sure. Daniel raised an eyebrow so she started to explain.

"That night I thought you were with Belle. I was looking for you and one of the parents said they had seen you two heading towards the house. Apparently you had an arm around her and she was giggling, a few people saw you and everyone was looking at me in pity and I thought.....Well when you said you were sorry about the Belle thing I thought you meant that you and her had been, well, you know." The words came out in a rush. Anna kept staring at his feet, unable to look up.

"Anna, she's just a kid." Daniel sounded annoyed.

"I know but you thought I was with Andrew and well you wanted me to forgive you for that so I thought you could forgive me for making the same mistake too. And earlier you said you wanted to try again…" Anna ran out of words and when Daniel still said nothing, she slowly raised her eyes to meet his, dreading what she would see.

"Does that mean you want to try again too?" He asked, his face was a mask.

"Well, if you haven't changed your mind or given up." She tried to smile, but her face felt frozen.

Daniel looked down for a second and then reached for her again closing the gap between them completely. One hand slipped around her waist whilst the other cupped her face. She looked up him, meeting his eyes finally relaxing as she saw that he was smiling.

"Believe me I hadn't given up; I just wasn't going to spoil your party." The amused smile gave way to a groan as he lowered his mouth to hers and kissed her deeply, leaving her in no doubt of his feelings. How long they stood in the lane she wasn't sure, but Daniel eventually pulled back, "Come on I'm taking you home."

Anna could only nod. Happiness bubbled through her as they made their way slowly back to his house, his arm firmly around her, whilst his words and kisses were promising what was to come.

"You know I was just thinking about what mum said about how you were brave enough to go out there and get your dream life and just how much it has benefitted us all," he said with a smirk making Anna blush.

His lips brushed hers, "I'm definitely feeling the benefits, but was meeting a gorgeous man part of the dream?" He asked innocently, although the corner of his mouth twitched.

"Maybe." Anna laughed, swatting his arm "but I seem to have ended up with you instead," she teased.

They had now reached his house. He opened the door, letting it swing wide so the two dogs could run inside.

Turning to Anna, he lightly picked her up. Daniel looked down at her as she slid her arms around his neck. He lightly brushed his lips with hers. "You know dreams are all very well but I'm going to show you just how good reality can be," he promised carrying her inside.

Thank you to everyone who has helped and listened and encouraged me to finally finish this book, you all know who you are, you lovely people.

Thank you also for choosing this book and I hope you have enjoyed reading it as much as I have enjoyed writing it. If you have a spare five minutes, please can I ask you to leave a review. They help more than you can know.

Printed in Great Britain
by Amazon